Praise for

"Greenwood's mix of sweet romance and sensuality, blended with an engaging plot and charming characters, is certain to enchant readers. The feisty heroine and dark hero…are perfect, as is the dialogue between them."

—*RT Book Reviews*

"This beautifully penned story is rife with emotion, sensuality…tender romance, and true love, providing readers with a tale they will not soon forget… A must-read for lovers of historical romance!"

—*Romance Junkies*

"Lovely…a wonderful plot that is entertaining and emotional."

—*Kiltsandswords*

"A delightful historical romance. Emily Greenwood engages you from the first page."

—*Fresh Fiction*

"Greenwood weaves some unique threads into her Regency romance, heightening the sexual stakes and rendering a wholly satisfying happy ending for this touching love story."

—*Kirkus*

Praise for *A Little Night Mischief*

"Tantalizing reading...the honest, natural fun and the playful then consuming love that emerges are best of all. Great entertainment!"

—*Long and Short Reviews*

"There's a certain whimsical nature to the plot, the hero is quite devastatingly gorgeous, and the writing is well crafted."

—*All About Romance*

"A delightfully charming read, sprinkled with mischief...refreshing, fun, and entertaining."

—*Lily Pond Reads*

"Filled with humor, passion, and a lovely ending!"

—*Proserpine Craving Books*

Praise for *Mischief by Moonlight*

"With engaging characters and an intriguing story line, Ms. Greenwood has created a story that is fun, light-hearted, but passionate, filled with mischief, honor, and the power of true love."

—*My Book Addiction Reviews*

"A delightful read; it gives new life to a story line as old as time… A beautiful, and sexy, novel."

—*Maggie Hite, Librarian*

"A witty historical romance…a tale of moonlight, mischief, and magic in a Regency setting."

—*Romance Junkies*

Praise for *Gentlemen Prefer Mischief*

"Emily Greenwood's delightful characters that are so well developed and the humor that threads through the plot make *Gentlemen Prefer Mischief* captivating."

—*Long and Short Reviews*

"A devilish, charming ex-army captain, a righteous young woman, mysterious haunted woods, and a cast of delightful supporting characters make for a mix of delicious sensuality in Greenwood's nicely written read."

—*RT Book Reviews*

"Greenwood makes you fall in love with the secondary characters and keeps you wanting more."

—*Historical Romance Lover*

"Intriguing, sexy historical romance."

—*Romance Junkies*

Also by Emily Greenwood

A Little Night Mischief
Gentlemen Prefer Mischief
Mischief by Moonlight
The Beautiful One

HOW TO
HANDLE
a Scandal

EMILY
GREENWOOD

sourcebooks
casablanca

Published by Sourcebooks Casablanca, an imprint of Sourcebooks,
Inc.
P.O. Box 4410, Naperville, Illinois 60567-4410
(630) 961-3900
Fax: (630) 961-2168
www.sourcebooks.com

Printed and bound in Canada.
MBP 10 9 8 7 6 5 4 3 2 1

For Nora and Pete

One

ELIZABETH TARRYTON WAS SEVENTEEN THE NIGHT she finally understood that some mistakes could never be undone.

The fateful day started in a manner that was, regrettably, becoming familiar that summer of her first season in London.

"Lizzie, why am I reading about you in the newspaper *again*?" her uncle and guardian, Will Halifax, Viscount Grandville, asked as they breakfasted at his London town house.

Lizzie bit her lower lip. It was a lip that had had at least three odes written to it that summer. Five had been written to her red-gold hair, which was in truth the sort that Renaissance painters had lived to capture, and ten had been written to her deep blue eyes, which would have done credit to an angel but for the sparks of mischief that often danced in them.

"Um…" Lizzie wasn't certain which incident might have made it into the paper. There had been the midnight serenading under the window of handsome young Captain McKinley last week, though Lizzie hadn't been the only person involved in that. And then there was the little incident at the Cullivers' party two nights before…

"What the devil can you have been thinking to jump into a fountain in an evening gown?" Will said gruffly. "And with two men present!"

The party, then.

"Oh, Lizzie." Anna Halifax, the other occupant of the breakfast table, looked pained. A year before, when Lizzie had become Will's ward, Anna had become first Lizzie's governess and then Will's wife. Anna and Will were like the older siblings Lizzie had never had, but they could be ridiculously concerned with propriety, considering Will was only thirty-three and Anna a mere twenty-four.

But Lizzie loved them dearly, and she knew they meant well—and just as important, she knew they'd never send her away. Being sent away was the one thing that worried her, but they'd promised she'd always have a home with them, and she trusted them. She had to, since she had no one else.

Will put down the paper and fixed her with a penetrating gaze. He was tall and darkly handsome, with brown hair and deep blue eyes, and his serious air lent him the right amount of gravitas to be a very fine viscount. But when he looked at her with what she privately called his "shrewd" look, she always wanted to squirm.

"I assure you the gown is perfectly fine," she said, stalling for time.

"The gown is irrelevant beyond the fact that it was likely made of something flimsy and thus entirely transparent when wet."

"But it didn't matter," she hurried to explain. "When Cicely dared me, I agreed on the condition that she and the gentlemen tie scarves over their eyes and turn around. So all that happened was that they heard a splash. I wrapped right up in a blanket, and nobody saw anything."

Will groaned, and Anna pressed her lips together. Anna was an unusually beautiful woman, with black hair and sherry-colored eyes, and she had once been the center of an enormous scandal herself. But that had been different, because the scandal hadn't been her fault.

"Lizzie," she said, "we *know* you are an extremely intelligent young lady. Your reading tastes are sophisticated, and you probably know more about the issues of the day than any other young woman in London, let alone many of the gentlemen."

"I'm two-thirds of the way through the complete works of Shakespeare," Lizzie pointed out, hoping to distract them. She'd discovered a love of reading when Anna was her governess, and could not believe she'd once scorned it.

"But that just proves my point," Anna said. "You're smart, which is why we have so much trouble understanding why you keep doing these senselessly scandalous things. They may seem harmless to you, but they're chipping away at your reputation, and they could make it hard for you to marry well."

Lizzie didn't understand herself why she needed to keep doing scandalous things, but she couldn't seem to stop. She knew she *should* stop. The sentence uttered by her stepmother two years before should in itself have been enough to make Lizzie stop, but it was almost as if, despite everything that had happened, those words compelled her to misbehave more.

"Oh," Lizzie said, waving a hand dismissively, "reputation. Surely the dullest word in the English language."

She thought she heard the sound of two sets of teeth grinding. They wanted her to look to the future, but Lizzie had never liked to think about the future. *Now* was what interested her.

The truth was, Lizzie *didn't* want to get married. She needed excitement, and the idea of settling down with one man for eternity made her want to weep. To Lizzie, nothing was as addictive as the company of men—plural. She simply adored them, and she had since she was a little girl.

"My darling Lizzie, who could deny you anything?" her beloved, widowed father would say with a fond smile whenever he looked up from writing his sermons to find Lizzie, at six or seven, scampering through his study in another new frock. He'd indulged her in whatever she wanted, perhaps partly to make up for the mother she'd never known. With a papa who was so wonderful, Lizzie had rarely minded not having a mother.

When the two of them moved to the island of Malta for his work, he'd said he was glad his little Lizzie could live somewhere free of the petty rules of English life, and he'd smiled as she'd run free over the island, charming the inhabitants as though it were her mission in life.

"She's made friends with all the sailors in port and the shopkeepers," their housekeeper informed the Reverend

Mr. Tarryton when Lizzie was thirteen. *"The men in town all call her the little angel. It ain't genteel."*

"Nonsense," Papa had said, curling his arm affectionately around Lizzie's shoulders. *"My Lizzie is special."*

"She's a flirt," the housekeeper had pronounced, and she'd promptly been sacked.

"Never mind about her," Papa had said as they watched the woman march away from their house with her ugly black valise. *"She's just jealous because you're going to break hearts someday."*

Lizzie had looked up at him, hoping he could see the love shining from her eyes. *"I'd never break yours, Papa."*

"I hope not, poppet," he'd said cheerfully and kissed the top of her head.

And she hadn't; he'd been the one to break hers.

The day her unconventional papa married a very proper woman was a dark day for fifteen-year-old Lizzie, who soon realized his loving gaze was no longer fixed on her.

Seeking to fill the hollow space where once her father's love had been, she'd taken to spending more time with the handsome young naval officers who sailed into Malta's port. They listened to her as her father once had, and she'd loved making them smile—until her outraged stepmother had sealed her doom.

"Your daughter," Lizzie's stepmother, Marian, had said to Papa one night when Lizzie returned to find them waiting for her, *"is a-good-for-nothing trollop, and you should be ashamed of the way you've indulged her."*

The words had cut, but what had hurt far more was that her father had just stood there as his new wife told him his selfish daughter was going to cost him his position, and that she must be sent away to a proper English school where she could learn how to behave.

And he'd sent her away.

Lizzie had arrived in England bitterly unhappy, and more unhappiness followed when she received a letter informing her that her father and stepmother and new baby brother had died of a fever.

It was through this tragic turn of events that she'd become Will's ward. His steadying influence had brought her a measure of happiness, while his position in society offered her entrée into a glittering world of parties and balls and...gentlemen. Everywhere in London there were handsome, charming gentlemen.

How she loved their mischievous smiles. The little notes they slipped furtively to her as she stood talking with friends. The thrilling things they said to her while dancing. The endless stream of flowers they sent to Halifax House with her name on them.

The only thing she didn't like about gentlemen was when they grew serious and wanted to propose. It was quite delightful to be sought after and do things like jumping into fountains, and she didn't want any of it to end, which it surely would as soon as she married.

"I know you want to enjoy your season without the pressure of needing to find a husband," Will said. "And certainly there is no need to rush into an engagement, never mind that we will want to be certain of any man you choose because your dowry will make you the object of fortune hunters—"

"Exactly!" Lizzie interrupted with cheerful relief. "So it's best to take my time."

"But," Will continued firmly, "you must have a care about your reputation."

"I will," she said easily, and smiled. "Trust me."

"We do trust you, Lizzie," he said seriously, making her feel so warm inside. And though the memory of her stepmother's sharp voice tried to tear down that secure feeling, Lizzie refused to listen. Will and Anna loved her; what could go wrong?

"Tommy's back in Town," Anna said after a bit.

"Oh, lovely." Tommy was Will's younger brother, although he was not a blood relation to Lizzie since she was related to Will through his first wife, her aunt Ginger. Tommy Halifax was perhaps Lizzie's favorite gentleman of all. He was four years older, handsome enough to turn the head of every young lady in London, and as fond of fun as she was. They had wonderful talks about all kinds of things.

She would almost have said he was her closest friend, except that he wasn't quite like her other friends. None of her girlfriends gave her the giddy feelings that Tommy sometimes did. But she never gave those feelings any thought, because Tommy was nearly family. She could flirt and laugh with him to her heart's content without worrying that he'd propose.

"Is he coming to the Cattertons' ball tonight?" She hadn't seen him for a week, since he'd been off on some errand for Will at Longmount, one of the family estates.

"I believe so."

So they would dance and have fun, just as they always did.

❧

Tommy watched Lizzie from just inside the doorway to the Cattertons' ballroom, having just arrived.

She was dancing with his cousin Andrew, and Tommy's eyes followed her in her pink satin gown, which made him smile. Pink was her favorite color, and she nearly always wore it. Her gown was embroidered with gold flowers that set off the rich gold tones in her reddish hair, and a pink ribbon circled her neck, the single diamond dangling from it drawing his eyes to the milky loveliness of her bosom. She was so beautiful that she made everything around her seem like nothing but a blur.

God, he'd missed her, and it had only been a week since he'd last seen her.

Ever since Lizzie had come to live with his brother the year before, Tommy had found himself increasingly fascinated by her. How he felt about her now went far beyond attraction, but he'd kept his attentions chaste, not only because he respected her, but because Will would have had his head if he'd known the kinds of thoughts Tommy was having about her.

Tommy had kissed his fair share of willing women. Since meeting Lizzie the year before and falling under her spell, however, other women had ceased to hold any interest for him, and he was still a virgin. He knew he wanted to be with Lizzie always.

But Lizzie was younger, and she'd had a hard time, having lost her family two years before. He knew that she'd been dreaming of her first season all during the last year, and she deserved her chance to be the belle of the ball, even if Tommy secretly wanted to keep her all to himself.

So he'd held back, and gone away when he couldn't stand to watch the way other men's eyes lit up when she was around.

But it was July now, and she'd been in Town since May. Having been presented at court, she was "out" and thus ready for any man who wished to win her. Though she might be in no hurry to find a husband, Tommy knew it was only a matter of time before some man snapped her up. Especially now, when nearly every fellow in London knew what a firecracker she was and would be wondering what she'd be like in bed.

Tommy ground his teeth. He'd heard about the fountain incident because one of the two men present was a friend of Andrew's. Lizzie had a natural boldness—some might call it willfulness—and she was impetuous, qualities that were part of her charm. But this wasn't the first such incident, and she was treading a thin line between being a little outrageous and becoming a true scandal.

Fortunately, he had the perfect solution to the little problem of Lizzie's adorable outrageousness: he was going to marry her.

The idea still made him a bit light-headed, because he hadn't thought to marry for years. He was not yet twenty-two, and if asked even the year before whether he might marry soon, he would have roared with laughter. But then he'd met Lizzie.

A twinge of conscience prodded him; he should probably have discussed his plans with Will first. But that was a conversation he didn't want to have yet. And they were brothers—there was nothing but respect and affection between them, so Will had no reason to object to Tommy's suitability.

The dance was over, and Andrew was leading Lizzie to where Will and Anna were talking. Before Lizzie could go off with anyone else, Tommy made his way to her, pleased that her face lit up when she saw him.

"There you are!" she said, coming close to give him a quick embrace. She smelled of that soft rose scent that was uniquely hers.

Andrew clapped Tommy on the back jovially, Anna embraced him, and Will asked after Longmount. After all the pleasantries had been gotten through, Tommy, his heart beginning to race, looked toward the open terrace doors, where few people seemed to have gone despite the warmth of the summer night. He held out an arm to Lizzie.

"Let's go outside and cool off. You can tell me about everything I missed."

She agreed and chattered happily as they walked, telling him about what had happened while he was away. When they stepped through the doors and onto the terrace, she looked up at the dark summer sky and sighed happily. Her capacity to be nearly always happy was one of the things he loved best about her.

"Isn't it the most splendid night?" she said, and as he watched the starlight mingle with the gold lights in her hair, he was pierced by her beauty. He murmured his assent as he led her away from the manor and into the quiet, deserted space of the garden, which was lit with torches.

"It *is* a splendid night," he said to the side of her face as she gazed at the stars. He took a deep breath. "But do you know what makes it truly splendid for me? Being here with you."

There was a longish pause, then she turned to look at him. He'd never said something so personal to her, and he was dying inside waiting to know how she would take it.

"You must be in the mood to flirt tonight," she said lightly.

"I'm not flirting. I'm serious."

She frowned. "I'm not good at being serious, Tommy."

"Nonsense," he said. "You can be serious when you choose."

"Er…thank you," she said, sounding puzzled.

He'd never once kissed her, though he'd wanted to desperately, countless times. But now that he had such serious intentions toward her, and considering how well they knew each other—surely it wouldn't be inappropriate now?

"Lizzie," he said, huskiness creeping into his voice, "I want to kiss you. May I?"

She seemed surprised by his request, as though all the days and nights they'd spent talking and flirting hadn't been leading in any particular direction. But there was a bond between them, built of affection and friendship. And attraction—he felt as certain of it as of his own breathing. They were meant to be together.

"Erhm." And then she smiled. "Yes. I'd like that." The words, breathy wisps that hinted at awakening emotions, inflamed him.

She tipped her head up and his heart thundered. When his lips finally—finally!—met hers, he *felt* it: she was going to be the love of his life.

Her mouth opened to him, and her tongue gently sought his, which gave him the unwelcome awareness that he wasn't the first man she'd kissed. How many of the gentlemen of the *ton* had tasted her? he wondered with a surge of jealousy.

He pushed the thought away. It didn't matter, because he meant to be the last.

A little whimper escaped her, and she hugged him closer as though she needed him. The awareness touched him in the most welcome way. She *needed* him, just as he needed her. He forced himself to break the kiss.

"Lizzie," he murmured, "we can't go on like this."

"Like what?" She sounded adorably dazed.

He smiled a little. "Stealing kisses in the garden."

"Who would know if we did?"

"Trust me, we can't. I won't survive the experience."

"What do you mean?"

"I mean, dearest Lizzie, that you make my head spin."

"Do I?" She laughed. "Will said the same thing yesterday when I told him I loved champagne."

"You make my head spin in a *different* way."

An inscrutable emotion flitted across her face. "Er…" She mumbled something that sounded like, "Me too." But it might also have been something that ended in "you."

Then she smiled brightly, as if they'd been talking about any old thing, and said, "Do you know, I should quite like a lemonade."

And before he could say a word, she'd stepped away from him toward the ballroom.

He stood blinking for a moment at her abrupt departure. That kiss…it had been amazing, but it hadn't been amazing just for him. He'd felt the thrill pulsing between them, heard the wonder in her voice.

He moved to the doorway. She'd found her way to Will and Anna, who were standing with the rest of his cousins near the edge of the ballroom. It occurred to Tommy that this was perfect: most of the people they loved best were right here. What better moment could there be to declare their love for each other?

❦

Lizzie swept into the ballroom wondering if she had a silly smile on her face. But Tommy had just kissed her! And it had been a little wonderful.

He was a *much* better kisser than Lord Hewett, who'd stolen a kiss in an alcove at a house party last month, or young Mr. Fletcher, who'd quickly pressed his lips to hers under the mistletoe at a Christmas party. She wasn't even going to count the lieutenant she'd kissed in the garden at the Rosewood School the year before, because that had really been about something besides kissing.

Her smile slipped a little as she thought of what Tommy had said afterward. He *had* made her head spin a little, but she didn't want to talk about it. Talking made things too fixed, like they were all decided, when really she just wanted everything to be *possible*.

She hoped the kiss wasn't going to make it

impossible to go back to the way they'd always been, because she needed Tommy to be her friend.

She hoped… No, surely it wasn't necessary to hope anything. Surely *Tommy* wasn't going to be like the other gentlemen who'd wanted to be serious. This was Tommy, with whom she always laughed and teased with no consequences. Surely it had only been a kiss, even if it had been a little amazing. But she decided right then that they mustn't do it again.

"And what have you been up to, Lizzie?" asked Will's cousin, Louie Halifax, who only months before, on the shocking death of both his uncle and his cousin, had become the Earl of Gildenhall.

Lizzie thought "Gildenhall" was the perfect title for him, since, with his dark blond hair and extremely handsome looks, he seemed gilded. And since he'd been a commoner his entire life, he was not at all stuffy—which wasn't to say that he didn't have quite a bit of presence. He was certainly considered the catch of the season by all the mamas of the *ton*, even if despite being over thirty, he seemed in no hurry to be caught.

"Oh, nothing," Lizzie said. "Are there any cakes left?" She strained to see beyond Louie's shoulders.

He chuckled. "There were three left last I saw, unless Andrew ate them."

His brother rolled his eyes. "Why would I do such an uncouth thing?"

Emerald, their younger sister, cocked her head. "Have you ever noticed how we say people are uncouth, but we never say they are 'couth'?"

Emerald was the same age as Lizzie, and, with eyes as purely green as Tommy's, perfectly named. Thanks to the dramatic reversal in her family's fortunes, Emerald and her older sister Ruby were enjoying the kind of lavish season they could never have had with the burden of debt that had once pressed on them all.

"Or 'ept,'" Ruby pointed out. "People are inept, but never 'ept.' Maybe we should make it a word. This could go down in history as the 'ept' season."

"You can't just sprinkle your conversation with made-up words and think everyone will start using them," Andrew said.

"Can't I?" Ruby said with the light of challenge in her eyes. Ruby Halifax might look haughty, but she had a competitive streak when it came to her brothers, and Lizzie found their squabbles entertaining.

From the moment she'd met them, Louie and his brothers and sisters had treated Lizzie like one of the family, and getting to know them had been one of the best parts of becoming Will's ward.

Someone tapped her on the shoulder. She turned, and there was Tommy. He looked funny, but not in a humorous way. Something fizzed unpleasantly inside her.

"You left so suddenly, Lizzie. I had an important question to ask you."

She'd heard that kind of thing before, and it wasn't good. *Oh no. Oh no, no, no, no.* He wasn't going to do the very thing she desperately didn't want him of all men to do—he *mustn't.*

She had to lighten the tone immediately and keep him from speaking serious words he would regret. But before she could speak, Will said, "What's going on, Tommy?"

Oh please, she thought desperately, *don't let this be what it sounds like.*

Tommy's green eyes pinned her. He had black hair with a rogue blade of white slashing through at his forehead, and she'd seen more than one young lady swoon over his striking good looks. But to Lizzie he was simply Tommy. And he wasn't supposed to say momentous things to her.

"I'm sure Tommy doesn't have anything to say to me that can't be said in front of all of you," she said, giving him a smile meant to encourage him to keep things light.

But his face was serious.

"You're right, Lizzie. The words I have to say, while especially for you, will mean something for all of the family. Because what I want to ask, dearest Lizzie," he said, taking her hand and dropping fluidly to one knee as his eyes held hers and her stomach plummeted, "is if you will do me the very great honor of becoming my wife."

All the breath rushed out of her. She could feel that Will had gone still next to her, and she heard Anna's quick intake of breath and knew that the others were watching as well. Behind them, people were glancing curiously their way, doubtless drawn by the sight of Tommy Halifax on bended knee.

Panic rushed through her, making her light-headed and off balance. She felt startled and also a little angry that he was ruining the friendship they'd shared. No—he was ruining everything, because how would his family ever look on her the same way again, now that he'd chosen her? Already excitement was beginning to brighten the beloved faces around her. She felt as if the parson's noose were already slipping over her neck—and everything within her revolted against it.

Which was how, unable to stop herself in that terrible, awkward, panicking moment, she did the one thing she should never have done.

She laughed.

In the stunned moment that followed, she heard Ruby gasp and saw a terrible dark look come over Tommy's face, changing it so she felt suddenly that she hardly knew him. He was still holding her hand as though frozen. She struggled to find something to say, but she couldn't say yes, and she couldn't disappoint him, so she said nothing.

His eyes turned into shards of sharp green glass that cut her, like a knife paring a rotten part from an apple. He dropped her hand and stood up, but now he would no longer look at her, and she understood with a terrible finality that nothing would ever be the same.

Without a word to her or anyone else, he turned and left the ball.

She wrote him two different letters that night and tore them both up before crawling into bed, desperately unhappy and confused and wishing she'd never even gone to the ball.

The failed proposal was the talk of Town, but Lizzie supposed Tommy didn't care or, more accurately, didn't notice, because three days later he boarded a ship for India.

Two

WHEN CAPTAIN TOMMY HALIFAX—SOON TO BE Captain *Sir* Tommy Halifax—caught his first sight of England from the bow of a ship after six years away, he was surprised to find himself grinning. Good old England. He'd barely given it a thought all this time.

He'd left the country still practically a youth, and he was returning—just for a visit—as a man who'd seen quite a bit of the world. He hardly felt like the same fellow.

He had skills now that he hadn't possessed when he'd left, gained while working on behalf of England's interests in India: he could speak Hindi fluently, undertake complex diplomatic relations, withstand punishing conditions for days on horseback across vast stretches of uninhabited lands, and charm females of all ages with little more than the arching of a black eyebrow over his distinctive green eyes.

In addition, he'd become adept with a sword, which had been a good thing during the long voyage from India, since the ship bringing him to England had been set upon twice by pirates. Tommy had aided the crew in repelling the brigands both times, the second time coming to the rescue of the ship's captain as he was about to be felled by a terrifying beast of a man.

This last episode had earned Tommy the undying gratitude of the crew and the small number of passengers, and considering that one of the purposes for Tommy's return to England was to be knighted for service to the Crown (in recognition of, among other feats, his diplomatic efforts with a powerful rajah that had averted an all-out war), he seemed to his shipmates to be quite covered in glory.

The sailors, in fact, had created a song in his honor that they'd taken to singing while scrubbing the deck, with bawdy verses that rhymed such things as "manly thighs" with "darkening skies," which made Tommy hide a smile whenever it rang out over the sea. But he was honored to be called a "lion for England," and he was happy to serve his country.

And happy, he realized as the September sun gilded the spires of London, to return for a bit, even though this visit home was taking him away from work he wanted to be doing in India. And he was eager to see his family. He'd missed his older brother, Will, and his sister-in-law, Anna, and his Halifax cousins.

It was too bad that his stepmother, Judith, was away tending to her ailing mother, and that his cousins Andrew and Emerald would still be in Switzerland while Tommy was in England. But he was eager to meet Will's young son and daughter. Not being near his family had been the only thing he'd regretted about living in India.

On the other hand, family—of a sort—was also the reason he'd originally left.

Six years before, he'd been naive and foolish enough to mistake lust for his brother's niece for love. His life had felt ripped apart when Lizzie rejected him.

Now he could acknowledge that she'd done him a favor. But for her laughing at his proposal, he might have stayed in England and missed out on the most amazing experiences of his life. He might almost have wanted to thank her.

Almost.

❧

Anna, Lady Grandville, had been stirring her tea for far longer than the addition of a spoon of sugar required, and Lady Elizabeth Tarryton Truehart, formerly known as Lizzie but now called Eliza by all those who cared for her, supposed she knew what was coming. She'd just been hoping they wouldn't have to talk about it.

"Dearest," Anna began, but then she frowned as though not sure where to begin. Eliza couldn't blame her.

They were sitting in the drawing room in Truehart Manor, which Eliza had inherited upon the death of her husband, Sir Gerard Truehart, two years before.

Anna cleared her throat and began again. "People are starting to notice that you haven't been to any of the events held since Tommy's return."

The crisp September breeze slipped in the window behind Eliza, stirring the long curtains against the skirts of her demure blue-and-white-striped gown and brushing the tops of her plain black ankle boots. Her hair was styled in a simple knot, and she wore no jewelry save a pair of pearl earbobs Will had given her as a birthday present. The breeze was perhaps a little chilly, but even in the winter months she preferred that the windows be cracked to let in fresh air.

"If people are gossiping about me and Tommy not being in the same room together, then they have far too much time on their hands. I'm just an old widow anyway."

Anna rolled her eyes. "You are *twenty-four*, Eliza—younger than many ladies who've yet to wed once, and you're the lovely niece of Viscount Grandville, so your movements will always be of interest to society. But it's not the gossip I care about."

Although Anna was an artist with an excellent eye for the beauty of nature (and she'd once been known as the Beautiful One), her appearance always had an absentminded quality. Today was no different. She was wearing red shoes with a bronze gown that no one else would have paired for fear of clashing, but on Anna, somehow the ensemble looked very fine and rather ahead of its time. Eliza hid a smile as her eyes lingered on Anna's slightly messy coiffure, guessing that her aunt had dispensed with the services of a maid and simply jammed her boisterous black hair into a knot in lieu of wasting time she preferred to spend crawling around on the floor with her young children.

"Good," Eliza said. "There are far more important things."

A blast of cold autumn air came in through the window, and Anna pulled her blue shawl more snugly around her shoulders. Eliza ignored the discomfort from long practice.

"What I should have said is that *Will and I* think it's odd that you and Tommy have yet to meet since he returned from India, because both of you mean so much to us and we want to have the whole family together. And what must Tommy think, with you not even present at the celebration for his knighthood?"

"I was not in London when he returned from India."

Anna sniffed. "Yes, that trip to visit an ailing friend came up *quite* suddenly. However, you've been back for several days, and you haven't been to a single one of the dinners or parties we've held for him. And since he's only going to be in England for a few months, there's a limited time for all the family to be together." Her eyes settled on Eliza's. "Or are you avoiding him?"

"Why should I be avoiding him?" Eliza said. "That would be silly of me."

Which didn't mean it wasn't also exactly what she was doing.

After Tommy left for India, she'd finally managed to set down her thoughts and sent him a letter of apology. But she'd never had a reply, and she'd taken that to mean he wanted to forget what she'd done—and her. Which she'd understood.

He couldn't know how bitterly she'd regretted her behavior. Nor how guilty she felt when Will had said quietly, "I don't think he's coming back for a long time. If ever." Though neither Will nor any of the family had ever behaved any differently toward her after Tommy left, for the first two years, Eliza had lived in daily fear that everyone was secretly furious and disgusted with her, and that Will would send her away just as her father had.

"You're a beautiful and charming young lady," her father had written in the only letter she'd received from him after he sent her to the Rosewood School, *"but beauty and charm can't bring your life meaning and value. You have to make something of yourself."*

The letter had forced her to accept that, just like her stepmother, her father had thought her worthless. Hurt and angry, sixteen-year-old Eliza had set about proving just how important beauty and charm were in life. Every man who'd come under her spell had been one more reason to believe she wasn't the good-for-nothing person her father had so clearly thought her—until the disaster of Tommy's proposal.

After Tommy left for India, she'd finally taken her father's words to heart and begun to make a new path for herself. Marrying Gerard when she was nineteen had been part of that path. A kind, serious, older gentleman, he'd helped her focus on the important things, like self-discipline, and forgiven her frequent mistakes. Their marriage had been a beneficial friendship that had left her in a better place when he had, sadly, died after two years, leaving her enough money to be independent.

And though Will was too noble ever to send her away, with the birth of each of his and Anna's children, Eliza had felt a little guiltier that their Uncle Tommy wasn't there to meet them. She'd known that she could never strive hard enough to earn the love Will and Anna so foolishly bestowed on her.

"Well," Anna said, "you can see Tommy at the Cowpers' dinner party tomorrow night. I know he's going, and you've been invited as well."

"I declined the invitation."

Anna waved a hand dismissively. "You can change your mind. Aren't you curious to see him? I'm told there was a ranking system devised by this year's debutantes. Lord Bernard was listed as Most Likely to Marry Quickly, and that nice Mr. Caruthers was deemed Least Likely to Steal a Kiss." She paused. "Tommy was voted Most Swashbuckling."

A spark of interest niggled Eliza, but she ignored it. "That's fairly outrageous, making a list like that."

"It's just the kind of thing you would have done at their age."

"Exactly—a bad idea."

Anna frowned thoughtfully. "Eliza, I think it's wonderful, what you and Meg are doing here with the girls you're helping. But…I worry that you don't have any fun anymore."

Eliza and Meg Cartwright, who'd been her closest friend since the season they were seventeen, had gotten lost one day in a part of London where they'd never ventured before—and found street upon street where children sat neglected and begging. Their hearts went out especially to the girls, who would have the least opportunity to better themselves, and before they'd even returned to Mayfair, the two friends had begun planning how to help.

Education would be key, they knew, but girls who'd been living on the street were hardly in a state to begin attending school. Meg and Eliza finally came up with the idea of making Truehart Manor into a sort of halfway point, a place where destitute, orphaned girls could come to stay for weeks or months, depending on how long they needed to acquire the skills, polish, and basic education that would allow them to blend in at a school in Bath run by Eliza's friend Francesca. Meg moved into Truehart Manor, and they began work. So far, they'd sent eight girls to Francesca.

Eliza took a sip of her tea. "Helping the girls at Truehart Manor *is* what I do for fun."

"But you need a life apart from that, too. You should go out to parties and dinners sometimes."

"I really don't feel the need."

Anna smiled encouragingly. "You might meet an interesting man. I know any number of nice gentlemen who would like to meet you."

Eliza laughed. "I'm not interested in meeting men, Anna. I've already tried marriage."

"You were married to Gerard Truehart for two years. That's hardly a vast experience. And Gerard…" Anna's brown eyes settled on Eliza with the weight of seriousness. "We always worried he wasn't the best match for you."

Eliza's marriage to Gerard had been…pleasant. If their time together had sometimes seemed a little boring, Eliza reminded herself that life couldn't be thrilling all the time.

Anna didn't say anything about how the couple hadn't had children because she knew that Eliza couldn't; Eliza had told her so. Though Gerard had religiously made an effort several times each month to produce an heir and Eliza had dearly wanted a baby, there'd been no result. Gerard had had a son with his first wife—though the child eventually died—so they knew the problem wasn't with him. A doctor had pronounced Eliza infertile.

Her lack of a baby was the secret sorrow of her days, but she didn't allow herself to dwell on it because she already had so much for which to be grateful.

"Listen, Anna, I really don't think it would be very nice for Tommy if the two of us met. I'm certain I'm not his favorite person."

"It's been six *years*, Eliza. He can't possibly be holding a grudge. I'm sure he's forgotten about it."

Eliza wasn't. Certainly he might no longer care that she'd laughed at his proposal. But forgotten? She highly doubted it.

Anna hadn't been the one pinned by Tommy's fierce glare six years ago, nor had she been the very good friend who'd shared a kiss with him.

And that kiss… There'd been magic in it.

Unfortunately, Eliza had discovered that affection for a person you'd liked and admired wasn't something that could be turned off like a tap. She'd dreamed of him for years after he left, even though she'd been married to another man. And no matter how many times she'd sternly told herself that one kiss was no indicator of anything, something in her had remained stubbornly unconvinced.

"I'm sorry, but I really can't go to the Cowpers'," Eliza said. "I've already committed to attending a lecture with Meg."

"You'll have to see him sometime, Eliza. It will be difficult not to."

Eliza was rescued from the necessity of a reply by a heavy thump in the corridor outside the drawing room, followed by a cacophony of girlish voices and the thundering of feet on old floors.

"That will be Mrs. Trinkett with the girls," Eliza said, referring to the middle-aged widow who'd moved in a few months before to help Meg and Eliza with the girls. "They're doing grammar today."

The two ladies waited out the racket as Eliza poured more tea for them. The sound of a door closing greatly reduced the noise.

"How many girls are there now?" Anna asked. "It sounded like hundreds."

"Only four. You've met Mary, Susie, and Thomasina. Franny came two weeks ago. She is, well, a bit hard. She lost her parents in a fire last year, and she's been living on the streets all this time, trying to stay out of the poorhouse."

"The poor child." Anna shook her head. "Will and I are so proud of what you're doing. It's hard to believe you are the girl who was expelled from the Rosewood School for climbing out her bedroom window to meet a man."

"Thank God I'm not like that anymore."

"Oh," Anna said, an almost sad look coming into her eyes, "but you were charming."

"I was a careless flirt without a thought in my head."

"That's not true. Perhaps you made some mistakes, but everyone does. You're far too hard on yourself."

Not hard enough, Eliza thought.

There was a knock at the door and Meg poked her head in.

With her straight brown hair and honest brown eyes, she looked as pretty as a porcelain doll—until one's eyes drifted downward to her attire, which was generally odd. She favored badly mismatched clothes; today she had paired a pale buttercup-yellow silk gown with a russet shawl. If the shades of the colors had been different, the outfit might have looked interesting, but it was as though Meg had sought out the most jarring combination of colors she could find.

"There was ice in the girls' washbasins this morning," she said. "Maybe we should close the windows now that it's getting cold."

"Nonsense," Eliza said cheerfully. "Cool air is good for the circulation."

Meg's eyes slid meaningfully to where Anna sat huddled under her shawl. "And we need to discuss your insistence that they read five books a week. I think it's too much."

"The girls need challenging goals if they're going to make progress."

Meg looked like she had more to say, but she just pressed her lips together and closed the door.

"Five books a week?" Anna said. "Don't you think that's a little excessive?" She rubbed her hands together as if to warm them. "And honestly, it *is* chilly in the house."

"Builds character," Eliza said. "How will they make something of themselves if we're soft on them?" Experience had taught her that self-indulgence and leniency led to disaster, and what she wanted for the girls who came to Truehart Manor was a better life. "Really, it's for the best."

It was nearly lunchtime the next day when Eliza stepped out of Smithson's Fine Papers. She'd had a productive morning purchasing supplies for the schoolroom, including new maps and a writing tablet. Susie, at eleven, was only just able to form her letters, and they had to find a way to get her to focus more efficiently. Eliza had also ordered chemises for the girls from the dressmaker, who'd brought out a new rose fabric that she insisted was made for Eliza's coloring. Though pink had once been Eliza's favorite color, resisting the temptation to dress garishly was now child's play, and she smiled peacefully as she declined.

She did find herself slightly exasperated, though, to overhear no fewer than three ladies discussing Sir Tommy Halifax and his many fine qualities (handsome, witty, and swashbuckling—apparently no one had ever had a chance to use the word until he'd come home). But realizing she was being unfair to him, Eliza let the feelings go. When a wide-eyed young lady had approached her and shyly asked if Eliza was related to Sir Tommy, Eliza was able to say in quite a nice tone, "No, I'm not."

As she moved down the street, a mother came toward her with a baby in her arms. The baby was beautiful, with rosy cheeks and dark eyes, and the sight tugged at Eliza with the old, aching emptiness. Lately it seemed as if everywhere she looked, there were mothers with babies. The girls at Truehart Manor were almost like daughters to her, but their place in her life was temporary. A child of her own would have been someone to love forever. But she had no intention of ever marrying again, so there would be no baby.

Though she'd accepted all this long ago, she couldn't seem to stop envying women with children—another flaw she needed to work on. She strived harder every day to do more good and be a better person. Which was why she was still thinking about something that had happened that morning.

She'd come upon Franny and Thomasina standing in the upstairs corridor, discussing, of all things, prostitution. In a better world, neither girl would know the first thing about the topic, but any child forced to live on the street quickly learned of the compromises people made to survive. Just the day before, Eliza had received word from Francesca that one of the older girls sent to the Bath school had left to work as a high-class prostitute.

It was a sad fact that an astonishing number of girls and women worked in the trade, which ran the spectrum from cheap encounters in alleys to lucrative work in high-class brothels and for a select few, a unique position in society as a courtesan who might command astonishing sums and even a measure of respect.

Apparently, both Franny and Thomasina had cousins who worked in brothels.

"Florrie earns pounds and pounds every month," Franny said as Eliza paused unseen around the corner behind her. "Much more than any maid or governess."

"My cousin Nancy says she'll never, ever go back to being a scullery maid," Thomasina said. "At Madame Persaud's there's a party every night, and the ladies dress up in fancy clothes and wear masks so the men can't see who they are. Doesn't it sound exciting?"

"It sounds like an easy way to live like a queen, is what it sounds like," Franny had said. "And with all the fine airs we'll be learning, I'll wager Madame Persaud would be glad to take us on in a year or two."

Eliza had nearly gasped at the idea of Truehart Manor and Francesca's school functioning as some sort of prostitute training academy. She'd stepped forward and said, "That's enough, girls," in a stern voice. "You're making things up, and I don't want the others hearing this kind of nonsense. A brothel is not some grand place to work."

"I didn't make anything up," Thomasina protested earnestly. She was a sweet girl, though easily led. But Franny gave Eliza a challenging look.

"A brothel is a dangerous place," Eliza said.

Thomasina blinked. "But my cousin is happier and healthier than ever. She's not poor anymore."

"Begging your pardon, ma'am," Franny said, not sounding at all remorseful, "but a fine lady like you would have no idea what it's like at a brothel."

"Yes, I—" Eliza had caught herself, surprised at the rush of forgotten memories from her girlhood in Malta, when she'd flitted about the sun-kissed grand harbor chatting up sailors, shopkeepers, and prostitutes. Everything in Malta had felt magical to the happy child she'd once been, from the toast-colored buildings of the town to the deep blue of the Mediterranean Sea, which framed the view in every direction.

With its open, warm-hearted people and beaches scattered with sea daffodils and rockroses, Malta had meant freedom and joy to a child who'd grown up amid the rules of chilly England. The girl she'd been couldn't have imagined anything like desperation behind the gaily painted faces of the women who called to the sailors from their doorsteps.

But Franny was right: aside from her vague memories of the harbor's boisterous women, Eliza knew almost nothing of what the lives of prostitutes were like. The girl's words stirred something in her…the forgotten thrill of a challenge issued.

You'd never jump in a fountain, Lizzie.

Females aren't allowed in gentlemen's clubs.

I'd wager you wouldn't dare to meet me at midnight in the garden.

She'd pushed the memories of her wild days aside as she dismissed the girls, but now she kept turning over what they'd said. Maybe she needed to educate herself. Maybe she needed to find a way to see for herself what it was like in a brothel so she could better steer their girls away from any illusions offered by its false promises.

As she crossed the street and entered Hyde Park, she decided that she must find some way to try. Apparently the brothel was called Madame Persaud's—could Eliza send some sort of anonymous note there to Thomasina's cousin Nancy, asking for help in return for money? If what Franny had said about the nightly parties and the women wearing masks was true, it could be a way for Eliza to sneak in and observe.

She knew that what she was considering was completely scandalous and risky—which was why she wasn't going to tell even Meg about her plans—but it would be nothing like the wild things she used to do. This time she wouldn't be following the lure of the forbidden. She'd be acting for the benefit of others.

A series of sharp barks pulled her out of her thoughts. A large dog was racing toward her across the greensward. It stopped in front of her, barking excitedly.

She'd always loved dogs, and this one's exuberance made her smile. But as she looked at him, she realized there was something about this dog that was familiar. *He* certainly seemed to know *her*, though awful looking as he was, he was hardly the sort of dog usually seen in Mayfair.

He was enormous, for one thing, a dark brown beast whose head reached the middle of her waist. He had a torn ear that flopped against his head with each deep woof, and the end of his tail was clearly missing. There was also a bald patch near his rump that suggested he'd been in a fight. But his fur was a beautiful chocolate color, as were his eyes, and looking into them, she suddenly knew who he was.

"Traveler!" she cried. Dropping to a crouch, she let her packages slide to the ground as she wrapped her arms around him. He licked her neck enthusiastically, making her laugh.

She sat back on her heels. "You were but a slip of a thing the last time I saw you. And you were in much better shape." She gently ruffled his ear, its torn edges clearly an old injury. "Which isn't to say you're not still adorable. But what are you doing here in the park, all alone?"

"He's not alone," a voice said from behind her—a

voice she hadn't heard for six years. It had deepened in the intervening time, but voices had personalities, and she knew this one. She turned her head, and there was Tommy.

If it hadn't been for the white blade of hair that fell across his forehead amid the slashes of his longish, unruly black hair, she might not have known him immediately. He'd always been remarkably handsome, but now... Something fluttered in her chest.

India's sun had tanned his skin, and his features had lost any youthful softness. His shoulders and chest had filled in with what was clearly hard muscle. Like his Halifax cousins, he had green eyes, but his had a clarity she'd forgotten—along with a knowing light that hadn't been there before, as if he'd seen and done just about everything possible. His dark blue tailcoat made her think of a foreign sea at night, and though it was as elegant as any London gentleman's, it didn't suggest sophistication and elegance, but rather trade routes conquered and booty taken.

Most Swashbuckling indeed.

She stood up. She'd thought it would be awkward to see him, but suddenly she was so happy.

"Tommy! What a surprise to meet you here." When he didn't respond as she paused to breathe, she kept going. "Though considering Traveler is here, I ought not to have been surprised. Perhaps *you* were surprised to see *me*?" She was babbling, but the steady way he was looking at her with those unwavering green eyes was making her feel off-kilter.

"Lizzie," he said, tipping his head in greeting. His

polite expression gave no hint of how he felt about seeing her. "Anna said you'd come back to Town."

She cringed a little at the old nickname but didn't correct him; it wasn't surprising that he'd called her "Lizzie" since it was the name by which he'd always known her. But if he displayed no irritation at seeing her, neither did he seem at all glad.

As he stood there looking at her politely, she almost wished he was angry, because then maybe there would be the chance to speak of what had happened, to apologize properly and put to rest some of her guilt. The proposal lay between them—at least, she thought it did—but she couldn't just blurt out an apology for laughing at him after not seeing him for years.

Yet they were *almost* family, and her conversation with Anna had pointed out the impossibility of them avoiding each other entirely. It would be so much easier, she now saw, if there wasn't awkwardness between them. She stepped a little closer.

"I'm sorry I missed your knighthood ceremony. I suppose I should call you Sir Tommy now?"

"That's not necessary."

She'd been teasing, but he hadn't smiled, and he didn't look like he wanted to chat. Was he simply unamused? Why couldn't she read him anymore, as she'd once been able to do? "Well…anyway, congratulations, and welcome home. It's really quite lovely to see you."

"Thank you," he said politely. "It's nice to see you as well." He dropped to his haunches and deftly scooped up her packages, then stood and held them out to her. "I hope Traveler didn't cause anything in your parcels to break."

She shook her head and repressed a bizarre, sudden urge to step forward and simply embrace him as she would once have done, never mind that she hadn't touched a man since Gerard died.

She tried again to glean the state of Tommy's emotions from his polite expression, but without result. What if he *had* forgotten what happened—and forgotten her as well, and all the good times they'd shared? Though she ought to be relieved if he'd forgotten their shared past, some of those memories were happy ones for her, and she didn't like the idea that they might now be nothing to him.

"Are you in the park for a walk with Traveler?"

"I was on an errand."

"Ah." Her mind whirred. Should she say something? Or would it be best to let sleeping dogs lie?

If for nothing other than your own self-respect, her conscience insisted, *you owe him a proper apology. Go on, he's not going to bite you.*

Though what if he did bite her—metaphorically? What if bringing up the past made him angry?

You deserve his anger. Stop wasting time.

Right. Maybe it was an odd moment to do it, but she had to say something. She cleared her throat. "Tommy, did you get the letter I sent you years ago, right after you left?"

The barest hint of a frown tugged at his mouth before disappearing—or had she imagined it?

"Please, Lizzie," he said reasonably, waving a hand dismissively, "that was years ago." He gave her a polite, impersonal smile. "Now, if you'll excuse me," he continued in that maddeningly reasonable tone, "I'm afraid there's somewhere I must be." He dipped his head in a sketch of farewell and left her standing there.

Had he known she was about to apologize and not wanted to discuss the old incident? Or did he just not care about anything from so long ago, even something that had left such a big imprint on her?

Seeing him had made her feel like she was suddenly seventeen again, unsure and emotionally stormy, and she gave herself a sort of mental shake. She wasn't that girl anymore, and her life now had meaning and purpose that had nothing to do with men.

❧

Tommy strode away from Lizzie with Traveler trotting at his heels. He'd been to Whitehall that morning to deliver some sensitive documents he'd brought from India, and now he was headed to the house of his cousin Louie, the Earl of Gildenhall. He and Louie and Will planned to ride out of the city for a few hours. Tommy had only been in London for two weeks, and already he felt penned in by all the gentility, so a bruising ride seemed like the very thing.

It wasn't that he didn't enjoy balls and dancing and lively dinner conversation; he did. It was just that he missed *action*—the kind of action that his life in India provided. Hell, even the boat trip over, while it had left him frequently pacing the decks like a caged animal, had at least offered the entertainment of pirates.

It was a shame his cousin Andrew was away, or the two of them might have found a way to jaunt off into the country for a week or so, sleeping rough and hiking the hills as they'd often done. But Andrew was in Switzerland, probably exploring the Alps, the lucky bastard.

Tommy was a little amused that Lizzie had wanted to bring up the proposal. Not that he wanted to talk about it, he thought with a shudder. What a fool he'd been. Idealistic, too trusting, and blind, as young men often were, to faults in the beautiful women who captured their attention.

He supposed she still lured unsuspecting males by the cartful. She was more gorgeous now than she'd been when he'd left, though she was dressed more demurely today than he'd ever seen her before. The years had sculpted her features with loveliness and enhanced her blue eyes with a gracious, if deceptive, warmth. The color of her hair had deepened to the rich golden red of sun-kissed autumn leaves, and her voice now had a pleasing hint of huskiness.

He'd known she'd married Gerard Truehart—Will had sent regular letters—and the news had at first made him furious. Even though the man had been a harmless older gentleman, Truehart had had what Tommy had not, and he'd hated him for it.

It was easier now to feel sorry for the man. Having been her victim once, Tommy could easily imagine how she'd beguiled Truehart. He could even conjure a little pity for the poor fool who would be her next victim, because if there was one thing he knew about Lizzie, it was that she'd never be without admirers.

It was almost comical now, how angry and bitterly disappointed he'd been six years ago. But finally, after a year in India pining for her while hating himself for being under her spell, he'd awoken to the awareness that the world was filled with lovely women.

He'd come to understand that she was simply a shallow person. Realizing that he'd only been one of the many admirers she'd been stringing along that season—and that Lizzie had been as addicted to the attention they gave her as an old sot was to drink—had finally freed Tommy of his enslavement to her.

It had also taught him the wisdom of never again listening to the whims of emotion. Now he knew that love—what he'd thought he'd known at twenty-two—was simply lust mingled with weakness and foolishness.

Oh, he knew that some people did find love, or what they believed to be love. He would never suggest that his brother and Anna weren't going to be blissfully, mutually, and eternally happy. But that kind of thing was rare, and not for him.

Why would he need marriage, anyway, when the world was full of willing women? If he ever married, it would be years hence, after he'd done everything he wanted to do and there was little left but to surrender to domesticity.

At his side, Traveler bounced about excitedly, as though still happy about meeting Lizzie. Tommy ruffled the fur on his head.

"She's a siren, old boy. You know what that means: lovely package, imminent doom. Most definitely to be avoided."

When Tommy arrived at Louie's town house, his cousin and Will were standing by the hearth in the drawing room.

"I see you've brought the beast," Louie said dryly as Traveler bounded over to him. "Did Graves swoon on your way in?" he asked, referring to his butler.

"The merest flicker of an outraged eyelash," Tommy reported. "He seems to be growing accustomed to us."

"You say *us* as though the two of you were an old married couple," Will said, dropping to his haunches to pet the dog.

Tommy had noticed that Will liked to insert references to marriage into his conversations with him, but he refused to rise to the bait of discussions he didn't intend to have.

"You're not meaning to bring the old fellow with us today, are you?" Louie said.

"He's staying with me," came a feminine voice from the doorway as Louie's sister Ruby entered the room. She was dressed, as always, in a shade of red and in a gown so striking that it could only be the height of fashion.

At twenty-nine, Ruby had settled into a clearly contented existence that revolved, as far as Tommy could tell, around attending balls, buying clothes, and visiting friends. Her features were too strong to be called beautiful, but she was a very handsome woman, and as the sister of the Earl of Gildenhall, she would still be considered a catch. But marriage was not in her plans; once Louie had become earl and the pressure for her to find a husband was off, she'd declared that she'd remain single. "I'll be the aunt all the children love best," she liked to say.

Ruby took a seat on a yellow divan, and Traveler trotted over to be petted. She pulled a small biscuit out of her pocket and offered it to the dog, who took it with enthusiasm.

"Biscuits?" Tommy said. "You'll make him soft."

"Pish," she said. "I'm sure any creature who's been dragged all over the world by you and been half baked and half frozen on any number of occasions deserves a treat." Tommy's family had naturally been eager to hear more about the adventures he'd described so briefly in his occasional letters, and they'd reacted with varying shades of delight and horror to his escapades. "Why you wish to be hideously uncomfortable, dirty, and hungry most of the time when you might be sitting by a cozy English fire with a glass of brandy in your hand and a grateful dog by your feet, I'll never understand."

"Where's your spirit of adventure, Ruby? Besides, Traveler loves voyages. Only consider his name."

She gave Tommy a dry look.

He turned to Louie, mockery tweaking the corners of his mouth. "And you should watch whom you're calling *old fellow*. Why, I almost feel I ought not to drag you two old men out on what will likely be a very punishing ride for you."

It was true that Will was thirty-nine and Louie was thirty-seven, but no one looking at the men's tall, firm physiques would have described either as old, let alone aging. Louie retained the air of the roguish golden boy he'd always been, and Will still moved with the athletic grace of a man who knew how to fix a roof and pound in a fence stake, and had done both on his estates on occasions too numerous to count. But what would be the fun in admitting any of that?

Louie's eyes glittered. "Trying to cry off now that you've realized you won't be able to keep up with us?"

"We'll see who can keep up," Tommy said.

This kind of banter had been going on for decades among the Halifax men. Riding out for hours at a punishing pace was something they'd done often when younger. Tommy spent plenty of time in the saddle in India, and while those long hours could be grueling, he missed them. When he was on horseback riding out beyond the outskirts of Hyderabad, the world was his oyster, and nothing was required of him but finding his own way.

Will sent his eyes heavenward and Ruby laughed softly. He was the oldest among all the cousins, and unlike Louie, who'd unexpectedly inherited his earldom and estates in his early twenties, Will had known from an early age that he would be viscount and responsible for much. Duty and honor had always been of utmost importance to him, and while Will was in no way humorless, there had always been something more serious about him.

"Racing?" Ruby said. "Name-calling? Will you boys ever grow up?"

"Who wants to grow up if it means abandoning races and name-calling?" Louie said.

Will gave an exaggerated sigh. "Hasn't anyone ever told you, Louie, that an earl must have decorum?"

"You, about twenty times a month," Louie said. "But as you *are* older, I suppose I ought to consider deferring to your wisdom."

"You'll be deferring to my dust," Will said as they headed out of the room.

Tommy shot Ruby a grin on his way out. "See you at the Cowpers' tonight?"

"If you have time to clean up—you do realize that it rained last night? Louie's valet moaned about mud for days after the last time he and Will went riding. I believe he despairs of Louie ever really being the sort of fellow an earl ought to be."

Tommy laughed as he passed through the door. After days cooped up in proper, tasteful drawing rooms, dashing across muddy fields with the autumn wind whipping at him sounded like bliss.

They rode sedately out of the city, then as soon as the houses fell away switched to a pace that would spare their horses but was nonetheless tiring for the riders. There was little chance for conversation over the beating of three sets of hooves, save for shouted taunts and masculine laughter. But they hadn't come to chat anyway, and as they rode under a brilliant blue sky over open fields and past trees showing the first yellows and oranges of autumn, their grins grew wider.

Eventually they passed the edge of a wood, and before them in the distance gleamed the thin line of a stream.

"The tree on the left," Tommy called out, indicating a pair of enormous oaks that stood by the stream's edge. "Race you!" He kicked his horse into a gallop as his companions did the same.

First one of the men would seize the lead, then another, the sound of thundering hooves filling the air along with splats of mud. They held to no rules of politeness when going neck-or-nothing, so when Louie edged Will toward a cluster of small branches that whipped him as he passed, Tommy laughed and did the same to his cousin.

Will, however, took the dubious honor of most obnoxious when he thundered past both of them just as they drew near a puddle, showering them so liberally with mud that Tommy and Louie both got it in their hair.

Tommy saw his chance as the path narrowed between two stands of trees. He pushed his horse ahead and had made it almost to the oak tree, but Louie came from behind to cut him off at the last moment, arriving first, followed seconds later by Tommy and Will.

"Ha!" crowed Louie as his horse danced beneath him. "Victorious over His Majesty's newest knight."

Tommy snorted. "Enjoy it. It's a long way back to Mayfair, and your old bones will be feeling it."

"Nonsense," Louie said. "I feel invincible. I've never been in better form, wouldn't you say, Will?"

"I'd say that you're within a whisper of sounding like the most conceited earl in the *ton*."

Filthy and winded, the men dismounted and walked their horses along the stream and watered them. Louie handed out sandwiches his cook had packed.

Will said, "Last night, Heck thought it would be amusing to lean out a second-floor window and shoot pebbles at the flowers in our garden."

"And he's only six," Tommy said with wicked glee. "Too bad I won't be around to watch him vex you as you try to form him into the responsible heir of a viscount."

Tommy felt his brother's eyes lingering on him at the mention of not being around in coming years. He should have kept his mouth shut. "I suppose I'll have a taste of what Father must have suffered when he was training me," Will said. "I remember him telling Mother it couldn't be done, but you know Mother—she was endlessly optimistic."

"She was," Tommy agreed with a trace of that old emptiness. She'd died when he was seven, their father a few years after. The world was full of dying, Tommy had discovered early on; he meant to *live*. To behave with no regard for risk—that was his way of thumbing his nose at death.

Louie polished off the last hunk of his sandwich. "So, Tommy, have you considered staying? You know the whole family is happy to have you back, and India won't miss you for a year or two. Why take a long boat journey again after only a few months at home? It seems like pure madness."

"Really, *madness*?" Tommy laughed. Though it was true that he wasn't exactly looking forward to the long return voyage, and it *was* quite fine to be somewhere that had an autumn after all the years in India, where the seasons were more along the lines of either monsoon season or not monsoon season. But England was…tame. "I do have things awaiting my attention in India."

He was, though, looking into buying an estate in

England for the time—still far in the future—when he was ready to settle down. But he wasn't going to mention this to his family yet, because he knew they'd see it as a sign he might stay, when it would simply be a place to put some of the considerable money he'd made.

"Anna wants cousins for Heck and Vic because she had none," Will said. "She says she quite envies us Halifaxes, with there being so many of us."

"If anyone should be busily filling a nursery with heirs," Tommy said, "it's the Earl of Gildenhall."

"One more word about filling nurseries," Louie said, "and both of you are going for a swim."

Their brief repast completed, the men mounted and turned toward Town, guiding their horses at a walking pace to start.

"So," Louie asked Tommy, "have you seen Eliza yet? Ruby and Anna are quite interested in the fact that the two of you have yet to be seen in the same room."

Tommy knew he should have expected his family's interest in how he and Lizzie would get on. Fortunately, he could now put this subject to rest. "Actually, I ran into Lizzie in Hyde Park earlier today."

"Why didn't you say?" Will said.

"Why would I? It was just a brief encounter with an old friend."

"Just an old friend…" Louie said with a teasing note in his voice that Tommy chose to ignore.

"She goes by Eliza now, as I think you know," Will said.

Tommy shrugged. "Old habits. Why did she change it, anyway?"

"I think it was Gerard who started calling her that, and it stuck."

"Well," Louie said, "how did the big reunion go? Ruby will want all the details."

Tommy shot him a disgusted look. "For the love of… I don't see why it should be of interest to anyone else, but it seems I've forgotten about the Halifax fascination with family gossip. We ran into each other, talked briefly—nice to see you and all that—and parted. That's it. No story."

Louie lifted an eyebrow. "So everything's forgotten and forgiven after all this time? You were—understandably—pretty angry when you left."

"I was twenty-two, Louie. It would be ridiculous if any of that still mattered to me."

Will nodded slowly, but his gaze didn't leave Tommy's face. "She's a very different person now, Tommy."

Tommy nodded noncommittally. He very much doubted that his brother, Lizzie's one-time guardian and fond uncle, could be unbiased in his judgment of her.

He spurred his horse to a trot, and his brother and cousin followed suit.

Three

A BOOKSELLER'S SHOP SHE NEVER FREQUENTED HAD seemed like the perfect meeting place to Eliza when she'd proposed it in her note to Thomasina's cousin Nancy, but she hadn't expected Little's Books and Fine Papers to be so crowded so early in the day. There hadn't really been much choice, though, since Nancy couldn't have come to Truehart Manor without being noticed.

They had to squeeze themselves far to the back of the shelves of travel books in the rear of the store so they could converse unnoticed. As soon as she'd checked to see that no one else was around, Eliza slipped Nancy the generous tip she'd promised in her note written on behalf of a "shy, curious friend" who wanted to observe the beguiling ways of the ladies at Madame Persaud's so she might better beguile her husband. (Eliza actually did wonder what men found so compelling about prostitutes.) She'd signed her name as Mrs. Williams.

"You really think my friend wouldn't be noticed?" Eliza asked as they stood amid the volumes about

Italian holidays. Nancy, who was pretty and looked to be about twenty-five, had a blunt way of talking, but at least she was dressed unobjectionably. Though Eliza's note had urged discretion, saying she'd gotten Nancy's name from a friend of a friend, she had worried that the woman might look like, well, a prostitute.

"There are always new girls coming through, and all the girls will be wearing masks," Nancy said, "so your friend won't stand out. That's what makes Madame Persaud's special—every night, the women all wear masks at the start of the evening. The clients like the mystery."

"Do the men wear masks?"

Nancy shook her head. "And none of the gents can choose a lady to go upstairs with until the choosing time at ten o'clock, which sometimes leads to bidding wars." She gave a husky chuckle. "Madame Persaud loves it when that happens."

This was even better than Eliza could have hoped! It had occurred to her that in trying to pass herself off as a prostitute, she might attract the attention of a client, but it seemed that even if she did, all she had to do was leave the brothel before ten.

Though an insistent little voice demanded that she recognize this whole idea was beyond foolish and that sneaking into a brothel would be returning to her outrageous old ways, she silenced it with the knowledge that what she would be doing was for a very good cause.

Nancy told Eliza about the layout of the house, what Eliza's "friend" should wear to blend in, and the location of the back entrance where she could enter the brothel unnoticed.

Nancy smiled. It was not a sweet smile, but Eliza supposed, considering the life Nancy must have led, that she had grown rather cynical. "Maybe your friend really just wants to see for herself what goes on. Maybe she thinks it's exciting."

"No, she doesn't," Eliza said, not sure why it mattered what Nancy thought. Perhaps, after she understood more, Eliza might find a way to help Nancy. Though the woman's confident, tough manner didn't suggest someone needing help.

Their business concluded, Nancy left the travel section. They could not depart together, which would defeat the purpose of meeting in this neutral environment, so Eliza meant to wait a few minutes and then be on her way to meet Meg at a coffee shop nearby.

Lingering among the travel books, she had just picked up *Travels through Venice* by Mr. Thomas Jones-Thomas when she heard the sound of a now-familiar voice.

"I'm sure it must be here somewhere," Tommy's disembodied voice said from the other side of the bookshelf next to which she was standing.

Damn.

She shrank back against the slim space of wall at the rear of the travel section, as if that would help should he appear at the end of her aisle.

A quivery woman's voice said, "I know it must be around here somewhere. I put it down when I was talking to Mr. Hannay earlier."

Eliza knew this speaker as well—it was Mrs.

Dombrell. A woman of about sixty, she was an impoverished spinster who spent a good portion of her day sitting on benches in the local parks and talking to birds. Not because she was insane, though she was certainly odd, but because she was kind and she liked birds.

She also loved to read and talk about books, which Eliza knew from having sat with her on more than one occasion, and Eliza had a soft spot for her. But many people regarded Mrs. Dombrell as a nuisance. She was known to scavenge near bakeshops, looking for crusts to feed her beloved birds, and she was not averse to talking to herself. And, with her cloud of loose white curls and her musty, threadbare frocks, she was a bit disreputable.

Mrs. Dombrell sighed. "I'm afraid"—she lowered her voice—"that the shop owner won't be very happy with me. There was already that trouble about the bird that came in last time on my hair—really, I didn't know it was there!—and made a bit of a mess on one of the books."

"Never fear, dear Mrs. Dombrell," Tommy said kindly. "We'll find it." How did he know her? He'd barely been in London two weeks, and Mrs. Dombrell was hardly the sort of person whose acquaintance one hastened to make.

"I do hope so," she said. "Mr. Widdershin," she said in a stage whisper, "said that I wouldn't be able to come into the shop again if there were any more problems."

There followed the sound of books being shifted, some muttering, the scuffling of feet. Intensely curious, Eliza carefully inched *Travels through Rome* halfway out of its place on the shelf and peered through the opening. She could just see the back of Tommy as he leaned close to the shelf opposite and probed among the books.

He was wearing buff trousers and a bright blue tail-coat that made her think of spice-scented marketplaces and exotic birds. She supposed he must have had it made in India. His broad shoulders filled out the coat in a way that made her want to stare. Still poking about among the books, he lifted his arms and reached the highest shelf.

"You surely wouldn't have put it here, Mrs. Dombrell—or would you have?" he asked playfully, and the older lady giggled. He was flirting with her! With musty, odd, sweet Mrs. Dombrell, who surely hadn't had kind attention from a handsome gentleman in who knew how long.

Something squeezed in the region of Eliza's heart as she remembered how genuinely charming he'd always been toward females who were ignored for reasons such as age, lack of beauty, or general awkwardness. It had been one of his most endearing qualities, this innate kindness, and she was glad that life hadn't burned it out of him.

"Oh, Sir Tommy," Mrs. Dombrell said delightedly, "how you jest. I could never reach that high without long arms like yours."

The arms in question were certainly appealing. The tropical blue fabric of his coat strained against them, defining firm curves here and there. Being able to watch him unobserved was quite nice, because although he'd been perfectly—maddeningly—polite the day before, his manner had been reserved and hidden, not open and warm as he was being with Mrs. Dombrell. Eliza had to suppose that was because he hadn't been happy to see her.

The realization stung, because clearly, from his behavior toward Mrs. Dombrell and the adulation that seemingly every other female in London was heaping on him, he was still capable of being one of the most charming fellows in the world if one were in his good graces. Which she clearly was not.

She reminded herself that she was no longer interested in either charming or being charmed by men and told herself to stop looking at his arms.

He turned to the side to reach for a shelf that was perpendicular to the one in front of him, and Eliza drew back a bit from the book slot to avoid being seen. But if she tilted her head, she could still see him through the space just above the tops of the books on the shelf. His expression bore a look of affectionate amusement with Mrs. Dombrell.

He'd always been so fun and lighthearted—it was one of the things Eliza had loved best about him. And dear God but he was handsome, even more so than he'd been years before. The taut planes and curves of his face under his bronzed skin seemed fascinating, suggesting experiences about which she knew herself to be curious.

Longing pierced her. What if, instead of laughing at him years ago, she'd said yes to his proposal? Her life would have been entirely different. For one thing, there would be no Truehart Manor.

But even now, she didn't see how they could have

grown up together as well as they'd grown up apart. She'd needed to learn things that she might never have learned if she'd been married to him at the age of seventeen.

He plucked at something amid the books on the opposite shelf, a greasy-looking packet of the kind that contained meat pies sold on the street. It looked disreputable, but Tommy presented it to Mrs. Dombrell with a flourish.

The older lady blushed and accepted the packet. "Thank you ever so much, Sir Tommy."

"It was nothing, my dear Mrs. D. Only"—he glanced briefly behind him, toward the front of the shop—"I would put that away on your person somewhere until you leave the shop."

Mrs. Dombrell promised faithfully to keep her greasy packet secret, going so far as to stuff it into the pocket at her waist, and after several rounds of effusive thanks, she departed.

Tommy, however, lingered among the shelves, pulling off books and appearing to read bits of them. It was remarkably pleasant watching him, though Eliza knew she ought to stop. Also, it was possible that someone she knew might pass by and address her, and Tommy would hear. Or, more likely at the rate he was plowing through books on sculpture and architecture, he might shortly move along to the aisle where she stood. She needed to leave.

Quietly she began making her way out of the aisle, intending to turn left at the end to avoid his direction.

Her efforts at discretion were ruined when her reticule brushed against a protruding book as she moved past it and the book fell to the floor with a thud. Tommy, who apparently had the reflexes of a cat, was on the scene in a heartbeat.

He did not look delighted when he saw who was standing in the aisle next to his.

"Lizzie?" he said in a voice that held none of the playful warmth he'd showed Mrs. Dombrell. "What are you doing here?"

She decided on misdirection as her best course. "It's Eliza now, actually. I haven't gone by Lizzie for years. Are you shopping for something in particular?" It was a stupid question that made her sound as though she worked at the shop and was offering assistance, but with any luck it would distract him.

It didn't, and his eyes narrowed. "Were you there the whole time I was with Mrs. Dombrell? Were you *spying* on me?"

She flushed. "What a thought!" she said, managing a laugh. "I'm simply passing the time before I meet a friend. But perhaps *you* are up to something nefarious that you wish to hide by attacking *me*."

He just stared at her for several long moments, an effective method of intimidation that made her want to squirm.

"You must have been lingering in that aisle for some time—and very quietly, too—because I have perfectly good hearing, and the only person I've noticed around that aisle was a lady who emerged several minutes ago. Perhaps she was a friend of yours?"

Eliza willed herself not to flush again. The last thing she needed was to make Tommy interested in who Nancy was.

"I don't know who you mean. I was simply looking for books about Italy," she said. "I've always wanted to go there. Now, if you'll excuse me, I must be on my way." She stuck her nose in the air and took a step forward, but he grabbed hold of her arm and drew her close.

"You're up to something, aren't you? You might have my brother charmed into thinking you've changed into a virtuous woman, but I'm not so easily fooled."

This was all wrong, the way things were between them. Maybe he'd known she wanted to apologize yesterday and he hadn't wanted to hear it, but he deserved her apology—and she really needed to offer it.

Besides, at this rate, they wouldn't even manage to be pleasant when Will and Anna eventually thrust them together, as now seemed inevitable. And, equally important considering what she was planning to do that night was that Tommy not be suspicious of her. She looked him in the eye.

"Tommy, I want you to know that I'm very sorry about what I did six years ago when you proposed." She thought he flinched at the word *proposed*, but she made herself keep going. "I sent a letter to apologize, but I don't know whether you ever received it."

"I did, nine months later."

She winced, but she'd known it would take a long time for a letter to reach India. Her letter had been stiff and formal, because she hadn't known how else to express herself.

"A letter was inadequate as an apology, and far too easy for me. I hope you'll accept my apology now for the way I behaved. I was young and, frankly, scared about the idea of marriage. You deserved so much better from me."

❧

Tommy never thought he would hear Lizzie speak to him as she just had. What might he have done if she'd written something like that to him years ago?

Probably nothing, he thought, because time and his own choices had moved him beyond dwelling on what had happened. But there had been those painful, dark first months in India.

He wanted to accept her words graciously. And yet, he didn't trust her. He didn't think people could change so much. Lizzie had been all about fun and flirting, and it wasn't until he'd stepped out of her fascinating orbit that he'd seen she was someone who needed to be the center of attention.

Plus, he was certain she'd been loitering in the bookshop to watch him. He'd had the sensation that someone was watching him when he was talking with Mrs. Dombrell. But why should Lizzie be so interested in him? And why apologize now for what happened years ago?

He crossed his arms and propped a shoulder against the end of the bookshelf. "Did Anna put you up to this? I know she's keen for everything to be as though we're all one happy family."

Lizzie shook her head. "This doesn't have anything to do with Anna and Will. And I don't have any secret motives. It's just an apology, plain and simple, for having behaved badly years ago."

She seemed sincere, and he would be a bastard to hold a grudge. "Very well, I accept. And perhaps my public proposal was too dramatic a gesture." What a mooncalf he'd been. Thank God he wasn't like *that* anymore.

He considered the idea that like him, Lizzie had changed from the person she'd been back then. She looked different, of course. Her face was more interesting, her demeanor more assured and relaxed, her figure a touch more lush in all the right places even if her clothes were far less dramatic. He'd have been lying if he didn't admit he found her extremely attractive. She was twenty-four and a widow, he reminded himself. Of course she wasn't the same person she'd been.

But then he watched as her eyes drifted beyond his, and he glanced behind him and saw Lord Benchcombe talking to a woman. It was the woman he'd seen pass by the bookshelves earlier and who must have been in the aisle with Lizzie when he was talking with Mrs. Dombrell.

Eliza smiled. "Your public proposal was a sweet idea," she said, but all her attention seemed to be on the man and woman and not on discussing the event she'd supposedly felt such a need to apologize for.

"You seem very interested in that woman," Tommy said.

Lizzie seemed to start. "What?"

"The woman behind me you keep looking at. The one who was in the aisle with you a few minutes ago. The one you said you don't know."

She flushed. "Er…no. I don't… Er, well, that is, it's Lord Benchcombe. I…have a tendre for him."

Tommy absorbed this bizarre admission. Benchcombe was a handsome fellow. Young and tall, with the kind of hair women liked to call golden. But a tendre? Wasn't that the province of silly young ladies of sixteen?

"You admire Lord Benchcombe?"

"Exceedingly!"

He glanced at Benchcombe, who was now looking at them, perhaps having noticed Eliza's gaze. Tommy had always thought the man dull-witted, if nice enough, and the ladies did seem to find him handsome. "And does he know?"

"Oh, no."

"Have you admired him for a long time?"

"Er, no. That is…"

"Just last week you were smitten with someone else?" he supplied.

"Yes!" she said, looking oddly relieved. "Have to keep things moving. You know how it is."

He didn't, actually. It was one thing to keep company with different partners, but flitting around like a giddy sixteen-year-old, consorting with every available person of the opposite sex? No. Good God, Lizzie was a widow now—hadn't she grown up at all?

He found himself more than a little disappointed in her, and then surprised that he was disappointed, because after all, this was Lizzie, who'd gotten herself thrown out of school for kissing gentlemen and made such a scandalous name for herself during her season by jumping into fountains and sneaking into gentlemen's clubs. In short, she'd had a wonderful time doing just as she liked without a care for the consequences. He'd once though he might be an answer to the wildness in her, but he'd discovered he was not.

He didn't care much about propriety, but he'd seen enough of trouble and death and sacrifice to know that life wasn't all parties and giddy notes slipped under guest-room doors.

Or maybe for Lizzie it was.

At least now he understood that regretful though she might be about how she'd behaved years ago, she hadn't really changed. It was sad, really, though he doubted it felt that way to her. She was so lovely and lively that she'd always have men dancing to her tune. No doubt Benchcombe would shortly be one of them, if he wasn't already.

Tommy wondered briefly if she was as scandalous as she used to be, but that only made him want to think about what kind of interesting trouble she might be getting into, which he didn't need to be pondering.

He tipped his head politely at her, feeling a little sorry for her that she'd never really grown up. "Then I'll leave you to charm him," he said, hiding a smile.

She blinked, then smiled tentatively back at him. "I'm glad we had a moment to speak candidly."

"I as well." At least now when they inevitably met again, it wouldn't be awkward.

They both began walking toward the door.

"Leaving before any of the adoring ladies of London discover you're here?" she teased. "I heard that this year's debutantes have deemed you the Most Swashbuckling man in London. Perhaps in the world."

He might tell himself that he was unaffected by her, but a spark of that old mischief had come into her eyes, and it took him back to a time when she could make him smile like no one else. And dream; she'd filled his dreams, both wicked and sweet, and those dreams had tormented him for ages, even after he'd decided she didn't deserve his affection.

The memory of the torments she'd been able to inflict on him made him crave to pay her back, even if only in a small way, and as they were passing Benchcombe, who was now alone, Tommy tapped the man on the shoulder. Benchcombe turned and dipped his head to Tommy and, with a smile of real pleasure, to Eliza.

Tommy leaned closer. "If you ask Lady Truehart to dance at the next ball, Benchcombe," he said, "I have it on good authority she'll say yes."

Tommy heard a quickly indrawn breath from Lizzie, but he merely inclined his head at her in farewell and left the shop with a grin.

❦

What on earth had possessed her to tease Tommy, Eliza thought as he left her standing with Lord Benchcombe, when she'd long since trained herself to abandon the urge to flirt? Being in his presence seemed to have scrambled the wits she normally kept so well trained.

Lord Benchcombe promptly began to quiz her about when she would next attend a ball, looking quite pleased at the idea that she'd been dreaming of dancing with him.

When Eliza had noticed that Nancy was still in the shop and talking to him, she'd been so agitated that she'd given Tommy the first excuse she could think of for staring at them. Now Tommy thought she was a ninny, but that was the least of her problems.

"I'm afraid I recently turned my ankle, my lord," she told Benchcombe regretfully. "And though I'm able to walk, my doctor insists, disappointingly, that I do nothing as vigorous as dancing for several weeks."

"You hide it well, dear lady—I noticed no limp when you walked."

"Vanity," she said regretfully. He was a nice man, and he didn't deserve to be made to feel as though she was toying with him.

He nodded. "It is my fondest wish that you will be improved soon. Perhaps I might send my own physician to you?"

She assured him there was no need and thanked him, then sedately left the shop with a cheerful wave as he looked on.

Once out of sight, she had to nearly run to the coffee shop so she wouldn't be terribly late meeting Meg. When she arrived, Meg was already installed at a small table by a window.

"Sorry I'm late," Eliza said breathlessly, taking the seat opposite her. "I lost track of time at the bookseller's."

Meg leaned across the table and said with a sly look, "So what's all this about you having a tendre for Lord Benchcombe? And Sir Tommy Halifax playing cupid?"

"*What?*"

Meg laughed at her expression. "I passed Mrs.

Tate in the street. She was in Little's when Sir Tommy told Benchcombe that you were hoping to dance with him."

"You don't have to call him Sir Tommy," Eliza grumbled. "He's only Will's brother."

"What else am I supposed to call him, since thanks to you avoiding him, I've yet to see him?"

"He's just a man."

A serving girl arrived to take their order for coffee and cakes and left to fetch their things.

"Mrs. Tate was nearly clicking her heels at the idea that Lady Eliza Truehart, with her beauty and wealth, might be back on the marriage mart. She's on her way now to spread the word around Town."

Eliza groaned. "I'm *not* getting ready to marry again, and I can't believe Tommy did that—it was incredibly embarrassing. Besides, Lord Benchcombe is a nice man who doesn't deserve to be used as part of a joke."

Meg laughed. "Don't worry about him. He's probably just excited that you talked to him, since you generally treat men as if they make little impression on you."

"So do you."

"No I don't. I simply like worthwhile men, and they're hard to come by. I'm an educated, sensible woman, and I don't want a husband who only knows how to dance. Give me a man who's *done* something with his life—designed a building, or sailed the oceans."

"Then maybe you would like Tommy."

"Ha! I'm sure he's an interesting fellow, but there's

too much history between the two of you to make that idea comfortable. Besides, I thought he was only in England for a holiday before he returns to India."

"He is."

Meg nodded thoughtfully, then waited as the serving girl brought their coffee. Once she was gone, Meg took a sip of her drink and said, "So, what were you doing talking to Tommy? Aren't you just about his least favorite person because of what happened years ago?"

"We've met by accident twice now, and this time I took the opportunity to apologize."

Meg's eyebrows shot up. "You've talked to him twice and you didn't tell me?"

Eliza shrugged as casually as she could, considering that she was still thinking about how he'd made her knees weak. It was ridiculous that she was having trouble getting herself to focus on Meg.

"I ran into him briefly in the park, and just now at the bookshop. I realized it was silly for there to be awkwardness between us."

"Do you think he's truly forgiven you?"

Eliza stirred her coffee. There had been something in his manner, as though he still didn't trust her. "He accepted my apology, but I doubt that it's made me rise much in his estimation. So maybe now I'm only *one* of his least favorite people."

"Hmm."

"Why 'hmm'?" Eliza said.

"Just that you two were once very close. So maybe now that he's returned, whatever was between you will be rekindled."

Eliza repressed an unwanted tingle at the thought. She shouldn't care what Tommy thought of her, but she'd long since forced herself to cultivate truthfulness, and she knew that for some reason, she did care. Not that it mattered. "We're both entirely different people now. And that prank with Benchcombe is hardly the sort of thing a man would do to a woman he liked."

"Perhaps, though it just sounds mischievous to me." Meg grinned. "I was at the lecture on temperance this morning, and Sir Tommy Halifax was all any of the ladies could talk about. He's very swashbuckling now, apparently, whatever that means, though of course he always was a charmer."

"At the *temperance* lecture? Couldn't they find something more suitable to talk about?"

"Why shouldn't he have been a suitable subject? He's not addictive, after all." Meg paused, and her eyes twinkled. "Or is he?"

Eliza rolled her eyes. "I have better things to do with my time than flirt with swashbuckling fellows. He's part of my family, for goodness' sake."

"Not your blood family. He's not *related* to you. And apparently he's the most interesting man in England. Maybe you're secretly hoping he'll propose again."

"Don't be ridiculous. Anyway, you of all people know that I won't get married again. I'm the happiest widow in London."

"Maybe," Meg said. "Or maybe you just haven't found the right man."

This was a conversation Eliza definitely didn't want to prolong. She gestured to the bag by Meg's feet, from which was protruding the spine of a book. "Have you been to the lending library?"

Despite her practical demeanor and deep suspicion of men who were charming, the books Meg loved most to read were gothic novels full of romance and drama. Eliza, who'd once loved just that sort of book, never read them anymore and thought Meg would be happier if she stopped as well, but Meg insisted she only read them to mock them.

Eliza tilted her head and read the spine. "*The Dangerous Baron of Darkness*. Why's he dangerous? Does he refuse to provide candles, leaving his guests to trip over furniture in the dark?"

"Ha. He's dangerous for ladies to know, as usual."

"So you're enjoying disliking him, as usual?"

"Exactly."

It wasn't hard to understand why Meg held such gloomy views on the opposite sex. Her mother had had terrible taste in men, and the last thing Meg wanted was to ever be like her. After Meg's kind but feckless father died when Meg was young, her mother had managed to marry not one but two men who were already married to other women.

"Two bigamists!" Meg had told Eliza. "Two! Who else but my mother could succumb to charming seducers *twice*?" She'd shaken her head, the vexation clearly still fresh though her mother had been dead for years. "My mother couldn't be happy without a man in her life—it was as though she was nothing without one."

Which meant that as far as men were concerned, Meg was impossibly picky. And, though Eliza wouldn't want to point it out, getting older.

Though Eliza had no intention of ever marrying again herself, she knew what she was giving up. Meg didn't. Marriage could be very pleasant, Eliza had learned, and an important opportunity for people to grow and change. She'd more than once told Meg she ought to try it. At which point, Meg would always remind her that most of the time, marriage wasn't something people could just "try," since barring mishap, it lasted for life.

But still, strong marriages were the foundation of a healthy society, and Eliza hoped that the girls who came through Truehart Manor would one day find spouses who would be good helpmates.

Eliza did wish Meg would make a little effort with her appearance, though, because underneath her mismatched clothes and careless coiffures, she was quite lovely. Eliza's eyes wandered over the pale green spencer Meg was wearing, an unattractive choice with her dark brown gown. It was as though she chose her clothes as a sort of hedge of thorns that any potential mate would have to slash through to see the woman underneath.

"Dearest," Eliza said, "wouldn't you like to go shopping with me? I'd be happy to advise you…"

"No," Meg said.

"But our girls—"

"Don't need me to look fashionable."

"No, of course not. But we do want them to appreciate the importance of a polished appearance."

Meg pressed her lips together. "Do you hear yourself, Eliza?"

Eliza blushed. "What do you mean? I'm only trying to be helpful."

Meg heaved an exasperated sigh. "You know I love you. We've been the best of friends since your first season, when you jumped in that fountain at the Hartwells' party and needed a towel."

"Ugh. That wasn't a good time in my life."

"Wasn't it? Because you seemed a lot happier then."

"I don't know what you're talking about. I wasn't happy then—I was making myself into the most scandalous girl in the *ton*."

"Very well, you couldn't have gone on forever like that. But now…"

"Yes?" Eliza said with more than a little irritation. First Anna and now Meg—why was everyone insisting they liked her better when she was a disaster?

"Did you have to go so far in the other direction?"

"How can you suggest that I'm not going in the right direction—that what we're doing at Truehart Manor isn't of the utmost importance? What could be more important than having a life filled with purpose?"

"I agree it's important, but what about laughing? Dancing? Playing?" Meg said. "Making mistakes?"

"You're not making any sense."

Meg sipped her coffee. "I'm just beginning to feel that you've set some sort of impossible standard for us all—the girls, me, and especially you. None of us will ever measure up to the ideal of perfection you have."

"We have to set high standards for the girls if they're to improve enough to go to school."

"But reading five books a week?" Meg pressed. "Some of them don't like to read, and pushing too hard may extinguish any moderate interest they have."

When she was a girl, Eliza had told herself books

were for boring people and given herself permission to become the biggest flirt in Malta. "Nonsense. They just need more exposure."

Meg frowned. "What about our meals? Cook says you told her not to cook with salt anymore."

"Dr. Henley says it's better not to eat salt," Eliza pointed out, though she missed it as well.

Meg huffed. "Fine. All those things are just details, but this makes me truly worried: you told Mary that if she laughed too much, people would think she was a flirt. She's ten years old—she's supposed to laugh! We all are."

Eliza frowned more deeply. Mary was a sweet girl, but she could be unbridled, and she didn't yet under-stand that needing to capture other people's attention was a road to becoming ever more outrageous. "I just want the girls to be happy in life. People need self-discipline to be happy."

"I agree. But I think you're being too hard on them. It's as though somewhere along the line, you decided pleasure was a bad thing."

That was because it *was* a bad thing. Her self-indulgence had cost her Tommy's friendship and driven him away from his family. But Meg was making her sound like someone who couldn't enjoy herself, and that wasn't true.

The serving girl arrived with a plate piled with treacle tarts, shortbreads, and cakes slathered with cream. Meg took two cream cakes and a tart, which she dolloped further with cream. Eliza selected a piece of shortbread and nibbled it.

"See?" Eliza said. "I like to indulge."

"You chose the dry cookie instead of the creamy delight," Meg said over a mouthful of cake.

"I happen to like shortbread."

"Or you've taught yourself not to want more."

"Than shortbread?"

Meg groaned. "Eliza, I can't help but feel that the single most important thing in your life is starting to be self-discipline."

Eliza flushed. "I thought you liked being my friend."

"I do! If I didn't love you so, I wouldn't say anything. It's not pleasant telling people difficult things, you know."

"So what do you want me to do?"

"Go to a party or a ball. Go to someone's house for dinner. Say something stupid and frivolous."

"You mean go back to the way I used to be? I won't do it."

"Of course I'm not suggesting that you behave like a sixteen-year-old." Meg poked her fork into another chunk of cake. "But don't you ever think of taking a break from Truehart Manor? What we do can be challenging, and neither of us has had a holiday for a long time. You have money—you could see the world, meet some new people."

"*You* haven't taken a holiday either," Eliza pointed out testily.

"But I mean to. You know I've been making plans to go to Italy this winter. Maybe you should come with me."

"Who would stay with the girls?"

"Mrs. Trinkett could manage for a few weeks."

Italy sounded lovely, and it was true that Eliza

hadn't taken a holiday for years. But the thought of a holiday—with no schedules and nothing to do but try to enjoy herself—sounded foreign, and she knew she'd be a drag on Meg's fun. Still, she appreciated that Meg meant well.

"I'll think about it," she said, smiling a little.

"Good," Meg said, looking relieved.

Eliza felt tempted to tell her friend about her plan to go to the brothel that night—Meg would certainly see *that* as a sign that Eliza wasn't always focused on being perfect—but she knew she couldn't. If Meg didn't decry the whole idea as insane, she would want to come as well, and Eliza couldn't let her take that risk. As a widow who would never marry again, Eliza could afford a hint of scandal. Meg could not.

Four

LATE THAT NIGHT, ELIZA PAUSED BEFORE THE DARK back entrance to Madame Persaud's brothel. She wore a black velvet mask and a deep-pink satin gown with a low bodice that she hadn't worn since she was seventeen. The gown was snug and cut lower than the dresses she wore now, and she'd kept it as a reminder of the person she didn't ever want to be again. At least now it would serve a good purpose.

She'd powdered her hair heavily and pulled it into a loose knot, turning her red-gold tresses into an indistinguishable pile of white on her head, but she'd decided against any face paint, hoping to look unremarkable among the other women, who would doubtless look more purposefully enticing. With the black mask on, Eliza didn't think she looked recognizable. She hoped, with a giddy sense of unreality, that she'd pass as a prostitute, if only one who wouldn't attract much attention.

Her conscience made one last effort to restrain her by pointing out that if she was discovered and became a scandal, the work of Truehart Manor would be ruined, but she ignored it. If they were going to continue losing girls to the lure of prostitution, their work would have little effect anyway.

Since the brothel catered to the tastes of wealthy gentlemen, it was in a respectable part of town. Eliza had her coachman drop her a block away from the large house, with instructions to drive around the neighborhood and check back for her at intervals. She made her way to the deserted mews behind the row of houses, found the back entrance Nancy had told her about, and slipped in, unnoticed as far as she could tell.

She moved along a narrow corridor, following the sounds of voices and music. The prostitutes would gather in the drawing room to welcome the clients early in the evening, which allowed the men to circulate as they arrived and ponder which women they would choose for the evening. It was nine thirty, so Eliza had half an hour to step into another life and ferret out the sort of details that would help her take away the glamour that places like this held for girls like Franny and Thomasina.

She emerged into a long foyer with two doorways and a staircase that led upstairs. There were two women in the foyer dressed in boldly colored dresses like Eliza's and wearing masks. Her stomach dropped at the sight of them—this was her first contact with anyone in the house—but when they merely glanced at her and went back to talking to each other, she repressed a sigh of relief and kept moving.

Masculine laughter issued from the far room, which had to be the card room. As she drew close to the nearer doorway, she confirmed that it led to the drawing room and moved inside. As she made her way toward a large plant that she hoped would offer a little concealment, Eliza counted a dozen women standing about in groups, laughing and chatting. The prostitutes' lips were rosy with lip paint, and rouged cheeks peeked out from the bottom edges of their masks. They were all nearly falling out of their gowns, and Eliza could feel her cheeks burning as she realized the tops of their nipples had been rouged as well.

She stationed herself behind the plant without drawing more than a passing glance from anyone and prepared to take an inventory of tawdriness. She had expected cheap furnishings and bad taste, but as her eyes lingered over the room and its occupants, she was disappointed to find that everything was remarkably tasteful. There was a handsome carpet on the floor, and several beautiful landscape paintings adorned the walls. The settee that stood near her would not have been out of place in her own drawing room.

Neither did the women seem coarse, aside from the exaggerated allure of their clothes and faces. Their hair was prettily styled, and though she had steeled herself to withstand the sort of odors to be expected from a place that employed desperate women to fulfill the desires of men, she smelled nothing but the sorts of floral scents favored by society women. She frowned.

A group of three women moved closer to her as they cleared a space for a couple who had started dancing the waltz. Here, at last, was something she might use to discourage the girls, because the dancing prostitute, whose pretty lips and softly rounded jaw suggested she was about twenty-five, was dancing with a fat, balding man of at least sixty. She might even have been Nancy, though because of the mask, Eliza couldn't have said for certain.

As the couple passed near Eliza, she was startled to see that the man was Lord Renfrew, a prominent judge. Renfrew was a nice man married to a very nice woman. What on earth was he doing in this place?

What he was doing, apparently, was enjoying himself. He was smiling at his partner, and the woman had curled her hand over Renfrew's shoulder in what looked like affection. But how could it be? She was being exploited.

The three women standing on the other side of Eliza's plant laughed.

"Millie will keep him busy tonight," said one of them, a brunette with full, painted lips.

"Oh, be serious, Daniela," said one of the others, a blond whose petite nose peeked pertly from the bottom of her mask. "You know Renfrew just wants to talk and rub her feet."

Rub her feet? Eliza nearly burst out laughing. Why would he want to do that?

But instead of laughing, the three women shook their heads sadly. "The poor, sweet man," the brunette said. "To think that when his wife told him she wouldn't lie with him anymore after the spare heir was born fourteen years ago, he just accepted it. All she wants to do anymore is shop. I wouldn't have their wealth for all the tea in China."

"If you had their money, you could *have* all the tea in China." They laughed again, and Eliza wondered at them. They were driven by poverty to sell their bodies—how could they be so jolly?

The blond spoke again. "Look, there's Steventon." The three women turned their gazes to the doorway and emitted a collective sigh as a tall, handsome gentleman entered.

"*He* doesn't need to pay," the blond said. "I tell you, what that man can do. There's kissing, and there's better kissing, and there's the *other* kind of kissing." Husky laughter greeted this comment, and Eliza frowned. The woman was clearly talking about something sexual, but Eliza didn't know what she meant.

She found herself mortally curious. What was this other kind of kissing? Gerard had kissed her many times, but it had never made her want to sigh with husky delight.

In truth, Eliza would never have used the word *delight* about what had happened in her marriage bed. Still, she hadn't minded submitting to Gerard's brief attentions. He'd been endlessly respectful about the whole thing, as though he hadn't particularly cared for it either.

"Sorry about this, my dear," he'd say several times a month, *"but we've got to make the effort for an heir."*

Listening to these women, though, Eliza couldn't help but wonder if there was more to sexual relations than she'd experienced.

"Steventon's the reason I've so much put away for later," the brunette said. "I'll be buying that house by the sea before too long, see if I don't."

Eliza frowned. This sounded too much like the way Franny and Thomasina had painted prostitution, and she knew it couldn't be right. Aside from the risk of pregnancy and disease, a woman who sold her body risked being a social outcast, never mind the reality of having to make herself available to all kinds of men who might do whatever they liked with her body.

"Now then, my dear," said a male voice from just behind Eliza, "you must be one of the new girls. I like your look. Shy, aging virgin, is it?"

Eliza's stomach dropped. She slowly turned her head and saw that there was now another man in the room, who'd apparently found his way to her. He was perhaps forty, with brown hair and the well-fed air of a nobleman. A playful smirk hovered at the edges of his thick lips.

As his words registered more thoroughly, she repressed a spike of irritation. *Aging?*

He was waiting for her to reply and flirt with him, and if she didn't respond, she would appear suspicious. How ironic: in attempting to accomplish something of worth, she was going to have to revert to the flirt she'd once been.

"Oh, my lord," she said, adopting a breathy, girlish voice to disguise her own and also play into the *aging virgin* that she apparently looked like. "I can't begin to imagine what you mean."

He laughed. "Can't you, dear, innocent lady? Tell me, what is your name?"

"Er…" She said the first name that came into her mind, which was, appallingly, "Victoria."

Wonderful. She'd just used the name of Will's three-year-old daughter as a cover for herself in a bawdy house. Good God, if he ever found out about any of this…

"Victoria. Very nice. I'm Roundswell, and very pleased to make your acquaintance. Sweet, innocent Victoria, allow me to say that I would be pleased to be your guide in all things unknown to you." He grabbed her hand and looked intently into her eyes.

Dear heaven, she had an interested customer!

"Oh, my lord," she said as alarm raced through her, "I'm not ready for such…" She racked her brain for what to say, but everything seemed awkward and she finally blurted, "doings."

"Doings?" He guffawed. "Innocent and diverting. And you're blushing, too. Don't know how you manage that on command, but I must have you." He consulted a watch hanging from a chain over his substantial paunch. "Good—it'll be time for the choosing in ten minutes."

Oh no, the choosing! She must find a way to discourage him so she could escape before then. She laid her free hand over her heart in a fearful gesture and tugged at the hand he still held. "In truth, my lord," she said, "you will wish to choose someone else. I am clumsy and unschooled in the arts of the bedchamber."

His eyes glittered, and he squeezed her hand. "Even better," he said in a low voice. "I shall enjoy teaching you everything. Already the evidence of my desire—" he began, but then shut his mouth with a wicked smile. "But such words are not for shy virgins. You shall discover for yourself."

"Oh, er, yes," she whispered hoarsely, her mind recoiling at the thought.

"I have to collect something from the card room,"

he said. "Wait here, and I'll be back before ten." He squeezed her hand again before finally releasing it. "I've reserved room number six."

She nearly shuddered, but she forced herself to smile feebly. "Until then."

At which point, thank God, he turned and made for the door to the corridor.

She had to get out of this place. She might not have discovered the kinds of things she'd hoped to find, but now she had an admirer whom she wouldn't be able to escape if she wasn't gone by ten.

Eliza was almost to the door that led to the corridor when her arm was caught in a sturdy grip, and she spun around, her heart hammering, certain she was about to be exposed.

It was Lord Adderbrooke. She knew him from church.

"Where are you off to in such a hurry, missy?" he asked in that voice she'd heard pronouncing "Amen" and singing about the day of the Lord. *He* was here too?

"Oh," she said in her breathy strumpet's voice, "er...the retiring room."

It almost came out as a question, but he didn't seem to care, or maybe that was why he laughed.

"It's not that direction. You must be new."

"Yes, sir, I am."

"And your name?"

Oh, not again. Surely at any moment she was going to be felled by the gods of propriety. But then, she would never have been a favorite of theirs anyway. "Victoria."

He smiled. "Well, Victoria, I've reserved room

number four. We can retire there together after the choosing. It's only a few minutes away."

Another customer? What was wrong with these men? She looked like a dusty virgin, apparently.

She remembered then what Nancy had said about how there would be a bidding war if two men wanted the same woman. She had barely two minutes left before ten, but how was she to escape? The only thing that came to her was to simply rush into the corridor and make for the exit, praying she reached her carriage before any pursuers could catch her. But such a desperate measure would draw attention.

She was saved by the arrival of a gentleman who hailed Adderbrooke. When Adderbrooke turned to greet him, she quickly moved into the corridor to escape. But she immediately saw that the way to the exit was blocked by a party of men talking to each other.

Panic crashed over her. Any moment, Adderbrooke was going to turn around, or just as bad, Renfrew would emerge from the card room. In the drawing room, the music came to an end and there was an expectant murmur that could only be the beginning of the choosing.

Inspiration struck when she saw a serving girl going up the stairs to the second floor with a pile of folded linens. Spying her only means of immediate escape, Eliza scrambled behind her and made her way upstairs.

Once in the second-floor corridor, Eliza opened the first door that wasn't marked with a six or a four and peered inside. Wildly relieved that the room appeared to be unoccupied, she rushed inside and closed the door with her heart hammering. She could not expect to be safe in there for long, but she could gather herself to make an escape plan. Maybe once everyone was assembled in the drawing room, she could sneak back downstairs and make a run for the exit. If nothing else, the room had a window, though as she peered out at the ground two floors below, the prospect of leaving by that route did not appeal.

∽

Tommy hadn't intended to end up at Madame Persaud's that night, but he was with two old friends—Matthew Dearden and Stephen Elliot—and they seemed intent on visiting every gaming spot and club in London.

Tommy didn't mind Madame Persaud's. The place had a fine card room, as well as a lounge where gentlemen could converse undisturbed. It was a place he'd been more than once when he was young and eager for the kind of experiences a man could have there, even though he'd never gone upstairs with any of the prostitutes. He'd liked looking at the women, though, and talking to them.

But he wasn't much interested in bawdy houses anymore, and he could easily have done without coming there. He did, however, enjoy cards and gambling.

But now, as Tommy and his friends stood in the corridor talking, Matthew leaned close to say in a low voice, "Nitwet's here. In the drawing room."

Tommy muttered a curse. He'd played Nitwet at a club a few days before and taken quite a bit of money off him. The man had been angry when

Tommy had refused to play further that night, but it had become apparent to Tommy that Nitwet was in dire financial straits.

"He'll insist you play him here and now. Depend on it," Matthew said. "But he hasn't a chance. He's good, but you're better."

Stephen nodded. "And you'd be in a fair way to winning his last farthing and his estate as well."

Tommy frowned, knowing he wouldn't take any more of the man's money, however much Nitwet might, idiotically, insist it was a matter of honor.

"We ought to leave before he sees us, then," Tommy said.

His friends agreed, but before they could make their way to the front door, which was beyond the card room, Nitwet emerged from the drawing room. With the crowd in the corridor, Tommy wouldn't make it to the door in time to avoid him.

"Damn." He cast a glance behind him toward the stairs and saw his only option. "Go on to White's," he told his friends. "I'll duck upstairs until he's gone and meet you later."

His friends nodded and he quickly made for the stairs, taking them two at a time.

Once in the upstairs corridor, he looked around and, knowing he still risked meeting Nitwet if he lingered in the corridor, he knocked on the first door he came to. When there was no reply, he went in and, remembering the custom, plucked the charm that hung from a black ribbon on the inside knob and draped it over the outside knob to indicate the room was occupied, lest some pair of lovers think to use the room after Madame Persaud's vaunted choosing. He turned the key in the lock.

The room was dim, with only the light of a low fire in the hearth, but it smelled pleasantly of sandalwood. Madame Persaud's being a fairly tasteful establishment, there was a handsome if narrow bed, which was festooned with pillows and bore a crisp, white coverlet that proclaimed the freshness of the furnishings.

Chuckling a little at how he'd ended up there, he sat on the bed, then swung his legs onto it and stretched comfortably out on his back with his hands behind his head. He felt pleasantly alone and unreachable, a sensation that, as a guest of one household or another, he'd not experienced since returning from India.

ىے

Though it was dim in the room, Eliza nevertheless knew who was now lying in apparently relaxed contentment on the bed. When she'd heard steps in the corridor, she'd quickly hidden herself by the side of the large wardrobe near the window. When the door opened, making her knees tremble as she tried desperately to make no sound, she'd seen the side of Tommy's face lit by the corridor sconce.

What was he doing here—in this room, in this bawdy house? Was he waiting for a woman? She desperately hoped not, but she didn't see how it could be otherwise. Really, though, did he need to frequent such a place? From the reactions of pretty much every female in London, Eliza would have supposed feminine favors would be his for the taking.

Remaining rigidly unmoving in her hiding place

behind the wardrobe, she wondered if she might simply wait him out. Though if he was waiting for someone, which seemed likely, the immediate future did not bear thinking about. And yet, she'd thought she'd heard him lock the door.

"I can hear you breathing, you know," he said in a mild voice from the bed.

A startled gasp escaped her.

"Oh," she said, making her voice higher as she'd done downstairs so he wouldn't recognize it. But then she was at a loss as to what to say.

He laughed. "Aren't you going to explain yourself? Come here where I can see you."

Gad.

But resisting his request would only make this worse. And she *was* wearing a mask and hair powder—she'd even fooled Adderbrooke. Plus, it was dim in the room with only the glow of the fire and a few threads of moonlight curling around the edges of the curtains. She must simply brazen it out.

She moved out of the shelter of the wardrobe. "Please excuse me, my lord. I'm new here."

"Ah," he said softly, turning onto his side and bending his elbow to prop his head up on his hand. "I'm not a lord, my dear. Just a man. Is this is your first night?" And there it was—playfulness and warmth in his voice, exactly what had been missing from everything he'd said to her since his return.

"Yes," she whispered.

"Is it perhaps," he continued, "that you're not certain you've chosen the right path?"

"Er, perhaps."

"It's not a bad life here, I think. Or at least, it isn't for the women who have generous and considerate patrons. But it's not for everyone. Come, is there nothing else you might do?"

This got her dander up—men were so terminally blind to the crushing forces working against women. "No, there isn't," she said tartly, then bit her lip as she remembered that she mustn't make herself too distinctive or she'd risk piquing his curiosity, or even revealing her identity somehow. "I…failed as a governess, and the pay I'd receive if I took work as a maid is atrocious." She tried to ignore the realization that she had just espoused Franny's argument for becoming a prostitute.

He chuckled. "You express yourself ably. I see that you're well educated. So, you've fallen on hard times?"

"You could say that." Though he didn't know who she was and this situation was ridiculous, somehow lying outright to him felt wrong.

"And so you made a study of the possibilities and concluded that coming to a place like this was your best hope?"

"It seems to be the way many women find to provide for themselves."

He was silent for long moments, and she began to worry that he'd recognized her, or her voice, even though she'd made it breathy and girlish, or that he was examining what she'd said carefully. None of those possibilities were good.

She'd be better off getting him to talk about himself—and in truth, she was curious. "What brought you here tonight, sir?"

"Some friends," he said. "It's a decent establishment, but I would as soon have gone home to my bed. However, there was an awkward situation about to develop downstairs with a fellow who wants to take revenge for rather a lot of money he lost to me at cards. He has hardly a farthing left, and he'll want to stake his estate. It seemed easier to simply avoid running into him in a place where people gamble. So here I am"—he chuckled—"hiding."

Admirable of him. But then, he'd always been a good man.

"It seems we both are," she said because it seemed unnatural not to reply since he was being friendly and she was supposed to be a woman in need of a kind word.

"So, are you coming to any decisions here in your hiding place?" he asked.

"Decisions?"

"As to your plans for the immediate future. Do you mean to acquire a protector?" He sat up and swung his legs to the floor. He seemed to lean forward, as if to make her out better. Even though he was sitting, she sensed the breadth of his shoulders and chest as they moved nearer to her space.

"I…don't know," she said.

"Come closer and let me see you. I'm as red-blooded as the next man. Shall I predict your likelihood of success?"

"Er," she breathed. *As red-blooded as the next man…* She hardly wanted to risk getting closer to him when any minute he might discern something familiar about her. But his words gave her a shiver of the kind of excitement she didn't allow herself anymore.

"Don't be shy," he urged in a kind voice. "Tell me your name."

With an inward sigh, she said, "Victoria." She desperately hoped that she'd somehow escape without running into Roundswell or Adderbrooke again, but just in case, it seemed wise to stick to the character she'd created. But here with Tommy, she was starting to feel less like the creation she'd dreamed up when she'd set out that night, and more like she used to feel when she was young and ready to do anything.

She forced herself to mentally recite an aphorism about self-discipline that Gerard had taught her.

"Victoria," Tommy repeated. "I have a niece with that name. You may call me Tommy. But I can only just see you, Victoria, with the poor light in here. Come closer. I won't bite." He chuckled softly. "Unless you want me to."

"No!" she said too forcefully and in her own voice. To cover the mistake, she stepped a little closer and said in the girlish voice, "I'm sure I won't need any, er, biting."

He laughed again. She'd forgotten what an irresistible laugh he had.

"Closer," he urged again. Then, in a voice that held a note of suspicion, "Unless there's something you're trying to hide?"

"Of course not." She forced herself to move nearer to the bed. In for a penny, in for a pound, and if he recognized her, well, he already had a terrible opinion of her. What would it matter?

Although she had really begun to hate that he didn't like her anymore. They'd once been such good friends, and being with him now, while he didn't know who she was, was quite nice.

But *nice* was the wrong word. He made her heart flutter, and her lips felt warm, as though they were buzzing. It was the magic of attraction—that old, unpredictable magic she'd told herself she must do without if she wanted her life to be on the right course.

And her life *was* on the right course. She was accomplishing good things, helping people, leading a worthwhile life. It was all good, except for that stray feeling of emptiness that sometimes dogged her, the ungrateful sadness over the child she'd never had even though she had everything else.

Well, maybe not *everything* else. She thought again of the prostitutes talking about the men who made their hearts race. Of the things they liked doing with men—things that were mysterious to her.

The fire snapped as a bit of sap heated, and she nearly jumped. But she ignored the tension that was making her feel like a tightly strung wire and forced herself forward to stand right in front of Tommy. He regarded her steadily in the low firelight, then gave a soft whistle.

"Your figure alone would assure your appeal, Victoria. But you also have lovely eyes, a pretty chin, and a very enticing mouth. I don't suppose you wish to remove the mask so I can assess the rest?"

"No."

He smiled, and she did too. She liked that he could see her smile and little else of her face.

"I suppose your hair is a light color under that unnecessary powder?"

"I like the powder."

He made a skeptical sound. "There's something about you... I like what I've seen of you so far. But if you'll forgive me for saying so, I wonder if you'll be comfortable working here. A certain boldness is required."

"I can be bold." Lack of boldness had never been her problem, although this seemed to be a new kind of boldness he was talking about.

"Really," he said with that same note of skepticism. "Well, it's certainly bold for a former governess to decide to take on a lightskirt's role. But will you be bold in the bedroom arts?"

Eliza flushed from her head to her toes. As a widow, she was used to people speaking more plainly than they might around debutantes, but nobody had ever said the words "bedroom arts" to her.

Hearing these words from Tommy now made her feel as though she knew nothing at all about what went on between men and women. There had never been anything about Gerard's hesitant touches that she would have described as skillful. She swallowed.

"I'm certain I shall manage. I have been with a man before."

"Is that what turned your mind to this way of life? An affair with the lord of the manor perhaps?"

"Something like that. I know that I cannot conceive."

"Oh?" He took her hand, and the touch of his large, warm hand sent excitement through her. He tugged her a little closer.

"Would you like to practice your boldness a little before you become a professional? I propose a kiss.

As one who has something of a history of kissing, I believe I might offer you an estimation as to how well you will fare."

She ought to resist. She knew there were costs to indulging herself, and she made better choices now. But tonight she'd begun to see that maybe there were experiences she'd missed.

Temptation, thy name is Tommy Halifax.

She stared down at the wicked tilt teasing the edge of his mouth and knew that whatever he was proposing was a terrible idea. He'd said a kiss, but who knew if he meant to stop there? And even if he did mean just a kiss, was she insane, to be tempted to kiss him when she was probably the last woman in the world whose lips he'd want to touch with his own? She'd read hatred in his eyes that night years ago, and though he'd said he accepted her apology, she wouldn't be surprised if some of that feeling still lingered, hidden by a polite veneer.

Yet, she yearned to touch him. She wanted him to enjoy her company as much as he once had—as much as he was clearly now enjoying Victoria's.

And how could Victoria decline his request anyway? She was supposed to be a woman seeking to be a strumpet—wouldn't he be suspicious if she turned prudish?

Mischief sparkled in his eyes and her heart thumped in thrilling reply. Mischief was something she'd never been able to resist.

"Of all the nerve," she said lightly, smiling. His invitation had given her permission to be bold, and she placed her palm along the hard jaw that had so fascinated her.

One black eyebrow rose in a pirate's misbehaving slant, and the white of his teeth flashed as he grinned. "If there's one thing that I've never been said to be lacking, it's nerve." With a tug on her arm, he pulled her sideways onto his lap.

Her heart stuttered and she thought for a moment she might swoon. He smelled extremely good, a little like sandalwood, a lot like something that, if she'd had to name it, she would have called, with a giddy sigh, *swashbuckling*.

"I can see that," she said. She didn't even need to summon Victoria's breathy voice because her own had turned soft and hushed.

He looked at her intently, the color of his eyes indistinct in the semidarkness that would fortunately leave the color of her own eyes indiscernible to him, but the warm glow in his gaze made her light-headed.

"Do you feel shy, Victoria?"

She nodded slowly. It was true—she did feel shy and a little overwhelmed by him, but the feeling was exciting. And also surprising; she was hardly virginal—she'd kissed more than a few men, though none since Gerard had died, and she'd experienced the ultimate joining many times with her husband. But in each of those encounters, she'd been certain of her own power, of the upper hand she'd always held as the one pursued, the one allowing the attentions of an admirer.

For the first time ever, that wasn't how she felt. She knew Tommy no longer admired her. He might find Victoria attractive, but Eliza Truehart's beauty was nothing to him, and he certainly didn't admire her as a person. She felt shy and off-kilter, a new sensation for her.

He smiled, managing to look both kind and wicked, and her heart did a somersault.

He placed a fingertip against her lips, right at the bow. Lightly, he pressed downward, and the moist, hidden skin at the seam met the warmth of his finger. His finger moved along the plumpness of her lower lip, bringing the hint of moisture he'd gathered and spreading it with wicked slowness, and she read the message he was sending: he knew about her body and what it could do.

He took his finger away and bent his head. When his lips met hers, she knew instantly that this was something that could have power over her—that *he*, if she weren't careful, could have power over her...power she'd want to give him.

❧

Something kept teasing at Tommy, a sense that there was something familiar about shy, blushing Victoria. She was funny and smart and sweet, and the parts he could see were achingly lovely. But there was more to her, some gauzy memory like that of a dream.

He didn't want to pay attention to dreamy things, though, because she was here and real and luscious. Her breasts—tastefully, teasingly concealed compared to the other women there that night—had been drawing his eyes ungallantly downward from the moment she'd come closer, and he'd found himself aroused.

Despite her admission that she'd been with a man before, her kiss was unpolished and perfunctory, and he guessed whatever experience she'd had must have been brief and fumbling. The contours of her cheeks and faint lines curving at the edge of her mouth suggested she was perhaps twenty-five; she'd seen a bit of life. But for a woman who was thinking of selling her sensual charms, she had only the most rudimentary idea of how to kiss. Her lips had opened to his, but she was just sitting there as though waiting. She clearly had no idea what to do with her lusciousness.

It was like kissing a virgin, but without the guilt he would have felt for doing so, and his groin tightened further.

He stroked his tongue softly against hers and she quivered. But still she held herself back, not taking any initiative, and he felt challenged to arouse her further. He skimmed a palm over the front of her bodice, slowly circling his hand over the silky fabric until he felt the plumping of her nipple underneath. Her breath caught and he smiled against her mouth.

Her hand came to rest on the top of his shoulder, as though she was going to explore him, but she didn't. She seemed to have no idea that she might have a part to play. "Tommy," she whispered, and again he had the sensation that he knew her.

"Don't you want to take off that mask?" he murmured.

"No!" she squeaked.

"Very well," he said, teasing thoughts as to her identity fading, because really, how would he know her? Having been away for years, he knew hardly any women in England, and certainly no governesses. He kissed a trail down her neck and slid a fingertip under the edge of her bodice, nearly groaning at the satin fullness of her breast.

"Victoria," he murmured, "you have many, many charms. But if I may offer an observation…"

He stopped to dip his head and kiss the upward swell of her breast, and he heard her quick intake of breath. Clearly his touches were having an effect on her.

"Yes?" she prompted.

"I wonder about the ultimate success of your endeavor if you don't develop some contributions of your own."

"Contributions?"

"If I may?" he said, his fingers pausing at the edge of her bodice.

She nodded.

He tugged and her breast popped free. He leaned forward and captured her nipple in his mouth, and she whimpered. This little scenario of the innocent prostitute and her mystery initiator was arousing him almost unbearably. The scent of her warm woman's skin with its hints of floral soap seemed like the best thing he'd ever breathed in.

"It's all about pleasure," he said. "You would have to touch the man and seek to pleasure him, and in doing so bring pleasure to yourself. Or at least appear to be pleasured."

"Oh," she whispered, sounding genuinely surprised. Her breathing quickened as the hand on his shoulder began to move, tracing over him with little catches of hesitation that made him burn.

"Men like to be touched as much as women

do," he pointed out, nearly groaning as she shifted in his lap.

"I...didn't know," she said, sounding oddly remorseful.

She moved her hand to his neck and stroked him with what felt like affection, this woman who hardly knew him. She pulled his head down for a kiss that now had its own sensual agenda, because her tongue met his and stroked with a newfound eagerness.

If a protector was what she wanted, maybe she'd need look no further. He hadn't had a woman since he'd left India, and there had been that incident at the bookshop when he'd found himself, to his deep annoyance, attracted to Lizzie.

Perhaps Victoria was just what he needed.

⋞⋟

Now I know what lust is, Eliza thought as she kissed Tommy with everything in her that wanted him. This was what the women downstairs had been talking about. She was intoxicated, hot, and breathless, and she didn't care about the proper voice of her conscience that had been dictating to her for the last six years.

She tugged at the ties of his shirt until it fell open and slipped a hand inside. His chest was hard and warm, and his broad ribs tapered narrowly as she slid her hand lower over muscles honed to tautness.

He let out a sound that was half gasp, half laughter. "You seem to be catching on."

"I'm a quick study." She pulled his shirt out of his trousers, nearly dizzy with desire.

He responded by pulling her bodice down to bare both her breasts and feasting on them. She moaned and arched closer, not caring that she was being demanding. She began working the buttons on the front of his trousers, which was the first time she'd ever done such a thing because Gerard had always come to her in a nightshirt.

Had Gerard wanted her to do these things? Had she been selfish when she was married?

The thoughts niggled, but all she could think was that Gerard had never been like this—urgent and hot—and so she hadn't either. How would she have known?

Tommy's hand swept with slow arrogance up the inside of her thighs and made for the secret heart of her, the place that Gerard had always treated as though it was too pure to even speak of or really touch, a place that should only receive the most brief and functional attention.

Tommy Halifax felt no need for respect or distance; he intruded confidently among the curls between her legs and traced his fingers wherever he liked. Certainly he seemed to know what pleased her, drawing helpless moans from her as he made sensual circles over and over in one place that was turning out to be very special.

She wasn't a virgin, but she felt new, as though she were waking up. Maybe it was better this way; she'd seen what men had in their trousers, and experienced it already—she wasn't afraid of what would the joining would be like.

For the first time, she *wanted* it.

She pushed the front of his trousers aside and gasped at what she could see of him in the dim light. He was large, thick, and…absolutely not apologetic.

He gave a husky chuckle, but when she touched him, he groaned and pushed into her grip, hard as stone and pulsing with heat.

Before she knew what was happening, he'd pulled her to straddle him, the hem of her dress pushed indecently up over her thighs even as her breasts lay bare to his kissing. He took her nipple in his mouth and nipped her without so much a by-your-leave, and she loved it. What they were doing was rough and probably coarse and certainly wicked, and she wanted more—she *needed* more.

She scooted closer to his chest, her feet moving onto the bed behind him, her legs spread over his cock, which was a word she'd heard around the docks of Malta years before but had banished from her mind as she steered herself toward uprightness. But now she said the word in her mind, enjoying its frankness. Still gripping him, she brazenly rubbed the tip against herself.

He sucked in a breath. "Victoria?" he said hoarsely.

"Yes," she panted.

"You've caught on spectacularly. There should be some sort of prize," he ground out.

She threw her head back, feeling every inch the wanton. He was at her entrance now.

"Yes?" he asked, and they both knew what he meant.

"Yes!" she cried.

He needed no further urging but plunged into her with one forceful stroke.

"Tommy," she moaned, and it meant so much more to her than he could ever guess. She nearly wept from the pleasure as he filled her.

His breath grew ragged as he worked himself into her again and again, driving her pleasure higher with each thrust.

She felt herself aiming toward a blurry cliff at the edge of an unknown land, a place whose geography only Tommy knew. He tipped her backward, holding her securely as he stroked deeply inside her until finally—finally!—with what felt like fireworks exploding, she fell. Wonderfully and gratefully, she fell over a boundary that she'd never even known was there.

Through the veil of her own pleasure, she was aware of him still stroking inside her, grunting, his hands worshipping her body. He buried his face against her bosom, kissed wildly up her neck, rubbed his lightly whiskered cheeks against hers, and scrabbled his hands in her hair, until with a final plunge he sighed out his release.

His hands flew upward through her hair, taking the ribbons of the mask with them, and she just had time to see the pleasure lighting his eyes before he recognized her.

Five

TOMMY COULDN'T BELIEVE HIS EYES. IT WASN'T possible! It couldn't be.

And yet it was. The well-pleasured woman looking back at him with dawning fright was Lizzie.

Victoria the innocent, awkward prostitute was *Lizzie*?

How the hell could this have happened? And *why* was she even here?

His blood came instantly to a boil. "What the devil is going on, Lizzie?" he demanded.

Any last vestiges of bliss fled from her face and she fumbled to get off him and stand up, pulling her dress over her shoulders as her skirts fell to cover those shapely legs that had so inflamed him. Guilt crimped her features.

"I'm sorry," she gasped. "I'm so sorry."

"You're *sorry*?" he growled as he fastened his trousers with rough, quick motions. He stood, enjoying a bolt of angry satisfaction when she shrank back from him. He speared her with a furious glare.

"You're going to be so much more than sorry by the time I'm done with you." Even in the dim firelight he could see her blanch. He stepped closer and alarm rippled over the lovely face that had put him under a spell years ago and that had clearly worked its magic again on him tonight, no matter that he'd only seen part of it.

Apprehension pulled at the corners her beautiful mouth.

"I, um, I realize that me being Victoria is not a happy surprise for you," she said in a voice that was little more than a croak. "But you must see that this wasn't something I'd planned. It just happened."

He crossed his arms, rage curling his fingers into his locked muscles. "*I* wasn't the one wearing a mask. You *knew* who I was." He narrowed his eyes. "Was this some kind of trap?"

She laughed, a bitter sound. "How could it have been a trap when I had no way of knowing you would be here? Or that you would come into this room?" She spoke with a defensiveness she had no right to. "And what possible reason could I have for trapping you?"

"I don't know. What possible reason could you have for being here, in this house?" he asked with slow, dangerous menace. "*Why* is my brother's ward pretending to be a prostitute?"

"I am twenty-four years old, Tommy Halifax, and nobody's ward anymore. And though I behaved wrongly, you were a willing participant in what we did."

He thought his head was going to explode. "I had a damned good reason for doing what I did. I thought you were a strumpet! What was *your* reason? Damn it, Lizzie, we just had relations. I would never have done what I just did if I'd known that was you."

A spasm of what looked like hurt swept over those proud, perfect features, and for a moment he entertained the thought that this all had truly been some monumental mistake. But no, Lizzie was the Siren. He couldn't allow himself to be tempted to trust her.

Her shoulders slumped. "There's no excuse for what I did."

"You're damned right. You could have told me who you were at any moment since I came into this room and allowed me the choice. But instead you took the choice from me by trickery."

"I have behaved appallingly. There is nothing I can say to excuse myself."

He was startled by the remorse in her voice and the honesty of her words. Was it possible that she was sincere and truly humbled? But then he remembered how she'd apologized so earnestly at the bookshop and reminded himself that she was very good at manipulating people, and his jaw hardened.

"I'll ask again," he said, hearing the dangerous note in his voice and not caring. "Why are you here, and why are you pretending to be a prostitute?"

She inhaled, as if to gather herself. "Because I wanted to see for myself what a brothel was like. The girls we help at Truehart Manor—one of them has just abandoned everything we tried to do for her and taken work as a prostitute. Apparently, many of our girls think it's a profession with wonderful advantages. I wanted to understand better what we're fighting to keep them away from."

His brows slammed together. "You want me to

believe you came to a brothel dressed as a prostitute just so you could observe what it's like to be a prostitute?"

Her spirits seemed to sag further. "Yes."

The subject was serious, but a scornful laugh escaped him. "And you were going to do what—solve the problem of the world's oldest profession? Convert all the brothels to convents?"

Her jaw tightened and her chin tipped up, which ought to have looked ridiculous considering she was wearing a rumpled, low-cut pink dress and heavily powdered hair, but he grudgingly admitted to himself that there was something a little majestic about her spirit.

"I don't think there's anything laughable about women being in dire straits and needing help."

His lips thinned. "I don't either. And there are plenty of women in bad situations, but this isn't one of them. The women here know they will be treated well and compensated handsomely. But that doesn't mean a woman like you should ever come to such a place, never mind pretend to be one of its denizens. What would Anna and Will think if they ever heard that you were here? What would *anyone* think?"

"I wasn't going to be here very long. I was just going to gather the kind of information that would help us make sure our girls won't be enticed by the lure of prostitution."

He snorted. "You might tell yourself that's why you came here, but I don't believe it. You have everyone fooled, don't you, Lizzie?"

"I'm not trying to fool anyone."

"You want everyone to think you've turned over

a new leaf," he sneered, "but underneath that veneer of propriety—underneath the muted clothes you've been wearing and those do-gooder's plans—you're still the same girl I knew. Hell, I'll wager that 'work' you supposedly do at Truehart Manor is nothing but a way to make yourself look good. You've got my brother and Anna and everyone else fooled with your ruse of respectability, don't you? But I know better."

She recoiled, as though his words had actually wounded her. "I've tried to set my life on a respectable course," she said in a shaky voice, "and I don't care if you believe the worst of me, but our girls are decent, good children in need of help."

Her words suggested someone who truly cared about those girls and poked at his idea of her, but he told himself this was just more of her trickery. He crossed his arms. "And what would you have done if it had been another man who'd come in here instead of me? Would you have seduced him as well?"

"Of course not." Her brows drew together in a deep wrinkle. "Things here are not as I had thought they would be. The women here seem almost content with their lot."

"Some of the women here fare better than the wives of the men who come here. And they earn enough that, if they wanted to leave, they would have enough to take care of themselves."

"It's still a choice no woman should be forced to make. There are consequences."

"Exactly," he ground out. "Like a *baby*. You could be carrying my child this very moment."

"No," she said firmly. "It's not possible. My

husband and I had normal marital activities for years with no result. He had a baby with his first wife. Our doctor agreed the problem lay with me."

How the hell had this happened? He never had intercourse without French letters, and in India, there were savvy, beautiful courtesans very happy to share his bed. With no eye to marrying for a long, long time, he never consorted with English women. If he was ever tempted by a woman who would expect an engagement, he needed only to look around him at all the disastrous marriages among his friends to lose interest. The marriage of his closest friend in India, Oliver Thorpe, had been a prime example, and now Tommy couldn't think of the poor devil without all kinds of conflicted feelings he didn't want.

"A doctor isn't God," he said. "A doctor can't see into the future. He could have been wrong. And now you've dragged me into your little game."

❧

Eliza was shaking. Clearly she was not only wicked but also insane to have done what she'd just done—and with Tommy of all men. She'd somehow given herself permission to abandon years of walking the upright path she'd chosen and given into temptation. Although what she'd done had been wrong, it had felt so intensely right at the time because she'd been so attracted to him since his return, even though in truth she didn't really know him anymore. But she'd been weak, and she'd indulged herself at his expense.

He seemed to think that her presence there that night and her work at Truehart Manor were all just a way of gaining attention for herself. How shallow and worthless a person he thought her.

But she'd wronged him tonight, quite seriously. She'd given herself permission to do something reprehensible because she thought she could manage it without anyone being affected, and she certainly owed him an explanation.

"This wasn't a game," she said. "I came here for the reason I told you—to better understand this thing that entices our girls. But some of the men thought I really was a prostitute, and I had to escape them before the choosing, only I couldn't get down the corridor, which is how I ended up hiding in this room."

He muttered a curse. "Did anyone touch you?"

"No!" Putting aside the moral implications of the way she'd behaved, how had she ever thought what she'd done tonight with Tommy could be accomplished with no consequences? "It was just a bizarre coincidence that I was in here at the same time you were. You came in, and you didn't know it was me, and"—she took a deep breath, hoping the awkward truth would resolve this disastrous situation—"and you were being so kind and fun that I couldn't resist what started to happen between us. It was like old times."

His eyes narrowed dangerously and she rushed to finish.

"I mean, obviously we never did anything like this before, but still, we used to be so close."

His face darkened; clearly she'd said the wrong thing. "Funny you would bring up old times. They're exactly what have made me not want to spend a single extra minute in your company. Nothing ever really touched you, did it? It was all flirting and games with no consequences for you back then, and it still is. And now you've ensured that I might never be able to get away from you."

His words cut horribly. He didn't understand that she'd tried to make amends over the last years and become a better person. Still, she more than deserved his scorn.

"I understand your anger. But as to any consequences for you, I assure you that there will be none. I'm not some fragile poor virgin whose life has just been ruined. I'm a wealthy, established woman who makes her own choices. I understand that you may have no wish to accept my apology, but I see no reason for us to discuss this further."

She reached toward the bed and snatched up her mask. "Of course I won't say a word of this to anyone. No one will ever know. It seems inevitable that we'll meet at family events while you're in England, and I assure you that I will behave with nothing but politeness toward you."

When he made no reply, she tied the mask over her face and turned to go, but he caught her roughly by the arm.

"You will send me word if there is anything I need to be told." It wasn't a question.

She nodded once.

"I will see you home."

"No," she said. "You can't. Someone might see us together and perhaps recognize me. No one expects to see me here, so if I'm glimpsed alone, I will attract little notice."

She could tell from the way his mouth hardened that he didn't like what she'd said but that he acknowledged the wisdom of it. "How do you plan to get home then?"

"I have a carriage—the driver was to keep an eye out for me in the mews. I'll go out the back door."

Tommy nodded tersely. "Wait here while I see if anyone is about."

He opened the door and stepped into the hallway, which seemed quiet. He was gone for a few moments and she supposed he was checking the stairs. When he returned, he held the door for her.

"Go. You'll be able to escape notice just now."

She slipped past him and down the stairs. From the quiet in the drawing room it seemed most of the couples had already disappeared into chambers together. Nobody was about as she found her way to the back door and the mews, where her carriage appeared almost immediately and she was whisked to safety, all but weeping with relief.

Six

THE DAY AFTER THE BROTHEL INCIDENT, ELIZA threw herself into a frenzy of activity. The last thing she wanted was even one moment to think about what she'd done the night before, and how, before everything had gone terribly wrong, it had been one of the most amazing experiences of her life. She'd stumbled and been enticed back into her old, wild ways, but she wasn't the needy young fool she'd once been, and she knew what the path of virtue looked like.

First thing, she took the girls on an hours-long march around the city, and forced herself to be frank and specific with them. After her night at the brothel, she knew that things were more complicated than she'd thought, but she felt now that at least she would be able to speak plainly.

She told them about Maria leaving the Bath school to take work as a prostitute, and said that Maria might very well make quite a bit of money as a prostitute. Her words brought gasps and startled looks from the girls, but Eliza pressed on.

"Perhaps you've heard that a high-class brothel is

mostly parties and wealthy gentlemen, and very possibly you are right. Some of the gentlemen might even be handsome, and they might treat you quite well."

She could tell from the shocked looks on the girls' faces that they never would have dreamed a lady would say such things. "But have you also heard of the diseases the women who work there get? I'm sorry to say it, but they're quite disgusting. Not to mention the risk of carrying a baby, and with no husband to help you. And what if you really cared for your gentleman? He could never accept you in his life."

"Why are you telling us all this?" Franny said sourly.

"Because I want you to make an informed choice for a path that will serve you well in life. We're trying to give you choices that will allow each of you to have a long, happy, and truly fulfilling life. So I would ask you to think very carefully about what you will be risking and sacrificing for the choices you make in life." She pretended not to notice that Franny rolled her eyes.

When they got back to Truehart Manor, she had them write essays on the topic "How discipline and hard work can help me succeed." Afterward, she reorganized the library until she was nearly dropping with fatigue, then rose early the next morning and attacked the dead flowers in the garden that the gardener hadn't gotten to yet.

Once the girls were up, she pushed them through a day of grammar lessons, then sat with them at lunch, offering corrections to their table etiquette. Meg had planned to work with them on sums, but Eliza couldn't bear the idea of time on her own, so she encouraged Meg to take the afternoon off and worked with the girls herself. After dinner she had them take turns reading aloud until bedtime, then turned her attention to the linen closet, refolding everything into perfect squares.

The next morning, Meg insisted that Eliza let the girls have a break. "You've had them so busy the last few days that they're beginning to look glassy-eyed, and it's not doing anything good for their dispositions. There was quite a lot of bickering early this morning."

Eliza reluctantly agreed that the girls could have a few hours free, though she'd already planned out the day and the thought of unfilled time made her anxious.

She and Meg were in the library later that morning, going through the household accounts, when a maid appeared to announce that Lord Quimble, their next-door neighbor, had come to call.

Meg and Eliza stood, raising their brows at each other in surprise—they only knew the man in passing—and then Quimble entered. His face was red.

"My lord," Eliza said, "how kind of you to favor us with a visit."

"It's not out of kindness I've come," he said tightly. "It's about those miscreants you have living with you."

Eliza blinked. "Miscreants?"

"The girls," he said impatiently. And then he went on to inform them that he'd been about to get into his coach earlier that day when a pair of girls who were hanging about Truehart Manor had approached him. One of the girls had mocked him, and when he'd tried to correct her behavior, the other one had kicked him in the shin. He'd had to depart immediately, or he would have come right away to report this behavior, he told Eliza and Meg. But now he wanted to see the girls punished.

Eliza and Meg looked at each other with dawning horror as he described Franny—the kicker—and Mary, who'd apparently mocked him. Knowing Franny, it was all too easy to imagine her kicking Quimble, though Eliza would have expected better from Mary. She sent a maid to fetch the girls so they could apologize.

"I'm not the only neighbor who's had trouble with these miscreants you harbor," Quimble continued. "We've all had enough."

"They're not miscreants, my lord," Eliza said firmly. "They are merely children who've known a great deal of hardship, and they are deserving of our compassion. That's why we've brought them here—to help prepare them to be productive members of society."

"Clearly you're failing."

The maid returned then to say that the girls were gone.

"Gone?" Meg said.

"They left a note."

Eliza scanned it, then pressed her lips unhappily and handed it to Meg, whose face paled as she read it.

"Well?" demanded Quimble. "Where are they?"

Eliza cleared her throat. "It seems they're gone. They've taken employment as ladies' maids in training, and they won't be back."

Quimble looked furious at being deprived of his chance for retribution. "You don't even know what they're up to," he sneered. "Which just proves my point. Children like them do not belong in a fine neighborhood like Mayfair, and if you don't abandon this preposterous enterprise, I'll have the magistrate on you."

Eliza sucked in a breath and felt Meg tense beside her. "That's quite unfair."

But he didn't care, and he left.

Eliza and Meg both slumped onto the divan. "Oh dear," Meg said.

"Yes." Eliza's hands were shaking.

"What I can't understand," Meg said after a minute, "is why the note mentioned not going in for prostitution. Why on earth would we think they'd gone to a brothel?"

"Er, it may have been something I said. I thought it would be better if they knew about Maria and what being a prostitute might truly be like so that they wouldn't be tricked into thinking it's an easy way to make money."

Meg's brows drifted up. "That must have been quite a conversation."

Eliza sighed. "Much good it did. Now Franny and Mary have gone into service. How could they leave when we were offering them so much more?"

"Well, their note said they expected to get better food as part of Lady Tarnower's household," Meg said.

Eliza groaned. "I insisted Mary not have seconds at meals because she was growing so plump. But I just can't understand making such a foolish choice."

Meg stared at her for long seconds. "Maybe living here is too much of a change for some of these girls. They're young, and they need to play and eat cake in addition to learning grammar. Maybe they feel as though they'll never be good enough for the future we envision."

"I don't expect them to be perfect!" Eliza said, so frustrated. "I'm not perfect. But we have to strive."

"Actually, Eliza, I don't even want to strive to be perfect. And I just want our girls to know they're loved."

Eliza couldn't understand how everything had gone so wrong when she'd tried so hard to make it right. "But that's what I want, too—for them to feel happy and loved."

"I believe you want that. I just don't agree with how you've been going about it."

They sat for several minutes in silence. "Maybe Trueheart Manor isn't the best place for these girls," Eliza finally said in a small voice. "And now, with Quimble's threats, I'm not sure we could carry on anyway, if any of the girls really want to stay."

"Perhaps it would be a good idea, once we take Thomasina and Susie to Bath, to reconsider our approach."

Eliza swallowed a lump of disappointment and had to agree.

∽

Early one morning a few weeks after the night at Madame Persaud's, Tommy was awoken from a dream featuring Eliza by a knocking on his bedchamber door. Even as he came to consciousness, he was plagued by visions of her, alternating between Victoria and a very prim governess, both apparitions making him hot. He hadn't heard a thing from her since that night, and though he supposed this was a good sign, he wondered if he ought to contact her to be certain. The idea was not appealing.

"A visitor here to see you, sir," announced Ringle, Louie's butler, when Tommy opened his door. (He was staying at Gilden House.)

"Who is it?" Tommy asked.

"A Mr. Tippet, sir—a lawyer. And a boy."

"A boy?" Tommy muttered as he got out of bed and began pulling on clothes. Why should a boy visit him? Or a lawyer, for that matter? Unease crept down Tommy's spine as he hastily pulled on clothes. It couldn't be possible…

But it was. Rex Thorpe was standing in Louie's drawing room. And there could really be only one reason he was there.

"Rex," Tommy said, forcing down an ignoble jolt of dismay at the sight of the boy, "it's good to see you. Though I confess"—he managed a smile—"to being *surprised* to see you."

Rex greeted him in the arrogant manner Tommy remembered from the few occasions he'd encountered him previously.

The boy had grown since Tommy had seen him last, at Oliver's funeral in India. Tommy supposed Rex was about thirteen now, and he was beginning to grow into his height, his wiry legs like two billiard cues. His straight, white-blond hair was sticking out in places all over his head, and his mouth wore a dissatis-fied expression. Clearly, Tommy thought, repressing a sigh, some things about Rex hadn't changed.

Though Tommy had been good friends with Oliver, the company of his son had never been a pleasure.

Oliver was a key adviser in the East India Company who worked nearly all the time, and he hadn't known what to do when his wife abandoned the family to take ship for France and subsequently died on the way, leaving him with a boy of nine. Oliver had hired an ayah to look after the boy and gotten back to work. Tommy had suspected, as the years passed, that Oliver had found it easier to leave his son's care entirely to servants.

Tommy exchanged greetings with the lawyer.

"Major Delancey felt the boy would be more comfortable in your care," Mr. Tippet said.

"I had thought the Major meant to adopt Rex," Tommy said. Tommy, Delancey, and Oliver's sister Diana had all been named in Oliver's will as possible guardians for Rex. Tommy had been quite relieved when Delancey had agreed to take Rex on, because no one had heard from Diana Thorpe for some time, so Tommy would have been next in line. As clearly he now was.

Rex snorted. "That old windbag? As if I would agree to be his son. Anyway, he needed to get rid of me because he got himself engaged, and the lady didn't want anybody else in the household but them."

Even though Rex was behaving as though it didn't matter that Major Delancey had as good as discarded him, Tommy could guess that under his bravado, the boy felt passed around like a basket of dinner rolls. Tommy hoped Aunt Diana was a good sort, because surely it would be best for the boy to be among family again once they found her.

"Well, you are very welcome here, of course, though being a guest myself since I'm only in England for a brief stay, I haven't exactly got a home in which to welcome you properly."

Mr. Tippet gave Tommy a packet with information regarding the trust that Oliver had set up for his son. "And this," he said, handing Tommy a slip of paper, "is the last address that could be found for his aunt. She's the wardrobe mistress for a traveling theater company."

A peculiar occupation, but at least there was an address at which to reach her.

Tommy gave directions for Rex's trunk to be brought into Gilden House, and Tippet took his leave. Tommy knew his cousins wouldn't mind if Rex stayed there, but clearly the best thing would be for the boy to be reunited with his only surviving family member as soon as possible. Tommy would send someone out in search of her immediately.

Rex, who'd been wandering around the room as Tommy examined the papers he'd been given, picked up a music box Tommy happened to know Ruby had brought back from a trip to Germany. He hoped the boy wasn't going to damage it accidentally.

Tommy cleared his throat. "I'm sorry about this," he said. "I imagine you would have preferred to stay in India."

Rex just shrugged, but at least he put the box down.

"And I'm sorry about your father as well."

"You said that already, at the funeral." Hardly a polite response, but Tommy reminded himself of all the boy had been through in the past year. And even before then, having lost his mother. He resolved to be understanding with Rex. But what on earth was he supposed to do with him until his aunt could be found?

"Whose house is this?" Rex asked.

"It belongs to my cousin."

Tommy's life was all so temporary. True, he had just bought an estate in Kent, but his man of affairs was still seeing to the final details of the sale, and Tommy himself had yet to even visit the place. The estate was to be an investment, and eventually, in a decade or two, a place to call home when he finally returned to England. And apparently it was in need of much work before it would be quite habitable. So really, he was currently nearly as homeless as Rex. Which wasn't good for the boy, he told himself. What Rex needed now was the sort of stable home Tommy couldn't offer him.

"Would you like an ice? Shall we go to Gunter's?"

The boy shrugged again, but Tommy decided they might as well go. They could hardly sit around making awkward conversation for hours.

Gunter's was not a particular success. Rex consumed his ice in a matter of moments, then fidgeted while Tommy finished his. Several people Tommy knew stopped to greet him, and Rex replied sullenly to each introduction.

"Is this what you do all the time in England—eat ices and chat?" Rex asked as Tommy settled the bill.

"Sometimes," Tommy said, making an effort not to clench his teeth.

"Seems dull."

"I'm only here for a few months, and then I'm to return to India."

"Good. I like India better."

The thought of bringing this obnoxious boy with him to India was far from appealing. "Well, your aunt may have other ideas when we find her. She'll probably want you to stay with her."

The boy smirked and began to kick the table legs.

The rest of the day passed in similar fashion, and Tommy was nearly at his wits' end by the time he decided to pay a visit to his brother. "He has children," he told Rex as they made their way to Halifax House, "and toys."

"I don't play with toys," Rex said tartly. "I'm thirteen."

"Nevertheless," Tommy said in a steely voice, "we'll go see him."

Will and Anna were at home, for which Tommy was extremely thankful. Anna had hardly heard more than the barest outline of the boy's story when she offered, as Tommy had been urgently hoping she might, for Rex to stay at Halifax House.

"He'd be around Heck and Victoria here with us, even if they're younger," Anna said. "Gilden House really isn't an environment for children. If only Marcus wasn't away at the Thorntons' studying with their tutor, he might be a friend to Rex, since they're about the same age. But just now, it's nothing but adults."

"Exactly," Tommy said with what he knew was a shameful amount of relief. But it was better this way.

❧

Truehart Manor was quieter with only Thomasina and Susie left—a fortunate circumstance, considering Lord Quimble's threat—but as the days went by, Eliza realized this was a good thing, because she was finding herself far more tired than usual. Since she was used to pushing herself, she didn't at first think much of it. However, when she arose for the third day in a row and had to race for her chamber pot to cast up her accounts, she knew she couldn't hide from the truth any longer.

Her always-regular courses were late. Food sickened her. She was exhausted.

She knew the signs because she'd looked for them so fruitlessly in the years she was married.

She was going to have a baby.

She should have been in a panic. She, an unmarried woman, was expecting a child. If her state were discovered, the scandal would be tremendous, never mind what Tommy would say if he found out. She ought to be ashamed, but she wasn't. All she could feel was wonder and gratitude.

The baby was an answer to the secret prayers she had not even allowed herself to say.

Already she was dreaming of taking her baby for walks and sitting in a garden together in the sunshine, her tiny son or daughter laughing and babbling. The thoughts made her so happy—though not so unrealistic that she didn't acknowledge that her situation was something of a disaster.

Her baby would have no father—or at least, not a father who acknowledged him or her—because she wasn't going to tell Tommy. He was leaving for India in a month or two, and from everything she knew, women rarely looked as though they were increasing until well after that. All she needed to do was keep the baby secret until sometime after his departure. When he found out at some future date that she'd had a baby, he'd be thousands of miles away and, considering what he thought of her, very likely to think it was the child of some other man. She certainly couldn't imagine him returning to England simply to force her to marry him.

Anyway, it had been abundantly clear that disastrous night that sharing a child between them would be an undertaking fraught with anger and resentment, and she would never subject her child to such a life. She was at fault for what had happened, and it was only right that Tommy should not be affected by any consequences. Never mind that she didn't *want* him to be affected; this was *her* baby, and she already loved her little one so much.

Telling her family and friends about the baby without lying or mentioning a father was going to be a challenge, but surely she could come up with something, and she still had time to decide what. She was hardly the first unmarried gentlewoman to find herself expecting a child. She was wealthy and resourceful, and she and her baby would find a way to be happy.

She made dreamy plans to go away for a few months somewhere nice to have the baby, perhaps in a little house by the sea, and ignored the reasonable voice that said this wasn't going to be as easy as she wished. All that mattered was that she was going to be a mother.

Over the next days, she went around with a secret smile, keeping up with her long lists of duties while secretly dreaming of the future. But fatigue dogged her, and when she overslept a week later, she was surprised that no one had come to wake her—until she remembered that Meg was taking Thomasina and Susie to the Royal Menagerie. The two girls had progressed to the point of being ready for Francesca's school, and when Meg had insisted they should have some treats before they went, Eliza could only agree.

She rang for a breakfast tray, which arrived bearing toast and tea. But though she normally enjoyed her morning tea, the mere sight of it that day made her queasy. She forced herself to nibble a bit of toast and had managed half a slice when there was a knock at the bedchamber door. To her surprise, Anna came in.

"You're not dressed," Anna said, clearly dismayed.

Eliza covered a yawn. "Good morning to you, too. I'm just getting up. What on earth are you doing here so early?"

"It's not that early. And you'll have to hurry, or we'll be late for the Bridewell luncheon."

She'd forgotten the Bridewell luncheon. Caught up in her enforced busyness, and not wanting to see or hear about Tommy, she'd been avoiding Will and Anna, along with any social engagements. She'd accepted the invitation to the Bridewells' yearly event weeks before. Was forgetting things part of increasing as well?

"Actually, I don't know if I, er…" she began.

"The Bridewells are expecting all of us, as usual. And Will and I haven't seen you in what seems like ages."

"I've just been terribly busy."

"Knowing you, I'm sure you have. But you have to make time for fun." Anna smiled with extra cheer. "Tommy will be there."

Wonderful.

"Um…" It would be rude to bow out at the last minute, but the thought of tables of food sickened her, and she was definitely not ready to see Tommy. But before she could come up with a tiny white lie (and she meant it to be very tiny, since she hated fibbing to Anna), a look of concern came over Anna's face.

"Are you ill?" She drew closer and peered at Eliza. "You do look a bit pale. Are you feverish?" She pressed her hand to Eliza's forehead. "You don't *feel* hot."

"I'm fine." Eliza forced a smile.

But Anna ignored her and examined her face, as though she might diagnose something merely from the state of Eliza's skin. "Is it some kind of female trouble?"

Eliza almost succumbed to a nervous laugh, but kept herself in check. She wasn't yet ready to say anything about the baby. "Really, it's nothing."

"Perhaps we ought to call Dr. Henley, just be to certain."

Eliza nearly squeaked. A doctor would certainly have ideas about what was wrong with her. "Truly, I was only being lazy. But now that you're here, I feel just the thing." There was nothing for it; she would have to go. "If you'll give me a minute, I'll get dressed."

Anna, looking relieved and a bit smug, left Eliza to dress, admonishing her not to take too long, though she needn't have worried on that score. Eliza knew Will was waiting in the carriage, and the less time she kept him, the better, because she didn't want to have to answer questions from him as well.

But she wouldn't be able to keep this kind of thing up much longer, she thought as she slipped into a brown silk gown.

The Bridewell luncheon was a sort of unofficial gathering for those who lingered in Town into September, and while Eliza always made time for this chance to see friends who would soon leave for their country homes, it was invariably a long repast full of great quantities of food, which, given her current state, was not an appealing prospect.

Nor was the prospect of seeing Tommy appealing, considering their last meeting and the fact that she was secretly carrying his baby. At least the luncheon would be crowded, and since he hated her, he'd be unlikely to want to spend more than the briefest moments in her company.

Ten minutes later she was settling onto a seat in the Grandville coach with a cheerful look pasted on her face.

"What's the theme food this year?" she asked. The annual luncheon featured a different food every year. It had been exotic vegetables of the world last year, and Eliza was crossing her fingers for fruits this year.

"Game meats," Will said, rubbing his hands. Eliza nearly moaned.

"Wonderful," she said, forcing a jolly note into her voice.

"Isn't it?" he said. "I was out for a ride this morning with Louie, and I'm famished."

❧

Tommy was in the Bridewells' drawing room with

the hordes of other luncheon guests when his brother, Anna, and Lizzie arrived. He'd known she would be there—it was why he'd agreed to come. Tommy hadn't seen her since their midnight encounter, nor had he received any note from her, so surely there hadn't been any consequences from their encounter.

Still, he needed to be certain.

He went over to join his brother's party, asking first after Rex, and hoping the boy had settled in after two days in his brother's household. Anna said that Heck seemed to have taken to him, which sounded good.

"I've dispatched someone to look for the aunt," Tommy said, "but it will be a few days at least before there is any news." With luck, the issue of Rex would be resolved before Tommy left Town at the end of the week to visit the estate he'd just bought in Kent, which was now officially his.

"Who's Rex?" Lizzie asked.

"He's the son of a friend from India," Tommy said. "I'm looking after him, in a way." Then Tommy asked if he might borrow Lizzie for a moment.

"Surely I don't need to be checked out like a book from a lending library," she said. Though she was making a joke, her voice was carefully neutral, which was just as well. The last thing either of them needed was to make Will or Anna think something suspicious was going on.

He steered her toward a portion of the large room where no one else had wandered, probably because it was at the farthest distance from the hearth and the room was chilly.

"Well?" he said.

She was wearing a silky brownish gown, which looked nice enough on her, though it wasn't doing her usually glowing complexion any favors. Her hair was carelessly arranged, as though she'd simply twisted it into a knot and jabbed pins in it randomly, and he wondered with a spike of something he didn't want to examine whether she'd been out late the night before and had little time for her toilette that morning. Looking into her eyes, he suddenly recalled the vulnerability that had been there that night they'd…

Stop thinking about that night, he told himself firmly. But it wasn't the first time he'd recalled it. How could he not, when along with being a disaster, it had been so incredibly erotic?

Her chin lifted. "I'm not a child to be corrected, Tommy."

"You know what this is about. I want to know whether my life is about to change."

"It's not," she said, and there was no mistaking the sureness of her reply.

Thank God. He'd dodged a bullet. Hell, they both had, and the grateful knowledge made him feel almost charitable toward her.

"Good news, then." He luxuriated for several moments in the relief. He hadn't realized what a weight the possible dramatic change in his fortunes had been, hanging over him like a dark cloud of doom. He was in no position to marry, even if he'd wanted to marry Lizzie, which he certainly didn't.

But practical considerations had hounded him, and he'd kept imagining a hazy future with her, and then he would think of all the marriages he knew that were disasters. Really, except for his brother, Tommy didn't know anyone happily married, and he was a keen enough observer of the obvious to know when a gamble wasn't worth taking.

Lizzie didn't look as relieved as he felt, but then, she'd known for however long—a week or two, he supposed—that she wasn't increasing. He should have insisted she tell him either way as soon as she was certain, but he'd only insisted that she contact him if there were consequences, and so she had not. Perhaps she only just knew, though he didn't in the least want to consider the physical details of any of this business.

"If I might," he said, "as an almost-relative, offer advice about any future such risky undertakings—"

"Don't," she said. "My affairs are my own, just as yours are your own. All we need do is be civil to each other, and I think we can manage that."

He nodded.

Luncheon was announced at that moment, and he allowed himself to express a little of his sudden lightheartedness.

"Are you ready for the marathon of conversation and food that is the Bridewell luncheon?"

A grim look came over her face that seemed out of proportion to his comment.

"Gad," was her only reply, and they went into the dining room.

Seven

ONCE SEATED AT THE BRIDEWELLS' LONG LUNCHEON table, Tommy found himself next to Mrs. Parfitt, a mannish, vigorous lady of fifty with whom Tommy's stepmother, Judith, had once traveled in Egypt. He remembered Mrs. Parfitt as a great lover of dogs.

Lizzie was across the table and several seats away, next to Mr. Hawke-Jones, a distinguished-looking older gentleman, who'd looked extremely pleased to be sitting next to Lizzie.

Eliza, he thought. Distrustful and angry as he'd been with her, he'd made no effort to acknowledge that she preferred this name. It actually *was* hard to remember to call her that, because she'd been Lizzie in his mind for years, even if he'd tried never to think of her. But she was older now, and it made sense that she'd want a more sophisticated name. And maybe, he allowed grudgingly, she *had* changed a little for the better. He had to admit to being impressed at the relatively reasonable way she'd handled the conversation with him about what had been a very awkward subject.

"Finally came home to England, did you?" Mrs. Parfitt said to Tommy in the sort of loud, firm tone one used when summoning dogs from across a wind-swept moor. Apparently age had not diminished her memorable assertiveness. "Looking for a wife, I'll wager. Unless you've taken one of those Indian ladies to wife?"

"I am not married, ma'am," he said pleasantly.

"So you are seeking a wife in England," she announced in that dog-calling voice. Tommy felt the eyes of everyone at their end of the table swing toward him.

"Indeed I am not," he replied. "I have come on business and to visit family."

She nodded. "Yes, the knighthood. But you'll be wanting a wife," she insisted in her loud voice. "You're of that age, and you're the man of the moment. Best strike while the iron's hot and find a pretty gel."

He was saved from the necessity of a reply by the arrival of a footman offering a dish of venison, which Tommy declined. He and Louie had had a late evening the night before (and though Louie had been up in time for a ride with Will, Tommy noticed that his cousin had managed to avoid the luncheon). Tommy had barely managed to choke down a cup of strong coffee that morning and get dressed in time to leave for the Bridewells'. His stomach had not yet awoken to the point of desiring venison.

Nor did he wish for the sliced boar that came around next, though he took a little of the grouse to be sociable. But he drew the line at a dish of mysterious-looking meat in murky brown sauce that was billed as "mountain hare" but which he suspected might be badger. Why anyone should wish to pass badger off as hare, Tommy couldn't have said, save that Lord Bridewell was known to have an impish sense of humor.

Lizzie—no, *Eliza*, he must make the effort— laughed at something Hawke-Jones said, and Tommy couldn't help but recall how much he used to love her laugh. It was throaty, and when she really got going, it came out as a cascade of husky notes that was pretty much the essence of uncontrolled delight.

Ridiculously, he felt annoyed that he wasn't the one making her laugh.

Why should he care? He had no intentions toward her, and especially not now that they weren't going to be forced into marriage. He hardly knew her anymore.

Except, that wasn't exactly true. Some things about a person didn't change. The sense of humor, for one thing, and now that he could relax about the whole thing a little, he had to admit that she'd been extremely fun at Madame Persaud's—which had been, of course, why he'd kissed her. She'd been so irresistibly playful and unbelievably sensual…

He shifted uncomfortably in his seat as memories of that night worked a predictable effect on him. Her innocent-seeming eagerness had been almost unbearably erotic, as though what they were doing was new to her. But how could it be, since she'd already been married? Still, it had been one of the most satisfying sexual encounters he'd ever had—until he'd realized who his partner was.

A bony elbow in his ribs dragged his attention back to Mrs. Parfitt. "What about Miss Ablewhite over there?"

Poor, oblivious Miss Ablewhite, hearing her name being bandied about from several seats away, glanced up with a startled look.

"She'd make you a very nice wife."

Tommy sent an apologetic smile in Miss Ablewhite's direction. The young lady looked to be all of fifteen, and she blanched shyly as she stared at him with a sort of awe. The pointy elbow dug again into his ribs; apparently Mrs. Parfitt required a reply.

"Miss Ablewhite is all that is lovely," he said with a brotherly smile in the girl's direction, "but she need hardly be looking to an old man such as myself for a husband."

Mrs. Parfitt cackled.

Anna smiled at him across the table. "Tommy, you ought to tell about riding an elephant," she said. "You're surely the only one present who's done so."

He obliged her. Most of his end of the table listened, and laughter greeted the part of his story at which the elephant stepped on the picnic lunch that had been the whole purpose of the outing. How foreign India would seem to these people—the way the heat of the day spread the scents of cardamom and curry through the streets, the chatter issuing from a zenana, where the Indian wives and mistresses of Englishmen lived with their slave girls and eunuchs. He missed everything from the talk of Hindoo gods to the riotously colored flowers. He missed how different it was.

Not that he begrudged the *ton* the predictable,

contented way its members spent their time managing their estates and gathering at house parties. He just didn't want to be one of them. Or at least, not for decades.

Though Anna and Will had refrained from pressing him in any way, he knew they were hoping he might be tempted to return to England for good. But he couldn't do it. Just last night, he'd met with the Minister for Foreign Affairs to discuss Tommy's perspective on various political situations in the regions surrounding Hyderabad, and he'd have a great deal to address when he returned to India.

A footman came around with a "surprise treat" reputed to be salted bear meat imported from America, and Tommy repressed a shudder.

He could see his brother, at the very farthest end of the table, piling some of the bear onto his plate while talking to a government minister. Fatherhood seemed to have given Will an even larger appetite than he'd had before, though Tommy couldn't see where he was putting all the food he ate, because he was still in excellent form. Running after his children, as he so often did, probably kept him trim.

It was funny how different two brothers could be. Will, as viscount, had an enormous number of people who depended on him, a situation that Tommy felt certain would have suffocated him. But his brother always seemed like a man who couldn't believe his good fortune. Good thing, then, that Will was the eldest.

He ought to see about doing something nice for Will and Anna, as a thank-you for hosting Rex.

Tommy devoutly hoped the boy wasn't being too much trouble.

"I see you haven't had any of the meat dishes, Sir Tommy," Mrs. Parfitt announced. "Did you turn against meat in India, as is customary there?"

Out of the corner of his eye, he saw Eliza stifling a laugh at his expense.

He smiled at Mrs. Parfitt. There was something clarifying about her that he liked, even though she was bandying his unmarried status about as though it were a topic for general discussion. Though tempted to agree that he'd given up meat and thereby save himself in case the next course was something like roasted rat, he knew doing so would only lead to future dinners at people's houses consisting of far more vegetables than he'd want. He loved meat. He just didn't want any at that moment, and certainly not salted bear.

"No, ma'am," he said. "And many in India do eat meat."

The pointy elbow returned, revisiting a spot on his ribs that was growing tender from the repeated abuse. "How about Miss Vale, then, for a wife?" She jerked her chin at a plumpish, startled woman of perhaps twenty-five whom Tommy didn't know. "She looks a likely contender, and she has a fine rump."

"Mrs. Parfitt, please," Anna said with gentle firmness as Miss Vale blinked furiously. "Let us remember that some observations are too personal."

The lady merely nodded at this, as though accustomed to commentary about her commentary. Which was doubtless the case, given how free and loud she was with her opinions.

"Oh look," Mrs. Parfitt said. "Lady Truehart is only having the turnips and carrots. What's going on with the young people of today? Don't they need to feed their blood with good meat?"

Eliza blanched at these words, turning so pale that she looked a bit green. "I, er, think it's good for us all to eat lightly of meat at least once a week. This is, unfortunately, my light day."

Tommy thought her voice sounded strained.

Mrs. Parfitt sniffed. "When I was a girl, I ate meat three times a day and was the better for it. No wonder you're so pale and slim." She peered at Eliza. "You might be a widow, but you're still a mere child. You need guiding." She turned to Anna. "Do you offer her your wisdom, Lady Grandville, as the wife of her uncle?"

Anna looked startled at this question, but before she could frame an answer, Eliza said, "Ices!" in a breathless voice. "I hear there are to be ices. The last of the season, don't you suppose?"

Mrs. Parfitt was happy to give her opinion on ices as well. (They were a waste of money and in no way as nourishing as a good syllabub, but when she was a guest, she ate what she was served with pleasure whether she liked it or not.) Getting Mrs. Parfitt to expound on her opinions, Tommy realized as he saw Eliza's expression relax, had been her intention; she seemed eager to move the topic away from her eating habits and her pale appearance.

The observation gave him a stirring of unease.

"Lady Truehart!" Mrs. Parfitt said, as if coming to a sudden understanding. She turned to Anna. "Don't you think, Lady Grandville, that Lady Truehart would make the perfect wife for Sir Tommy? They can both eat vegetables together."

"Er…" Anna began.

Mrs. Parfitt's brow wrinkled as though she were reaching for some memory, and Tommy knew with a feeling of inevitability what was coming.

"Wasn't there something about an engagement between them a while ago?"

"Oh look, Mrs. Parfitt," Anna said with brilliant timing for which Tommy was grateful, "syllabub!"

By the end of lunch, he had decided that he needed to speak to Eliza again as soon as possible and in more detail, because her increasing pallor during lunch had begun to make him anxious.

What if she was mistaken about the possibility of a baby after all? What if she didn't quite understand how to determine whether she was increasing? If she'd had her courses, that ought to be definitive, but he'd heard there could be false or confusing signs as to whether a woman was expecting. Indian women were far more open about bodies than English ladies, and he knew a bit more about such things than when he'd landed in India. Apparently, women could have irregular courses, or, astonishingly, not even realize they were pregnant until the baby was arriving.

He really didn't want to think about any of this.

Still, it had only been a month or so since that fateful night, and he himself couldn't see how a woman could know for certain if she was to have a baby until an enormous belly was present. Though he did know that ladies who were increasing were likely to be pale and queasy.

But what if *she* didn't know all the right signs? As an

unmarried woman, she might feel she couldn't consult a doctor who, while he ought to be trustworthy with such information, was nonetheless human and a risk for gossip. And she might hesitate to ask a friend for guidance—particularly Anna, who would likely ferret out the truth. Of one thing he was certain: neither he nor Eliza could want Anna and Will to know any portion of what had happened.

He caught up with her as the guests were milling about in the drawing room after lunch, most of them, save Eliza and Tommy, moving very slowly with the weight of too much heavy food.

"Eliza, we have to talk," he said in a low voice.

She looked startled. "Why? We've already talked."

"I think there may be more to discuss."

"No, really," she said, but he ignored her and pulled her into the empty corridor.

"I just want to be absolutely certain there won't be any consequences from that night," he said.

❧

Eliza's stomach flipped over. She'd told herself that she hadn't lied to him before lunch when he'd asked whether his life was about to change, because it wasn't. He didn't want a baby and she did. Since that was the case, she saw no need for him even to know. Why was he asking again?

"I told you there wouldn't be."

"Yes," he said, "but then it occurred to me that perhaps you might be mistaken. That the, er, signs might not be easy to interpret, unless there was something definite to indicate otherwise."

She flushed. He meant her courses. He wanted to know if she'd had her courses. She would have to lie.

"Um," she said.

"Eliza," he said sternly, "I need to be absolutely certain you're not increasing." He paused, as though something had just occurred to him, and his eyes narrowed. "And if there *was* some outcome of our joining, I have a right to know. Besides, it's not as if you could keep such a thing a secret."

"But I could!" she blurted out before she could stop herself. "I could keep it a secret."

His jaw hardened instantly. "So you *are* increasing. You lied to me." The lethal rasp in his voice reminded her that dispatching dangerous pirates was all in a day's work for him. "I should have known."

She tugged at the arm he held, but he didn't release her.

"Very well, yes! I lied by omission," she said, aware of the need to keep her voice low, with people just inside the drawing room. "But only because I mean to take care of everything so you *won't* be affected. It's my fault this happened. I have a plan—I mean to go away to have the baby."

But he didn't seem to be listening to her explanation. "I should have known you would lie to me. Did you make up all that business about being infertile too?" he demanded.

She shook her head. "I was simply wrong about being barren. Gerard and I tried for years to no avail. I dearly wanted a baby—"

"So the truth comes out!" he broke in. "You used me as some sort of stud!"

"What? No! It was an accident."

But his jaw had only grown harder. "Why would I be foolish enough to believe that when you've already lied to me?"

"Because it's the truth! I wanted to spare you."

"No, you wanted this all to work out neatly for yourself."

"I thought," she nearly snarled, "that since you were going back to India before long, you need never have known."

"Good God," he growled.

She tamped down her emotions, trying to find a way to keep this conversation from veering out of control. "Look, this situation isn't your fault—we both know nothing would have happened that night if you'd known Victoria was me. But I have resources and plenty of money of my own—I shall simply go away for a few months, somewhere I'm not known, and then, after a while, I can come back to London and say I adopted the baby from an orphanage."

Tommy stared at her, his jaw so hard it might have been made of stone. Though he'd seemed to soften toward her over lunch, whatever tiny bit of goodwill he might have developed had clearly disappeared.

"Leaving aside the *ridiculous* notion that this baby is yours to do with as you wish and not mine as well, your plans are absurd and irresponsible. You can't simply disappear somewhere, have a baby, and return to your old life as if nothing had happened."

"Of course I can. Women have done things like this countless times before. What choice have they had? I at least, as an educated, well-off woman, can do for myself. And if I have to share some of the troubles that other women have endured, so be it."

"Save the philosophizing, Elizabeth. You're carrying my child, so you're going to be my wife."

Outrage and fear burned through her in equal measure. "No, I'm not," she said through her teeth.

"Yes, you are. I'll drag you to the church if I have to."

"But you can't make me say the words."

She turned away quickly and escaped back into the drawing room, where Anna and Will were chatting about some crumbling old estate in Kent that Tommy had apparently just bought, though Eliza couldn't manage to pay attention because she was worried that Tommy was going to follow her and try to browbeat her.

She kept her eyes surreptitiously on the door, but long minutes passed and he didn't reappear. She could only be grateful.

Anna pressed her to come back to Halifax House for tea, but Eliza really needed to go home and figure out a plan. She might have won the battle she'd just had with Tommy, but he was clearly furious, and she needed to find a way to keep this from turning into a war.

❧

Eliza was thoroughly shaken by the time she arrived at Truehart Manor, and she went right to her bedchamber and ordered a bath. The day was chilly and she sank into the steamy heat gratefully, wishing it could wash away all her mistakes. How had things come to this? She was pregnant and unmarried, with the furious father demanding she marry him so he could be angry at her for eternity.

And the place she'd worked so hard to establish as a refuge for disadvantaged girls—the undertaking around which she'd been building her life—was being rejected not only by the girls she wanted to help, but by the community in which she lived.

Her life was a mess. But she was going to have a baby, and nothing could diminish the joy that knowledge brought.

She reached for the towel the maid had left. She needed to talk to Meg.

Once dinner was over and Susie and Thomasina had gone to their rooms, Eliza pulled Meg into the breakfast room and closed the door.

"This is intriguing," Meg said, taking the maroon-striped chair by the fire. "Is something going on?"

"Er," Eliza said, coming to sit in the opposite chair, "yes."

Meg waited with a pleasant look on her face. Eliza bit her lip, hesitating. Meg laughed. "Heavens, but I'm growing interested. Do you want me to guess?"

"I don't think you'll manage," Eliza said. "I'm expecting."

"Expecting what?"

"The usual."

Meg just looked at her for several seconds. "Are you expecting a *baby*?" she said in a hushed voice.

"Yes."

"But how? Why?"

"I suppose the answer to both questions is also 'the usual.'"

Meg reached for Eliza's arm, a stricken look coming over her face. "Oh, Eliza, has someone harmed you? Were you molested?"

"No," Eliza said quickly. "It was nothing like that." And then she began to explain, starting with how and why she'd gone to Madame Persaud's.

"You went to a *brothel*? What on earth can you have been thinking? What an insane thing to do!"

Eliza's lips twisted wryly. "I see that now, obviously." She explained the rest of what had happened, leaving out the details but giving Meg the gist.

"My God," Meg gasped. "Sir Tommy Halifax is the father of your unborn child? Does he know?"

"Yes. I wasn't going to tell him, because I plan to take care of the baby on my own and he's going back to India, so I thought he would be gone before it would be apparent that I was increasing. But he figured it out at the Bridewell luncheon today. He's furious, and I can't blame him. But that doesn't mean I'm going to let him tell me what to do."

"What did he say?"

"He demanded I marry him."

"As well he ought!"

"I'm not going to marry him."

Meg's eyes widened. "*What?* Why not? You're an unmarried woman who's increasing—what else can you do but marry the father?"

"He doesn't want this baby, and he as good as hates me. Marrying each other would be a recipe for disaster, for both us and the baby. I mean to go away and have the baby somewhere else, on my own."

Meg's eyebrows lowered. "This sounds like an

even more insane undertaking than your trip to the brothel."

Eliza smiled. "That's why I need your help. When you take Thomasina and Susie to Francesca's tomorrow, I want to go to Bath with you. Since we won't have anymore girls in our care here"—she sighed a little over the failure of her hopes for Truehart Manor—"I thought I could stay with Francesca and help out at her school until Tommy goes back to India. And then I would go away, before I started to show."

Meg crossed her arms. "What if he finds out you're in Bath?"

"How would he, if you don't tell him?"

"Anna and Will, for instance, will wonder what happened to you."

"You can tell them I went to stay with a friend who needed help. I'll send them a letter when I get there. Then once Tommy's gone, I'll come back to London and sort out my affairs. I could even join you in Italy," she said, the idea just occurring to her, "and perhaps stay and have the baby there."

Meg pressed her lips together. "This is an entirely mad scheme."

"I know," Eliza said quietly. "But I don't know what else to do."

Meg sighed. "You *know* I'll help you, and I suppose it just might work. But…don't you think you should sort things out with Tommy?"

"You didn't see his face today—he looked ready to swashbuckle me. Trust me, this is for the best."

❧

Eliza and Meg were on the road very early the next morning, along with Thomasina and Susie, who were sleepy but also excited. The girls chattered giddily about what Bath and the school would be like, and Eliza could only hope that what she and Meg had tried to do for them at Truehart Manor wouldn't ultimately turn out to be a waste.

Once their carriage cleared the outskirts of London and she could tell herself she'd managed to evade Tommy, Eliza began to relax, although it was difficult to feel entirely at ease since her stomach was queasy. But still, she'd taken the best possible step for the future of herself and her baby.

They'd just passed through a village when their coach slowed to a stop.

"What can it be?" Meg wondered aloud.

Eliza rapped on the roof of the coach and called out to the coachman. "Why are we stopping?"

But there wasn't time for him to reply, because the door opened abruptly, and there was Tommy.

"Oh dear," Meg murmured.

"Good morning, ladies," Tommy said, sweeping them a gallant bow. "I apologize for interrupting your progress. I am Sir Tommy Halifax. Miss Cartwright, I presume?" he said to Meg.

"Yes," she said, sounding a little breathless. His black hair shone in the midmorning light, and his face looked freshly shaved. He was wearing a brilliant saffron-colored coat he might have stolen from a rajah, along with a striped blue-and-white waistcoat that set off the slash of white at his forehead. Though his gracious manner was that of a gentleman, the tilt of his lips whispered "rogue."

"Very pleased to meet you," he said to Meg. "My sister-in-law, Lady Grandville, has sung your praises to me on many an occasion."

Meg blushed, clearly charmed, and Eliza wanted to pinch her.

His gaze move on to Thomasina and Susie, who were both staring at him slack-jawed, as though they'd discovered themselves in the presence of a friendly pirate captain. "And you must be two of the accomplished young ladies from Truehart Manor, of whom I've also heard."

"Thomasina, sir," the girl said in an awed voice.

"And Susie," the other girl whispered.

He swept them each a bow. "I'm honored to meet you both."

He turned to Eliza, and a hard glitter came into those green eyes that had just charmed the rest of the carriage's occupants into a stupor. "And of course I am already well acquainted with Lady Truehart. In fact," he said, giving Eliza a smile that doubtless only she was able to see was evil, "I have pressing business with her."

He held out a hand. "My coach is just behind, Lady Truehart. If you would come with me?"

She wanted to tell him to take himself off in the strongest terms imaginable, but Thomasina and Susie were there, and Eliza didn't want to be a bad example to them or create a scene that would be interesting enough to become gossip. She forced a laugh.

"Goodness, Sir Tommy, the idea!" she said breezily. "I'm already on my way somewhere. Surely we could chat in London when next we meet."

"I don't think so," he said, his eyes boring into hers.

Eliza's eyes flicked to Meg, silently beseeching her for help.

Meg leaned close. "He has a stake in this," she whispered. "I'm sorry, but I have to agree that you must talk to him."

Eliza wanted to howl with frustration, but instead she allowed him to help her down. His coach stood behind hers, the horses waiting patiently.

Tommy leaned into Eliza's coach and said, "No need to linger, Miss Cartwright. I'll see that Lady Truehart gets where she needs to go."

"What?" Eliza squawked, aware that Meg and the girls could see them out the window of her coach. "But my trunk," she protested. She supposed he meant to return her to London, and what did it matter now if he did, since the point of her flight had been to avoid him? Still, it was going to be an awkward, unpleasant ride back, and she could only think he meant to renew his insistence that they marry. She would simply have to put him off until they got to London.

"No time to unload it," Tommy said. "Besides, I have a valise for you."

He did? "Why? How could you possibly?"

He ignored her and gave Meg a cheery wave. She waved back, and Eliza's coach took off, leaving her standing with Tommy.

"After you," he said, gesturing toward his coach.

"This is ridiculous," she said through her teeth, aware that his driver could hear their conversation. "What do you think you're doing?"

"I suggest we discuss this where our conversation will be private."

She wanted to offer him a few choice words, but she just clamped her lips together and got into the coach. She noticed, with a fleeting feeling of consolation, that Traveler was curled up on one seat, but before she could sit next to the dog, Tommy climbed in, closing the door behind him, and beat her to it. Traveler opened one eye and gave her what looked like a pitying glance before going back to sleep. She took the opposite seat, Tommy rapped on the roof, and they took off.

"Where do you think you're taking me?" she demanded.

"To get married. I have a special license."

"*What?*" she gasped, and then was simply speechless for several seconds. "Stop the coach this instant and let me down! You're out of your mind."

"No, *you're* out of your mind if you think my child is going to be a bastard." Though he'd been so charming to Meg and the girls, it was clear to Eliza that under that polite facade, he was seething.

"Don't use that word."

"Why not? Everyone else will, once they find out."

She threw up her hands. "This is ridiculous! We can't marry. Neither of us *wants* to marry." When he didn't reply, she said, "We just need to be reasonable about this."

"I *am* being reasonable," he said, though with his hard jaw and his bitter mouth, he looked anything but that. "There is no other choice. Besides," his eyes settled on her, sharp green ice chips, "I already told Will that we were eloping. I told him we'd been secretly courting, and that we'd discussed marriage like the two rational adults we are. And I told him that you'd agreed—but that it's your fondest wish to have a grand, romantic gesture, so I was going to sweep you off your feet."

"This is so outrageous, I don't even know what to say."

He looked out the window. "Will was surprised at my news—though it's probably more accurate to say he was suspicious. But he seemed to accept the idea. Anna was certainly thrilled—apparently she's been entertaining some bizarre notion that we were always meant for each other. I wouldn't have thought her prone to that kind of nonsense, but there you are."

Eliza's heart was racing. How could he have done this? "You told Will and Anna we were getting married? What on earth were you thinking?"

But he simply turned his head and gave her a level stare, and she knew exactly what he'd been thinking. If she refused to do as he asked, not only would she disappoint Will and Anna, she'd also have a great deal of explaining to do.

She finally understood just how big a mistake she'd made that night at Madame Persaud's. She'd tangled with a man who'd spent the last six years riding around a land of tigers and scimitars, a man who dispatched pirates and negotiated with princes. The hopes, wishes, and dreams of one English lady were nothing to a swashbuckling brigand used to taking what he wanted, and clearly kidnapping her was all in day's work.

"Anna was quite insistent about packing a valise for you so you wouldn't be without something to wear, once I swept you off your feet," he said.

"Apparently, she had some of your old clothes that you'd discarded."

Eliza nearly groaned at the thought—the only clothes of hers Anna could have had were the things from when she was younger, the garish clothes of her first, disastrous season, which she'd given Anna to share with her maids. She'd had no idea Anna had kept them all this time.

"Tommy," she said, struggling for an even tone though his domineering manner was making her furious, "I really am sorry about what happened. I wanted you not to be affected."

"And yet I am affected. You're carrying my child, the child you schemed to have."

"I didn't scheme to use you so I could have a baby," she insisted, though she knew from the set of his features that she was wasting her breath. He clearly meant never to believe a thing she said. "The two of us marrying is a *terrible* idea. We can barely even say a reasonable sentence to each other."

"It will hardly matter. We'll marry, the baby will have the protection of my name, and I'll return to India. Our lives will in most ways go back to being just as they were."

What a strange future he was describing. And yet, furious though she was to admit it, when he'd told Will and Anna they were eloping, he'd taken away her choice as surely as she'd taken away his the night she'd fooled him at the brothel. If she refused to marry him, she'd have to explain why to Anna and Will, and after the way she'd laughed at Tommy's proposal all those years ago, how could they ever understand if it seemed she'd led him on and rejected him again? Never mind how suspicious they'd be when her baby was eventually born.

"Very well," she said tightly. "We'll marry."

He grunted at her acquiescence. "We'll be continuing on to my new estate in Kent afterward, as I have yet to see the place." He paused. "I have already let Will and Anna know that we'll be spending our honeymoon there together."

Apparently he'd seen to everything. Bitterness settled over her at his high-handed behavior, but what was the point of saying any more about it? "What's it called, this new place of yours?" she bit off, determined to take back some modicum of direction for her life.

"Hellfire Hall."

Surely she'd misheard him. "*Hellfire* Hall?"

"It used to be owned by pirates," he informed her with a nasty smirk.

And wasn't that just perfect? She was apparently headed for Hellfire Hall, the ideal place for a wicked brigand to take his kidnapped bride. Her stomach, already sloshing unpleasantly, took a deep dip and settled into her shoes.

At the next town, they stopped and found the vicar. Tommy presented him with the special license, and in a matter of minutes they were standing before the altar in the small village church.

As Eliza struggled not to succumb to a daze of numbness, woodenly speaking to the vicar when necessary, Tommy stood stiffly, doubtless looking like a nervous groom instead of a man furious about the way his future had suddenly changed.

Forsaking all others until death do us part, she repeated after the vicar. The words were timeless, honoring the goodness and love that marriage was meant to bring, but she and Tommy didn't share love, and the only good thing they had between them was the baby. She vowed to herself in that moment, for the baby's sake, to do her best to try to be decent toward Tommy.

His mouth seemed to barely open past the teeth she supposed must be clenched as he said his own vows. At the end of the ceremony, he leaned down and pressed his mouth against hers, doubtless so the vicar wouldn't guess there was anything awry between the bride and groom. His lips were dry and warm, and surely the softest part of this hard man.

Something squeezed in her chest as he stepped back. While his eyes told her that she was nothing to him, he wasn't nothing to her. Despite everything, she was very attracted to him, but it wasn't only that. He'd certainly changed over the last six years, but though he'd spared little warmth for her since his return, she knew that, to everyone but her, he was charm personified, an even more appealing version of the smart, witty, good man whose company she'd once so loved.

She couldn't forget that night they'd shared. Their touching and joining had opened something vulnerable in her that she couldn't seem to close up again. But their lovemaking had clearly left no impression on Tommy, and she knew that living with him for whatever time they would have together would put her in danger of being hurt by him.

She must simply find a way not to let that happen.

Eight

IT WAS EARLY AFTERNOON BY THE TIME THEY TOOK leave of the vicar, and Tommy announced that they would have lunch at the inn before resuming their journey.

The idea of eating anything had only grown less appealing as the day wore on, and Eliza told him she wasn't hungry. "I'll wait in the coach while you eat."

"You will not," he said, taking hold of her elbow and steering her toward the Grizzled Hare. "You will come inside and eat lunch."

"Goodness, what a gracious invitation." She attempted to tug her arm free with no success. "But I'm not hungry just now."

If she'd forgotten how hard his chiseled jaw could look, she was now reminded. Just the sight of her seemed to make him instantly clench it. "We will not be stopping again until this evening, when we reach an inn where we will pass the night. Therefore, you need to come inside and eat something now."

Her heart sank at the thought of all those hours in the coach, both because she didn't want to spend them in his company and because her stomach was churning, but she forced herself to look unaffected. "As I don't wish to eat anything, I don't see the point in coming to sit inside at a table so you can glower at me."

He leaned close and dropped his voice to a low growl. "You need to eat, whether you wish to do so or not. The longer a woman in your condition goes without eating, the more likely she is to cast up her accounts. Poached eggs and dry toast seem to help in such cases."

Since she hadn't been able to eat anything that morning, Eliza doubted she had any accounts to cast up, but she didn't like that he seemed to be knowledgeable on this subject. "And you have a great deal of experience with 'such cases'?" she said frostily.

His eyes flashed with irritation. "It's general knowledge."

To anyone who doesn't spend all her time on frivolous things was clearly the part he didn't say. He thought all she did was go to parties and do charitable works to make herself appear caring, that the changes she'd made since he left years before were all a ruse. He even believed she'd used him like some sort of breeding animal so she could have a baby.

Realizing she was clenching her teeth, she forced herself to relax. In truth, a poached egg and toast sounded a little appealing, though she was annoyed at the idea of consuming them in front of his likely smug face.

"I do believe," she said, tipping her chin up, "that I shall take a little something after all."

He let her arm go and they stepped inside the Grizzled Hare.

略

Tommy had no trouble avoiding conversation with Eliza during lunch since she clearly didn't wish to speak to him either.

They sat alone in a private room, the serving girl having left after bringing their food and stirring up the fire against the briskness of the afternoon. Eliza ate her egg and toast in small, slow bites while he worked through a plate of sandwiches, and they both stared at fixed spots on the floor as though they were a long-married couple already bored with each other.

It was a dismal thought, but far better than the others he was having. For instance, how did he know she hadn't done something like the Victoria-the-prostitute stunt with other men?

God, if he'd ever meant to marry, it would never have been to someone like Eliza. He'd had years of watching marital disasters play out among his friends, of observing how nearly impossible it was for most people to be content with their spouses, whether because of infidelity or other weaknesses. The one thing he'd known for certain was that he'd never marry a woman he didn't respect and trust—and ideally, not until they'd courted at least a year to ensure they suited.

He thought of Rex, whom Anna had cheerfully agreed to keep while Tommy and Eliza eloped and had their "honeymoon." It was hardly remarkable that the boy was a trial to be around, considering that his parents' marriage had been so poor.

Even Tommy's beloved father had betrayed Tommy's mother, and while Tommy loved his stepmother, Judith's arrival had caused years of bitterness in his family. Why would he want to set himself up for the unhappiness marriage always seemed to bring?

But now he'd done exactly that.

He'd always intended that when he did marry, one day years in the future, he and his wife would be faithful to each other—that, like Will and Anna, they would only *want* to be faithful. But what about Eliza? How could he trust her not to flirt—and more—with every man she met?

He didn't even want to think about what being faithful to Eliza was going to mean in terms of his own needs and desires.

He fixed her with a hard look. A hint of vulnerability at the edges of her pretty pink mouth tugged at his attention, but he just gave her a bitter smile.

"You do understand," he said, "that we'll be keeping those vows we took today. There will be no infidelity in our marriage."

Vivid red swept into her cheeks. "Your suggestion that I have other plans is incredibly insulting."

"Words are easy. Commitment is hard. You and I are now stuck together, and I don't plan to be the only one affected by the change," he said, letting steel into his voice. "I'll not have my child mothered by a woman who doesn't know the meaning of restraint."

She put down her serviette and stood up.

"Where do you think you're going?"

"To the coach. I have nothing further to say to you."

In a flash he was upright, and he grabbed her arm before she could leave.

"I didn't hear any assurance from you."

Her eyes flashed at him, those blue eyes that had haunted dreams he'd never wanted to have and that now belonged to a wife he hadn't wanted. "If you think this baby means anything less than the world to me, you don't know me at all."

"That's right, I don't."

She jerked her hand away and made for the door, and he let her go.

❧

Eliza managed to climb back into the carriage with her head held high, but she was shaking.

She heard him talking to the coachman and making arrangements for the next leg of their journey, and when they set off again, she was alone in the coach with Traveler while Tommy rode alongside.

The food had helped a little, though she certainly wouldn't admit that to him, and when Traveler hopped up onto the seat next to her with what looked like compassion in his large brown eyes, she laid a grateful hand on his soft head and slept. When she woke up late in the afternoon, she ran through baby names while petting him.

"What do you think, Trav?" she asked him. "I like Georgiana for a girl, and James for a boy."

He licked her hand. "Though I wonder if your master and I are going to have terrible arguments about this as well." She sighed. "Probably," she said, leaning her cheek against the dog's head. But she also knew she'd do anything for the tender life growing inside her, and that was obviously going to include matching wits with her baby's father.

They stopped late at night in the courtyard of an inn. Eliza and Traveler got down from the coach, and Traveler made for the stables while she told Tommy they must have separate rooms. He just looked at her for a long moment, then strode into the inn, where he was greeted with enthusiasm by the innkeeper, who clearly knew a wealthy gentleman when he saw one.

"I'd like two rooms, please, one for my wife and one for myself." Tommy made a regretful face. "She has a tremendous snoring problem. You may even wish to isolate her from the other guests lest they be unable to sleep through the sound."

Eliza had to restrain herself from kicking him in the shins.

The innkeeper declared himself terribly sorry, but there was a harvest festival occurring in the town and hardly any rooms were available. Sir Tommy and his wife would be obliged to share a single room, he said, giving Tommy a look of deep sympathy.

The innkeeper promised to have a tray of food sent up and led them to a small room at the end of a narrow passageway. It held a table, a chair by the hearth, and a bed that looked far too small to share. Nearly dropping with fatigue, Eliza managed a weak smile of thanks.

As soon as the door closed behind the innkeeper, she said, "I'm quite exhausted and I should like to retire. You may take the bed—I'll take the chair by the fire."

Tommy rolled his eyes. "No, you won't."

She forced herself to say in a reasonable tone, "Would you please stop behaving as though I'm twelve? I was merely being polite. Since that bed is too small to share, one of us will have to take the chair, and I'm perfectly happy to do it."

He lifted a hand to rub his eyes as though he'd had a tremendously trying day, which made her want to yell at him. "Anyone who tried to rest in that chair would be far too uncomfortable to sleep. The bed is small but we'll manage."

She was too tired to argue. "Fine," she said, sitting on the edge of the bed and pulling off her shoes.

A knock on the door signaled the arrival of a supper tray. Eliza was far more interested in the bed than the food, but Tommy said, "Eat first, then sleep." When she didn't move, he grabbed her arm and tugged her upright.

"I really don't want anything," she muttered.

"You need to eat something for the baby."

She knew he was right, so she forced down some milk and a few bites of a buttered roll.

Afterward, she eyed the bed, ready to crawl into it with her clothes on. But with her stomach so delicate, she knew she'd be more than just uncomfortable trying to sleep buttoned into the fitted bodice of her gown. It made her fume to know she'd have to ask Tommy for help, but she stood and turned her back to him.

"Could you undo my buttons, please?"

He didn't reply, but after a few moments she heard him stand, and then she felt him pushing the buttons through their slits with the sort of perfunctory haste one might use in tossing unwanted items into a dustbin.

When he was finally done, she glanced over her

shoulder and saw that he had already turned away from her. She removed her gown and laid it over the back of the chair, then climbed into the bed in her chemise and stretched out under the blanket with unutterable relief. The last thing she did before dropping her head to the pillow was to pull the pins out of her hair and drop them on the bedside table.

A few minutes later, Tommy blew out the candle and the bed sagged as he got in on the other side. She was grateful for the exhaustion that pulled her into sleep.

❧

As Tommy lay next to Eliza, the even sound of her breathing told him that she'd fallen asleep almost immediately. He was not so fortunate. She might be an infuriating woman whose actions had forced him into a marriage he didn't want, but she was also the woman with whom he'd shared a passionate sexual encounter that his body hadn't forgotten. Unbuttoning her gown had been a torture he'd pushed past as quickly as he could, but at least the light in the room was dim. He'd kept his eyes on the back of her head the whole time.

When he'd come to blow out the last candle, he'd seen that she'd taken her hair down. She looked different with her hair loose—younger, vulnerable, and achingly lovely, and he'd known that his efforts to ignore her appeal had been useless. He still wanted her, and he was hugely annoyed with himself for it.

He rolled closer to the edge of the bed, pulling the blanket tighter over himself against the damp autumn chill, and refused to think about the fact that Eliza was sleeping next to him in only a chemise. He felt like a trussed chicken lying there in his breeches and tailcoat. In India, most nights he wore nothing to bed. Not that he missed the extreme heat or the swarms of flies and mosquitos, but he did miss what he did there: riding out to far-flung royal courts to conduct talks, intervening in diplomatically sticky situations, evading capture when the tables suddenly turned. He'd even negotiated his own release from prison on one occasion.

While often sweet, life in England had never offered him anything like that.

Eliza rolled over onto her back and began to snore softly, and the last thing Tommy thought before falling asleep was, oddly, that the sound was peaceful.

He awoke early the next morning, predictably aroused by the awareness that there was a beautiful woman in his bed. Eliza was still sleeping, and he rolled his head on the pillow and took in the head beside him. Strands of reddish-gold hair lay across her cheek, drawing his attention to the way her eyelashes brushed the fragile skin under her eyes and the hint of fine lines at their edges. She looked…real.

He got out of bed.

While she slept on, he called for breakfast to be brought in along with hot water. Having done for himself so often on his travels, he rarely felt the need for a valet. He was adept at packing garments so they didn't wrinkle, he'd become handy with a needle after all those months aboard ship watching the sailors sew, and he could certainly shave himself.

When the hot water came, he was not particularly

quiet as he set out his soap and razor, and after a few minutes he heard Eliza shifting in the bed.

"Tommy?" She sounded sleepy.

"Time to get up and eat. We're leaving in twenty minutes."

"Twenty minutes—" she began in a way that sounded like she had a great deal of outrage to express, but she swallowed whatever she'd been about to say and sat up, pulling the blanket around her. He caught a glimpse of her in his looking glass, and the sight startled a laugh out of him.

She frowned. "What?"

A clutter of curls flopped dizzily across one side of her forehead and stood up in a lion's mane around her head. Her big blue eyes were still soft with sleep, her lips pink. He reminded himself of her shallowness.

"Your hair," he said gruffly, focusing his eyes on the reflection of his own cheek as he dragged the razor along the skin.

"If you will leave the room," she said, "I will see to my hair and change my clothes."

"You can change behind the screen," he said, guessing that she simply wanted him to leave. Perhaps it was childish of him to want to thwart her, but he couldn't seem to help himself.

A few seconds passed. "Very well," she finally said. "Close your eyes."

"I'm shaving. Or perhaps you would *like* me to slice myself open?"

She made an exasperated sound. "Clearly you would have to pause in your shaving while your eyes were closed."

"And yet I prefer not to. I *am* your husband, after all. And you'll be behind a screen. Besides, it's not as if I haven't already seen most of you." Though not *all*, not anywhere near as much as he wanted, and the knowledge plagued him constantly.

"You're being a beast," she grumbled, but he could hear her pulling the blanket around her as she got out of bed while he went to work on the other cheek. He spared barely a glance for her as she made her way to the trunk that Anna had sent for her, a length of blanket trailing behind her like a queen's train. She opened the trunk, poked through the clothes inside for a few moments, then closed the lid without taking anything out and reached for the blue gown she'd worn the day before.

"What, don't you like the things Anna sent?"

She ignored him and disappeared behind the screen. After some minutes of rustling, she emerged at the edge of the screen. She'd tidied her hair by pulling it into a simple knot high on the back of her head, and she was holding her blue gown closed at the neck in back. "I need help with the buttons again," she said. "Please."

She turned around expectantly, displaying the line of buttons he'd undone in near darkness the night before. Now the daylight gave him a fine view of gauzy white chemise where the gown gaped, and what seemed like yards of buttons to be gotten through little slits.

"Isn't there one of those kinds of gowns with the drawstring neck in that trunk?"

"No. They're just party clothes, things from a long time ago."

He snorted. "And they're not good enough for your wholesome widow image, is that it?"

She just stood there with her back to him, waiting.

He gritted his teeth and got to work, keeping his eyes on the back of her head. Looking at his fingers was not a good idea, since as they moved upward, her hand gripping the gown closed let go, revealing the soft, fair skin of her nape, where a few strands of hair lazed against her milky skin. *Siren*, he reminded himself.

❧

Eliza could feel Tommy doing up her buttons with determined speed, as though he couldn't wait to be done with being so near her. It was just as well he was treating her as though she had the plague, because she was tempted to spin fantasies of something positive perhaps coming out of their forced marriage, something good for their baby. She knew that wasn't going to happen.

He thought the life she'd made for herself in the last six years had been nothing but a mask for the selfish, careless flirt he believed her still to be, and maybe it was better for her if she let him think her so shallow. "Maybe I'll wear the clothes if there's anyone at your estate worth impressing," she said.

"If that's how you want to look at it."

They were both quiet as he finished the buttons. When she turned around, she let her eyes skip over his rumpled suit and forced herself to adopt a haughty tone.

"You're hardly dressed to impress."

She was certain she heard the sound of teeth grinding. "I'm about to change." He put his hand on the waist of his trousers with a glint of challenge in his eyes, and she gave a shocked gasp (which was not entirely for his benefit) and turned away.

While he was behind the screen, a knock sounded and a maid entered with a breakfast tray. Once she'd left, he said from behind the screen, "We've a long way to go today, so you have about five minutes to eat."

She knew it would be best for the sake of her stomach to eat something, and she picked up a roll, but she couldn't seem to make herself take a bite.

"You'll need to actually put the food in your mouth for it to benefit you."

She turned and saw he'd come out from behind the screen. "You do realize that I'm not some fragile young thing who's going to quiver at your every command?"

He gave her a dark look. "In fact, as your lord and master, I *can* order you about if I choose." He moved toward the looking glass and began tying his cravat in a simple knot, which she supposed was necessary since he had no valet. Though she couldn't really imagine him wearing some elaborately tied confection.

"Lord and master?" she scoffed. "Whether you believe it or not, I do want what's best for the baby. It's just hard to eat with a queasy stomach."

He gave a sharp nod and went over to his valise.

She did her best to eat some of the roll and drink a little tea, since apparently they were going to be on the road for hours again, a prospect she tried not to think about.

"Will we arrive today?"

"Yes."

"How long do you mean to stay at Hellfire Hall?" He didn't look up from his valise when she spoke, and she thought that perhaps those moments when they weren't looking at each other were the best times to attempt conversation. Not that she wanted to engage him in chat, but there were things she needed to know.

"A while."

Which told her nothing. He held so much power over her now, power she hadn't wanted to surrender, and the knowledge infuriated her.

"Do you mean several days? Weeks?"

"I haven't decided."

"And then you'll return to India?" A horrifying thought occurred to her: he could compel her to return to India with him. Though why he should wish to do such a thing short of sheer bloody-mindedness, she couldn't imagine. "Alone?"

"Alone. My passage is booked for two months hence. You will stay in England." He paused. "It was what you wanted anyway, wasn't it, to have it be just you and the baby."

"Yes," she muttered, though everything was different now from what she'd dreamed of, and she knew, stupidly, that she was a little disappointed that he clearly was not even the tiniest bit tempted to stay in England and meet his child, never mind being a part of his or her life.

She was being foolish, because it was for the best that he was leaving.

She stood and began to pack up the few things she'd taken out of her case. She had a life in London.

She had Meg and Will and Anna and her friends, and *they* would be her baby's family since Tommy would not.

And he was not abandoning her. Except for the detail of their marriage, they'd made no promises to be with each other.

She rested a hand on her still-flat belly. She was going to have a baby to love, a baby who wasn't going to be born on the wrong side of the blanket, and she was *lucky*. If Tommy didn't want to share in that, it was his problem.

When he turned away from the looking glass, freshly shaved and dressed in a peacock-green tailcoat, she instructed herself to ignore how handsome he was. Also, how tall. Nor should her eyes linger for even one moment on his thighs, whose rock-like muscles were suggested by the snug-fitting cloth of his buff-colored breeches. She averted her eyes when he turned around to put something in his valise and refused to care that his back looked extremely good.

Nor did she allow herself to remember that lying in the same bed with him last night, just before she fell asleep, she'd experienced an entirely misplaced feeling of comfort.

They departed the inn, with her and Traveler again in the carriage and Tommy riding his large chestnut stallion.

It was a very long day, during which she, surprisingly, didn't feel as ill as she had for the past few days. She distracted herself from thinking about all the ways her life had changed overnight by talking to Traveler and looking out the window. The scenery at least was beautiful, everywhere the crimson and gold of autumn, and people working in the fields.

When they finally arrived at the manor, it was evening and very dark. Eliza could see little of the building, but by then she couldn't summon the energy to care. Her limbs felt like weights as she climbed down from the carriage.

The housekeeper, Mrs. Hatch, greeted them warmly at the door and was all smiles when Tommy introduced himself and told her that he'd recently married and brought his bride to see his new estate.

Eliza, who'd never felt so exhausted in her life, asked if she could be shown to her room.

"Of course," Mrs. Hatch said. "The bedchambers for the master and mistress have been cleaned and aired." She looked a little hesitant. "Though of course the furnishings are very…simple."

Eliza wouldn't have cared if the furnishings were nothing but a blanket thrown on a cold floor at that point, as long as she could stretch out her cramped, aching body and sleep.

With the help of a maid the housekeeper sent to her, Eliza undressed and fell gratefully into bed.

In the middle of the night, she awoke to the awareness that something was very wrong.

∽

Eliza did not make an appearance at breakfast the next morning, though Tommy, dining alone, was not surprised. When he saw Mrs. Hatch later that morning, the woman, clearly thinking that a newly wedded husband hungered for every morsel of news about his beloved, told him that a maid had been dispatched with a tray for the mistress, but that Lady Halifax had sent the girl away and asked not to be disturbed.

Though he tried to convince himself that Eliza was playing the martyr, or perhaps the princess for whom nothing in his crumbling manor would be good enough, his conscience prodded him. She'd looked drawn and pale when they'd arrived, and she'd retired immediately.

He went to her room, but there was no answer to his knock, so he went in.

"Time to start the day, Eliza," he said, advancing into the room, which, like his, looked suitable for an inhabitant who was either austere or destitute. His agent had not exaggerated when he'd said the estate was in need of renovation. Hellfire Hall would clearly need quite a lot of attention before it would be truly presentable, and if nothing else, Eliza could help with that. She certainly owed him. "You've a manor to play mistress to."

She was still in bed, lying on her side facing away from him, and she didn't turn when he spoke, but what had he expected? Though he acknowledged a grudging respect that she hadn't crumpled under the less-than-generous manner in which he'd been treating her, he knew that developing soft feelings for her would be a mistake.

The fire was dying and the room was colder even than the rest of the drafty manor. He threw a few logs in the hearth, then moved toward the bed. As he did so, he caught sight of an empty washbasin on the room's small table and, on the unwelcoming old wood of the floor, a single, startling drop of blood.

A sense of foreboding came over him and his eyes flew to the bed. "Eliza?"

She finally turned over. Her face was ashen and her lips bloodless, but it was the flatness in her blue eyes that struck him most.

"I lost the baby," she said in an emotionless voice. Then she turned on her side away from him again.

He stood there speechless.

Mrs. Hatch had clearly known nothing of what had happened, nor surely any of the servants, which told him that Eliza had dealt with the miscarriage entirely on her own. Alone, in the dark of night, in an unfamiliar house.

Perhaps she hadn't rung for help because she hadn't wanted to make it known that she'd been increasing, since they were so recently married. Or perhaps she'd felt alone among people she hardly knew. He felt bad, though, that she'd been on her own.

"I'm sorry," he said quietly, moving closer.

When she didn't respond after several long moments, he said, "Should I call a doctor?"

"No. It's not necessary."

"Is there anything you wish? Anything you need?"

"Please just go away."

He felt instant relief at her words—relief that she didn't expect anything from him. This was followed by an unwelcome feeling of self-disgust. He might be furious with her, but she was clearly very much affected by the loss of the baby. However, she wanted him to go, and he certainly didn't want to stay there when he didn't know what to do, so he obliged her and left.

He would let Mrs. Hatch know that the mistress was exhausted from the journey and a bit unwell, and that she should be left to rest.

~∞~

The soft click of the door closing told Eliza that Tommy was gone.

She didn't seem able to do anything beyond stare at the bare stone walls of her chamber. The room's windows were starkly unrelieved by curtains, and she could feel a thin current of cold air seeping through their old frames. The furnishings, though they were clean and tidy, were ancient, and the small carpet was threadbare. The room looked like a dungeon cell.

She didn't care. The only thing that mattered was that her baby—her sweet, tiny, fragile, miracle baby—was gone.

Her throat closed with the heavy weight of sorrow, and her tears soaked her pillow.

Nine

By the next morning, Eliza still hadn't stirred from her bed and Tommy was concerned. She hadn't touched the tray he'd delivered to her room the afternoon before, though she did appear to have drunk some of the tea Mrs. Hatch had brought her in the early evening. But tea was nothing.

He was beginning to think she needed a doctor.

He went to her room again, clearing his throat to announce his presence in case she was sleeping. But as he drew near the bed, he could see she was awake and lying on her back.

"How are you feeling?" he asked.

"Tired," she said, not looking at him.

"You should see a doctor. I'll send for one today."

"No," she said, rolling her head on the pillow to look at him. "I don't need a doctor. It was a…normal occurrence," she said dully. "It happens. It happened to Anna, a year after Heck was born. She was fine."

He hadn't known that had happened to Anna. It was hardly the sort of information one put in a letter, but perhaps if he'd been at home, Will would have shared the news with him.

Eliza's words reassured him somewhat, though she didn't exactly seem to be "fine," but he supposed a day or two of recovery would be needed.

"Very well, but you must try to eat something." He gestured to the tray at her bedside. "It will help build your strength." He sounded like a damned nursemaid, but he didn't know what else to do. What did he know about women's needs or caring for ill people? He almost never got sick, and when he did, he retreated to his rooms and preferred to be left alone.

"I just need to rest," she said, and turned away from him. He didn't like it, but he left.

Two days later, he overruled Eliza's wishes and sent for a doctor.

She looked daggers at Tommy when he brought Dr. Hall in to see her, and Tommy was glad to escape the room and leave her in the care of someone trained and knowledgeable.

After his examination, Dr. Hall assured Tommy that Lady Halifax had recovered physically from the event and that she could certainly have another baby. But he also said that some women took losing a baby very hard, even one that had barely had time to grow.

The next morning, her tray was again sent away with hardly anything missing. Mrs. Hatch said to Tommy, "Poor Lady Halifax must be quite unwell. She's not eating enough to keep a bird alive." He couldn't agree more.

He made his way to her bedchamber, knocked once, and entered, closing the door behind him.

She lay in the bed as usual, though now she was dressed in a fresh white chemise that he suspected the maid had helped her into, and her hair looked freshly washed and still a bit wet. But her skin was pale, her cheeks sunken, and her eyes flat. Pity stirred in his chest, along with the banked embers of his longtime anger with her.

He strode over to the bed. She turned away from him, pulling the blanket over her shoulder as if to seal herself off under its protection.

"You need to get up," he said. "It's not sensible to lie in bed like this for days."

She made no reply, but he was prepared for that. He grabbed the edge of the blanket, pulled it briskly off her, and tossed it over a nearby chair. She yelped and sat up.

"What do you think you're doing?" she demanded hoarsely. She drew her legs up and hugged them, and her teeth chattered for a moment before she clenched them.

"Helping you get ready for the day."

She just stared at him, though perhaps that was a hint of anger beginning to brighten the flatness in her eyes? Good. Anything was better than that detached, emotionless look.

Tommy went over to her wardrobe and examined the dresses. The silks and velvets of a fashionable woman, they were all too pretty and impractical for the chatelaine of this rustic home. One even had jewels sewn all over it. He knew what Anna had been thinking when she packed such things for an eloping couple, but now he wished he'd let Eliza bring her own trunk from the coach, because he guessed it had been full of those plain gowns she'd been wearing in London.

He'd assumed those sensible frocks were nothing but a costume, part of the veneer of propriety she'd created. But though he'd been so convinced she'd been acting the part of a demure, caring widow, he didn't feel comfortable judging her so harshly now.

"It's cold today," he said needlessly. "You'll want something warm." Hellfire Hall's name promised warmth, but instead the place seemed to absorb any heat generated by the well-tended fires that were kept lit in most rooms. Though today, by his order, her fire had been allowed to go out. "You can put on that gown you were wearing when you left London."

"I'm not getting up."

"Oh, but you are," he said firmly. He might not be a good nursemaid, but he definitely knew the value of getting on with things even when you didn't feel like it.

He thought of his friend Jonathan Tartt, a captain in the East India Company, who'd embraced the Hindoo religion and delighted in holding nautch parties full of dancing girls. Though Tartt had a wife in England, his true love was his Indian mistress, and when she died delivering his child, he'd shut himself in his house with crates of wine. By the end of the fourth week, it had become apparent that if somebody didn't force Tartt to take up his duties, he'd lose everything he'd worked for. He'd yelled like an ogre when Tommy had gone through his house collecting every last bottle, but it had forced him to get out of his house and start going through the motions of living again.

"You're the lady of this manor, and you have a household to manage."

"I'm not well. Mrs. Hatch can see to things until I'm better."

He spotted the blue gown she'd been wearing when he stopped her coach and brought it with him as he returned to the bed.

"You can put this on."

"No, thank you," she said stiffly.

His jaw tightened. "Either you put it on, or I'll put it on for you."

"I just lost a baby, Tommy," she said in a ragged voice.

"You did," he said quietly, "and I'm sorry about that." He cleared his throat. "But the doctor says you're fine, and that there's no reason you can't have… He said that someday maybe you could have another one."

He *really* didn't want to talk about this. The idea of another baby—a baby that wouldn't be an accident—was so distant from his thoughts that it was best left for some other decade. But it wouldn't be fair for her to think that part of her was damaged.

He tossed the dress on the bed. "Now, who's doing the dressing?" he said, though he really hoped she wasn't going to test him on this.

"I'll do it," she bit off. "Just get out. And send a maid."

He nodded and started for the door. "I'll return in twenty minutes. If you're not presentable, *I'll* get you dressed."

❧

What the hell had come over Tommy? Eliza thought

angrily, hugging her legs tighter for warmth and mentally piling on him several choice words she'd picked up at the Malta docks as a girl but had never allowed herself to use—even in her mind—in recent years. How could he treat her this way? The man was an unfeeling beast!

Clearly he meant business, though, and the thought of him dressing her… She shuddered.

The fire in the hearth had been allowed to burn down that morning as it hadn't on the other mornings, and now she guessed that he must have ordered it to be neglected as another means of forcing her out of bed. With her blanket gone, she was freezing.

"Grr," she muttered, swinging her legs off the bed. Her bare feet hit the icy floor and she forced herself to stand up. She felt limp and weak as a kitten, and she needed something warm immediately, but she ignored the dress he'd picked and made her way to the wardrobe.

Anna had packed her a bouquet of beautiful gowns. Eliza trailed her fingertips over the myriad shades of pink she used to wear—deep roses and the palest pastels, and lustrous ashes of roses for when she was feeling more serious. They were all the kind of beautiful, attention-seeking colors she never wore anymore. Anna, who hardly even bothered about her own clothes, often urged Eliza to wear pink as she used to, or to put on some of the jewels she'd once worn with such pleasure. But then, Anna had thought Eliza should marry again.

And now she had.

The little voice of conscience that had been such

a constant companion in recent years directed her to put on the sensible blue dress. For years she'd listened to that hard voice of discipline, but now, with a feeling of bitter anger, she ignored it and plucked a rose-colored silk dress from the wardrobe. Crossing the small, threadbare carpet, she stepped behind the ratty old screen.

The screen was covered in a fabric that might once have been nice but was now faded to the color of sunbaked dirt and stained with alarming dark patterns that looked like dripping liquid. Perhaps it had been part of some horrible midnight event involving pirates and captives and knives and blood. Probably some smuggled rum as well, and doubtless chains and ropes.

Or just disgusting, clumsy men, she thought as her eyes roamed anew over the ugly room that had been her only view of the world for the past several days. Perhaps every woman who'd ever come to this manor had, like her, been brought here against her will—possibly countless women sold or forced into marriage, their wishes of no value in the transactions men undertook.

She was being absurdly dramatic, she thought as she pulled the dress over her chemise. While she *had* been forced into marriage, she was the one who'd set the stage for it. The little scolding voice pointed out that she'd made her own bed, and now she'd have to lie in it.

Preferably alone, she thought, though judging by the cold expression that came over Tommy's face whenever he was in her presence, she wasn't going to have to worry about him finding her so irresistible that he'd force himself on her.

The thought shouldn't have made her spirits sink any lower, but it did. Against all sense, and even as she'd been outraged by the heartless words he'd just spoken, she'd also dearly wanted him to take her in his arms and hold her. She told herself that she was merely starved for human contact after days alone in bed.

She started on the buttons she could reach while she waited for the maid, but she was too weak to make much progress. When the maid arrived, she was the same young woman who'd sometimes brought her trays. She'd brought a cup of chocolate with her now, Eliza noticed with the first stirrings of appetite she'd had in days.

She accepted the cup and warmed her hands on the hot drink, then took a small sip and asked the maid, who said her name was Lucy, to do up her buttons.

"Would you like me to do your hair?"

Eliza was about to specify her usual boring, severe coiffure, but she didn't feel like having her hair pulled back tightly. When she lived in Malta, she'd run about with her hair floating in the wind, and she'd been happy and carefree. Coming back to England had meant the end of carefree ways and the need to forget the pain of her father's abandonment and death. As she'd grown older, she'd come to think of her wild younger self with shame.

For the first time now, she looked back on the girl she'd been with a feeling of loss.

"I'll just leave it in a plait," she said, pulling her hair over her shoulder and separating it into three strands.

"Oh," Lucy said, clearly surprised that the new mistress should wear such a casual coiffure. But when Eliza asked her for a ribbon to tie the end of her plait,

Lucy produced a small length of blue satin with a smile. "It will look very pretty with your hair, ma'am."

Eliza thanked Lucy and dismissed her. She brushed a hand over her silky, richly colored skirts. The bodice was lower than what she was used to wearing, and it was snug after six years. Her inner scold insisted that she looked like she was trying to attract a man, but she was tired of telling herself pretty colors were a mistake, and she wanted to wear pink because she liked it. If some man found her attractive, it was his own damned problem, because she just didn't care.

A sharp rap on the door indicated the return of her husband, exactly twenty minutes after he'd left.

Would she ever get used to the idea that Tommy was her husband? They'd taken those vows, and now they were sealed together, their destinies tied until death, even if he was planning to spend much or maybe even all of that destiny on his own in India.

If they'd only waited a few days, there wouldn't have been any need to marry. If only Tommy hadn't kidnapped her and made it nearly impossible to refuse…

No. He might have been overbearing, but she couldn't fault him for not wanting his baby to be born a bastard.

The pain of grief still tugged at her, but she pushed it down as another sharp rap sounded at the door. She let him in.

His eyes traveled over her gown and hair, and his brows drew down. No need to worry that *he* would find her attractive. "I thought you didn't like the things Anna sent."

"I changed my mind."

He looked like he wanted to say more, but he just frowned and came into the room with all the cheer of a rain cloud. She supposed having black hair must be useful when needing to create a sense of doom. The cold glint in his clear green eyes suggested there'd be no warmth for her. "Luncheon will be served shortly in the dining room. I am going out."

"You forced me out of bed so I could eat lunch alone in the dining room?"

"You needed to get up."

This was true, but she wasn't going to agree. His mouth was set in a commanding slant she never would have dreamed him capable of six years before, and it made her wish she knew more about what he'd done in the intervening years in India.

When she didn't say anything, he said, "You're the mistress of Hellfire Hall, Eliza. Or do you plan to shirk your duties?"

She crossed her arms. "Of course I don't plan to shirk my duties. I mean to speak with Mrs. Hatch shortly. And since we're talking of plans, how long will you be gone today?"

"A little while."

"Which could mean an hour, a day, or a week. I'll need to know this sort of information, now that I'm the mistress of Hellfire." She liked that: *mistress of Hellfire*. It made her sound ferocious.

"I have business to conduct in town," he said stiffly, no doubt irritated at the idea of answering to a wife he hadn't wanted. She wondered what the "business" was. It might even be a visit with a mistress, for all she knew. They had, after all, been there several days, and she had no idea how he'd been spending his time. The thought of him consorting with a female companion while she'd been in bed made her feel both depressed and angry. And he still hadn't told her anything.

"Should you be expected for dinner?" she pressed.

"No."

He offered no explanation as to where he would be, and Eliza sucked her teeth. "Well," she said, "I can't function effectively as mistress without access to funds. I will certainly need to buy things for the manor. For that matter, our whirlwind wedding left me with no financial settlements whatsoever."

He waved a careless hand. "I'll have my lawyer make arrangements with your lawyer. You may spend what you need to and have the bills sent here," he said in the voice of someone who'd clearly spent very little time or thought on the estate he'd acquired. And why should that surprise her, when he wasn't going to be living there for years, apparently?

She crossed her arms. "If the rest of the hall is anything like my bedchamber, this whole place needs a great deal of redecorating."

"It needs a little work, but it's not that bad. I like it."

"Not that bad?" She jabbed a finger toward the carpet they were standing on, where portions had been worn down so thoroughly that the floorboards were visible. "This carpet wouldn't keep a flea cozy, there's so little of it left. Never mind that the bare walls make the room feel like a dungeon."

A hint of a smile hovered at the edge of his mouth

before disappearing. "And what's wrong with that? The place has character. It's manly."

A growl stirred in the back of her throat. "As you will apparently not be in England to enjoy Hellfire Hall for some years to come, its lack of comfort may be of little import to you. But *I* will need to stay here now and again when I visit the estate, to say nothing of any visitors, and it's totally unsuitable."

Apparently thoughts of her staying there or visitors arriving didn't please him, because he glowered at her. "I had thought to rent it out. But I suppose the place would benefit from attention in some areas. Do as you see fit."

∾

The dining room was, Eliza decided on entering, very possibly worse than her bedroom. A long room with the same bare stone walls as her chamber, it had a cold, bare floor, an enormous battered table with deep gouges that suggested it had been used as a cutting board, and several large windows draped in a hideous nubby brown fabric that created gloom by the yard while doing nothing to keep out the October chill.

In short, it looked like a place where bearded, unkempt brigands might have paused to grab a fistful of meat on their way out the door to their next voyage of doom.

While Eliza was taking all this in, a door at the opposite end of the room opened and Mrs. Hatch came in. She wore a plain blue frock and white cap, and she was carrying a tray that held a pitcher of lemonade and a pile of sandwiches. Eliza's stomach grumbled at the sight.

Though she'd met Mrs. Hatch the first night, and the woman had twice come herself to bring a tray to her room, Eliza had taken little notice of her. Now she saw that the housekeeper was only a few years older than she was and attractive, with dark blond hair and warm brown eyes. Eliza wondered briefly why she wasn't married to some nice farmer and watching over her own household.

Mrs. Hatch greeted her and dropped a curtsey, which couldn't have been easy to do while holding the laden tray. "I hope you are feeling better, ma'am."

Eliza said that she was and thanked her. She thought she detected a hint of relief on Mrs. Hatch's face and wondered if the woman had been worrying about what sort of person the new mistress was.

"Might I have one of those sandwiches?"

"Of course." Mrs. Hatch held the tray out for Eliza to make a selection. "Cook made them for Sir Tommy, but he's had to go out."

Eliza nodded and nibbled the edge of a ham sandwich. "I believe you and all the staff were only recently hired." Mrs. Hatch nodded. "Do you know anything of the previous tenants?"

"No one's lived here for a good ten years, since the place belonged to Flaming Beard."

"*Flaming Beard?*" Eliza helped herself to the other half of the sandwich. She hadn't realized how ravenous she was.

Mrs. Hatch chuckled. "The pirate. Well, privateer, since he did have a letter of marque to attack enemy ships, but he had a penchant for drama, and he was a fierce adversary who made quite a lot of prize money from his captures. He had a reddish beard, and he liked to tuck lit paper twists into it when engaging with the enemy."

"I like him already," Eliza said. Her irritating inner voice threw up its hands in disgust with her.

"We were all over the moon when we heard Sir Tommy had bought the estate. I do hope you will both be very happy here…though I understand Sir Tommy may return to India before long."

The poor woman looked concerned, as though Eliza and Tommy hadn't figured out that it wasn't the best thing for a newly married couple to immediately put an ocean between themselves. Of course, the servants depended on their positions at the manor, and if the estate were merely a forgotten possession, things at Hellfire Hall would soon turn to rack and ruin. Or, more accurately, remain in rack and ruin.

"Yes, but I shall remain in England." Eliza smiled a little and realized it was the first time she'd done so in a very long time. "I look forward to many visits here." If Tommy didn't insist they rent it out, that was.

She asked Mrs. Hatch if she was married, since the custom for housekeepers to use "Mrs." obscured whether the women were single or married.

"I am unmarried. I used to work for the vicar, but if you'll forgive me, he's tight with a penny and has no interest in a home being run properly."

"Well, I like a home to be run properly," Eliza said because it was true, actually. She was sick of the austere measures she'd adopted for Truehart Manor. She'd pinched and strived and withstood deprivations and discomforts for six years as a sort of penance, and what had it gotten her? The mission of Truehart Manor seemed doomed, and she was married to a man who thought she was a selfish ninny.

She realized then that she didn't feel anymore like she owed Tommy a penance. And as to what she owed Will and Anna—who'd been deprived of his company for the last six years—she ought to care, but she could no longer make herself do so. Perhaps this was because she was angry with Tommy, but she didn't really care why.

She decided that making this gloomy old place into something pleasant would be a worthy goal, and maybe it was just the sort of challenge she needed right now. Plus, if Hellfire Hall were spruced up, maybe *she'd* live here. Tommy could hardly need the money from renting the place since she'd brought him an enormous infusion of funds when they married.

Maybe she'd forget about trying to make something pure and good out of Truehart Manor again. Maybe she'd live at Hellfire Hall and just indulge herself con-stantly, with lavish baths and good meals and lively, outrageous dinner companions. The sea was nearby, and though she'd yet to see it, she'd caught a whiff of salt air now and again. She'd missed the sea, which had been one of the best parts of living on Malta. Meg could come stay. With no girls to worry about, they could do as they liked. They could…have fun. When had she last allowed herself to have fun?

"I'm very glad you're here, Mrs. Hatch. As you've

no doubt observed, there is a great deal of work to be done if the manor is to be habitable."

Mrs. Hatch looked pleased. "In truth, I have a few ideas."

Eliza and Mrs. Hatch spent several hours making an inventory of the manor. All of the rooms had bare, smudgy stone walls that seemed to drink up any light coming in from the windows, and the general feeling everywhere was of cold gloom. In addition to the bedchambers for the master and mistress, there were a dozen smaller bedchambers, each exactly the same: plain stone walls, a sturdy wooden bed with a puny mattress, and a simple oak table and chair.

The kindest thing that could be said about the furnishings was that they were serviceable, and though the drawing room had a nearly comical amount of furniture, none of it matched.

"Were all these things in here when you arrived?" Eliza asked as she ran a hand over a maroon brocade divan that clashed with a pair of bright-blue-and-white-striped chairs. There were, puzzlingly, two large tables in the room, along with a pianoforte that might have been acceptable if its surroundings weren't so crowded.

Mrs. Hatch nodded. "Apparently Flaming Beard bought a number of furnishings when he first acquired the manor, but then lost interest in decorating."

"He had terrible taste," Eliza said as her eyes came to rest on a chair upholstered in a vomitus color.

"I found Flaming Beard's account book when I was tidying one day," Mrs. Hatch said. "He seemed to spend most of his money on great quantities of food and drink. It seems that many of the men who sailed with him lived here as well." She stopped. "Please excuse me—"

Eliza held up a staying hand. "Feel free to read any of the books you find here. In truth, your interest makes you an invaluable resource. Was the manor always known as Hellfire Hall?"

Mrs. Hatch shook her head. "Before Flaming Beard bought it, it was called Heaven's Repose, and it belonged to a very religious man. I think Flaming Beard took special pleasure in defiling it, as it were, with wild parties. From what I can tell, he had quite a sense of humor." A smile tugged at the corners of her mouth. "And he was handsome. There's a portrait of him in the attic."

A handsome pirate sounded like just the sort of unsuitable man whose company Eliza currently felt in need of. "We'll hang it somewhere prominent."

As they moved through the house, Eliza approved Mrs. Hatch's suggestions about wall hangings and made a note to venture into the town to see what might be available.

They inspected the closets, storerooms, and cellar, then visited the library, whose shelves had large gaps. "I suppose pirates aren't much for reading," Eliza said with a disappointed sigh.

They finished the tour in the kitchens, where two scullery maids were at work on a pile of dishes amid an even darker gloom than the rest of the manor.

"Let's have this room whitewashed immediately," Eliza said. "It's so murky in here that I don't see how anyone can tell when the dishes are clean. Never mind how it must depress the spirits."

The scullery maids, their arms deep in pans of water, looked extremely grateful at this pronouncement.

Behind the manor, a gardener was at work harvesting apples, of which there were massive quantities.

"Do we have a cider press?" Eliza asked.

"I believe so," Mrs. Hatch said.

Perhaps she could have a cider-pressing party in November, after Tommy left. When had she last thrown a party? Never. By the time she'd had her own household, she'd decided parties were nothing but an opportunity for people to eat and drink too much and misbehave.

She asked about the menus for that week.

"Sir Tommy said he didn't care how we prepared the meats, and that there was no need for much in the way of fruits, or vegetables either, with the exception of potatoes. The only other preference he expressed was that he not be served fish. Otherwise, he insisted he didn't care what was served."

"Hmph," Eliza muttered, visions of dry crusts and meat boiled past flavor dancing in her head. The fare at Truehart Manor had been plain, and they'd rarely had dessert, but at least the food had never been nasty. She was through with things being plain, though. "Never mind what he said; meals are of the utmost importance."

Mrs. Hatch looked pleased. "I myself love to try all the latest recipes, but I know there are some who don't particularly care what they eat."

Eliza had spent years telling herself she was one of those people, but she wasn't. Despite the ample funds she could have been spending on food, she'd told herself that self-discipline was good and indulgence was bad, and she'd felt like a better person every time she said no to what she really wanted. And where had that gotten her?

She was going to have wonderful meals. And wine. As much wine as she wanted.

"Whether or not my husband is one of those misguided people," Eliza said, "I certainly am not."

Mrs. Hatch looked briefly surprised that Eliza didn't know much about her new husband's tastes or wish to cater to them. But she just smiled encouragingly, as though she imagined Eliza would eventually catch on to understanding her man.

"Please see that there are plenty of fruits and vegetables. I am partial to desserts with cream. And fish should be on the menu," Eliza said firmly.

"Er... Doesn't it seem that Sir Tommy dislikes fish?"

Eliza enjoyed an inward grin. "He doesn't know what's good for him. Please order some salmon if there's any to be gotten," she said, wondering how he felt about eel.

It was nearly dinnertime when they finished. As promised, Tommy had not returned, but Eliza refused to spare a thought for where he might be.

After ordering a tray for her room, she stopped by the library. The pickings were slim, but she was such a compulsive reader that she'd often resorted to any printed matter she could find. The small stack of books on the sea she discovered were certainly an improvement on the labels of lotion bottles.

She also collected some extra candles, which she brought to her chamber with the books and lit against the room's inhospitable dark, making it somewhat cheerier. She put the books away for a late-night treat (if that was the word for volumes with names like *The Sea Captain's Lament*) and started making lists of things to be bought for the manor. Thick carpets were first on the list, because the cold of the floors was so powerful it even penetrated her shoes.

She worked for a while until her dinner tray arrived, bearing a golden chicken pie whose decadently thick crust looked richer than anything she'd eaten in years, apple compote, and a generous portion of… Could it be? Yes! *Trifle*.

At Truehart Manor, their dessert was usually an apple, or if everyone had been very good, some simple bread pudding or a small plate of biscuits. She would never have so indulged as to serve trifle, with the thought that what you never ate, you didn't miss.

She snatched up her spoon and scooped up an enormous bite. Who cared if it was childish to eat her sweets first, or if she would become plump? Not she.

Her eyes closed in pleasure as the sherry-flavored custard and bits of cake filled her mouth. It was heaven, absolute heaven. She took another marvelous bite, then guzzled some of the red wine, which was excellent. Then she licked her spoon and broke greedily into the crust of the chicken pie, which gave way in luscious, fragrant chunks.

She put a spoonful in her mouth, feeling something crumbling inside her. All those years of denying herself, all the times she'd said no to the girls at Truehart Manor—why had she needed to be so hard? She'd made so many rules to live by. What a waste.

She sniffed and drank some more wine, which

eventually made her feel a little better, and she finished the chicken pie, the apples, and the trifle.

Cook was clearly a marvel, and it was nothing short of amazing that she'd come to work at Hellfire Hall, a place with a reputation as the derelict lair of pirates. She supposed the news that the recently knighted and oh-so-handsome Sir Tommy Halifax was the new owner had enticed the woman, along with several other of the more capable servants, to take employment at the hall. The knowledge shouldn't have annoyed her—after all, she was benefitting from the high-quality staff. But it felt good to give herself permission to be annoyed with Tommy after all those years of atoning.

The next morning, she arose early and breakfasted alone in the dining room, stifling any urge to ask after the whereabouts of her husband.

"I hope to purchase quite a few things to make the manor more comfortable," Eliza told Mrs. Hatch as she pulled on her gloves, having called for the carriage.

"Er," Mrs. Hatch said, "I think Sir Tommy may have arisen, if you were wanting to wait for him to join you." The poor woman seemed dismayed that her newlywed master and mistress appeared to be uninterested in each other. Eliza appreciated her hopefulness—what servant wouldn't prefer working for a happy couple rather than an unhappy one?— but she knew Mrs. Hatch was going to be sadly disappointed.

"Can't delay," Eliza said breezily, stepping outside.

She was glad to find that the town was a place of significant size, and as she passed through the streets, she felt cheered by the numbers of people bustling about amid handsome shops and rather a fine auction house.

Though sadness over what she'd lost lingered, she kept it at bay by focusing on the changes she planned to make at Hellfire Hall. She briefly wondered if they ought to change the name, in the interest of presenting a better public face. But she doubted Tommy would want to—he seemed to like it. And truth be told, she *liked* that it sounded wicked.

Though she had thought to make purchases just for the drawing room and her own bedchamber and Tommy's, when the master of the auction house revealed that they'd just taken delivery of the goods from a substantial estate, she decided that she liked the idea of Tommy getting a bill for enough carpets to cover every room in the hall.

In the draper's shop she found lengths of a rich sage fabric that she thought would look quite fine on the walls, along with some other handsome fabric in deep pink, and she bought large amounts. She chose heavy cream brocade for the curtains in the bedchambers, and she was just settling with the draper about sending the shockingly large bill to her husband when she glanced out the storefront window and saw Tommy standing in the street.

He was not alone. With him was a brown-haired woman wearing a fashionable hat and cloak, and even from inside the shop Eliza could see that she was pretty.

As Eliza watched, Tommy threw back his head and laughed at something the woman must have said. The only time Eliza had made him laugh had been when he thought she was Victoria.

Eliza sucked her teeth, wondering who the woman was. What if they were lovers? Though would he really have had the time, she asked herself, and then called herself a fool. For how much time, really, would the handsome, swashbuckling Sir Tommy Halifax, toast of all England, need to charm a woman?

"Lady Halifax, will there be anything else?" the shopkeeper asked.

She asked if he could have everything sent to Hellfire Hall (she thought he flinched at the name) by early the next morning, and when he assured her he could, told him to include a large tip on his bill.

She left the shop, and Tommy saw her approaching, which was doubtless why his companion moved on before Eliza reached him.

"What are you doing here?" he asked.

"Buying things for the hall."

He nodded once, then seemed at a loss for words. Finally he said, "You're looking better."

She nodded. Here they were, the two of them nodding at each other as though they had nothing to say.

Oh, there were certainly things to say, but the most important of them were words she could never speak to him. How could he understand the love she'd developed for her baby over the brief weeks of her pregnancy? And why would he care about the hopes she'd cherished, the visions of a sweet infant in her arms, the happy thoughts of her baby's first word?

He hadn't wanted the baby, and he certainly hadn't been filled with fancies of love and hope. For him the whole thing had been nothing but an unwanted fork in the road of his life.

And now they must somehow move forward, which meant establishing some reasonable state for this marriage in which they found themselves.

"Who was that you were talking to?" she asked.

"Mrs. Clarkson."

"Making friends already?"

"She's staying with some of the neighbors. I met her at dinner the other night."

She pressed her lips together, annoyed at her peevish-sounding words. But she *did* feel a little peevish that he'd been out making friends while she'd been lying unhappily in bed.

She tried for a pleasant tone. "Perhaps we should have your new friends to dinner, once the manor is fixed up. It's a good idea to get to know the neighbors."

"Maybe," he said, though his tone told her it wasn't going to happen.

She sighed. They were on the main street of the town, and people were coming and going all around them. "Tommy"—she dropped her voice—"we're newlyweds. Don't you think we should act as such, at least for appearances?"

The corners of his mouth tilted in mockery. "You always were concerned with appearances."

She could feel her mouth tightening with hurt that he thought so poorly of her, but she knew he had good reason, and she forced her expression to remain mild.

"What do you intend, then?" she pressed. "We're married, and we're sharing the same house for the time being. Will it be heavy silences and avoiding each other until you leave for India?"

"Is that how it was in your last marriage?"

"No," she said. "Gerard and I were very good friends." And she was beginning to think that she and Tommy must find some way to be friends of a sort as well. Or at least something a little better than barely civil.

Something flickered in his eyes, but he didn't reply.

"We need to talk," she said in a low voice, aware that any scene they made would provide juicy gossip for the people of the community, none of whom knew her yet. Though she was ready to abandon her allegiance to propriety, that didn't mean she wanted to make herself into an outcast. "But not here."

He crossed his arms and propped a shoulder against the tree behind him. "Here is fine for me. What did you want to talk about?"

"Nothing that can't wait until we are both at—"

"Home?" he supplied with a meaningful smirk.

"Yes," she said crisply. "Home is what couples usually call the place where they're living."

"It's just a house, Eliza," he said. "Don't think you're going to make it into anything more."

She watched as he walked off in the direction of the tavern. Then she went into the bookshop and bought several shelves' worth of books from the shopkeeper's storage. If she couldn't make any impression on Tommy's mind, at least she could make one on his pocket.

Ten

TOMMY LEFT THE TAVERN LATE THAT AFTERNOON, having bought several rounds of ale for those present and met more of his neighbors. He knew he'd lingered in the tavern to avoid Eliza, which was a stupid thing to do since he'd shortly see her at Hellfire Hall. But he was having trouble accepting that he had a wife.

Wives were for settled men. They brought wifely concerns, like talk of dishes and cutlery. And babies, of course, though now that was no longer an issue.

It wasn't that he was glad about what had happened with the baby, which he supposed was what she thought. He just hadn't been able to make peace with the idea of becoming a father before she'd had the miscarriage.

He'd dreamed of her last night, the first time that had happened since he'd left for India as a besotted youth, and he'd awoken with his teeth clenched in refusal.

Now that she'd gotten up from her sick bed, she seemed different. Contrary. She certainly wasn't trying to maintain a decorous look now; she'd been wearing another snug pink gown that showed the tops of her breasts. And her hair had been in a girlish plait that had made him think of untying the ribbon fastening and running his hands through it, damn it all.

She stirred far too many feelings he didn't want: attraction, the need to protect her because she now carried his name, and the dregs of his anger. He was sorry about what had happened with the baby, but he damned well didn't want to talk about it, if that was what she had in mind.

He took the long way back to Hellfire Hall, stopping by the houses of several tenants to visit with the families and check on the progress of some repairs he'd commissioned. The estate had been sorely neglected, which he'd known when he'd bought it, but the buildings had all been solidly constructed, so while the tenants' homes were old, they were at least sturdy.

He'd already told his manager to arrange for new roofs and paint and fencing for most of the houses, and he was pleased to see, as he rode past several of the homes, that work had already begun.

By the time he'd turned his horse toward the manor, it was late and the weak autumn light was beginning to fade. As he drew near the hall, the welcome scent of hot, fresh bread mingled with a delicious roasted aroma met him, the best thing he'd smelled since he left behind the curries of India.

After stabling his horse, he made for the door that led to the kitchen, where his appearance surprised Cook.

"Sir Tommy!" the woman said as she turned from a hot oven with a roasting pan in her arms.

There were plates of various foods on the table—quite a lot more than would be needed by one gentleman and his wife—and among them was a plate of fresh rolls. He swiped one and took a bite.

"Delicious." He gestured with the remaining portion of roll. "What's all this, then? Looks like enough for a feast."

"Mrs. Hatch and her ladyship had some recipes to try, sir."

And then he saw the mountain of vegetables behind her.

"Those aren't for dinner, are they?" he said, indicating the mound of turnips and carrots.

"Well, yes, Sir Tommy. Mrs. Hatch ordered turnips, carrots, and mushrooms." Cook beamed, unaware she'd just named three of his least favorite foods. "They're to be roasted with thyme. And there will be a nice salmon as well."

Salmon? Vegetables? Since he'd made his preferences known to Mrs. Hatch, who'd prepared the menus accordingly until today, he had no doubt as to who was ordering all this food he disliked.

He stalked upstairs in search of his wife, who was nowhere to be seen. Instead, when he walked into the upstairs corridor, he discovered a vast collection of rolled-up carpets and two footmen engaged in picking one up.

"What's going on?" Tommy asked.

"Carpets were delivered this afternoon, sir, with more to come tomorrow," one of the men said. "Lady Halifax asked us to start putting them in the bedchambers right away."

He barely managed not to growl as he asked, "And do you know where Lady Halifax is at present?"

"She was in the drawing room not long ago, sir," one of the footmen said hesitantly, as though he would have preferred not to divulge her whereabouts to her angry-looking spouse. Evidently, Eliza was already charming the staff.

When he entered the drawing room, however, instead of his wife, what Tommy found was that his previously dark and manly sanctum was now draped in pink hangings.

Pink!

Feeling murderous, he sent an anxious-looking maid in search of Eliza. She returned to say that the mistress was in the garden.

Teeth grinding nearly to powder, Tommy went out to the garden behind the manor, where dusk was settling in. The place was hideously overgrown, with tall weeds and ugly shrubs everywhere. Drooping clumps of hollyhock stalks and tangles of raspberry canes took up a large portion of the rear of the garden, where Eliza was kneeling in front of a scraggly shrub. Not far from her, one of the footmen was hacking at a small tree that appeared to be dead.

She was wearing a blue coat against the early evening chill and a brimmed hat and gardening gloves. Her plait lay over her shoulder prettily and made him annoyed that she'd been working like that with a footman nearby to look his fill if he wished.

Eliza looked up at his approach, then returned to what she was doing. Her coat was decorated here and there with bits of dried leaves and debris, and he tried not to notice the way the garment shaped itself to the curves of her waist in her bent posture, or that there was something very feminine about the motions of her arms as she yanked at some weeds near the base of the rosebush.

He stopped just in front of her, and she looked up at him. "Just what do you think you are doing?" he demanded.

She turned to the footman, who was still hacking at the tree. "Thank you, Robert. That will do for today."

Robert—Tommy admitted with irritation that he hadn't known the man's name—tried to hide his horrified expression at the way his employer was addressing his bride and left.

"Well?" Tommy said.

She stood and brushed herself off. His eyes were drawn reluctantly to the open front of her coat, where her gown clung to the lush curve of her bosom. He swallowed. The crease between her breasts teased his eyes downward toward a seductive, shadowy depth, and he chalked his instant flare of heat up to those months and months of wanting her when he was younger.

He adored Anna, but she'd done something diabolical to him when she packed Eliza's valise.

He tore his gaze away from her chest and realized his teeth were clenched again. He needed to stop doing that or there'd be nothing left of them by the end of a week in her company.

"I'm gardening, obviously," she replied.

"I can see that, though why you feel the need to do so when it's nearly dark, I can't guess."

"Since no one has cared for this estate for years,

there is rather a lot to be done. Though I was just about to stop for the day." Her reasonable tone only made his temperature inch higher.

"Why are you wearing your hair like that?"

She just stared at him for a moment. "Because I wish to."

He supposed he should be glad she chose to ignore his question about her hair, but if she glanced down, the front of his trousers would tell her he was far too affected by the way she looked.

"There is a massive pile of carpets in the upstairs corridor," he ground out, "and Cook is under the mistaken impression that mountains of vegetables and fish are wanted for dinner. Don't you think it would have been appropriate to discuss your plans with me?"

"I did discuss my plans with you, yesterday morning. You said I could do as I saw fit. So I'm making a few changes."

Lust and irritation warred in him, making him even more cross. "A few changes? There's pink fabric on the drawing room walls! And now you're ripping out the bushes. The next thing I know, there will be flowers everywhere."

She gave him a look, and the corner of her rosy mouth quivered saucily. "It's October, Tommy. You don't have to worry about flowers blooming any time soon, though you know, some people like them. But if you have a particular fondness for weeds, by all means, I can leave them."

He crossed his arms. "What about the fish for dinner? I don't like fish, as I've already informed Mrs. Hatch."

"Doubtless you've only had fish that was either not fresh or badly cooked. Salmon is delicious when it's been cooked nicely, and it's good for you."

He just grunted.

"I *am* the new mistress of Hellfire, as you yourself have already pointed out," she said in that reasonable tone. "These are the sorts of decisions I'm supposed to make."

"The garden is satisfactory as it is," he said. "As was the drawing room."

"I suppose so, if one is intent on living in a mean way. But I"—she tipped her chin up, as if asserting something—"don't wish to live in a mean way."

He disliked a cheeseparing household too, and had never been stingy about expenses. But when he'd bought the estate, he'd envisioned making a few improvements and renting the place for a number of years until he was ready to live there—not making it into something that felt like a home.

And he hadn't thought Eliza would be quite so energetic about making changes, especially considering how poorly she'd looked yesterday morning. He was glad that the color had come back to her cheeks, though; it made him feel better about arguing with her.

"And the wall hangings—how much did they cost?"

"Practically nothing for one as wealthy as you. Or is it us?" she said. She shook her head. "No, no, it's you. I lost my personhood when we married, so for the purposes of the law, *we* are Tommy Halifax."

"That's an odd way to put it."

"But accurate. Society allows you, as a man, to go

where you please and do as you wish. As a widow, I enjoyed quite a bit of that kind of freedom, but now that I'm a married woman, all my property and my considerable wealth are yours."

He pressed his lips together. "I won't stop you spending what you wish, within reason."

"But don't you see that now I'm meant to live my life in relation to you and your choices? What does that sound like to you?"

"If you're waiting for me to say 'slavery,' you'll wait forever," he snapped.

She sighed and pulled off her gardening gloves, tucking them into the pocket of her coat. "You and I are in a situation that neither of us would have chosen. We've pledged ourselves to each other, and now we're stuck together until death do us part. I think we'd both be better served if we could try to be friends of a sort."

Friends?

How well *that* had worked out the first time around.

He knew it was senseless to consider that time now; they'd both been so young. But it was part of his memory of her. And he'd hardly been back in England a fortnight when the Victoria episode had occurred, an episode that had seemed like just another of her scandalous larks, another play for attention.

His conscience pointed out that he'd been a very eager participant in what had happened at the brothel, and that maybe she'd meant well by trying to handle the consequences on her own, even if she'd been entirely wrong to try to exclude him.

But he didn't need help from his conscience right now—he needed to keep distance between himself and Eliza. In another month or two they were both going back to their own lives, and the less they got entangled with each other, the better.

"And what if I don't wish to be friends?" he asked.

She looked at him steadily. "Then I think it would be best if I returned to London immediately."

His jaw hardened. "You know you can't do that. Anna and Will would be devastated if they discovered we're not besotted newlyweds. Never mind the questions they would have for both of us."

"Maybe it would be easier on everyone if we just told the truth."

He didn't like that idea, and he especially didn't want to discuss any of what had happened between himself and Eliza with his brother. "It wouldn't be easier. And you can't just go about as you like now."

"And yet you can."

He sucked his teeth. She was right; it was unfair.

He'd always felt that marriage, if it was to work at all, ought to be a partnership like his brother and Anna had. They were united by affection and the desire to see the other one happy, which meant that neither of them would ever want to be more important or freer than the other. But those sorts of happy partnerships were impossibly rare, one in a million.

He shrugged. "That's the way the world works. You know that."

"We don't have to go along with the way the world works," she said. "We can make our own way."

Her gaze held steady, as though she had faith in her own opinion, and he felt a grudging acknowledgment that perhaps Eliza had grown into a person with some reasonable, well-founded ideas. He hadn't wanted to believe that under the cloak of propriety she'd fashioned for herself, she might have truly changed. But now he couldn't reconcile his idea of her as a selfish siren masquerading as a do-gooder with the woman who'd been so profoundly affected by the loss of the baby she'd barely known. Or this woman with the backbone to stand up to him and speak as forthrightly as she'd done.

There was something for which he owed her an apology.

He cleared his throat. "That night at Madame Persaud's—you really were there just to gather information, weren't you?"

She blinked, clearly surprised he'd brought it up. "Yes. Going there didn't seem very different from going to the poorer parts of London where Meg and I found orphaned girls we could help at Truehart Manor."

"I made harsh judgments about your reasons for being at Madame Persaud's, and I'm sorry."

She had gone very still. "I understand why you thought the worst of me. Of course I accept your apology."

❧

Eliza didn't know why Tommy had apologized, but she was grateful for this sign that he saw her as someone possibly deserving of respect.

"You really wanted the baby," he said quietly.

"Yes. I thought I'd accepted that I'd never have children, but it turned out that I hadn't." She looked away as huskiness crept into her voice. She'd felt some power growing in her since she'd realized she didn't care about being perfect anymore, but the baby was a loss that was still painful. "The baby meant so much to me."

"I really am sorry about what happened." His voice held a gentleness she wouldn't have expected him to use with her. She looked into those green eyes she'd known for what felt like forever and knew that he truly was sorry the baby had been lost—for her sake anyway.

Dusk was turning to dark and the chill deepening. Tommy had no cape or overcoat, but he didn't look cold in just his faintly shimmering cocoa tailcoat and tan breeches and boots. He looked a little exotic, and also commanding and handsome, a man as capable of carrying the weight of national hopes as of dispatching pirates and charming ladies. He wasn't trying to charm her now, nor had he been since coming home— except for the Victoria incident—but he still made her heart thump erratically in her chest.

Not that it mattered.

"You've changed from the selfish person I thought you were," he said. "You do seem to have some quite worthy goals."

"Did," she corrected, and gave a mirthless laugh. "What we were doing at Truehart Manor is finished."

His brows drew together. "What do you mean? I won't stop you from continuing the work you were doing—as long as there won't be any more brothel visits and you promise to take a footman with you into the bad parts of London."

"It's nothing to do with you. I made too many rules for the girls, pushed them too hard, and they started leaving on their own. In addition, it seems that our neighbors were outraged about us bringing 'miscreants' to live in Mayfair. So there's not really anything left to do."

Tommy frowned. "Of course there is, if you still want to do that work."

"I don't really know what I want. All I know is that the girls didn't like me, and I didn't even really like myself very much." She sighed. "Do you know, I haven't eaten cake for six years."

His eyebrows rose. "Cake?"

"It was too indulgent. I was going to lead us all down the path of virtue with cold rooms, plain food, and work."

A wry smile hovered at the edge of his mouth. "Couldn't you perhaps have done something in between that and the scandal you used to be? Why did you decide you had to be so virtuous anyway?"

She looked away. "Partly because I felt guilty. When you left years ago, I knew it was my fault. I knew that Will really missed you, and that you never would have stayed away if it hadn't been for me."

"Really," he said dryly. "You had that much power over my life?"

Her head snapped to him. "But…weren't you furious? Didn't you stay away because you hated me and you knew Will was too noble to abandon me, no matter that I'd hurt his brother?"

"I left because I was an angry, besotted young man who didn't know how much he needed to grow up. I stayed in India because I loved it."

"Oh," she said, feeling something lift in her…guilt fluttering away like a black bird departing.

His eyes softened. "Let it go, Eliza. It was six years ago, and it doesn't matter now. We were both too young. It was a mistake, just like what happened at the brothel. I suppose we'll never manage to be civil to each other if we don't both put those incidents behind us."

"I… Thank you." He couldn't know the release his words had given her.

His lips twisted in a half-smile. "Maybe you're right that we need to find a way to be friends of a sort, at least so our family and friends don't suspect we're not besotted newlyweds. And the servants as well. I think Mrs. Hatch is beginning to despair of us."

"That's the most sensible idea you've had since I married you." For the first time since he'd come back to England, she felt relaxed with him.

But she wished he hadn't just made her like him more.

⁂

Tommy was at breakfast early the next morning when Eliza came in, and he managed a cheerful smile despite the fact that the way she looked in her gown made him want to groan. It was a delicate pale pink, with little rosebuds decorating the rise of her breasts like the icing on an irresistible cake. He turned his gaze to his kippers.

"I've been considering quite a bit of redecoration for the manor," she said. "Why don't you come around with me today and we can make some decisions together?"

He looked up to find her piling lemon curd onto her toast. She bit into it, licking a stray dab from her top lip. He swallowed. Going around the house with her sounded like torture considering the effect she was having on him, which only seemed to be more acute now that he wasn't angry with her anymore.

In fact, he thought as she closed her eyes in apparent pleasure after another bite of her lemony toast, he was remembering all too many of the things he'd always liked about her, like her honest pleasure in small things. And her fondness for lemon curd.

"Er, that sounds like a fine idea, but I need to see to repairs at some of the tenants' homes, so I don't think I'll have time."

She looked a little disappointed, but she nodded. "Of course—that's certainly more important. Maybe I should come with you."

"I'm sure you'll be needed here at the manor," he said, envisioning himself sitting uncomfortably on horseback with lust pounding through him while she bounced up and down next to him on her horse. "Isn't it best to divide and conquer as far as the mountain of things to be done?"

"I suppose," she said, her pretty brow crimping, "though I really would like to know what you think about the decisions for the interior of the manor."

"Perhaps soon," he said, thinking of procrastinating indefinitely, which reminded him, with an unwelcome pang, that he'd all but forgotten about Rex. He supposed he ought to explain about the boy, considering he was, at least for the moment, legally responsible for him.

"There's a small issue I forgot to tell you about earlier. Do you remember that boy I mentioned at the Bridewells' lunch—Rex? He's the son of my friend Oliver Thorpe, who died in India last year. Just before you and I married, I became his guardian. He had been in the care of a Major Delancey, but Delancey sent him to me, and it's up to me now to find the boy's aunt."

Eliza blinked at this information. "Wait—what? But where is he?"

"Rex is staying with Will and Anna. It seemed best to put him in a household with other children."

"You are the guardian of a boy, and you forgot to tell me?"

"He's thirteen—practically all grown up."

She gave him a look. "Were *you* practically grown up at thirteen?"

"Very well, no. But still, it's not as though he's some tender wee thing in need of constant care. Besides, you and I *have* both been fairly preoccupied with other urgent matters in the last few days. In any case, it's only temporary. I can hardly be an effective guardian to him while in India, and I certainly couldn't bring him back there with me, so once his aunt is found, he can go to her."

She squinted into the distance as though turning over ideas. "Perhaps I might be of some assistance to him."

"I'm sure it won't be necessary. Rex has been bounced from one person to another ever since his mother died a few years ago. Oliver left him mostly in the care of an ayah who I doubt ever said no to him. I really do think the best thing will be for Rex to be with a family member. His aunt is Oliver's sister."

She nodded slowly. "I can certainly understand that he might wish to be with family."

"Exactly. I'm a sort of holding-place guardian for him until my man finds Aunt Diana. She's the wardrobe mistress in a traveling theater troupe roving about England."

"A traveling theater troupe?" Eliza frowned. "That doesn't sound good at all."

"Nonsense," he said. "She's just sewing costumes."

"Hmm," she said. "I don't know."

"There's nothing to worry about—it's all being taken care of. I just thought you should know." He put down his cup and stood up; fortunately, all the talk about Rex had had a quelling effect on his desire. "I'd best be going. I don't think I'll make it back in time for dinner."

She looked genuinely disappointed about this, but she just said, "I understand. There certainly is a great deal to be done around the estate."

"Exactly," he said gratefully on his way to the door. He just needed to avoid her as much as possible while still behaving like a contented husband. The contented part wasn't hard now; he liked being with her. It was the husband part that gave him pause, because husbands had privileges of intimacy…privileges he had no business even thinking about.

❧

Eliza spent a satisfying day seeing to the installation of the carpets throughout the rest of the manor and sorting the books that had been sent for the library.

Knowing Tommy wouldn't be home for dinner,

she thought of taking yet another tray in her room, but she realized she would feel as though she were hiding, or as though she didn't deserve to enjoy a nice meal. Instead, she told Cook she'd be eating in the dining room on her own. She didn't say "alone" because that would have sounded as if she'd been abandoned, when what she wanted was to do exactly as she wished, heeding impulses she would once have crushed.

She changed into a carmine silk gown, put on a pair of the earrings Anna had sent, and sat down at the table in the now much-more-appealing dining room with a sigh of satisfaction.

Dinner was a leisurely affair as she sipped her wine and savored the hearty roast and the billowy popovers with their soft centers. She lingered over each bite of the cake Cook had prepared, which was piled with cream and delicious.

Meals had been just more items on her daily list for so long that she'd forgotten the pleasures of simply paying attention to her senses. With a feeling of contentment, she nibbled cake and listened to the quiet crackling of the fire and the discreet bustle of the servants moving around beyond the closed door to the dining room.

From his new home above the mantel, Flaming Beard looked down at her, handsome and swarthy and a little disreputable. His dark eyes had wicked glints, but the suggestive expression teasing his mouth inspired her to lift her wineglass to him in a silent toast.

After dinner, unsurprisingly, she felt rather full, and as she looked out the dining room windows into the early evening darkness, she decided a walk would do her good.

She took a lantern and strolled briskly down the front drive, enjoying the chill of the night and the pure dark of the country sky. It was, she discovered, extremely fine to walk aimlessly about, enjoying herself without feeling as though she was wasting time. For years her goal had been to fill every moment with purpose. But now all those days of constant industry seemed pointless.

When she returned to the manor, she refused to listen for the sound of manly boot heels on the floor and retired to her room with another glass of wine and a stack of novels that had come with the library order. As she luxuriated on her bed with the wine in one hand and a book in the other, she told herself this was just the kind of thing she needed to do.

And she did enjoy herself. But she also had a thick head when she awoke the next morning.

At breakfast, she discovered that Tommy had already gone out, which meant that he'd gotten up quite early, and she'd slept so heavily that she hadn't heard him rise. But he'd politely left word for her with Mrs. Hatch that he was going for a long ride and also meant to see about workers to fix a hole in the stable roof.

Apparently, though, he would be home for dinner—Eliza supposed he knew it would defeat their purpose of looking happily married if he was never there—and she decided to make sure a nice meal was waiting for him.

She worked in the library well into the afternoon,

accompanied by Traveler, who dozed by the hearth, then spent time with Mrs. Hatch making arrangements for a kitchen garden to be dug in the spring. Afterward, she indulged in a long, hot bath, then put on a luxurious velvet gown of pale purplish-pink.

Dusk was blanketing the manor in gold-tinged shadows as she stood in the foyer with Mrs. Hatch, arranging some bittersweet in a vase. Tommy returned just as she stepped back to admire the effect.

"Did you have a good ride?" she asked as he handed Mrs. Hatch his dusty hat. His black hair was windblown and his cheeks red, and she suddenly wished that he would pull her into his arms the way another newly wed husband might.

His eyebrow quirked at her and she winked in the direction of Mrs. Hatch, who'd turned around. *Our audience*, her wink said. He smirked at her and said he was going to have a bath.

"Then we'll dine when you're done," Eliza said.

He cocked his head at all this wifely consideration, but then he smiled like a doting husband and said he would look forward to it.

Mrs. Hatch grinned hugely as he left, as though glad to see that the master and mistress had finally figured out how to behave like a happy couple.

Eleven

"A FEAST OF VEGETABLES, I SEE," TOMMY SAID WITH A theatrical sigh once the servants had brought in the platters of roasted cauliflower, along with peas and potatoes, and disappeared from the dining room. He did, though, help himself to all three, even if it was with an air of forbearance.

"*And* a substantial roast beef with Yorkshire pudding," Eliza pointed out, helping them each to slices of beef and pudding.

"The best part." He downed several mouthfuls of food. "Though potatoes are a vegetable I will always approve," he said.

"You have such an Englishman's taste for meat and potatoes," she pointed out. "I wonder how you've managed in India."

"I actually like many Indian foods," he said, sounding pleased with himself. "The spicy curries with lamb and the ones with chicken, and there are these stew things I love—though I'm not actually sure what's in them."

"Quite possibly vegetables."

"Very likely," he acknowledged gamely. "I suppose it's best if I don't actually know."

"Gives you a sense of culinary adventure, does it?"

"Exactly." He polished off his beef—she didn't know how he'd done it so quickly, since he had very nice table manners—and she helped him to some more.

"So," he said, "tell me about your marriage to Gerard. I only knew him in passing."

Her hand paused in carrying her fork to her mouth. "I wouldn't have thought you'd be interested."

"But I am. You said you two were 'good friends,' and he was quite a bit older than you."

"Thirty years," she said. "He was patient and kind, but he also had a strong sense of justice."

Tommy nodded, listening as she told him how she and Gerard used to take long walks, and how he'd brought her to lectures and encouraged her to do charitable works. Tommy was a good listener, which was another of his appealing qualities. As much as she'd always liked men, many of them liked talking about themselves far more than listening.

"I suppose it sounds…nice," he said.

She tipped up her chin. "There's nothing wrong with nice."

He gave a soft chuckle. "But it's not much fun, is it?"

"I wasn't interested in fun back then."

"And now?"

She decided it was better not to answer that, but just made a little hum and pushed away her plate. They'd both finished eating, and Tommy pulled the almond custard pie closer and offered her a slice before cutting one for himself.

He took a bite and closed his eyes with pleasure. "Another of your recipes?"

"Yes," she said, grabbing the cream pitcher. She poured an outrageous swath across her pie and devoured several bites, nearly moaning with pleasure.

"This tart is the food of the gods," he said.

"It is, isn't it?" she said, pleased he liked it. "Cook is a gem. Your man of affairs did find very good staff for the Hall. And Mrs. Hatch, of course. She's been invaluable so far with the redecorating—though really, I should say the decorating, since there was almost nothing here but mismatched furniture. And we've only just begun."

He arched a brow at her. "Well, clearly you've made a vigorous beginning. I've already gotten an astronomical bill from the auction house, and the one from the draper nearly knocked me over." When she cleared her throat meaningfully, he said, "And grateful I am for the carpet that's now in my bedchamber. Any more time walking in my stocking feet, and I was going to have nothing left but frozen stumps. I've never encountered floors so cold as Hellfire boasts."

She nodded. "At least our rooms and the dining room and the drawing room aren't quite so inhospitable now, with the wall hangings and new carpets. But those are just temporary—the manor needs major changes. For one thing, we need a plasterer, so the walls can be painted and wallpapered. And we ought to get some water closets, which would make everything more civilized. My thinking is to make the place tolerably comfortable for now, and then gradually undertake larger projects like the plastering over the coming months."

His lips pressed together thoughtfully. "When I bought the estate, I didn't imagine doing much more than making the manor habitable for tenants." She knew that he didn't want her to think of Hellfire Hall as a home, but she liked the idea of living there.

"But now you have a wife to see to things," she said. "No matter how the manor is going to be used, it's simply not sensible to let it languish in an appalling state fit only for disreputable people."

He sighed. "I suppose you're right."

"I'm right," she said firmly. "And while we're on the subject, you really should come around with me tomorrow and discuss the improvements. Some of them will be costly, and it's more sensible if we agree on how to spend *our* money."

He frowned a little, but he said, "Very well, I'll come around with you tomorrow."

"So," he said around bites, "was Gerard some sort of father figure for you?"

She made an outraged sound. "What a thought. He was simply a dear man."

Wickedness sparkled in Tommy's eyes. "Endless walks, lectures, charity—he sounds like he wasn't exactly the sort to set the sheets aflame."

"It's not all about flaming sheets in life," she said indignantly, and then wished she hadn't when, with the merest quiver of an eyebrow, he let her know he thought she was sadly mistaken. Something shameless in her responded to the devil in his eyes, but she tamped it down.

"I've heard of some fellows who simply don't care for sheet flaming," Tommy mused. "And then there are those men who prefer...well, men."

She'd heard whispers about men who liked other men that way, but she'd never thought Gerard was like that. "I don't think he liked marital relations," she said, blushing to speak of it.

Tommy just shook his head. "Can't at all understand not liking sex, but there you are. I find it pretty funny, actually, considering he was married to you, which would put ideas in most men's heads one hundred percent of the time."

Did that mean Tommy had ideas about her one hundred percent of the time? Though the thought was exciting, it was better if she didn't know the answer, because just sitting at dinner with him was making her feel fluttery and extra warm, never mind that her eyes kept wandering toward his shoulders and chest. They'd decided that they'd behave as friends, but friendliness wasn't the way to describe how she felt when she was with him.

"What would Gerard have thought of Victoria's charades?" he asked.

"He was very much in favor of helping those in need, which *was* my ultimate purpose in being at the brothel."

"I'm in favor of helping those in need as well, but don't think you'll ever do something like that again."

She sucked her teeth, realizing she'd let the happy intimacy of their dinner soften her toward him too much. "I thought we decided to be friends. Friends don't order each other around."

"You're my *wife*, Eliza Tarryton Truehart Halifax," he said roughly, and there was something about his naming her this way—as though he was acknowledging all she now was and had been—that made her heart skip, even though his next words were totally unacceptable. "And I won't have you putting yourself in that kind of needless danger again."

His eyes glittered at her dangerously, but in the past few days the two of them had moved beyond the mistakes that had brought them to where they were now, and she didn't feel guilty about asserting that she wasn't going to owe him that kind of obedience.

"We've agreed to be equal partners, Tommy. I'm not going to tell you to stay away from tigers, and you don't get to tell me what to do."

He was glaring at her, but she could almost have sworn there was heat in his gaze. The edge of his mouth twitched. "You don't actually need to tell me to stay away from tigers," he said, a husky note creeping into his voice. "I would do that anyway."

A soft whoosh of laughter escaped her. Something felt different between them. Was he flirting with her?

It didn't seem possible. No matter how much she was attracted to him, she knew he hadn't wanted their marriage and that his mind was set on India. She'd told herself that he couldn't possibly want anything more than friendly cooperation from her.

But...what if she'd been wrong? She wanted to be wrong, because the truth was that sharing dinner with him was the most fun she'd had in years. *Years*.

He frowned. "Eliza," he said in that husky voice that he couldn't possibly realize was making her heart melt into syrup. But then he looked away and turned his attention to folding his serviette. "I…think you should order some new gowns."

What? She'd almost thought for a moment that he was going to say something intimate. Clearly she'd only been indulging in fantasy, because she'd even imagined them standing up and moving together and kissing. Which she needed to not imagine.

"You don't like what I'm wearing?"

He waved a hand dismissively. "The things Anna sent are rather fancy for Hellfire."

"I like them, actually," she said, lifting her chin. "I'm tired of drab gowns, and pink makes me feel cheerful."

"But the Hall is ridiculously cold, and it's only going to get colder. It's October—you'll want some sort of high-necked wool thing."

He gestured vaguely at his neck and chest area, the place on her that apparently needed covering up. Was he trying to cover up her bosom? Could it be that he, too, remembered the desire that had flared between them that one night?

How she wished she could read his mind, because it was so hard to forget how it had felt being in his arms.

Yet he was frowning now, and clearly he didn't want to look at her.

She crossed her arms, reminding herself that she'd always been too good at spinning fantasies, even if in recent years they'd been about scaling the heights of virtue instead of winning the admiration of handsome gentlemen. "You don't need to worry about me being chilly, though I'm certainly touched by your concern. Anna packed me some wool shawls."

He just grunted.

She knew she ought not to probe him about the future, but she couldn't seem to help herself. Perhaps because now that she knew she could have a baby, a future without a child of her own seemed empty in a way it hadn't before. A baby would have changed everything for her, in ways that would have been so wonderful.

She cleared her throat. "I know my pregnancy was a shock, but hadn't you thought about having children sometime soon anyway?" she said.

He made a choking sound.

"After all, you're not *that* young anymore," she pointed out as he took a sip of water.

"I'm only twenty-eight," he said indignantly. "I've hardly needed to be worrying about marriage and babies."

"But don't you want children *someday*?"

He scratched the back of his neck. "Perhaps. I'm not sure I even especially *like* children."

"Nonsense," she said. "From what I've heard, Heck and Vic adore you. Children are better than anyone at telling who really likes children."

"Very well, let's say that I hadn't *envisioned* having children for a number of years yet, and I think it's a crime to bring children into the world if one doesn't intend to be involved with them."

"I agree."

"My work in India comes with peril. Life there is wild, and I would be a poor risk as a father."

"You want risk and adventure," she said. "Or perhaps you think you need it."

His jaw tensed. "It's not just adventuring for my own entertainment, you know. There's a great deal of necessary work to be done in India."

She forced herself to speak plainly, even though part of her wanted to let things remain unsaid, because if they never spoke of them, maybe it would mean they weren't true.

"And you don't want to be tied down." She might cherish the foolish wish that he could come to care for her, but she was done with glossing over hard truths and arranging things to suit herself.

He stuck a spoon in the little dish of salt on the table and lifted it, watching the grains fall back into the bowl. "India is hard on English marriages and families. And Hyderabad, where I put up, isn't like Bombay or Madras, which offer many of the pleasures of English society. Not many English women live in the hinterlands, and the ones who do are lonely and bored. It's a strain on a marriage, but it's equally a strain for a couple to live apart."

Though his regretful tone acknowledged that these were not words a wife would want to hear, Eliza understood that they were the truth as he saw it.

When he'd first insisted they marry, she'd panicked at the idea that he'd force her to go with him to India, simply because things between them were so acrimonious. Now it was different, and she knew she would likely love to live in India, even in the parts that would feel wild to an English person. Maybe especially in those parts.

Hadn't she loved living in Malta, with its different customs and climate? After she'd rejected Tommy's proposal, she'd taken to seeing her uninhibited years in Malta as one more unacceptable part of her that had to be rooted out, but now she found herself thinking of those years with gratitude. And she realized she wanted the chance again to have the kind of adventures that foreign places offered.

But would Tommy change his mind about taking her with him?

He had little faith in marriage, apparently. Considering her own merely pleasant first marriage, she had no reason to be particularly enthusiastic about it herself, but stupidly, she felt tempted to believe that she and Tommy might be different.

He replaced the spoon in the salt and moved on to squaring the bottom of his knife against the bottom of his fork. "I spoke to you once of fidelity," he said finally, "of how I'd always expected that marriage would mean that to me."

"I have always valued fidelity in marriage."

"And we've both agreed that men and women ought to be equal partners in marriage as much as possible. Yet ours was begun in difficulty, leaving neither of us a choice."

"Yes."

He looked at his hands as if they might hold some answer for him, then leaned back against his seat and crossed his arms. "My work will call me away for years—I don't even know how many. That might easily mean a whole lifetime lived apart for both of us."

And he wasn't going to take her with him,

obviously. Her heart trembled as she understood how this was going to be. "Are you saying we ought to agree that our marriage might not include fidelity?"

Something came over his face—she would have said it was regret, but she knew it couldn't be.

"If I sometimes entertained the idea of one day marrying wisely, I certainly never thought I would ever consider a marriage without fidelity," he said. "But now…isn't it for the best if we decide to go our own ways when I leave for India?"

She looked away. "So we would simply be two people who happen to be married."

"Yes," he agreed with what sounded like relief. "While we're together, until I leave for India, we'll be friends, just as we agreed. We behave as the newly married Lord and Lady Halifax ought to do, so that our family and friends and the servants all believe we are content. And that means fidelity while we are together. Once we are apart, though, I think we should go on as we like—discreetly of course."

She forced herself to reply. She owed this to him, as she saw it. "Very well."

"Then we are agreed to be reasonable," he said.

"Agreed," she said, struggling to force down the note of huskiness threatening her voice.

So there was truly no hope for their marriage being anything other than a friendly partnership. She knew she shouldn't have been entertaining any hopes, but… she really liked him. The friendship she felt for him made her want to spend more time with him, but it was more than that. He made her heart skip.

But clearly *she* wasn't making *his* heart skip.

A knock sounded at the door and Mrs. Hatch entered, looking fussed. "I'm sorry to disturb your evening, my lord and lady, but there was a small explosion in one of the privies."

Tommy absorbed this bizarre information, then said, "Why doesn't this surprise me?"

He tossed Eliza a rueful smile (she didn't know if it was for her benefit or Mrs. Hatch's) as he was going. Before he left, though, she reminded him of his promise to tour the manor with her the following day. She would probably regret spending even more time in his company, but she did need his thoughts on the work. And if she wanted to indulge herself foolishly by spending more time with him, that was nobody's business but hers.

⁖

Later that night, Tommy walked toward his bedchamber, having determined that an old stash of gunpowder had apparently been discarded into the privies not long ago and been ignited by a smoking pipe that someone accidentally dropped on top of it, thus necessitating the bizarre rule he'd just established that there was to be no smoking in the privies.

The incident was only the latest inconvenience offered by Hellfire Hall, but he knew he ought to be grateful for it, because when Mrs. Hatch had knocked, he'd been struggling mightily against the urge to pull Eliza into his arms and kiss her.

He wondered how she would have responded if he had. He didn't think he'd been imagining the light of attraction in her eyes, and he could hardly be the only one who remembered just how good their one fateful encounter had been.

He entered his bedchamber and began pulling off his boots. He could no longer find anything left of the spoiled, indulgent, superficial woman he'd believed Eliza to be. She was kind and resilient and funny, and so much more.

He *liked* her.

Not only that, obviously; he wanted her quite badly.

From the other side of his bedchamber wall came a few muffled sounds, the murmuring of two women. He supposed the maid had arrived to help Eliza prepare for bed. The thought was hotly erotic.

She was his wife and he wanted her. He was married to her for eternity, but she was not in his bed. Hell, they hadn't even consummated their marriage, if one didn't count that pre-wedding encounter. They were newlyweds who'd had no newlywed bliss.

He briefly wondered what she would think of French letters and discarded the idea with a curse as the thought of seeing the body hidden by all those teasing pink gowns worked a predictable effect on him. She was bewitching, but he knew she wasn't trying to entice him; she was just being herself. Now that he wasn't angry with her, though, it was impossible not to be extremely attracted to her. And to want the natural conclusion to that attraction.

But seducing Eliza would be a rotten thing to do, because it would draw them closer when he would be leaving her behind. They'd both agreed they would behave as friends, then go back to their former lives.

And he didn't want the encumbrance of a family. Making love to her, however much he wanted to, was a terrible idea.

He got into bed and pulled the covers over his head and groaned when an image of her bosom in the gown she'd worn to dinner popped into his head. By the end of another week living with her and not touching her, he was going to be nothing but a pile of smoking ash.

Twelve

"DO THE WALLS REALLY HAVE TO BE PINK?" TOMMY asked when he and Eliza stopped by the drawing room late the next morning as part of what she was calling "The Tour of What's Wrong with Hellfire Hall."

"The color is called salmon," she said.

"Salmon seems to be a theme of late."

She smiled. "I think it makes the space feel warm and inviting."

Pink, he knew, was her favorite color and always had been, which was doubtless why Anna had sent so much of it. He wondered if Anna had been tired of the dull clothes Eliza had been wearing. He supposed they had been part of her effort to be virtuous and austere.

She certainly seemed to have cast off austerity since coming to Hellfire Hall. She was wearing a fuchsia gown that had shiny overlays of some pearly fabric and fit her bosom in a snug way he couldn't seem to tear his eyes from. Her hair was piled in a loose style that made him think of rumpled sheets and would have been completely out of place in a London drawing room. She'd tied a fuchsia velvet ribbon around her neck with a black pearl dangling from it. He had to struggle to avoid looking at her as they moved around the house, because he kept thinking about doing completely inappropriate things, like backing her up against the wall and kissing her. And much more.

He wasn't supposed to be having thoughts that combined sex and Eliza, but how was he supposed to live with her when he kept remembering the warm, lush curves he'd traced that night they'd touched—curves he wanted to actually see, damn it all, and touch a lot more?

"We should go out to the garden next," he said, thinking it would be better not to be in such close quarters with her, because he kept catching little whiffs of her rose scent, and it was only making things worse.

"You want to visit the garden *now*? It's freezing this morning, and drizzling, too," she said as they moved on from the dining room. She'd proposed that after the dining room was plastered, they paint the walls blue with gold trim, and he'd agreed, just as he'd agreed to everything she'd suggested so far. All her ideas sounded smart and artful, and he knew he couldn't have found someone else to do a better job of making the house pleasant.

Once or twice when she'd looked at him that morning, he'd had the sense that she was thinking about him in the more-than-friends way he was thinking about her. But he told himself it was only wishful thinking, because nothing she'd said or done suggested that she wanted to do wicked things with him.

She frowned. "On second thought, maybe we

should go out to the garden and check it thoroughly. Traveler is fond of the garden, and there might be man traps or snakes or something like that."

"I doubt the brigands put any traps out," Tommy said. "Just their presence here was probably enough to discourage anyone from trespassing. And snakes are nothing new to Traveler. He would probably find himself right at home."

She laughed, and he tried not to notice how it made her eyes sparkle. "The rest of the things I bought from the auction house should be arriving today," she said as they stopped by the breakfast room. "Some green cloth for the walls in here, and a patterned carpet in red and gold."

She tapped her chin with her fingertip, drawing his eyes to her lips until he forced himself to look at the walls that he was supposed to be thinking about. "Or will that look too Christmassy, do you think?"

"Christmas is nice," he said. Nice… He wasn't feeling *nice* just then, and if they spent much more time walking around like this, she was going to notice that he was aroused.

"Hmm," she said, that fingertip tapping under her rosy lips again.

"Well," he said a little hoarsely, "I think we've seen just about everything, and I have to say, you've made a miraculous start. Really, the hall was nearly a shambles—if a clean one—when we arrived, and now it's not."

"Thank you," she said, so reasonably. So unaware of all the wicked thoughts he was having.

Or was she?

Stop wondering what she's thinking! Just stop thinking about her! he told himself sternly.

He was just about to go out to the garden on his own—surely yanking out bushes in the rain was the very thing he needed to take his mind off her—when a footman appeared with a note from Will that had just arrived. Tommy unsealed it while Eliza waited.

"Oh, for the love of…" he muttered as he read the first lines.

"Is there some problem?" she asked.

He looked up. "My brother informs me that we are about to host a family house party. *Here*. He means to arrive tomorrow with Anna and the children. He also invited my cousins, your friend Meg, and Rex."

Eliza gasped. "*What?* Guests? Here?" She sounded nearly incoherent. "*Tomorrow?*"

He couldn't help laughing at her horrified expression. "Will writes that the two of us have 'surely had enough of a honeymoon by now,' and that it's time to share our wedded bliss with the family."

Eliza just stood there with a dazed expression. "So many guests…here. This place still has all the welcome of a hastily pitched tent."

"I know," he said, wanting to strangle his brother. He suspected Will wanted to see for himself how things were going with his and Eliza's marriage. "They'll just have to take what they get. It's not as if they didn't know I bought a place whose last inhabitants were pirates."

Her brow wrinkled. "But what if any of them suspects something? I'd hate for them to know that our marriage isn't what they think it is."

"I'm sure it will be fine. They're family, after all."

She sighed. "Well, it will be good to meet Rex anyway."

"Mmm," he said vaguely. 'Good' and 'Rex' were not words he would have put together. But he didn't see the point in mentioning anything just yet. Besides, he was fairly certain that he saw the light of enthusiasm in her eyes, and they were going to need all the enthusiasm they could muster until the elusive Aunt Diana could be found.

"I've had lots of experience with girls of thirteen," Eliza said, "but I hardly know anything of boys that age. I suppose having him with us will be an adventure."

"That's one way of looking at it," Tommy said dryly. "Though maybe we'll get news of his aunt soon."

"Until then, Rex will be one more person we have to fool with our marital charade," she pointed out gloomily.

"Cheer up," he said. "It's not as if we hate each other."

"It wasn't so long ago that we did."

"But we're friends now."

"Yes," she said, though she sounded as though she wasn't entirely certain what that meant. He wasn't either, but now that hordes of people were descending on them, at least he would be too busy to spend time fantasizing about what was under Eliza's clothes.

"So we're already in a better place than most couples," he said. "All we need to do is smile a bit and look dreamy, and they'll take it for contentment."

"I suppose," she said with an exasperated little

smile, and something turned over in his chest, a forgotten sensation that moved with the sort of rusty groan that accompanied old dungeon doors.

Damn. Lust was doing strange things to him. *Was* she struggling with it too?

"Eliza," he said.

"Yes?"

He itched to kiss the elegant column of her neck and nibble downward toward the tiny ruffle at the bodice of her gown. And did her lips have to be such a pretty rose color?

"Never mind." His passage to India was already booked, and there were a number of delicate diplomatic missions he was to undertake on his return. He would be going back to a life he enjoyed, a life unencumbered by the responsibility he would feel if he and Eliza became too deeply involved.

But what if he came back to stay in England sooner than he'd originally planned? What if he gave himself, say, five more years, and then came home and tried to make a life with her? It could be a new plan.

But it sounded like a tremendously *stupid* plan. He loved his work in India. Why would he change his life on the slim chance that being with Eliza would offer something he couldn't even quite name?

Mrs. Hatch came around the corner of the corridor a moment later, and Eliza informed her that they were about to host a house party.

Tommy hid a smile at the poor woman's horrified gasp.

                                           ∽◈∾

With so little time to prepare for their guests, Eliza began organizing the household right away. Since there would at least be a mostly dry roof over everyone's head, she felt the next item of absolute importance was food, and she conferred with Mrs. Hatch and Cook as to the menus, then dispatched servants to purchase grand quantities of food and drink.

That settled, she decided they would focus their efforts on comfort, because more than anything besides a good meal, a tired guest wanted a welcoming space to relax. She sent a servant into town with instructions to buy mountains of the prettiest bed coverings that could be found, which would replace the plain, rather ugly linens currently adorning the guest bedchambers.

She sent Tommy into the town as well—to the auction house with instructions to buy some art.

"Art?" He laughed. "Do you really think a painting or two is going to help?"

"Yes. Get as many paintings as you can, and see if you can find some sculptures as well."

"Shouldn't you be the one making these decisions? I don't know much about art. Perhaps you ought to come with me."

The idea of buying art with Tommy sounded like more fun than she ought to allow herself, but there wasn't time anyway. "I can't. I've got too much to do here. Just get whatever takes your fancy. Anything will be better than empty rooms and miles of plain walls."

Tommy left, and Eliza and Mrs. Hatch turned their attention to the dishes and cutlery. There was enough of everything to accommodate their guests, except for a notable lack of spoons. They sent a maid to the attic to look through the chests stored there, and she returned with a large collection of them.

"Good heavens," Eliza said, turning over a silver soupspoon, "this handle is encrusted with little rubies."

"Are there any more?" Mrs. Hatch asked, looking through her own pile. "Oh! This one has emeralds."

"And I've one here with little pearls." Eliza looked up. "Such a ridiculous idea, putting pearls on something that has to be washed frequently."

"Maybe it was never meant to be used."

"I wonder if these were souvenirs Flaming Beard kept, or if he actually bought them." Eliza chuckled. "I like the idea that they belonged to some Spanish queen."

After the dining arrangements were sorted out, Eliza sent one of the footmen to cut back the ivy growing across the bottoms of the dining room windows. She herself went to the library and finished shelving the books she'd ordered.

Tommy returned in the late afternoon, followed by several laden carts. As two servants unloaded them in the front drive, Eliza stood with him, inspecting his acquisitions and indicating where each piece should go.

"How many landscape paintings did you buy?" she asked as the sixth one came off the cart.

"That's a seascape," he said. "It's different from the one with all the hills. And you did say to get a lot of paintings."

"So I did."

The next three were of dogs. She raised an

eyebrow at the last one, which showed a greyhound painted with all the care that might have been lavished on a king.

"I like dogs," Tommy said in an offended tone. "Besides, Traveler will appreciate it."

He'd also bought five busts of famous men and one large marble sculpture of a nude couple entwined.

"What were you thinking?" she asked as she watched a group of footmen carry the sculpture toward the door. The stone pair seemed almost alive, their passion for each other coming across so well that just looking at them made Eliza blush.

Tommy called out to the footmen, "Put it in the foyer."

"In the *foyer?*" she said. "It's really not appropriate."

He was standing next to her, and though the day was chilly, she could feel some of the warmth of his body. Or maybe that was just her own heat, a reaction to his nearness and to memories of what it felt like to be in his arms. He looked down at her with his clear green eyes.

"I bought it because they looked happy, which will make our guests cheerful."

"Happy?" she squawked as the servants disappeared inside, leaving her and Tommy alone. "That's not how I would describe it."

He smirked and she swatted his chest. They hadn't touched each other once since that brief, dry kiss on their marriage day, and she hadn't meant to touch him now. It had only been an old reflex of flirtation. Or at least, that was what she told herself as he captured her eyes with a gaze that seemed suddenly hot. Her hand lingered against the solid, warm wall of his chest.

It was as though just by touching him, she'd changed something between them.

His hand covered hers, warm and strong. He stepped closer. "How *would* you describe our sculpted couple?"

She couldn't think with him so close and holding her hand as though he wanted her to be there. He couldn't know just how much she wanted him to pull her into his arms. "Naked," she mumbled.

He chuckled, a husky sound that curled into her. "Observant of you. Are you suggesting that people can't be naked *and* happy?"

"'Happy' just seems like the wrong description," she managed to say, though it felt nearly impossible to speak sensibly just then. He smelled so good, familiar and exotic at the same time, and she could feel his heart beating. She wanted to let her hand roam onto the bare skin of his neck.

"Contented then?" he offered. His lids lowered and he looked at her from beneath thick black lashes. The wild slash of white in his too-long black hair and the shadow of the day's whiskers gave him the air of a pirate who knew charm might gain him far more booty than force. "Delighted?"

He wanted to suggest they were talking about more than just the statues. She shook her head. She felt that desire lay between them like an unopened letter.

"Enraptured?" he supplied, mischief glittering in his eyes. She would have been so much better off if he weren't so charming.

"Um," she murmured as his head dipped seductively closer.

"Wanting?" he whispered.

Wanting… There were all kinds of things she wanted. She wanted this man, and she wanted a family. She hadn't thought those two things could be reconciled, but she was having the craziest idea—and thinking that maybe it wasn't so crazy after all.

A heavy *thunk* sounded inside the manor, breaking the spell, and Eliza stepped away from Tommy as Mrs. Hatch rushed out with a dismayed expression.

"It's funny," he said as they watched the house-keeper approaching. "I feel as though I was about to ravish a virgin but was interrupted by a chaperone."

"You could hardly have ravished me in the front drive. And I'm not a virgin."

He didn't reply right away. And then he said, "But we never consummated our marriage."

"If you asked the average person whether we'd consummated our marriage, they would say that what we already did counted," she pointed out reasonably, even though all she could think about just then was whether he'd be outraged if she spoke the words she suddenly wanted to say.

"Shall I ask Mrs. Hatch her opinion?" he said.

Something wicked had come over him since she'd touched him, and now she was thinking that might actually be a good thing. But she needed to talk to him seriously, and she couldn't do it there in the drive. "If you do, I'll make sure you're served fish and carrots for dinner."

He only had time to give her a dark look before Mrs. Hatch reached them, distressed to report that one of the busts had been dropped and was now missing its nose.

"No matter," Tommy said. "You can put it in my brother's room."

Eliza left with Mrs. Hatch to inspect the disposition of the rest of the sculptures. There was still so much to be done that the rest of the day flew by in a whirlwind of activity.

While the maids made up the beds with the newly purchased linens, Eliza assembled a motley collection of chairs at the dining room table. There were, at least, plenty of chairs to choose from, thanks to Flaming Beard, even if they were a weird assortment. She also put fresh candles and towels in each of the bedchambers herself, and tall vases of bright-red flowering quince everywhere, along with dishes of fragrant dried lavender.

"It smells really good in here," Tommy said to Eliza as he passed her on the way outside to split some extra wood. "The pirates would be outraged at how hospitable the place is getting to be."

As the sun dipped low and Eliza checked on the completed tasks, she couldn't help pausing by the windows to enjoy the sight of her husband swinging an ax in his shirtsleeves.

It was dark by the time she'd sorted out which paintings would look best in which rooms and had a footman hang them. As the last landscape was being set in place in the room that would be Louie's, Tommy arrived in the doorway carrying his coat, his sleeves still rolled up to reveal strong forearms. She tried fruitlessly not to look at them.

"A great improvement, don't you think?" she asked him, indicating the room as Robert left with his tools.

"I do." Tommy grinned and picked up a flowered pitcher from the vanity. "And don't you want to compliment me for purchasing a vast quantity of these jug things when I was at the auction house?" They'd been delivered after Tommy arrived with the furniture.

She laughed. "It was quite brilliant of you to buy them, and they're lovely."

"I thought you'd like that they seemed the sort of thing to make a room less dungeon-like."

"And so they are," she'd said, pleased that he'd wanted to please her.

In fact, she thought as they finished a very late dinner of cold ham and potatoes and apple caramel cake (Hellfire Hall offered, if nothing else, mountains of apples for their guests to consume in one form or another), she was quite touched by his willing participation in the preparations. Here was a man—a *swashbuckling* man—who spent his days on daring missions of great import to those in power, who'd recently been knighted and might naturally expect, as men generally did, not to lift a finger in matters of household arrangements. Instead, he'd done a great deal of work.

It had been an exhausting day—and more remained to be done before their guests arrived tomorrow—but she could honestly say that she didn't know when she'd had such a satisfying day. They functioned well together. Too bad it wasn't going to last.

Tommy popped the last of a large piece of cake into his mouth and polished it off with a sip of wine, then pushed away from the table a bit and leaned comfortably back in his chair. He'd bathed before dinner and put on a tailcoat the color of a rajah's rubies, and his black hair fell carelessly across his forehead, the white slash angling downward with its usual boldness. A fire blazed cozily in the hearth behind him and created a little glow around his head. As if this golden man needed more burnishing, she thought.

"We've done well. Hellfire Hall looks decidedly more hospitable," he said, "though I don't suppose our pirates would have thanked us for making it less manly and brutal."

"I wouldn't have thought a home could be brutal, but that was before I stood on Hellfire's icy floors. The new carpets will mostly offer protection from frostbite, but what with the drafts and the occasional little leak when it rains, it's still a far cry from luxurious."

"At least it's just family and Meg coming. And Rex, of course, though being a thirteen-year-old boy, he's unlikely to care much about the state of the accommodations."

She nodded and they sat quietly for a bit, though Eliza's mind was buzzing with the idea she'd been entertaining seriously since that afternoon. She cleared her throat.

He looked at her quizzically and her heart turned over. She was more than halfway in love with him, but that could have no bearing on anything that was to come. She took her courage in both hands and said what she wanted to say.

"I want a baby."

Tommy blinked. "You want *what*?"

"I want a baby. The baby I lost…" Eliza began, then had to swallow against a thickness in her throat, "made me look at things differently. I'd thought I could never have a child. But now that I know I can, I want to try again."

He went very still. "What exactly do you mean?"

She could see he was wary, that he thought she was asking something huge from him, that she had expectations. But the last thing she'd do would be to make him feel she expected him to care more than he did, even if her own feelings toward him already ran deep.

"I'm not asking you to change your plans," she forced herself to say, though the words felt awful, because her heart wanted to spin so many fantasies about how things might be if he really cared for her. Perfect dreams of how they might make a big, happy family. That wasn't going to happen, but a baby she could love would make all the difference for her.

"You're going back to India before long," she continued, "and I'll be here in England, a married woman with no children. It's different for women. Surely you see how I might want a child?"

She sensed him stiffening and got up from the table to close the curtains, just to have something to do. And maybe so she didn't have to look at him when he said no.

"I thought you understood that I'm not ready to think about children," he said.

She brushed an imaginary smudge from the curtain cloth. "I do understand that, which is why I want to do this on my own." She forced herself to turn around and look him in the eye. "And I can. Lots of couples do things like this. How many of the men in India have families who live in England?"

His arms were resting on the sides of his chair, his hands steepled in front of him. Though his eyes were on her, she couldn't read any emotion in them. "Many. But they're not particularly happy families, and I never wanted to live like that. I always assumed that I'd have children much later, when I was ready to leave India. Why not wait a few years, until I move to England?"

"Tommy, I'm already twenty-four. If we wait too long, who knows whether I'll even be able to have a baby when you return to England for good? I want a baby now, and I promise that I'm ready to raise a child without making demands on you."

He gave her a look. "Anna was twenty-eight when she had Victoria. Women have children in their thirties all the time."

"But we can't know that it would work for me. And we can't know what life will bring, whether you might not come home for many more years than you think…if ever. I'm getting older, as are you."

"That may not be your best argument." He said nothing for several moments, and she waited, trying not to hope too hard.

Finally, he unfolded his body from the chair and came to stand before her. He looked down at her, his expression serious. "You truly want to do this? To be here in England, alone with our child if we have one? Because I can't bring a family to India—I *won't*. It's too dangerous, and I'm never in one place for long there."

"I wouldn't be alone here—you know that. I'd have Will and Anna and their children, and Judith would be a wonderful help. And Meg, too. The baby would have so many people who wanted to be family to him or her."

She paused, hoping she was using the right words to make him understand that she had thought about this and what it would mean for both of them. "It was the way I envisioned things working out before, when I was increasing and you didn't know. And now, with us being married, there wouldn't be any of the problems I would have faced. I can do this, Tommy—if you agree."

He drew in a breath and her heart hung in the balance. What if he said no? A window had opened for her with this chance to have a baby, and she knew she'd be terribly disappointed if he refused her.

"Very well," he said quietly.

"Really? Do you really mean it?"

"Yes."

"This is so *wonderful*!" she cried, and threw her arms around his neck. "Thank you."

He might not be excited about this, but he was willing to do it. And she was excited about it enough for both of them.

If she was ignoring the knowledge that the kind of relationship she'd just proposed would make her vulnerable to caring more deeply for him, she accepted whatever risk there might be. That trouble would come in the future, after he left, and she didn't want to think about it now. She'd spent the last six years living a narrow, circumscribed life, and she didn't want to live like that anymore. And maybe, if she was lucky, there'd be a baby to fill her heart with love.

꧁

Tommy wasn't entirely convinced of the wisdom of what he'd just agreed to, but Eliza apparently really wanted a baby, and not only could he not deny her this thing that was so important to her, he was burning to touch her.

He dropped his cheek next to hers, and just the nearness of her made him feel reckless, like he didn't know what he would do if he couldn't touch her. But he had to make certain she'd thought about this thoroughly.

"Don't forget, Eliza, that even when couples are hoping to have children, it doesn't always happen. You might be disappointed."

"Of course I know that—I've experienced it already. Whatever happens, I won't be disappointed."

"Are you sure that you won't feel abandoned when I leave?"

"I'm not going to turn into some sort of clinging, demanding wife." Her eyes glittered with something he couldn't quite read. "As you'll recall, I didn't want to get married either."

He glanced at the closed dining room door, then strode toward it, grabbing a chair as he went.

"What are you doing?"

He pushed the chair under the knob and came back to where she was standing.

"You've put yourself at my mercy," he said, slowly

backing her up to the wall behind her. "Now you're mine to ravish."

He took her hands in one of his and lifted them over her head, pinning them to the wall. He leaned into her, and she felt so good that it almost scared him. Thank God they were keeping things light.

"Beast," she muttered in a husky voice that made his blood heat.

"Guilty," he said, and kissed her neck. "I've already spent far too much time thinking about you spread out on this table. It's time for action."

"You've been thinking about me?"

"All the damned time," he said. "I was getting ready to buy you a sack to wear, because all those pretty dresses seemed designed to torture me."

Her eyes crinkled. "I'm…not sorry."

He kept his gaze fixed on hers as he ran a hand along the top of her shoulder, taking the edge of her gown and chemise with it and pushing the fabric to the edge of her shoulder, exposing her breast.

"How am I supposed to touch you?" she said.

"You can touch me all you want—later. Right now it's my turn."

He looked down at her breast and groaned as he cupped its plumpness. He pinched the rosy tip.

She whimpered.

"You like this," he said.

"Yes," she whispered.

He bent to graze her nipple with his teeth.

❧

Eliza sighed with pleasure and pressed herself against

him. She'd never been demanding about kisses until Tommy, but his boldness freed her to respond.

He dipped his head and captured her nipple in his mouth, and she moaned and pushed into him. She kissed him back urgently, their tongues meeting in greedy strokes that told of what was to come. Though she squirmed against his grip, he only smiled against her mouth and didn't let go. Dampness gathered between her legs.

His breathing ragged, Tommy nudged her legs apart and pushed between them, and his hard length pressed against her core. Lust—deliciously uncivilized lust—was taking them over in all its messiness, and knowing how much he wanted her only made her want him more.

He grabbed the hem of her dress and pulled it upward.

"Drawers," he muttered. "How nice." And then, which was not *nice* at all, he cupped her and rubbed her through the fabric.

She was desperate to touch him by the time he let her hands go. She pulled his shirt free of his breeches and ran her hands over the bunched muscles of his abdomen, nearly expiring just from the pleasure of finally touching his bare skin. She explored greedily, and his flat stomach twitched as her hands skimmed downward. She found the hard ridge straining against his breeches.

She was rewarded with the sound of Tommy's teeth gnashing. "God, Eliza."

They touched each other with abandon through their clothes, until he tore her drawers downward.

She paid him back by unfastening the buttons on his breeches, then gasped when he was exposed.

He laughed.

"It was dark at that brothel," she explained, "and I couldn't see you."

He gave her a wicked look, reached for the table behind him, and pushed the dishes aside carelessly. His hands slid to her hips, and he lifted her and put her bottom on the table. Cutlery clattered to the floor.

"When I was younger," she panted, "I thought you were so nice."

"An illusion. I wanted to do all this to you back then, but I couldn't." He pulled her legs around his waist and pushed her gown back from her knees. With no hesitation, he touched her between her spread legs. He rubbed her in slow little circles that made her nearly crazed with pleasure.

"Tell me," he said, still rubbing, and she knew she'd tell him anything if he only would keep doing what he was doing, "that night you were being Victoria, you said something about never knowing it could be so good."

Her cheeks heated as she remembered.

"What exactly did you mean?" he asked as his clever fingers robbed her of the last vestiges of her will. "You'd been married—surely you'd done the deed before?"

"I meant the bliss," she said, barely managing to get the words out.

His face lit up. "So you'd never known that bliss before?"

She shook her head.

If it was possible, the devilish light in his eyes turned wickeder. "But you liked it that night," he said.

"Yes," she whispered hoarsely.

He leaned over her and splayed his hands on either side of her head and moved into her slowly, impossibly slowly. She pressed against him, needing more, and he groaned but he wouldn't be rushed as he filled her. She'd never wanted anything as urgently as she wanted Tommy right then, and she wrapped her legs around him as he bent over her.

He captured her hands again and swept them over her head and continued his slow torture.

"Tommy," she murmured.

"Eliza," he said. "You've never been more beautiful."

Something in him seemed to break, and his strokes started to come faster, driving her nearly mindless until finally her release crashed over her. As she cried out, he captured the sound with his mouth, moaning as he found his own release.

A few moments later he slid onto the table, coming to rest at her side. "That was…rather wonderful."

"Yes," she breathed, still feeling a sense of awe. "It was."

Something had happened to her, along with the physical pleasure. The first time they'd made love at the brothel, she'd felt an unaccustomed vulnerability, and now she felt it again, only stronger, and it scared her. She told herself that if she didn't think about it, maybe it would go away.

Tommy leaned forward and collected her drawers and handed them to her along with his handkerchief. He fastened his breeches while she put herself to rights.

An enormous yawn stole over her. "It's terribly late, and we still have so much to finish before people start arriving tomorrow. We ought to get to bed."

"By all means," he said, "but you're sleeping in my bed from now on."

"If you insist," she said dreamily.

He held out a hand, and when she placed hers there, he kissed the back of her hand. "Though I warn you," he said as he pulled the chair away from the doorknob, "you're not going to get much sleep tonight."

She gave a silent cheer. "Oh well, there's always coffee."

Thirteen

THE HOUSEHOLD BUSTLE STARTED EXTRA EARLY THE
next morning as the staff hurried to put the final
touches on the manor. Eliza had already let it be
known that they could expect bonuses for their efforts,
and they were all working like fiends.

Eliza and Tommy breakfasted quickly, standing
at the sideboard in the dining room with cups of
coffee and slices of leftover cake from the night
before, a simple meal that left the kitchen staff
free to continue with their preparation of pastries,
breads, soups, and all manner of meats and vegetables for the guests who were expected to arrive
late that morning.

Eliza stifled a yawn and helped herself to more
coffee. Tommy had pounced on her almost as soon
as they'd tumbled into bed the night before. His
lovemaking was incredible, inventive, and unlike
anything she'd ever experienced. Though *she* was the
one who'd awoken *him* very early that morning.

"I hope there won't be fish on the menu today," he
said as he blew on his steaming coffee.

"Only a bit of trout at dinner." She nibbled a corner of cake, which was deliciously dusted with sugar.

"I thought wives were supposed to dote on their husbands, serving them only their favorite dishes."

She gave him a look. "We're also having a joint of beef. Most people like variety. And have you ever even tried trout?"

The edges of his mouth quivered.

"You haven't!" she said triumphantly. "And you such an adventurer. I begin to wonder at all this swash-buckling you are reputed to have been doing, if you haven't even had the courage to try different foods."

He downed the last of his coffee and stepped close. He smelled of fresh morning, of rich coffee and shaving soap and a new start. "I'll wager you'll find, Lady Halifax, that I'm not in the least lacking in boldness."

Her skin heated as she thought about all the places he'd touched her the night before. He leaned closer and his breath tickled her ear enticingly. "Keep remembering. Or better yet, come back to bed with me."

"Certainly not," she said, giving him a little push, though the primness she'd intended for her tone was compromised by her smile and the sparks dancing up her neck. "We have people arriving practically any minute."

He sighed. "It will have to be a stolen moment later in the day. Maybe in the stillroom."

She groaned. "You just reminded me: the stillroom is full of cobwebs. I'll have to send someone to clean it. Now," she said briskly, "since we still have no butler, please go down to the stable and check that everything is ready for the horses and coaches." She pinched the bridge of her nose. "I love Will and Anna, but I don't know what made them think we'd be ready for guests so soon."

"There's still time to hide all the food and extra wood. If we left Hellfire Hall to its own devices, it would probably drive them away in a matter of hours."

"As if that would work." She leaned forward and treated herself to a quick kiss on his freshly shaved cheek, then went to see to a thousand last-minute details.

Several hours later, she was settling the last bunch of flowers into a large crockery pot in the guest room meant for Meg when she looked out the window and saw the Grandville coach coming up the rutted drive to Hellfire Hall. She ran down the steps to the front door, calling out to Tommy that they'd arrived. He was standing in the drive with her as the carriage came to a stop.

"They'll want to talk about the wedding and our marriage," he said.

"I know."

He took her hand and squeezed it.

Will handed Anna down, and she rushed forward and embraced them both eagerly. "Did he sweep you off your feet?" she asked Eliza when they pulled apart. "Were you surprised?"

"I was definitely surprised," Eliza said. "We stopped at a little chapel in a village."

Will pulled her into a crushing embrace. "Congratulations, dear Eliza," he said.

"Thank you," she murmured thickly, feeling the

guilty weight of what their marriage meant to Will and Anna.

Will pulled Tommy into a hearty embrace. She noticed that Tommy had no trouble accepting his brother's congratulations with easy cheer.

"There was a sort of general outrage in Town," Anna said, "when it became known that the pair of you had eloped, thus depriving society of what everyone thought would have been the most exciting wedding of the year."

"We felt cheated as well," Will said, "so I'm sure you'll forgive us for wishing to come celebrate with you here."

"Of course," Tommy said. He looked entirely relaxed, which Eliza couldn't see how he managed with Will's dark eyes fixed on him as though waiting for Tommy to enlighten him about the real reason they'd eloped.

Will swung Victoria and Heck down from the coach. Vic promptly caught herself up in Eliza's skirts, hugging her legs and giggling, and Heck manfully extended a hand to Eliza, though the properness of the gesture was somewhat diminished by him saying, "Mama says I may call you Aunt Eliza now, but do I have to? I just want to call you Eliza."

She leaned down and swiped a lightning-fast kiss across his boyish cheek. "Of course you can still call me Eliza. Though I think it's pretty fine that you're now my nephew as well as my cousin."

"And here's Rex, of course," Will said, drawing Eliza and Tommy's attention back to the coach. "Do join us, Rex."

❧

Tommy watched as Rex got down from the carriage.

"Sir Tommy," Rex said casually as he shook his hand. Will caught Tommy's eye and arched a brow as if to convey that Tommy was going to have his hands full. Apparently Rex's stay at Halifax House hadn't worked any civilizing magic on him, but Tommy hadn't really supposed he could be that lucky.

He introduced Rex to Eliza. "Ma'am," the boy said, his eyes widening with admiration as he took her in. Tommy hid a smirk.

"So you knew Sir Tommy in India, Rex?" she asked.

Rex shrugged, as though this was a topic of little interest to him. Clearly, unlike Heck, Rex didn't think Tommy was all the crack. "He did the same sort of work my father did."

Tommy swept his hand toward the manor with a flourish. "What do you all think?"

"It looks really old and crumbling," Heck said with awe. "Can we explore it?"

"Of course," Tommy said. "It would be a sad waste of a former pirate's lair if you didn't. You will doubtless be glad that the place has been cleaned up a bit, but I'm happy to report, for those who are interested," his gaze included Rex, "that the dungeons have been left undisturbed."

"Dungeons," Heck breathed, his expression dreamy.

Rex rolled his eyes. "Is there a curricle? I should like to drive one. I'm known to be adept with horses."

A stunned silence greeted these rude, pompous words, though Tommy heard Eliza's softly indrawn breath. He summoned his most neutral tone—this was Oliver's son, and even if he was a brat, he was surely still grieving the loss of his father—and said, "I'm afraid we don't have a curricle here. But there's a pony cart. Perhaps it could even be taken for a ride in the woods."

"Oh!" said Vic, clapping her hands. "Are there foxes in your woods? I love foxes."

"Pony carts are for babies," Rex sneered.

"By the gods," Tommy muttered, nearly in awe of the boy's rudeness. He was saved from having to come up with some reply by a second carriage pulling up the drive.

"That will be Louie, Ruby, and Meg," Will said. "They had to fetch Marcus from the Thorntons', where he's been staying while Lady Gildenhall is away visiting friends." Lady Gildenhall was mother to Louie, Ruby, Emerald, Andrew, and Marcus. Ruby liked to say that Marcus, being so much younger than his other siblings, was like a prince with a bevy of attendants, but Eliza had noticed that, like the rest of them, Ruby was extremely fond of Marcus and enjoyed his youthful antics. Mostly.

"And they've brought David Holley's daughter, Susanna, as well," Anna said.

"You remember David Holley, Tommy," Will said. "He was Louie's conscience when they were at university together." Tommy laughed. "Louie offered to bring Susanna to give the girl a holiday while David and his wife tour the Lake District. Susanna's about the same age as Rex and Marcus."

Marcus and Susanna spilled out of the carriage like cannon shot, full of repressed high spirits.

"Tommy!" Marcus called, sprinting over. "What

a fantastic place!" At fourteen, Marcus was a bit taller than Rex and sturdier, with the confident air of a fellow who knew he was handsome, and whose brother was an earl. He had the Halifax green eyes and gold-colored hair like Louie, along with a nose that was currently a bit too big for his face.

"It does look…unusual," Susanna Holley said, curtseying to Tommy and Eliza as Meg, Ruby, and finally Louie emerged from the carriage. The girl was quite pretty, with honey-blond ringlets and fine brown eyes, and Tommy noticed Rex's eyes lingering on her when they were introduced. Rex and Marcus shook hands.

"We might take out the pony cart," announced Vic.

"I once drove a pony cart so fast, the wheels came off," Rex said.

Marcus guffawed. "That's something!"

"Really, Marcus," scolded Ruby.

Mrs. Hatch met the party inside and announced that there was lemonade in the garden. The young people all headed down the corridor that led to the back entrance, Marcus and Rex with their heads already bent together.

❦

Meg slipped an arm around Eliza's waist as they stood in the foyer and whispered, "When Anna told me they were coming here, I had to come too, to make certain you were all right. Did Tommy *kidnap* you that day we were on our way to Bath? I thought he was taking you back to London."

Eliza gave a rueful chuckle. "I guess you could say he swashbuckled me. But everything's all right."

"Hmm," Meg whispered back. "We have to talk later."

"Well," Tommy said to the group, "what do you all think of Hellfire Hall?"

"It's charming," Anna said. Will lifted a skeptical eyebrow and Tommy laughed.

"Well, it's vastly better than it was when we arrived," Tommy said, "but it's still a work in progress. We hope you'll all be comfortable, though."

"It's generous of you both to host us so soon after your wedding," Ruby said.

Louie snorted. "As if they had a choice. I'm willing to bet Grandville simply announced we were coming."

The corner of Will's mouth quivered briefly.

"Hellfire Hall does look a bit grim on the outside," Meg said, "though I thought I saw some pretty greenery hanging from the battlements."

"I had some holly hung there, which I thought looked rather nice," Eliza said.

"It spoils the whole brigand look of the place," Tommy said with a sigh.

Meg laughed. "And that's a bad thing?"

The foyer now looked much nicer as well. The walls had been hung with a stately old tapestry from the attic, a fire blazed in the enormous hearth, and a handsome table stood by the staircase, bearing a silver bowl piled with apples.

Meg's eyebrows rose as her gaze landed on the sculpture Tommy had bought. She squinted at it. "What is that?"

"Art," Tommy said. "Do you like it?"

"I couldn't really say."

"And isn't that a sign of great art?"

Eliza noticed the edges of Meg's mouth crinkling with suppressed laughter and smiled to herself. Meg was generally immune to charming men, but Tommy was awfully hard to resist.

"Well, Tommy," Will said, "Rex is an interesting fellow."

Tommy grimaced. "I suppose I owe you and Anna quite a bit for hosting him these last few days. Has he been an enormous trial?"

Anna glanced at her husband. "I'm sure we'd never describe a child in those words."

"Oh, I think you could describe this one like that," Will said. "He set fire to several of the rosebushes in the Halifax House garden."

Tommy winced.

"And he's the son of your friend?" Louie said incredulously.

Tommy nodded. "Oliver was an excellent fellow, but I did sometimes wonder if he'd neglected the boy. After Oliver's wife died a few years ago, he left the boy in the care of a very indulgent ayah."

Ruby said, "He seems unfortunately named, considering his temperament. And now you have your very own young king."

"Not exactly," Tommy hastened to say. "I'm merely looking out for him until his aunt can be found. She's the wardrobe mistress for a traveling theater troupe, and I've got a man looking for her."

Louie chuckled. "You'll be lucky if she doesn't meet the boy and decide not to take him."

"Louie!" Ruby said.

"He seems to have been both ignored and spoiled," Anna said. "With appropriate guidance, surely his better nature will emerge."

Eliza said, "He reminds me of some of the girls we had at Truehart Manor. They just needed extra understanding."

Will, Louie, and Tommy shared a look. "You may find that boys are much more annoying," Louie said.

"Do remember," Eliza said as she led them upstairs, "that the hall was abandoned for years before we arrived, and that its previous tenants were pirates."

"I'm not certain whether to expect cold, dirty rooms, or treasure chests everywhere," Louie said.

"Ha," Tommy said. "Though, really, Eliza's worked miracles. The place was nearly uninhabitable when we arrived."

Eliza felt warmed by his praise. "Tommy was the one who bought all the art," she said. "Including the sculpture in the entryway."

"Then Tommy can be the one to answer any questions Vic and Heck have about what the sculpted people are doing," Will said.

Meg was the last to be shown her room, and as she and Eliza and Tommy paused outside the door to her chamber, her eyes came to rest on Tommy.

"So," she said a little stiffly, as though leaving him room to account for himself.

He laughed. "I haven't done anything awful to your friend," he said. "Well, except for bringing her here."

Eliza sent Tommy off so she and Meg could have a few minutes alone. Meg's trunks had already been brought up, and Mrs. Hatch would send a maid shortly to help with the unpacking.

As soon as they had closed the door, Meg said, "I've been worried about you, even though Anna explained about Tommy's plans to sweep you off your feet."

"I'm fine," Eliza said. "But I lost the baby."

"Oh, dearest." Meg pulled her into an embrace. "I'm so sorry. What a terrible disappointment for you, even if the baby was the reason you had to get married."

"Yes," was all Eliza could manage as huskiness crept into her voice.

"And Tommy?"

"He's been very good to me since the miscarriage. And," Eliza continued, "perhaps there may be a baby after all."

"So it's not a marriage of convenience! I knew it! Didn't I say there would still be something between you two?"

"It's not exactly like that."

Meg's intelligent brown eyes settled on her. "What's it like then?"

"We've come to an understanding."

"Then he is staying in England?"

Eliza shook her head. "He'll go back to India at the end of next month."

"Alone?"

Eliza nodded.

"What exactly will that mean for you?" Meg's eyes narrowed. "You care for him, don't you? You care for him and he doesn't care for you. He's just going to do exactly as he pleases and abandon you."

"He's *not* abandoning me. He's simply going to go back to the life he was living before we married, just as I'm going to try to do." She tried for a smile. "Though considering how things at Truehart Manor have fallen apart, I'm not certain what the future holds."

Meg squeezed her hand. "Now isn't the time for you to be worrying about that. You need to focus on your marriage. Couldn't you make it work?"

"Even if I were tempted by Tommy," Eliza said, not wanting to admit even to Meg how much more than tempted she was, "how could I want to be with a man who's got his sights so clearly set elsewhere? I would be a fool, and you know I'm no fool."

"Being foolish or smart has nothing do with matters of the heart, as my mother demonstrated countless times. She was brilliant, and she repeatedly entangled herself with the most unsuitable men." Meg sighed. "It says something about Tommy that he's taken on such daring, difficult tasks in India. Clearly he doesn't want to be just the younger brother of a viscount."

"I know." Eliza had to respect him for making his own way in the world, even if that meant that he didn't see how such a thing could be accomplished in familiar old England. She looked away as emotion tugged at her mouth. Her feelings for Tommy ran deep, but she was doing her best not to let them overtake her, and talking about them with Meg would only make them feel more real.

"All will be fine, really," she said firmly.

"If you say so," Meg said, sounding unconvinced. "So, how was the journey here?"

Meg groaned. "You know I am fond of Ruby,

and Marcus is amusing, though of course he's only fourteen. But Susanna Holley is completely pleased with herself, which is a quality that is never desirable in a companion. Though she *is* thirteen, which was certainly not *my* best age."

Eliza shuddered. "Nor mine."

"But can you believe that Gildenhall rode with us for the whole journey? Five in a coach, and as the two tallest, he and I had to share a seat while the other three squeezed onto the opposite bench. So I had to endure his company the whole time."

"You were hoping he'd ride alongside?"

"Of course! You know I have never cared for him, and I don't see how he could have failed to notice, either. He is always so secretly mocking."

Meg considered Louie the very worst rake in the *ton* and deserving of no respect whatsoever, and clearly the hours spent together in the carriage hadn't improved her opinion. Louie seemed always to take Meg's stiff manner and silences in stride, though Eliza was certain that she'd caught him hiding a smile on several occasions. In truth, she sometimes wondered if there weren't some interesting undercurrents below the surface of Meg and Louie's non-relationship.

"If it's secretly done, how do you know he's mocking you?"

"You know what I mean—it's all very subtle, but whenever I'm with him, I'm certain he's enjoying himself at my expense. It's a struggle to be polite to such a man."

Eliza hid a smile. The Earl of Gildenhall was handsome, wealthy, charming, and one of the most sought-after gentlemen in the *ton*, and she doubted there was another woman in England who would have termed it a struggle to be polite to him. Though it was true that there was something of a cloud hovering over him of late; he'd fought a duel two months before with Viscount Marwich, a contest in which Marwich had lost an arm.

The duel had apparently had something to do with a woman, but there were only rumors and conjectures. Eliza had never liked Marwich, so she was inclined to believe that Louie had had a good reason to shoot him, but still, he'd maimed a fellow peer.

"Well, now that you're here and there are so many other people present, I hope it won't be too much of a trial to share a house with the earl," Eliza said, trying for a serious tone.

Meg gave her a look, but it was tinged with a hint of mirth. "Don't think I don't know you're laughing at me. And now that the earl is your cousin by marriage, you will doubtless feel you must champion him." She sighed heavily. "I shall try to do my best to be civil to him while I'm here."

Eliza laughed and hugged her. "You are the dearest creature," she told Meg. "What better wedding present could I have than a promise that you'll try to be pleasant to my new relations?"

Meg stuck her nose in the air. "I said *civil*. I didn't say I'd go as far as pleasant."

They collapsed in giggles.

Fourteen

THOUGH TOMMY HAD INSISTED THAT THEIR GUESTS could perfectly well eat lunch amid what Eliza called "the daytime dreariness of the Hellfire dining room," she was grateful for the fine weather that allowed them to eat in the garden, which was now being called "the wilds" thanks to Louie. He'd taken one look at the rioting vegetation, scraggly trees, and patches of bare dirt studded with rocks, and said, "You can't seriously call this a garden, Tommy."

"It just needs a little work," Anna said charitably as she and Eliza finished arranging the food and drinks on the large cloth that Louie had spread for them on one of the flatter sections of ground behind the manor.

Louie had guffawed. "It needs more than a *little* work. It needs someone to put a torch to it so you can start afresh."

Rex and Marcus, lingering at the edge of the group, seemed to think that idea was hilarious.

"I like this place," Heck had said.

Louie had grinned. "So do I, actually. Everyone has gardens. Tommy and Eliza have a wild land."

The day was warm for October, with a clear blue sky and plenty of sunshine, though it was still cool enough that the cups of hot tea served with the meat pasties and custard tarts were most welcome. The adults lounged comfortably propped up on their elbows or leaning against the odd rock and chatted as they watched the young people, who eventually began poking aimlessly about in the back of the wilds. Rex and Marcus kicked at bushes and trees, as though challenging them to turn into something more interesting.

"I suppose they're trying not to look like they're searching for signs of anything the pirates might have left or buried," Meg said as she selected a pasty. Tommy had casually let slip to the children that from what he understood, things had been buried on the grounds.

"Marcus and Rex probably consider themselves too old for such things," Ruby said. As usual, she was wearing red, a pretty garnet gown that was far too fashionable for such a setting, but for some reason, Eliza thought, Ruby Halifax never looked overdressed. She supposed this had something to do with the confident tilt of her chin.

"True," her brother said, "though I saw Marcus's eyes light up at the mention of the dungeon."

"Vic seems quite taken with Susanna," Eliza said. The little girl trailed after the older one as intently as a duckling after a mother duck, leaning close to peer at the ground wherever Susanna stopped to prod things with her feet.

Anna nodded. "Susanna has been sweet to her."

"Partly that's kindness," Ruby observed, "and partly, I suspect, it's showing off for the older boys."

"Rex has his own follower as well," Will said as Heck dropped to his knees next to where Rex had started to clear some underbrush. "Heck's been fascinated with India ever since Tommy came back and gave him a scimitar. He seems to think Rex is the luckiest boy ever, growing up in a land with tigers and elephants and full of men who are…" He flicked a glance at his brother.

"Don't say it," Tommy warned.

"Swashbuckling," Will finished with a grin.

Tommy tossed an apple core at him, which Will dodged, laughing.

A shout went up; apparently Vic had stumbled on something near the base of a rotting tree.

Louie squinted. "What is that—the remains of someone your brigands dispatched?"

"They're some ancient tools I found outside the old garden shed." Traveler, who'd been sitting beside Tommy, stretched and began making his way across the wilds to investigate. "I thought it might amuse the children to think the pirates left them lying around."

Eliza, sitting next to Meg, felt her heart squeeze at his thoughtfulness.

"Is there really a dungeon?" asked Meg, who had chosen a spot as far away from Louie as possible. Really, Meg was completely misguided about him, Eliza thought; the man was downright sweet. Hadn't he brought an extra child with him on holiday to give her a treat and the parents some time on their own?

"There really is," Tommy said, "but don't worry, I wouldn't send anyone down there unless hideously provoked."

"A competition seems to have broken out," Will observed as they watched Marcus wield a shovel under a carefully chosen tree. Susanna and Victoria were helping him by clearing the brush from the digging site. Perhaps fifty feet away, Rex was digging in the packed dirt next to a large rock while Heck cleared the loosened clumps.

"I wonder why they decided those particular spots would have to be treasure spots," Ruby said.

"They're probably just drunk with power since Tommy told them that if they want to look for buried treasure while they're here, they may dig anywhere they want in the wilds," Anna said.

"I like this place," Meg said, trailing her hand over a rock half-buried in the ground next to her leg. "It's a pirate's garden, wild and full of shadowy nooks and rough ground."

"I wouldn't have thought you partial to wild things," Louie said.

She lifted her chin haughtily. "I was speaking of the beauty of nature."

The corner of his mouth quivered and Meg gave him a dark look.

"Shall we go down to the sea?" Eliza asked. "I've been here all this time and not had a minute to visit it."

The adults all agreed, and they set off, leaving the children to their digging under the watchful eyes of Traveler. The path to the sea was overgrown, hardly more than a suggestion of a once-cleared trail, so the men went first, crushing down the high grass with their booted feet, tossing aside dead limbs, and bending branches to allow the ladies to pass without being scratched.

Tommy took the lead, though as he listened to Eliza laughing with Meg and Anna, who were a little distance behind the men, he wished he were with her, because she was so fun. She was witty and clever, and she kept him on his toes. He'd thought he'd known her years ago, but being with her now felt different. *They* were different.

He thought of the changes she'd made in the house and chuckled, deciding that if Flaming Beard and his brigands could have seen the rose fabric now softening the dining room's walls, they'd surely have gone on a rampage. Though in a sense, the pirate *could* see the room, since his portrait was now hanging over the fireplace.

"Something amusing you?" Will asked. He was behind Tommy, with Louie at the end.

"Just imagining what Flaming Beard would have thought about the redecoration of Hellfire Hall."

"I'll admit I was disappointed that the place is so comfortable," Louie said. "I was expecting a brigand's haul of grubby furniture and nasty old mattresses."

"And you still came?"

"I was willing to surrender comfort in the interest of adventure, or at least the chance to mock your impulsive purchase relentlessly."

"If you'd come a few days earlier, you'd have gotten your wish, though the furniture wasn't filthy; Mrs. Hatch is a demon for cleanliness. But it was barren and ugly until Eliza organized a massive redecoration effort."

Behind them, the ladies stopped to admire a colorful mushroom growing amid the mashed-down grass, but the men kept going, clearing the path further.

"She must have put in a significant effort to make it pleasant," Will said. "It will be a very fine home."

"Mmm," Tommy said vaguely. Will would want to talk about the future, and Tommy didn't want to have that conversation just then. He didn't want to have it at all, but considering how responsible and thorough his brother always was, Tommy doubted he'd escape entirely. He could only hope not to be pressed into giving too many details.

"I suppose this is nothing to the wilds of India," Louie said, crushing a tangled clump of juniper with his boot. "Do you miss it?"

"I do," Tommy said. "It's often hellishly hot there, and I don't miss that so much. But the variety of nature is amazing."

"Seen any tigers?"

"Several. And snakes enough to kill an army."

Louie made a face. "I don't know that I'd miss snakes."

Tommy laughed. "Very well, I don't miss the snakes. But the way it's all so different and exciting—I miss that. England is beautiful, and I love it, too, but the colors are muted, the sights familiar."

"It's not as though you've been all over England, Tommy," Will pointed out. "You've never been to the Lake District, for one thing, nor Yorkshire, unless I'm mistaken."

"I'm sure Yorkshire is a marvel to all who love it," Tommy said, "but it hardly compares to the splendor of the Taj Mahal."

"The pleasures of England may be more subtle, but they are no less compelling."

Tommy made no reply. England was lovely, but it was tame. How could he choose that tameness over the life that had fulfilled him for the last six years? He needed excitement. Maybe it wasn't a very admirable quality, but he knew who he was.

He stepped a little to the side to push a dead branch out of the way and saw that the ladies were closer than he'd thought; they'd simply been quiet. Eliza would have heard what he'd said, but he saw by her face that his talk of preferring India didn't seem to have bothered her.

Really, being married to her wasn't going to be bad at all.

Some minutes later they finally broke through the brush and trees, coming almost suddenly to the edge of a cliff that led down to the sea. They stopped in a jumble with nervous laughter as they realized how close some of them had come to pitching right off.

"You almost lost your husband to the sea," Louie pointed out to Eliza.

"Oh well," she said, "easy come, easy go."

Louie gave a bark of laughter, but Tommy noticed that Will didn't look amused.

"How beautiful," said Meg, gazing out over the sea, which was calm and mellow gold in the afternoon sunlight.

"Isn't it?" Tommy said.

They looked at the steep, overgrown path that led to the beach below and disappeared abruptly in a thicket of gorse that clung to the sheer face of the cliff.

"A trip to the beach doesn't look quite survivable, does it?" Meg said with a hint of disappointment.

"You've got your work cut out for you to make the trail passable," Louie said. "But think of the summers you'll have, frolicking on the beach and swimming."

It did sound nice—for the future. Tommy made a noncommittal sound, and they lingered over the view a little longer, then made their way back to the manor.

❧

Eliza's and Tommy's attempt to avoid probing conversations with Anna and Will lasted until just after tea, when they were waylaid by Will, who had slyly waited for the others to seek their chambers.

"Tommy, Eliza," he said, "do give us a tour of the library."

"Really, there's not much to it," Tommy said. But it was no use, and they were swept into the library, where Anna was poking through the shelves.

"So, how is married life treating you both?" she asked. Although Anna was hardly naive, she was also clearly quite hopeful about Eliza's and Tommy's marriage, and Eliza felt an inward slide of guilt.

"Married life is fine. *Very* fine, really," Eliza said.

"Yes," Tommy said enthusiastically.

Anna glanced at Will.

"Fine, is it?" he said, and Eliza couldn't miss the skepticism in his voice. "That's good to hear of a marriage that was entered into with such haste." He crossed his arms. "We both want nothing more than to see you two happy, and you certainly seem to get along well. But we've noticed the way you shift conversations to avoid any talk of the future. Do tell us about your plans."

For once, Tommy looked uncomfortable. "We've decided it will be best if Eliza stays in England while I return to India for the time being."

Will's eyes darkened. "And how long do you expect the 'time being' to last?"

"I don't know for certain. A few years at least."

Tommy's words fell into a silence that grew more charged with each passing moment.

Finally Will said, "Eliza? How do you feel about staying in England while your husband deserts you for an indeterminate number of years?"

"I'm not deserting her!" Tommy insisted. "We've discussed the possibilities, and this is our plan."

Eliza forced herself to speak. "It's really quite all right with me. We'll see each other again before too long."

More of the awkward sort of silence Will had always employed so well. She was deathly afraid that another few minutes and she'd break and tell them everything.

"The two of you are newlyweds and you're planning a major separation?" Will said incredulously. "What about loving and honoring and cherishing? How is that supposed to happen while you're not even in the same country?"

Tommy's jaw tightened. "Will, you may not have noticed this, but Eliza and I are all grown up now, and we're not in need of guidance."

"I think you are, if this is the choice you're making. What kind of family will you have, with the two of you apart? What about any children who might come along before Tommy returns?" He gave them a stern look. "You do realize it's possible, I assume."

"Good God," Tommy growled.

Eliza forced a smile. "We would hope that you two would be in their lives, of course, if we should be so blessed." She wanted to weep with the absurdity of the conversation.

Will looked tense, but Anna put a steadying hand on his arm. "Certainly we would be part of your children's lives. But with Tommy leaving, and so soon, children seem a little beside the point. If he really must return to India, couldn't you go with him, Eliza?"

This was twisting the knife. She would have loved to go with him, to share the adventure of India together. But he'd made it clear that he didn't want her to come.

"I'd prefer to stay in England," she said, and forced herself not to say anything further even though Will fixed her with the piercing look she used to think of as his "guardian stare." It had been years since he'd acted as her guardian, but she would always value his opinion and want his respect.

"We'll be no different from many other couples with a husband in India and a wife in England," Tommy said. "Everybody has sacrifices to make."

"But any couple who cared about each other would think spending years apart an unnecessary sacrifice," Will said. "Especially as newlyweds."

"I agree," Anna said. "I don't think you two have considered this from all sides."

"What sides do you mean, Anna?" Tommy demanded.

"Well, clearly you enjoy each other's company—anyone can see that. But loneliness can cause people to make desperate choices."

She meant the temptation to seek other partners once they were separated, which Eliza and Tommy had as good as agreed to do. But Eliza knew, deep in her heart, that no other man would ever tempt her, however lonely she would be without Tommy.

"I'm sure Eliza and I will find a way to manage everything ourselves," Tommy said firmly.

❧

Later that night after all the guests had retired, Eliza was tidying up the library in between yawns and gathering up some books the children had left lying around, while Tommy sat at the desk and dashed off a quick note to his man of affairs.

She had just picked up a book called *A Lady Gets What She Desires*, which had been suspiciously tucked under a volume on architecture, when Tommy's arm slid around her waist. She jumped.

"I didn't hear you," she said.

He leaned over her shoulder and peered at what she was holding. "Doubtless because you're over here reading wicked books." He plucked it out of her hand and read the subtitle. "*In Which a Lady and Her Lovers Make Discoveries.*" He snorted. "I'll bet. And did you find this instructive?"

She blushed. So far, she'd made quite a few new discoveries with Tommy. "It must have come with that shipment I ordered from the bookseller. Anna said she happened upon Marcus and Rex looking at something they seemed keen to hide from her, and I'm guessing this was it."

He winced. "Embarrassing, though I can't manage to feel sorry for them."

"I hope we're not going to be responsible for corrupting them."

"I'd be surprised if they haven't both stolen glimpses of such things before. Rex certainly seems as though he'd love to get his hands on anything forbidden."

She sighed. "I'm afraid you're right. Has there been any sign of his aunt yet?"

"No, unfortunately." He pressed a kiss to her neck. "But my man is persistent and resourceful."

"Poor Rex—I wonder if he's terribly worried about his future. Being worried never makes anybody behave well."

"No," Tommy agreed, sounding distracted.

"Maybe..." she began, turning her head to look at him out of the corner of her eye.

"Yes?" he said suspiciously.

"It's just that Rex has had a hard time of it—"

"What with being spoiled most of his life."

"Being spoiled is no advantage if it makes a person disagreeable. It's not Rex's fault his father ignored him and his nurse was too indulgent. He was a child. He could hardly have arranged sensible care for himself."

Tommy just grunted. "Never mind about Rex— the boy will be fine. Now, what say you abandon these dusty volumes, Lady Halifax, and come upstairs and let me see to *your* desires? I promise you I can do a lot better than whatever's in that book."

He didn't want to think about Rex or make plans for the boy that would involve himself, and why should she be surprised? Tommy wanted to sail through life unencumbered. She repressed a sigh of disappointment.

He tugged her toward the door. "We have work to do."

"Work?"

"Making-a-baby work. Though I'd prefer to think of it as giving a lady what she wants."

❧

Tommy nudged Eliza inside his bedchamber and closed the door behind them.

Putting his hands on her shoulders, he guided her backwards toward the bed. He captured her mouth in a kiss that immediately sent his body temperature up several degrees, then broke it to kiss along her soft cheek as she slid her hands over his ribs.

The curtains on the window by the side of her bed were open, and as he bent his head to her neck, something caught his eye, and he leaned closer to the window.

Fire. There was a small fire in the wilds.

He cursed. "Looks like Rex is up to no good."

Eliza turned to look out the window. "Oh no," she said softly.

"Stay here," he said. "I'll be right back."

Grabbing the pitcher of water that stood by his pillow, he quickly made his way outside, trying to keep a damper on his temper. He reminded himself that this was Oliver's son. But damn it all, did he have to be such a trial?

Tommy passed into the wilds, and there the little rotter was, facing away from him and warming his hands by the light of the fire, which looked to be confined to a shrub.

"What the devil do you think you're doing?" Tommy demanded as he strode over. The boy had to have heard him, but he didn't turn around.

"Just warming my hands, Sir Tommy. These bushes are nothing but trash. Eliza said so."

"*Lady Halifax* said they were weeds," Tommy said through his teeth. My God, but the boy could test the patience of a saint, and Tommy was no saint. "No one gave you permission to come out here and burn them."

The boy shrugged, though Tommy detected a quiver in the purposefully casual movement. "The earl said the place ought to be torched. What difference does it make if I burn a few shrubs?"

"The difference," Tommy said, stepping forward and stomping out the fire, "is that they're not your shrubs, and it's bloody dangerous to set a fire back here. The whole area might catch." Having put out the flames, Tommy dumped the pitcher of water over the smoldering remains.

"I had it under control," Rex grumbled.

"You are a guest in this house, Rex Thorpe, and you'd do better to say not one more word unless it's an apology."

Silence. Tommy waited.

"I'm sorry I burned your shrub," Rex said in the least contrite voice Tommy had ever heard. If he'd been able to see the boy's expression, he felt certain it would have been disrespectful. However, he also felt he could only push Rex so far toward civility just then.

"Apology accepted. And I don't want to see or hear of any more fires. Is that understood?"

"Yes."

They returned to the manor in the silent darkness. Tommy accompanied the boy to his chamber and made sure he entered before heading for his own room.

When he opened the door to his bedchamber, Eliza was sitting on the bed reading. She'd changed into a white nightgown tied primly at the neck. Apparently she was very engrossed in her book, because she didn't look up when he came in, and he remembered what a great reader she'd been when they were younger. He used to watch her secretly.

He closed the door. "You moved."

She looked up from her book and came over to him. "What happened? I watched from the window, but all I could see was that the fire went out abruptly."

"I put it out. Rex was there, enjoying himself. It seems he felt your dislike of the weeds gave him permission to burn them."

"Oh dear."

"I think I've made him understand that there will be no more fires."

"I hope you weren't too hard on him."

"I don't think that's possible."

She bit her lip thoughtfully. "He does seem as though he needs a firm guiding hand."

Tommy thought so, too. He'd once or twice wanted to say something to Oliver about Rex's behavior, but he knew he would have been completely in the wrong. Parents didn't welcome such suggestions from other people, and what did Tommy know about being a father? Nothing.

She looked like she wanted to say more, so he took her hand and tugged her closer. "Now, where were we?"

"But—"

"No buts, please. We have work to do."

He led her to the bed and tugged her down next to him, then started pulling the pins out of her hair. She sighed, closing her eyes and abandoning herself to his attentions. With a final tug, he released her red-gold hair so it fell loose down her back.

"Good lord, but you're beautiful, Eliza."

∽∾

Eliza snuck a glance at the side of Tommy's face. He looked so handsome that it made her heart ache. His dark lashes and the strong lines of his jaw and the masculine beauty of his lips all seemed like little arrows going straight to her chest. Would their baby, if they had one, have a mouth like his? A laugh like his?

"Now, why are you wearing this gown"—he tugged the string that tied her gown at the neck—"when I need you naked?"

She chuckled softly. Until Tommy, she'd never known how much fun sensual play could be.

She slid off the bed, clutching the gown to her chest. "If you want to see what's under this, you'll have to surrender something first."

A hot light flickered in his eyes, and the corner of his mouth inched back.

She jerked her chin at him, feeling deliciously rude. "The shirt. Take it off."

He complied with satisfying haste, and she looked her fill as his movements made his muscles bunch. His ribs were broad, his abdomen flat and dusted with black hairs.

"Well?" he prompted. "It's your turn."

She let her gown slip a few inches so it just covered her nipples.

"That's no better than some of the gowns you've been wearing," he pointed out.

"Of course it is, because there's nothing under this flimsy thing. Now, unfasten your trousers."

His mouth quirked. "You're full of demands tonight."

"I am, aren't I?" She was enjoying this. Maybe it was the chance to take a little power back from him. She was more at his mercy than she would ever have wanted to be, but he didn't need to know that. "And yet, if you want to see more, you'll have to come up with something."

He held her gaze with a seductively insolent look as he unbuttoned the fastenings of his trousers. The front flap fell open. It was too dark to see anything distinct, but the candlelight hinted at what the shadows held, and the thought was hotly erotic. She let her gown slip a few inches farther, so that it stopped in the middle of her nipples.

He groaned and started to move toward her.

"No," she said. "Stay there, or I'll pull my gown up." The effort to keep her gown where it was made her press her breasts up, plumping them and pushing them together, and she could see from the anguish on his face that he'd noticed. He pulled off a stocking.

She let the gown slip below her breasts, and he sucked in a breath. His gaze unwavering, he pulled off the other stocking and she dropped the gown to her hips.

"Your shape is so lovely," he said hoarsely. "Come here and let me touch you."

"Not yet," she said lightly, though she desperately wanted his hands on her. She was enjoying having him at her mercy too much to give in yet. "You're still wearing your trousers."

Hardly had she said the words when he'd whipped them off. And there he was, naked, masculine, and beautiful. He stretched out on his side on the bed, propping his head up on his bent arm, and gave her a roguish, eager grin. Dark hair swirled on his chest and pointed lower in a vee to the promise of secret pleasures.

"Golly," she whispered. He laughed softly, a thrilling hint of menace coloring the sound.

"I'm giving you to the count of three to drop that gown and get over here, or I'm coming after you."

She let him get to "thr—" before she surrendered and let the gown fall. He whistled softly in admiration.

"Come here, Wife," he said, still propped on his elbow like an arrogant Roman emperor. She moved slowly toward the bed, conscious that she had all his attention.

She sat down, and he skimmed a hand down her back all the way to her bottom, his touch making heat break out all over her in a trail of desire.

"You have a lovely arse," he said, and pinched a

plump part. His hand moved higher, over her waist. "And curves that nearly kill me." The wicked hand roved higher still to cup her breast. "And breasts that I rejoice in knowing are mine." He rolled her nipple between his fingers, drawing a moan from her.

Mine... She was his in more ways than he knew. She gave him a seductress's dark gaze and touched her fill of the armor of taut muscle on his back and ribs, then reached lower to settle on his erection. He jerked and started to sit up, but she was bold now, a woman who knew quite a bit about men and the world, and she pushed him back against the bed and lowered her head.

"Eliza?" he croaked.

The night before, she'd finally learned what the women at the brothel had meant by "the other kind of kisses," and Tommy had left her nearly delirious. Now, she wanted to do the same thing to him. Tentatively, she brushed him with her lips. His skin there was hot and smooth, and she lingered in several interesting places along his hard length. He groaned, sounding almost as though he was in pain, and she smiled and opened her mouth and took him in.

His breathing grew ragged, and when his hand moved to rest lightly on her head, she sensed that he was restraining himself from pressing her down. He muttered her name, ground his teeth, and made incoherent sounds.

She tortured him for as long as they both could take it, then climbed astride him, deeply pleased at the thought that *she* was taking *him*.

But not for long, because he began to set the rhythm, driving up into her, working her inside. His mouth took her moans as they rode together over the crest of magnificent, timeless waves. *He* was magnificent, the one man who'd ever claimed her so deeply, and she surrendered to the moment and, secretly, to him as she collapsed against his chest. She absorbed his final thrust, and he groaned and pulled her snugly against him.

Some minutes later, he sat up and arranged the pillows comfortably behind his back. "Do you think all our hard work in bed is having any effect?" He patted her stomach.

"As you've perhaps observed, it's not as though one must accrue points through effort before achieving the goal," she said dryly.

He laughed.

She fluffed up her own pillows and flopped back against them. The arrangement struck her as quintessentially domestic, and she imagined that all over England and other parts of the world, couples in beds were sitting up next to each other in darkened rooms, talking about the day's events or plans for the future, sorting out the ways they would meet life's demands together.

What if it could always be like this? She glanced at him out of the corner of her eye. His eyes were closed, a contented smiled hovering over his lips. Might he not want such domestic bliss, too? Might he not, after all, change his mind about what their marriage meant?

No, she told herself firmly. He wouldn't. Never mind that he'd given no indication that he had any intention of staying in England—she needed only to consider how assiduously he was avoiding being guardian to Rex to accept that he sincerely wasn't interested in anything that resembled family. What he and she were doing was about play and fun and making a baby, and that was all it could be. It would have to be enough.

Fifteen

ELIZA ROLLED OVER IN BED THE NEXT MORNING TO find Tommy just coming back into the room. He'd apparently gotten up, dressed, and left without her even noticing. From the quality of the light coming in the window, it appeared that the sun had only been up for a short time.

"You're up early," she said as he came near the bed. She tried not to feel disappointed that he'd been so able to abandon her. She missed the warmth of his body next to hers. Sleeping with Tommy was so much better than sleeping with a hot brick that she already worried about how deprived she was going to feel that winter when he left.

But since she didn't want to think about any of that, she didn't. She was now Unvirtuous Eliza, and Unvirtuous Eliza made bold decisions without fussing about consequences. Unvirtuous Eliza valued pleasure and happiness and indulgence, and she only cared about right now, which was, after all, the only thing anyone had. Why had she been such a fool before?

"Just thought I'd put out a few clues for the treasure diggers," he said.

"Clues?" He sat down on the bed and began tugging off a boot.

"A couple of pirate-type maps that lead to some buried clues out in the wilds. The usual sort of treasure-hunt things."

She pulled the blanket more closely around her shoulders against the chill and watched him pull off the other boot. "The children will love that."

He shrugged. "It was nothing." He dropped his boot on the floor, and when he pulled his shirt over his head, her heart gave a happy skip.

"It wasn't nothing," she pointed out, running a hand up his bare back, which was warm and so pleasingly hard. "You had to get up early to do it. Where did you get the idea?"

He turned around and leaned over her, the muscles in his chest and shoulders bunching. "It was something my mother did to amuse me when I was a boy."

Eliza smiled, imagining him as a boy. "Will was twelve years older—did you ever wish for siblings nearer your own age?"

"Not really. I guess my mother entertained me quite a bit. She was rather playful for an adult, now that I think about it." He shrugged. "Anyway, I thought the treasure hunt might entertain the children. Will always says that 'Happy children make for happy parents,' and perhaps we'll all have a better chance of finishing a conversation—and maybe keeping Rex from getting any bad ideas—if they have something to do."

She pulled him close and kissed him. "Very sensible and considerate of you."

He grinned. "It was, wasn't it?" As he kissed her neck, she thought about how he knew quite a lot about her island childhood and how she'd come to be Will's ward, but she knew very little of his early life. He'd never talked about it, even when they were younger.

She pulled him onto the pillow next to her. "What was your father like?"

His eyebrows lifted. "Why do you want to know?"

"Because I don't know anything about him, or your mother, really. You never talk about them."

He sucked his teeth. "That's probably because they died years ago."

So bluntly said. But she knew he'd been young when he'd lost them. "I've always had a sense that there was a great deal of love in your family in the years before your mother died."

He rolled onto his back and crossed his arms. "I had a very happy boyhood. My mother died when I was seven, my father when I was fourteen. I loved them both and have always felt lucky to have had them as parents."

"And yet, when I ask you about them, you cross your arms and stare at the ceiling."

He rolled his head on the pillow and looked at her. "Why are you quizzing me about this, and so early in the day?" He smiled, the corners of his eyes wrinkling and making him look so carefree and happy that she questioned her feeling that a shadow had come over him a moment ago. He rolled onto his side. "And when I've come back to bed specifically to ravish you."

He didn't give her a chance to reply, but applied himself so adeptly to ravishing her that she forgot about noticing anything but his body and his devilish charms.

❧

"I congratulate you on how civil you're being to Louie," Eliza leaned close to whisper to Meg two nights later as another lovely dinner drew to an end. Eliza and Tommy had invited the local doctor and his wife to join them for the evening, along with the Smythes, a neighboring family who had two daughters and a son of marriageable age. With dinner over, people were getting up to adjourn to the drawing room for dancing.

Meg gave her a look. "I hardly want to be a damper on the party."

Eliza glanced toward where Louie and Will stood talking with Dr. Hall, the Smythes' handsome son Adam, and Ruby. "I know you wouldn't do that." Which didn't mean she thought Meg was above giving Louie discreet looks of disgust, though Eliza didn't think she'd done so that night. "But really, Louie looked quite content to be sitting next to you. I'm sure I saw him smiling at you."

"Gildenhall smiles at everyone." This was just the sort of thing Eliza would expect Meg to say about Louie, but something about her demeanor looked different, and Eliza peered more closely at her friend. Good heavens, was Meg *blushing*? Calm, collected, in-control Meg, blushing at the mention of the most roguish rogue in the *ton*?

"You can remove that matchmaking gleam from your eyes, Eliza Halifax," Meg hissed. "I'm merely being civil to him, as you urged me to do. You know I have always barely tolerated him."

"True," Eliza said. Though it was possible that Meg might be persuaded to change her mind, because Eliza knew Louie could be very persuasive if he wished. Perhaps, with the proximity forced by the house party, something was developing. And if that *was* happening, Eliza certainly didn't want to interfere, because she found the idea of them together extremely interesting.

An arm curled possessively around her waist as Tommy caught up to them. "The waltz is mine," he said. "Don't even think about dancing it with Louie or that overly handsome Smythe boy."

"He's not a boy," Eliza pointed out, then laughed at the dark look coming over Tommy's face. "But he's not swashbuckling."

"Darned right," he said smugly.

Tommy needn't have worried about Louie dancing the waltz with her, Eliza noticed with a hidden smile as she twirled around the room a little later in his arms. Louie danced it with Meg.

Blissful days passed. With their friends and family around them, Eliza felt that the time was touched with a golden glow. The crisp, bright autumn days were spent exploring the countryside, hiking about all day and eating enormous meals when they got home. Nights they spent lingering at the dinner table with glasses of wine, then sitting around the drawing room fire afterward, talking and laughing. Eliza knew she wasn't the only one who felt that it was a fine thing to have the family all together. She'd caught Tommy's eyes lingering affectionately on his family many times.

And each night, she and Tommy made love.

Life with him felt like being a happily married couple—if she ignored the fact that, though she'd come to care deeply for him, she didn't know how he felt, or whether he might change his mind and stay. They simply lived in the moment and didn't talk about the future, which suited Eliza, because she didn't want to think about going back to the life she'd known in London without the purpose Truehart Manor had provided.

The children continued in their quest for treasure, having formed into two teams equally determined to strike pirate gold. Though Marcus and Rex both maintained a careless attitude, as though they were partaking because there was absolutely nothing else to do, they still applied themselves with competitive intensity to digging the deepest holes as fast as possible.

Rex seemed to have understood at least the virtue of not biting the hand that fed him, because he had not said or done anything terribly rude. Eliza had invited him to go walking with her on several afternoons, and she'd found him to be charmingly curious about nature, even if he hid his interest around the other children.

He seemed pleased each time she invited him, standing up a little straighter as though aware of special favor being bestowed. Though he also tended to talk almost entirely about himself. But he was young, and surely with guidance, he would grow to consider others more. If, that was, there would be someone appropriate in his life to guide him.

Eliza and Meg were watching the children's digging efforts one afternoon as they sat on the terrace with mugs of hot cocoa, wrapped in blankets against the chill of the autumn afternoon. The trees had changed into brilliant reds and golds and soft yellows, and the remains of a misty morning were finally burning off in the warmth of the sun.

In the near distance, Marcus, Susanna, and Vic were at work on a new hole whose location Marcus had determined by measuring off a precise number of paces from a nearby juniper bush. Rex and Heck were equally busy at the north end of the wilds, having paced themselves off as well using their own map.

"They don't seem to find it odd that both groups found treasure maps, both of which purport to lead them to the location of some buried treasure," Meg observed.

Eliza smiled. "Heck and Vic don't know enough to question it, and the older children probably think it's a lark. But I did overhear Marcus asking Tommy about what kinds of booty Flaming Beard might have been likely to have. And I'm sure that after what they all had to go through to get the maps, they want to believe they're real."

"It was brilliant of Tommy to hide them in the dungeon and drop hints at separate times to each group about how the pirates probably spent a lot of time down there."

"It was," Eliza agreed, then shuddered. "The

dungeon is horrible. I merely peeked down there once when I first toured the manor, and I saw a spider the size of my hand."

Eliza could feel Meg's eyes on her. "Tommy seems like a man who would really enjoy fatherhood."

"I know." Tommy might say he didn't like children, but he was wrong. She'd seen the sort of playful, thoughtful, good father he might be. But each time she was tempted to spin fantasies about the future, she reminded herself that arranging things for children to play with wasn't the same as committing to be a part of their lives day in and day out. Children needed guidance and got sick and grew into people their parents sometimes didn't understand. Eliza was ready to say yes to all of that, but Tommy wasn't.

"He's pretty irresistible," Meg said.

"He's a charmer." It would be so much easier if he weren't.

"He's more than that," Meg insisted. "He's smart and thoughtful and good-hearted. And let's not forget swashbuckling."

As if Eliza needed Meg to point that out. "I know."

"I suppose it's too early to know whether you're increasing?"

Eliza nodded. Whenever she allowed herself to think that she might already be carrying Tommy's baby, she got so dreamy that she could hardly pay attention to anything, so she didn't allow herself to daydream much. She'd just remind herself that Unvirtuous Eliza didn't worry about the future.

Meg slid a sideways glance at her. "Don't you

think he might change his mind, if there was a baby? Everything's different now."

Eliza sighed. "If he stayed, it would have to be because he wanted to stay. Even if there is a baby, I've assured him that I will be fine raising him or her on my own. I don't want him to feel trapped."

Meg stared at her uncomprehendingly. "But you care for him—perhaps more than you want to admit. Wouldn't it hurt to know that he wouldn't be sharing a child with you, the way Will and Anna do?"

Eliza could feel her throat begin to tighten and fought against it. "Yes. But I'm trying not to think about it."

Meg leaned closer, so that her shoulder brushed Eliza's. "I'm sorry," she said gently. "I'd been thinking for a while that you weren't really happy at Truehart Manor. The brothel incident put you in a difficult situation, but you're making the best of it, and there's an awful lot to respect in that."

"Thank you," Eliza said quietly. "But I wish I hadn't made such a mess of things at Truehart Manor."

"Helping the girls was a more complicated undertaking than we'd realized. We both made mistakes, but we meant well."

"I made far more mistakes than you did," Eliza said.

"You have to stop looking at it that way."

"I still want to help girls like the ones we were helping."

"Then you'll figure something out."

Eliza felt touched by Meg's faith in her, even if she didn't see how to make something out of the future. Which was why she wasn't going to think about the future—or at least not until after Tommy left.

But it was getting harder to tell herself she didn't care for him.

Eliza and Meg watched as Marcus and Rex began to dig faster, clearly showing off for Susanna. Though the two boys seemed to have become fast friends, Eliza supposed it was a good thing the house party wasn't going to go on for too much longer, or there might be trouble.

"So," she said, "is there something going on between you and Louie?"

When Meg didn't reply right away, Eliza looked at her. Did Meg's face look pink?

"Something between me and Gildenhall?" Meg laughed, and it *sounded* genuine. "Why should there be?"

"I don't know. But when you were dancing together the other night, you looked happy."

"It was just the wine."

"I see," Eliza said. Though Meg seemed emphatic, Eliza wasn't entirely convinced.

Meg excused herself a few minutes later to see to some correspondence, but Eliza stayed outside. The air was growing almost cold, but it was quiet in the wilds now because Vic and Heck had been led, protesting, inside for naps, and the older children had gone off to look for balls with which to bowl.

Eliza was fairly certain that Will and Anna were "napping" while their children napped. Louie and Ruby had announced after lunch that they were going into the nearby town and hadn't been seen since. Eliza loved the cheery clamor and bustle of all those people under her roof, and she knew she'd miss them terribly when the party came to an end in a few days, but she needed a little space to think.

Her roof. Hellfire Hall, despite its work-in-progress state, was a place she now yearned to call home. Fantasies of a little one wandering about in the wilds while she trailed behind had been teasing the edge of her intention to ignore the future and making it harder to be as carefree as she kept telling herself to be.

She wanted to share a baby with Tommy, to be a happy family together. Maybe, in some corner of her mind, she'd thought that once Tommy and she made love, he would come to care for her deeply enough that he wouldn't want to leave. But Meg's words were pushing her to be honest with herself, and she had to acknowledge that nothing Tommy had said or done had led her to believe he would change his mind and stay.

"Is there any tea for the master of the house?" Tommy said, startling her out of her thoughts.

"I didn't see you come out," Eliza said, glancing up. With the breeze teasing his black hair, he looked very handsome. "You can have some of the children's tea, though it's been sitting here for a bit."

He poured himself some tea and sat down next to her on the bench, close enough that she could feel the warmth of his leg beside hers. They both looked across the lumpy ground toward the area in the distance the children had taken over for their ridiculous game of bowling. The balls couldn't possibly roll straight, but that was probably a large part of the fun.

Tommy sipped his tea and made a face. "They won't want this now. It's nearly cold. Anyway, it looks as though they're quite taken up with one another."

He plucked one of the iced tea cakes off the plate and popped the whole thing in his mouth, followed in quick succession by several more.

"The children all love the treasure hunt you arranged."

When he just nodded absentmindedly, she said, "You're good with children."

He shrugged. "Perhaps it's just that I'm still a boy at heart."

She thought about that, and about how he loved adventure and had resisted settling down. Maybe there was something in this—but what did it matter? She couldn't change who he was and what he wanted. But she also couldn't seem to abandon the topic.

"I'm getting used to having Rex around," she said. "Will the theatrical aunt be a good guardian for him, do you think?"

"Why shouldn't she be? Or do you have something against theater people?"

"Of course not. It's just that we don't know her, and he doesn't either. She might be odd or something."

"Will it really matter that much if his aunt is odd?"

"How can you ask that? You, who had such a wonderful family? How would you feel if there had been no Will and Anna and Judith in your life? Or you'd never known your parents, whom you clearly loved?"

Something flickered in his eyes but was quickly extinguished. He crossed his arms. "Maybe you should admit that you can't be reasonable on the subject of orphaned children because of the way you were sent away from home and then lost your family. And you didn't like that school you were sent to, as I remember."

"None of that has anything to do with Rex."

He cocked his head. "Doesn't it? Your father remarried, then sent you away soon after. You must have felt there was some connection between the two events."

"Of course there was. I took his remarriage hard and behaved badly, making myself into a spectacle with the sailors in the port. Sending me away was the most sensible thing he could have done."

"But not the most sensi*tive*," Tommy said quietly. He softly brushed her cheek with his thumb. "Poor Eliza. You've taken all the trouble of that time onto yourself, haven't you? As though it was your fault that the father you'd adored became distracted by a new wife."

His words were seductive, but she knew better than to let herself slide into the ease they offered. "I behaved like a trollop," she said, needing to speak the truth of what had happened. "I was childish and selfish, and my behavior threatened his livelihood. How could he have trusted me not to do something truly scandalous?"

"He could have talked to you. Did he?"

She shrugged. "I don't think either of us was in a state for talking then."

"But you must have been close, after all those years when it was just the two of you. I was too young to know your father, of course, but Will always spoke of him as being a good-hearted man who'd been something of a scandal himself when he was young. Your father would surely have understood you."

A lump was growing in Eliza's throat. How

different would her life have been if, when her father had married Marian, he'd made sure that Eliza knew he still loved her and always would? If he'd made time to do special things with her, instead of giving every moment to his new wife?

She shrugged again. "I don't know. Maybe he didn't love me after all, or maybe he just didn't love me after I stopped being a little girl." She said the words carelessly, though they tore at an old wound. "I can't blame him. He was a vicar, and I couldn't stop myself from causing scandals that threatened his job."

"Because you didn't know what else to do. And at least your behavior got his attention."

"Until it got me sent away."

"And you never got to say all the things you needed to say to him."

She looked away, wishing he hadn't probed her about this. "Who knows if it would have mattered?"

"But perhaps it would have. For one thing, maybe you wouldn't have felt that a few mistakes meant you had to make yourself into the Queen of Virtue. Your father was a man of God. He can't possibly have meant you to go through life thinking you had to *earn* love."

His words shook her. Was that what she'd been doing? What he'd said touched close to a place that felt vulnerable. But she couldn't let him see that.

"Maybe," she said, forcing a light tone. "It's certainly benefitting you that I've abandoned virtue."

He grinned.

In the distance, Susanna laughed, a tinkling sound. "What a minx," Eliza said with a sigh. "I'm afraid poor Rex is already succumbing to her careless wiles."

"Why 'poor Rex'?"

"Because he's got Marcus the earl's son for competition."

"Hmm," Tommy said, not sounding particularly concerned.

Eliza looked at him. "Aren't you concerned he'll get his feelings hurt?"

"Not particularly. He's thirteen. All he knows of the world is what he's learning right now, which includes attraction, rejection, and perseverance. And," he said, finishing his cold tea in one giant gulp and standing up, "what really concerns me is our project."

She looked up at him from her seat on the bench, and her heart thudded at the spark glittering in his green eyes. "Our project?"

He took her hand and pulled her upright and bent his head close to hers. "The offspring project," he said. "How are we going to make any progress with all these uninvited guests around?"

"It was *your* brother who invited them all."

"True," he said, and bent closer still to nuzzle her neck.

"Tommy!" she whispered sharply even as tendrils of desire curled through her body. "Someone will see. Think of the children right there on the lawn."

"The 'children' are probably thinking about stealing kisses too. At least, the male ones are. And look, they're going inside now anyway."

He tugged her off the terrace and across the lawn toward the summerhouse. The ground was muddy and leaf-strewn, and she was wearing a pretty pair of cherry-colored satin slippers that matched her cherry silk gown.

The gleam in his eyes told her exactly where his thoughts were going, and already she felt fluttery. He was so irresistible, but now she was beginning to doubt the wisdom of what she'd set in motion with the baby plan. She made an effort to resist him. "My shoes are getting filthy, never mind that it's chilly and the sun's going down. We need to go back inside."

His only reply was to bend down, put a hand behind her knees, and sweep her into his arms, hardly breaking stride at all. She squeaked. "What if someone's looking out the window?"

"They'll think I must be a considerate husband who's trying to keep his wife's shoes clean."

She surrendered. Really, how was she supposed to resist him if she loved nothing better than surrendering to him?

They drew closer to the little stone summerhouse, whose trim had but a few flecks of whitewash left after years of rain and sun. Only two of the windows retained their panes.

"I had one of the footmen clear out the spiderwebs and pirate debris, which was mostly boxes full of empty rum bottles," Tommy said. "Rather predictable of our brigands, though apparently there were also two crates of books, much of it poetry."

"Really?" Eliza said. "Poetry? I'll wager it went well with the rum. I quite like the idea of a group of rough men sitting around in small groups, reading sonnets to each other."

"I'm sure that's not what went on, but if it makes

you happy to dream up such scenes, go right ahead. Though I think they were probably just using the books for kindling."

He pushed against the door with his shoulder, and it emitted a loud groan as it swung inward. He carried her inside and kicked the door closed.

In the fading sunlight, the summerhouse was chilly and shadowy, but not dusty thanks to Tommy's forethought, though a few leaves had obviously blown in after the cleaning. "It's freezing in here," she said.

"Well, yes," he agreed, walking over to a wooden bench with an angled back over which had been slung a thick red blanket.

"Your bower," he said, depositing her carefully on the bench.

"My bower is in a disgracefully neglected state." She pulled the blanket around herself, which made her feel instantly warmer and rather like a queen. "Which isn't to say that I don't like it. It seems like the sort of place someone would write a story about. Maybe a neglected little girl used to come here. I'm imagining a time before the pirates came, when a girl came here with her faithful hound. As a girl, I always wanted a dog, but I never had one. I think I felt that dogs made everything better."

He knelt down and pressed his lips against her collarbone, and his hot mouth lingered there while his palm made dizzying circles over her nipple that kindled warmth low in her belly.

"I'm sure Traveler would agree," he murmured. "Fortunately, he slunk in to nap with Vic, so we won't have to worry about him coming to look for us."

Eliza began undoing the buttons on Tommy's dark blue tailcoat. When it gaped open, she pulled it off him and laid it neatly across the back of the bench, where it was safe from leaf bits.

"I've been looking at you all day in that dress," he said, "and thinking about touching what's under it." He put his hands on the hem and pushed the dark pink fabric upward, sliding his hands over her stockings.

She drew his shirt out of his breeches and pulled it over his head.

"It *is* a bit cold in here," he pointed out.

"You'll warm up." Being with Tommy had given her a kind of confidence she'd never known before. Maybe that was because she knew he liked being with her, and that while he clearly found her attractive, his enjoyment of her was built on more than her beauty. They had a foundation of friendship.

She ran her hands over his bare chest, stealing the warmth of his skin even as the two of them generated more. The taut muscles of his abdomen twitched as her teasing touch crept downward. She leaned in to kiss his neck, but when she lifted her head, he captured her mouth in a demanding kiss.

"I'm dying to touch you," he murmured against her mouth.

"You'll live," she said, even though she was dying for him to touch her too.

His hard length jutted against the fabric of his breeches, and she leaned closer to slip a hand between them and rub him through the fabric. He groaned and pressed into her hand, his breathing thick with desire.

She moved her hand to the waist of his breeches

and loosened the fastenings, then pulled the opening wide. A little sound escaped her at the sight of him.

He laughed. "It's not like you two haven't met before."

"Each time I forget a little what you're like. However, there's a lot to be said for not being a tender virgin lady any more," she said, and wrapped her hand around him. He sucked in a breath as her palm swirled around the tip.

He caught her hands and lifted them away. "My turn," he growled. "No arguments."

"If you say so." The thrill of anticipation ran through her.

He urged her legs wider apart so he could move between them, still kneeling. But he was tall, so his head was nearly at her height. Reaching both arms behind her, he began working on the little hooks that held her dress together. In what seemed like seconds he had her gown loose enough that he could slide his large, warm hands down her back, heating her skin against the cold air and making her shiver at the same time.

He pushed her gown off her shoulders and gathered her breasts in his hands, then buried his face against them.

"Eliza," he said hoarsely. "I wish we didn't have guests. I wouldn't waste a minute not being with you. Not touching you."

If he only knew how she treasured every second with him.

He kissed down her breast, taking her nipple in his mouth and nipping her, making her need him more each moment. He gathered the pile of her skirts up and pushed them along her thighs toward her hips. "I want to pleasure you every way I can, everywhere I can."

He dipped his head lower, and she realized what he was going to do, *outside*.

"Wait—" she said, shyness overcoming her.

"Certainly not," he said gruffly.

Ignoring her squirming, he kissed attentively up each inner thigh, until she was shuddering. And then he was at the soft heart of her. When he kissed her there, she nearly wept.

"Tommy," she moaned as his tongue found all her most sensitive parts. He knew her, knew what would please her, knew when to push her. She would never find a man she cared for as much, she thought almost angrily, even as she rode the waves of hot desire.

Then he took his mouth away, and she nearly cried out from dismay until she saw that he was tugging himself free of his trousers.

He leaned back against the floor. "Come here."

She dragged her skirts up and climbed across his legs to straddle him. When she sank down onto him, she nearly expired with pleasure. He filled his hands with her breasts.

A stiff, chilly breeze blew through the place, bringing out goose bumps on the bare parts of their heated skin and whirling leaves past them forcefully, adding to the wildness of their mating.

She clenched around him as her own passion built, not holding anything back. Together they cried out their release, burying their faces against each other's necks to muffle the sound in the quiet little house.

He held her as she lay across him, still warm from their lovemaking, but it wasn't long before the cold made itself fully felt. She sat back on her heels and put her dress to rights while he buttoned his breeches.

"It's such hard work, this baby-making," he said, dropping a kiss on her forehead.

As they walked back across the wilds in the near-dark, the manor now lit up cozily before them with the glow of many candles, she finally forced herself to stop avoiding what she hadn't want to acknowledge: she loved him.

What they'd just done had felt beautiful and meaningful to her as nothing else could. What she felt for Tommy was the profound connection she'd been missing for what seemed like her entire life. And that was because he was so infinitely special to her. Because she loved him.

She glanced at him, wondering if his face might hint that he felt anything similar, that their lovemaking might have meant as much to him as it had to her. But his expression was unreadable.

Could he be thinking of changing his mind? She didn't feel she could ask. She didn't *want* to ask. But she needed to know.

She didn't have to say anything, though, because his next words answered her unspoken question.

"I'm going to miss having you around when I go," he said.

Not, she noticed, "I'm going to miss *you*."

Having her around entertained him, but that was all. She absorbed it like a blow.

She knew he cared for her—that he cared about her

needs and what happened to her. He certainly wanted her body, and he obviously enjoyed her company. But that wasn't enough for her. There was nothing deeper for him where she was concerned, and he didn't want there to be. His heart was set on grander things, on the world beyond the domestic. She would never be enough for him.

So he was still going to leave, and alone. Pride helped her force out a light reply.

"I'll send you a letter now and again, and kiss the paper before I put it in the envelope."

He chuckled, which wasn't the response her foolish heart so desperately craved, but she knew how things had to be.

If only she could make all the feelings she had for Tommy disappear. Then she truly wouldn't care what the future brought. But pretending all this time that she didn't care had been a fool's game.

She reminded herself that she was the one who'd proposed the baby plan, so it was wrong of her to feel unhappy now that it wasn't anything more than fun to him. The more she tried to push down her unwanted feelings, though, the more fiercely they seemed to rise up. Maybe that was because love was supposed to be a happy, bubbling-up feeling, but loving Tommy wasn't making her happy.

The baby plan had seemed like such a good idea. The playfulness and pleasure they'd shared had been irresistible, and her own desire for a baby was so strong that it had been easy for her to throw caution to the wind. But she hadn't been honest with herself when she'd made that proposal. Even then, she'd been falling for him, and the intimacy they'd shared had only pulled her deeper.

Now she could see how much getting closer to Tommy was going to cost her when they parted. Tommy was about keeping things light and moving on to the next adventure. Hadn't he disappeared for six years without a backward glance? He was very good at fun, but committing himself? No.

Dear God, she hadn't been trying to *earn* his love all this time, had she?

Had she somehow thought that giving herself to him would make him want her in a forever way, just as she'd once tried to earn love through beauty and flirting, and then by striving to be virtuous? The thought sickened her, but she didn't shy away from the truth of it.

When she discovered later that day that her courses had arrived, she knew it was time to take steps to protect her heart.

Sixteen

"DID IT REALLY HAVE TO BE THIS EARLY?" WILL ASKED the next morning as he and Tommy strode over the wilds toward the sagging gardener's shed that stood at the east side of the property. He was carrying a lantern against the early dawn darkness. "I left a warm woman to come out here and see my breath."

Tommy shifted the largish chest he was carrying to get a better grip on it. The thing was heavier than he would have thought it would be. He'd found it in the cellar and knew it would make an ideal treasure chest. "This kind of thing keeps you from going soft as you age. Besides, if we did this much later, the youth would be up and they'd certainly see us, even if they never left the breakfast room."

"I'll give you that," Will said. "Children have a way of finding out secrets. So, have you heard anything from Rex's aunt yet?"

"Still nothing, though my man thought he would catch up with the troupe shortly."

"Rex isn't the most agreeable of boys," Will said, "but he's been good to Heck and Vic. They've already begun wishing that we didn't have to leave in three days. No amount of reminding them how good it will be to return to their own home at Stillwell will convince them that leaving Hellfire Hall will be anything short of a tragedy."

They reached the garden shed. The door to the ancient structure was warped, and Tommy had to give it a ferocious jerk before it finally moved, scraping the ground and whining on its rusty hinges. A thick, musty cloud of dust wafted out.

"I hope that's not the powdered remains of a decomposing pirate," Tommy said.

Will waved at the air to clear it and went in first, the light from the door providing the only illumination in the shadowy space.

"If this place collapses on me," Will said, "tell Anna that Heck must go to Eton when the time's right and Vic should be educated in Latin, Greek, and maths."

Tommy laughed. "Since I'm right behind you, they'll be digging both our bodies out at the same time and scratching their heads over what the devil we were doing here at the crack of dawn. So at least we can perish knowing we left them guessing."

Will tripped over a wheelbarrow that had been left upside down on the floor. "Good lord, did the brigands just open the door and fling things in here?"

"Probably," Tommy said. "I can't imagine them caring about tidiness or hiring a gardener. Ah"—he bent over a pile of tools—"we're in luck." He grabbed two pickaxes. "These should make short work of that packed dirt."

They made their way out of the shed, collecting

the shovels the children had left outside, and Will followed Tommy to a spot he'd chosen. "Just what is this treasure we're burying anyway?" Will said.

"Some interesting things I found around the house."

"The children have been working hard. I hope they manage to find the treasure before we have to leave."

"They should. They're making steady progress through the map clues." Though Tommy didn't want to think about it, he was going to miss them all when they went.

"This treasure-hunt business has kept Heck and Vic more entertained than anything has in months," Will said. "Having them so happily occupied has left me and Anna more time for…other pursuits."

"I'm glad for you, but don't tell me any more," Tommy said, shuddering a bit. "Anna is a mother—and my sister-in-law."

"Motherhood isn't the end of sensual things for a woman, you know."

"Shh!" Tommy insisted. "Not one more word."

Will chuckled.

The treasure spot located, they put the lantern on the ground and got down to work. The dirt was truly packed, and they toiled in silence for several minutes, the morning quiet except for the thunks they were making.

Will grunted as he slammed his pickax into the ground. "Remind me why you didn't have the footmen do this while we distracted the children."

"Because if I asked the footmen, there would be the danger of the truth leaking out."

"You're certainly taking this treasure hunt seriously.

We must be approaching the level of cloak-and-daggering of your work in India."

Tommy snorted. "Almost."

When they'd finally managed to loosen the ground, they switched to the shovels the children had been using.

"So," Will said, "what are you doing?"

"Digging a hole," Tommy said.

He could feel the disgusted look his brother shot him in the shadowy light. "I *mean* what are you doing with Eliza?"

Tommy gave an inward sigh. After the initial conversation with Will and Anna, neither of them had said anything else on the subject to him or Eliza, and he'd thought that perhaps they'd accepted what he and Eliza had said. But he should have known better.

"We're a pair of newlyweds who are playing host to a collection of house guests. I'd say we're doing quite well."

Will slung a shovel full of dirt to the side. "You *are* doing quite well. That's my point. And only a blind man could fail to notice the smoking looks that pass between you."

"And there's a problem with that? Isn't it to be hoped that spouses will like each other?"

"The problem," Will said, sounding as though his teeth were clenched, "is that you have a splendid woman as a wife, and you're planning to abandon her for who knows how long so that you can make a dangerous voyage to a dangerous country. All for the sake of adventure."

"Thanks," Tommy said, slamming his shovel into

the earth. "Thanks for reducing my work to a frivolous entertainment."

Will expelled a breath and stood up. The first streaks of dawn were beginning to show on the horizon, threading the darkness with gray light. "I'm very proud of what you've accomplished in India, as should you be. But doesn't there come a time to put our own quest for glory aside and put more of our energies into the people in our lives?"

Tommy leaned on his shovel. "Marriage has worked out well for you. You and Anna are very lucky."

"It's not just luck, you know. There's a great deal of work involved in making a marriage work." Will paused. "Does your distrust of marriage have anything to do with what happened between Father and Mother, and how he had the affair with Judith?"

Tommy turned to thrust his shovel in the dirt again. "I'm not a child, Will. I know that people make mistakes." It was, he thought, what they mostly seemed to do.

And how could he trust himself not to stumble? His own deeply moral father had done so. Mistakes had costs, and life offered the greatest suffering to people who were attached to others.

He thrust his shovel into the dirt to avoid looking at his brother. The light was growing, and he could easily guess that Will's face held an expression he didn't want to see. "Just because it's all worked out neatly for you," he said, "doesn't mean I want to do things the same way."

"You forfeited the right to decide what to do for yourself when you married Eliza. It's your responsibility to consider what will be best for her as well, just as she must care about what happens to you."

Tommy did care about Eliza. More than made him comfortable, actually, because he was finding himself a little addicted to her—to the pleasure of their stolen moments, but also to the sound of her laughter and her warmth. She had a way of making him feel happy, even though he saw the feeling for what it was: a fool's trap.

He was clear-eyed, just as she'd been when she'd proposed her plan, and they both knew this would all shortly come to an end. If he sometimes found himself wishing to prolong their time together, he pushed the feelings away, knowing they would only lead to bad choices.

"I care about what happens to her, Will. Quite a bit actually, not that that's anyone's affair but mine and hers. I just haven't worked out all the details yet."

"You're leaving for India in a few weeks, unless you've changed your mind."

The sound of a twig snapping drew their attention toward the direction of the house. Apparently they'd been too busy arguing to register the arrival of Eliza. She was standing there with a small tray that held two glasses of what looked like lemonade.

"Er," she said. "I'm afraid I've been eavesdropping a little. Accidentally. But—"

"You don't have to explain anything," Will said tersely. "This is between Tommy and me."

"How could it possibly be between you two when you're talking about my marriage?" she asked.

"Because he's my brother and I think he's completely

wrong for wanting to leave." Will turned to him.
"You're very good at fun and adventure, Tommy. But
there's a hell of a lot more to life."

"I know that," Tommy said through clenched
teeth. Hadn't he buried more friends than his brother,
thanks to the dangers of India? Hadn't he lost his
parents while he was still growing? If he'd learned that
it was better to choose to be happy than to let darkness
take him, how dare Will criticize him?

"What happened between me and Tommy—it's
not what you think," Eliza said. She glanced at
Tommy, but he gave her nothing. Couldn't she see it
was better not to talk about this? "Tommy felt he had
to marry me."

"*What?*" Will's face darkened instantly.

"Eliza," Tommy said, warning in his voice, "this
isn't necessary."

"Yes, it is," she insisted. "I won't have Will thinking badly of you when I'm the one at fault." She
turned to Will. "I was at a brothel called Madame
Persaud's," she began.

"You were *where*?"

And then she told him everything, leaving out
the details but giving him a true picture of what had
happened even as Will's face darkened. "A few weeks
later, I realized I was increasing."

Will's eyebrows shot up. "Eliza? You're going to
have a baby?" he said, a note of joy exploding in his
voice. That joy tugged at Tommy, trying to seduce
him into being happy that she might now be increasing again, even though he knew he wouldn't be in
England for a baby.

"I lost the baby right after we married."

There was silence as Will took in everything that had been said.

But Will's initial joy had done something to Tommy, and now he found himself pushing away images of Eliza big with the child they might already have made anew, of his baby sleeping at her shoulder while he watched the two of them.

He couldn't allow himself to be trapped by the idea that such a future would work out with happy tidiness, though. Life wasn't tidy, and you couldn't trust it not to take away everything you wanted.

And yet, if there was a baby after all, Eliza would be happy. His own life in India would be filled with difficulties and hardships, but at least she would be in England, secure and happy with their baby, and…he liked that idea. Making love to her had been amazing, but through it all, he'd never thought once about what it might be like if she really had a baby. Of how, actually, he would really like to think of Eliza and a baby waiting for him in England.

Will turned to Tommy. "You had intimate relations with her at that brothel," he ground out, "and you two were barely speaking to each other afterward, weren't you?"

"The minute I knew who she was," Tommy said tightly, "I insisted she let me know if there were any consequences. And as soon as she told me she was increasing, I insisted we marry."

But Will wasn't interested in Tommy's sacrifice. "The best you could do when you found out who she was that night at the brothel was to say, 'Let me know if there's a problem'? What about going to visit her? What about getting to know her again as the person she is now?"

Tommy's face turned darker. "Don't," he said through clenched teeth.

"Or was that too much to ask because what you two had done was a complication you didn't want in your carefree bachelor existence?"

"That's enough!" Tommy said, his fists clenching.

But Will wasn't done. "I don't think it is, considering the way you're approaching your marriage."

"Stop!" Eliza said. "*Please* stop, both of you." She turned to Will. "I only told you what happened because I want you to stop pressing Tommy to stay. He was the one who insisted we marry once I knew I was expecting. I had been determined to raise the child on my own."

Will groaned. "That would never have worked."

"I know that now. But Tommy's behaved quite well, and I won't have you maligning him." Something warm poured over Tommy's heart at her selfless words, but he couldn't afford to think about what it might be. "He and I have an understanding between us. And we're the only people who need to agree about what goes on in our marriage."

Will pressed his mouth into a grim line. Tommy looked away.

"Very well," Will said. "I will say no more to either of you, save this: you have a chance at happiness together. Don't squander it."

There followed a heavy silence that no one seemed inclined to break, until Tommy finally said, "Is that lemonade?"

"Yes," Eliza said with what sounded like relief, and handed them each a glass. "Are you almost done here? The children will be awake soon."

Tommy downed half the glass of lemonade in one swallow, grateful for the mundane actions that would put the awkwardness behind them.

She insisted she could do a better job than they could at making the treasure sight look undisturbed, and by the time the three of them were done a little later, the ground looked no different than the surrounding area.

❧

Eliza and Tommy stopped by the shed to put the tools away while Will continued on toward the manor.

"You didn't have to do that," he said, closing the door behind them once the tools were stowed. "Telling Will. I can manage my brother."

"I know that," she said. "But it's better this way."

He just grunted. "Why didn't you come to my room last night? I stopped by your bedchamber when Louie and I finished with cards and knocked, but there was no answer."

She'd heard his soft knock and heard him call her name quietly, but she'd pretended to be asleep. She'd come to a decision after their time in the summerhouse, and the conversation she and Tommy and Will had just had only made her more certain that her best hope for her future lay in making choices that had nothing to do with trying to earn anyone's love. She'd swung wildly between being a scandal and being a prude, but maybe now she was finally learning the value of a middle path.

"I must have been asleep." She cleared her throat. "But we need to talk." Her heart twisted, and she wished she wasn't going to have to deny herself what she so desperately wanted, but she'd accepted now that she'd never have the future she wanted with him.

"Certainly," he said, stopping. He reached around her waist and pulled her close, brushing his cheek against hers before she could force herself to resist. His skin was prickly with unshaved whiskers that promised shivers she wanted so badly. "Right after we do a few other things. Come up to my room."

"I can't."

He chuckled, nuzzling her neck. "Don't be such a conscientious hostess. You can sneak up to my room for a few minutes."

"It's not that. I've changed my mind."

"About?"

"Trying for a baby."

He said nothing at first, just lifted his head and looked down at her. "You've changed your mind about wanting a baby?"

She swallowed a lump and nodded.

"How can you say you don't want a baby anymore?" he said in a low voice. "You said it was what you most wanted."

"I do want a baby, but not this way," she said, wishing her voice wasn't succumbing to huskiness.

"*What* way then? There is, as far as I know, only one way to create a baby."

Her hands pulled into fists at her side. "With me being the only one who really wants the baby. Why are you making this so hard? You don't want a baby.

It was *my* idea, *my* choice for the future awaiting me. For you it was just fun to oblige me."

His black eyebrows drew into slashes over green eyes that glittered with hard lights. "It was fun for you, too. Don't try to act as though you didn't like it."

"Of course I liked it!" she said angrily. "But I didn't realize what I was getting myself into. And now I've gotten my courses, and that means a clean slate. I don't want to try anymore. That's it. End of conversation."

She started to walk again, but she hadn't taken a step before he grabbed her arm and tugged her back to face him.

"You can't just decide that. There are two of us in this marriage, in case you've forgotten. And I haven't agreed to anything you've said."

"Are you saying you mean to exercise your marital rights and take your pleasure with me whether I wish it or not?" she demanded incredulously, the idea sickening her.

"Of course not!" he growled. He pushed a hand roughly through his hair. "But maybe I've changed my mind about the baby. Maybe I think it's a good idea after all."

She just stared at him. "You want a baby now? *Maybe?* What exactly does that mean?" Her heart was skipping wildly in her chest, pulled in a thousand directions, but she forced herself to stay calm.

"Our marriage started in a crazy way. We hardly even knew each other. We didn't know the people we'd each grown into. But now that we've spent some time together, it's obvious that we like each other. There always was a genuine connection between us, and it hasn't gone away. It was just buried under time and distance and hard feelings."

His words fell on her like a hail of small pebbles, well meant but painful. He *liked* her; he liked her friendship and spending time with her and making love with her. But he didn't love her.

"And it will be buried again when you go back to India," she said.

Storm clouds gathered at his brow. "I don't know what you want me to say. You don't *want* to come to Hyderabad, do you?"

It was the first time he'd even suggested he might entertain the idea of them being in India together, but she could see by his face that the idea still repelled him. "You're right. I don't want to go to India—at least, not the way it would be if I went. But you could decide not to go back," she said, forcing herself to speak the words though she felt certain he would refuse. "Stay here with me, if you want to be together."

She could see by the way his face fell that she shouldn't have said it. His eyes flicked away from her.

"Eliza," he began, but she knew what was coming, and she couldn't bear to hear words of pity.

"Don't," she said firmly. "We've discussed this and clearly there's nothing more to say. We must simply consider ourselves friends who are married. There are far worse things to be."

"Eliza, you can't—" he began, but he didn't have a chance to finish, because at that moment they became aware of the sound of hoofbeats and both turned toward the manor at the same time.

"What the devil?" Tommy said.

A cart had just come around the side of the stables and was gathering speed. The driver was Rex, and running behind him laughing was Susanna.

Rex was laughing, too—until he caught sight of Eliza and Tommy in his path. Jerking on the reins, he tried to divert the pony, but his inexpert handling sent the animal toward a large rock by the split-rail fence. One of the cart wheels caught on the rock, and the cart pitched wildly and came to an abrupt stop against the fence, smashing part of it.

Tommy was already running toward the scene, Eliza behind him, as the pony ran off, trailing the broken shafts. Susanna, stopped in her tracks at some distance from them, looked horrified.

Rex was climbing out of the remains of the cart when Tommy and Eliza reached him. "Are you hurt?" Tommy demanded roughly. Rex lifted his chin and shook his head carelessly.

"It was nothing."

"You're lucky this fence circles around ahead, or you'd be taking off after that pony right now," Tommy growled.

Rex, ever unwise, said, "It was just a bit of fun."

"Which is why you made sure to get up early, so you could take the cart before anyone noticed, isn't it?"

Rex looked mulish.

"Well?"

"It was just a nasty old cart," he muttered, "falling apart, like everything else here."

Eliza drew in a breath, aware, even if Rex wasn't, of Tommy's barely restrained fury.

"You've behaved with a selfish disregard for others

from the minute you arrived in England," Tommy bit off, "though having known you in India, I wasn't exactly surprised. But you're Oliver's boy, and I wanted to do right by you. And yet, you're making it so hard."

"So?" Rex said, and kicked at a stone.

Tommy's mouth tightened. "I expect you to make amends for what you've done this morning. The cart and fence will need to be fixed."

"I have a trust fund," Rex said. "You can take the money out of that."

"I don't want your money," Tommy said. "You're going to fix what you broke."

Rex's eyes went to the mess of the cart, which lay at an awkward angle with the shafts missing. It was a shabby old cart, but it must have been somewhat sturdy as well, because at least the wheels were intact. "I don't know anything about fixing things," he sneered, as if the very idea was beneath him.

"It's not complicated. Wood. Nails. Hammer. Measuring," Tommy said. Eliza noticed that, for a change, he had the boy's attention.

"Are you going to show me how, then?" Rex mocked, but Eliza read something beneath his bravado. She guessed that he was only sneering about what he didn't think he could allow himself to have: the attention of the man who'd been his father's friend and was now, temporarily, his guardian.

She tried to catch Tommy's eye and somehow convey that this was important, but he wasn't looking at her. "The carpenter will show you," he said.

The wisp of forbidden hopefulness disappeared

from the boy's face, replaced by his usual sneer. "What, do you think you're teaching me a lesson, Sir Tommy? Don't bother. You're just going to send me to my aunt the minute you hear from her. You're not going to be around for long—just like everyone else."

Though Rex was being terribly rude, Eliza's heart ached for him, and she wanted to say something. But she knew it would have little effect, because she wasn't Tommy.

"People will always be leaving you in life," Tommy said expressionlessly. "It's best to accept that early on, and then you won't be disappointed."

Rex blinked, clearly astonished by such harsh words. Eliza was astonished, too, and not a little horrified.

Without a word, Rex turned and dashed away toward the path to the sea.

"Aren't you going to go talk to him?" she said as they watched him go.

"We just talked. I imagine he wants to heap curses on me in private."

Eliza bit her lip. "I know I'm not a shining example of success when it comes to children, but what you just said was pretty grim."

He shrugged. "It's the truth. Won't he be better off if he accepts it, instead of going through life angry that his mother left him and then died, and then his father died as well?"

"I'm not certain that what you're talking about is acceptance. It sounds more like resignation." She paused for a long moment, realizing that perhaps she'd just come to understand something about Tommy. He always seemed so happy and fun, and he was so confident and strong and playful. It had never occurred to her that he was also completely pessimistic.

She cocked her head. "Almost right after your mother died, your father married Judith because they'd been having an affair, didn't he?"

His expression instantly grew wary. "Why on earth are you asking me about that now?"

"I just never saw it before: how what happened to you was maybe not so different from what happened to me."

His eyes narrowed. "Don't think you're going to distract me from what we were talking about before Rex came along."

"You were close to both your parents, and they died when you were young. Will was doubtless a fine older brother, but he was twelve years older than you. I know Judith was a good stepmother to you, but maybe a lonely, grieving boy might decide it was better to make life into a game than to let the hurt get to him."

He rolled his eyes. "And all this because I suggested to Rex that he not make himself unpleasant?"

"Maybe. Maybe that's what's familiar to you— getting people to like you, losing yourself in amusement and adventure. It can be a way of avoiding anything more serious. But I just realized what I hadn't seen all along: that underneath that playful exterior, you're a cynic."

Her words clearly took him by surprise. He frowned. "No, I'm not. I just prefer to face what's real."

"But do you leave room for things working out well just as often as they turn out badly?"

"I hadn't realized you found me such a gloomy trial to be around."

"I don't. I'm sure nobody does. You're the swash-buckling prince of fun. But underneath that, perhaps you don't really trust life to work out. You don't trust people not to die, marriages not to fail, families not to fall apart as Rex's did. As, in a way, yours did."

He scowled, his black brows twin slashes. "You're being ridiculous."

"Am I? You're a man now, so it's up to you whether any of this means anything to you. But Rex is thirteen. And I think you should go talk to him." She shaded her eyes against the now-bright morning sun. "He's taken the beach path, and considering the choices he's made so far, I wouldn't put it past him to decide to take that dangerous climb down to the beach."

He gave her a look, but she could see he hadn't considered that. "Very well, I'll go after him. But you and are going to talk when I get back. We have unfinished business."

✎

When Tommy found Rex, he was indeed standing at the edge of the cliff above the sea, looking like he was considering a descent. He turned when he heard Tommy approaching.

"I wouldn't recommend a trip down to the beach," Tommy said. "It promises more danger than most of us would want this early in the morning."

The boy just shrugged, a mulish, defiant look on his thin features. He looked as though he'd grown since he'd arrived in England, and his trousers now stopped above his skinny ankles. He ought to have had new clothes. But of course, Tommy hadn't wanted to think about anything as long term as clothes for a boy who was only passing through his care.

He wasn't proud to realize that he'd been thinking of Rex as little more than a parcel awaiting delivery. He'd told himself, as he always did, that the best thing for everybody was to keep things light, to keep moving, to stay streamlined and ready for action. But Eliza was right; his words to the boy had been too harsh.

Underneath that playful exterior, you're a cynic. She'd seen something in him that he didn't want to examine.

He cleared his throat. "I owe you an apology, Rex. I spoke too harshly to you a few minutes ago. I was angry that you'd been disrespectful, but you deserve better than a guardian who hasn't thought enough about you and your future."

Rex blinked, seemingly startled by Tommy's words. Then he frowned, as though discounting them. "Why apologize for speaking the truth? People *do* always leave."

"You've had a harder time than many people, Rex. There's no getting around the sad fact that parents sometimes die. My own mother died when I was a little younger than you, and my father a few years later. But I had it easier than you; I had an older brother to look out for me."

Something softened in the hard line of Rex's mouth, as if hearing someone acknowledge his hardships made them a little more bearable. But then the hardness returned. "I don't want your pity," he said, turning away.

Tommy was surprised to find that he admired the boy, admired his spirit and his pride and even the force behind his anger. "It's not pity," Tommy said to Rex's back, "it's compassion. I'm saying I've known some of what you've experienced, and I respect your grit." He laughed a little softly. "Even if it's cost me a bush, a cart, and part of a fence."

Rex turned, and Tommy had the satisfaction of noting that the boy looked truly surprised for the first time. "Aren't you angry about the cart and the fence?"

"Well, I'm not happy about what happened. But they can be fixed. And I think, as the one who broke them, you'll want to fix them. A man acknowledges his mistakes when he makes them, and does what he can to fix them."

"I…" Rex's eyes dropped to the ground. "I'm sorry I took the cart out and broke it and the fence. I knew taking the cart was a rude thing to do, but I didn't care."

Well, Tommy thought. *How about that.*

"Come," he said. "I'll help you fix it. We'll have breakfast and then get to work."

The boy looked up, his eyes clear, and nodded soberly. "Thank you, sir," he said, and for the first time, there was not the barest hint of mockery in his words.

Seventeen

IT TOOK THE WHOLE DAY TO FIX THE CART AND fence, and everyone came out at one point or another to watch the work for a few minutes. Will and Anna stopped by on their way out for a walk and marveled at the progress Tommy and Rex had made after only an hour. Louie sauntered by next and complimented Rex's hammer strokes, drawing a pleased smile from the boy. When Louie offered Tommy some advice on his efforts to measure a new beam for the fence, Tommy gave him a look that promised doom, and Louie walked off laughing.

The children stopped by on their way to the treasure dig, clearly wondering if they could in good conscience continue digging without Rex, but he manfully told them to get to work since there were only a few days left before the house party would break up. Visibly relieved, the rest of the children headed for the part of the wilds where they'd last been digging.

Eliza came out with sandwiches and lemonade at lunchtime and made an impromptu picnic for them, eating and chatting with them in the grass by the fence. Tommy itched to get her alone so he could make her see that she didn't need to abandon the hope of a baby—and that the idea of them keeping their hands off each other once her courses were finished was ridiculous—but it wasn't possible. Anyway, she directed most of her conversation to Rex.

It was dusk by the time they finished. Their work done, Tommy and Rex paused to admire the repaired fence and the cart, which was now stable again.

"The work looks good," Tommy said.

"It does," Rex said, sounding pleased. "I've never built anything before."

"Feels good, doesn't it?" Tommy said, looking at the boy. He felt differently now about what he owed Rex, and he was surprised to find that he didn't mind.

Rex nodded, his silent response saying more than words could have done.

They put away their tools and Tommy made for his bedchamber, where he bathed and dressed hastily, intending to find Eliza before dinner. But she seemed determined to avoid him, and with a house full of guests, it was easy to do. Before he knew it, they were all gathered for dinner, and he and Eliza could hardly speak privately there.

He finally cornered her in the drawing room afterward while Susanna was performing a seemingly endless series of tunes on the pianoforte for her captive audience. Eliza had stepped outside the room to speak with Mrs. Hatch, and when she reappeared, Tommy grabbed her hand and discreetly tugged her toward the doors to the terrace at the back of the room.

"What are you doing?" she hissed, a smile on her face for the benefit of anyone who glanced their way as Susanna played on.

"Talking with my wife. What did Mrs. Hatch want?"

"The cabbages seem to have spoiled. They were meant to be part of tomorrow's lunch."

"Oh. Even though I don't like cabbage, I suppose they would have been tasty, because all the meals you've arranged have been delicious."

Her eyes narrowed suspiciously. "Why are you being so nice to me?"

"Was I not being nice to you before?"

"You've been considerate, but now you're being extra nice."

"I like you and you're my wife—why shouldn't I be nice?"

She frowned a little. "I need to get back to our guests."

"Wait." He felt unaccountably awkward, even though they'd been so easy with each other until she'd announced she wanted to abandon the baby plan. "I've been thinking about Rex."

That got her attention. "Oh?"

"I've begun to feel that this roaming aunt may not be the best thing for him. That he might benefit from a more stable situation."

Her eyes lit up. "I agree. What did you have in mind?"

"Well, it would affect you the most at first, while I'm in India. And he'll be away at school a good bit, but when he isn't, I thought he could come stay with you, if you agree."

She smiled. "Of course I agree. I'm more than

happy to help. So I assume this means you plan to remain his guardian?"

"Yes."

She nodded thoughtfully. "And Will and Louie will be around to help guide him."

Tommy didn't like the idea that she was so ready to think of his brother and cousin as substitutes for him. "Actually, I was thinking I could delay going back to India for another few months and stay here." He leaned closer, his body drinking in her soft warmth. "With you."

Her expression was not enthusiastic. "I don't think you should do that."

"Why not?"

"Because going back to India is what you want, and it's what you should do."

Now she wanted him to leave? "Dammit, Eliza, I like being with you. We enjoy each other's company and we're married. You want a family, and I'm offering you that."

Her eyes held a mysterious light that twisted something in him. "I'm very glad about your plans regarding Rex. But I'm not getting back into bed with you."

His brows slammed together. She turned to go back to the party, but they weren't finished talking. Something had changed with her—she was keeping something from him—and he needed to know what was going on.

With one hand he pushed open one of the doors behind him and with the other he caught her hand and pulled her, spluttering, onto the dark terrace. He closed the door behind them.

"What on earth are you doing?" she demanded, crossing her arms tightly over the shimmering wine-colored gown she was wearing. "It's freezing out here."

"We need to talk."

Her face was shadowed, though he could see her eyes in the glow coming through the drawing room windows. "You just want to change my mind, but I won't be swayed."

"I want to know why you want to give up the baby plan. Don't you think you owe me an explanation, after all that's passed between us?"

"That's rich, coming from you."

"You see, that's just the kind of cryptic thing I mean. You're keeping things from me."

She didn't say anything for a several moments, and then she said bluntly, "I'm not going to sleep with you again because I've fallen in love with you, Tommy."

All the breath seemed to rush out of him.

She was in love with him?

She certainly didn't seem happy about it.

Love… He didn't believe in it. Love was a gamble, a fairy tale, insubstantial and indefinable. He knew about action and decisions, but love was an idea, a feeling. He couldn't buy it or touch it or slash it. He didn't trust it.

"I don't know what to say."

She smiled, a small, sad smile that made his jaw clench. "You don't need to say anything at all. Now we both understand where we are. And now you know why it's better that we go our separate ways."

Why was she acting as though she knew exactly

what he was thinking—especially when he didn't even know himself?

She turned to go inside, but he grabbed her arm. "You can't just say something like that and go."

"Of course I can." She tugged her arm out of his grasp. "It's my own business, and I'm not asking for anything from you."

The door to the drawing room opened then, startling them, and Meg poked her head outside. "Oh, there you are, Eliza. Can you come do your hostess magic and get Susanna to stop playing? I think Heck will riot if he has to sit listening to any more, and Louie and Will are looking pained as well."

Eliza went back inside without a backward glance.

Tommy felt like punching the stone wall of the manor, but he just followed her inside with his teeth clenched, wishing they didn't have a house full of guests.

At least Rex was glad when Tommy took him aside a little later to let him know that, once Aunt Diana was found, Tommy intended to insist that Rex stay under his care—if Rex would like that.

"Like it?" The boy's gaze dropped and a little color came into his cheeks. "I know I've behaved badly since I came, but I don't want to be like that anymore, and I should consider myself exceedingly lucky, sir, if I could stay."

"Then it shall be so," Tommy said, laying a hand on the boy's shoulder.

Rex looked up, a dreamy expression coming over his face. "And to think I'll be staying with Lady Halifax while you're in India. She's amazing, and not like any lady I ever met."

"She'll be like a mother to you," Tommy pointed out sternly.

"But ever so much more fun."

Tommy didn't want to think about Rex and Eliza and all the good times they might have without him, so he clapped the boy on the back and went in search of a brandy.

~❧~

Eliza arose early on the last day of the house party. After her conversation with Tommy, she'd had trouble falling asleep. Her jumbled emotions tormented her, but she didn't regret telling him the truth, because now they both knew where they stood.

Knowing that the party would be ending made her feel bittersweet, though at least Tommy seemed to have accepted Rex. She was happy about that for the boy's sake and her own; she would enjoy getting to know him better.

She decided that they should have a bonfire that night to celebrate the end of the house party—and also to fill the time so there wouldn't be a chance for any awkwardness with Tommy. And when everyone left tomorrow morning, she would leave as well.

Her time with Tommy had opened her eyes to all the ways she'd been untrue to herself, and now she felt ready to think about the future with new hope. She was going to try again to make a place to help orphaned, forgotten girls, and she'd already talked to Meg about her plan. They agreed that they'd been thinking too small before, and that Truehart Manor—with its location in a community of wealthy neighbors concerned about appearances—was the wrong place for girls who'd known lives that had been so different and hard.

She intended to buy a large house outside Bath, somewhere with room for at least a dozen girls. And they would hire more staff to help, perhaps former teachers. Eliza and Meg wouldn't need to live there. Instead, they could direct the work and, if it was successful, establish more places like it.

Leaving London would be an adjustment for most of the girls, but it would provide the break from their old way of life that they badly needed. The new place would be welcoming, with prettily painted walls, wonderful meals, and all kinds of fun to be had along with the lessons in grammar and manners. And a dog—at least one, and maybe two—and cats. Children needed pets.

She'd already come up with a name for the place that Meg loved: they were going to call it Redstocking House. Women who liked to read and learn were called bluestockings, but she wanted the girls they helped to feel proud of their accomplishments and to see the creativity and potential they possessed.

She felt like a different person from the woman who'd compulsively pushed the girls in her care toward unattainable perfection. And even though she'd be going forward with a broken heart, the brokenness didn't seem entirely a bad thing, because her heart felt so much more open and capable of love than it ever had before.

It was a relief that she didn't see Tommy that morning. Just before luncheon, she was in the kitchen talking with Cook when Vic ran through like a town crier, announcing that the treasure of Hellfire Hall had been found.

Eliza hurried out to the wilds, where Tommy was already standing with Louie, Will, Anna, and Ruby. Eliza sidled up next to Meg, and they all watched as Marcus and Rex worked to free the small chest that Will and Tommy had buried.

"What did you put in the treasure chest, Tommy?" Ruby asked. "Skulls?"

"You'll see," he said.

Once the box was finally raised from its hole and placed on the ground, Susanna theatrically brushed the dirt off it. Rex slammed a shovel at the lock, knocking it off to shouts of encouragement from all present. Marcus leaned forward and opened the box.

There was a heavy pause. "*Hats?*" he finally said. "We dug like fiends for hats?"

But Heck and Vic were already rushing forward with glee. "Pirate hats!" Heck shouted, grabbing a stiff, black hat of the kind Admiral Nelson would have worn. He put it on, and it sank below his eyes. Vic giggled and put on one with an enormous white feather that curled from the peak all the way down to her mouth.

Rex pulled out a chunky necklace made of shells.

"Shell jewelry?" Marcus said in a disgusted voice, his opinion of Flaming Beard clearly falling by the moment.

"And coins!" Heck said, scooping up a small pile of shining disks. "One for each of us."

Louie leaned close to Tommy. "Where did you find this stuff?"

"Where else but the dungeon?"

"Those coins might be worth something," Ruby pointed out.

"Perhaps, but they're small," Tommy said. "And they did deserve something for their trouble."

Marcus and Rex upended the chest and began to attack it, poking at various parts of it.

"What are you doing?" Heck called from underneath his hat.

"Looking for the rest of the treasure. What kind of pirate would have made a map for a bunch of hats and shells?"

Heck sniffed. "*I* would have, if I'd been a pirate."

Rex gave a shout of triumph. "There's a false bottom!"

Heck and Vic collapsed in giggles, undone by "false bottom." Susanna and Marcus hastened to join Rex, poking inside the chest.

"What else did you put in there?" Will asked Tommy.

"Nothing," Tommy said, clearly puzzled. "There must be a secret compartment, which makes sense now that I think of it, because the chest is much heavier than it looks."

With a shout of triumph, Rex held up a silver flask. He worked the cap loose and brought the flask to his nose. "It's rum!" he said excitedly.

"Let me have it," Marcus cried.

"Oh, great," Anna said as Rex handed it to him. "That's just what the children need—a flask of rum."

"I wouldn't worry too much," Tommy said as they watched Marcus toss back a swig and promptly turn green.

"Ugh, it's like medicine," Marcus said. "But still, *pirates* were drinking that. And look"—he reached into the chest—"there's a book." He opened it and read, "The diary of Flaming Beard, in which I detail my wondrous exploits."

"Golly," Rex whispered in awed tones, dropping the bottle, which released its liquid into the grass. He leaned close to look at the book.

Anna groaned. "That's bound to be wicked."

"And very likely the best treasure they've found," Will pointed out with a chuckle.

"Should we find some way to get it away from them?" Eliza asked.

"No," all three men said at once.

Heck scampered over, still wearing the hat. "I'm never going to take this off," he announced. "I can't wait to wear it to the bonfire tonight."

"Bonfire?" Tommy turned accusatory eyes on Eliza.

She forced a cheery smile. "To celebrate our last night together."

He gave her a look that said he didn't appreciate her making plans without him, but with everyone there, he couldn't complain.

"Can I burn a chair?" Heck asked.

"Hector Halifax! What a question," his mother moaned.

Marcus and Rex also looked quite interested in the answer to that question. "Actually," Eliza said, "I've put aside a number of worm-eaten chairs and things that can go on the bonfire."

Heck let out a whoop.

"This all sounds quite exciting," Ruby said dryly, but she was smiling.

"Doesn't it?" Tommy said meaningfully, his eyes still on Eliza.

"And helpful, too," Eliza said, pretending not to notice his simmering looks of doom. "We can get rid of broken old things. Could you see to the details, Tommy?"

She ignored the sound of his teeth grinding.

❧

Tommy spent the afternoon directing the removal of furniture to a patch of open, mossy ground in the wilds and organizing the building of the base for Eliza's bonfire, which he was perfectly aware she'd intended to be as much about offering their guests a happy final night as a way of avoiding him. Which he didn't like at all. She'd told him she loved him—how could she just ignore him?

Her admission had startled him, and he couldn't stop thinking about it. He would have expected to feel smothered, or as though she was trying to tie him down, but he didn't, perhaps because she so clearly wasn't. But also because the idea of her caring about him made him feel...good.

As he tossed an old chair on the growing pile, it occurred to him that maybe he'd been so focused on the life he thought he wanted that he hadn't been able to see he might now want something different.

The moment darkness fell, the children exuberantly urged the adults out to the wilds. Louie, whose mis-spent youth had given him more experience lighting large fires than anyone should have, took charge of starting the fire, and soon a roaring blaze was lighting up the crisp autumn night.

Eliza was laughing with Ruby, Meg, and Will when Tommy moved next to her and took her hand. She tried to pull away, but he held on firmly.

"What are you doing?" she muttered at him.

"We need to talk."

She frowned and glanced at Meg next to her, but Meg was staring off in the direction of Louie. "No, we don't."

"Yes, we do," Tommy said, and tugged, leading her to the skimpy shelter of a small tree. She clasped her hands in front of her. In the glow from the enormous fire behind her, she looked wary.

"I've thought about it," he said, "and I've decided that I will be back in England within three years."

"What are you saying, Tommy?"

"That I want to have a family with you. I'm asking you to wait until I return home for good."

She looked away. "Tommy, I'm your wife, and I'll always fulfill my duties to run our affairs in England and take care of Rex. We will make a very good marriage of friends."

"Dammit, Eliza, I'm talking about coming home to you. I'm talking about giving up my life in India within three years and coming to live in England for good. All I need is a little more time—just one more adventure. And then I'll be done. I'll want to be in England. I'll want a home. With you."

She looked maddeningly nonplussed. He'd just offered to change his life for her. He *cared* about her.

Was she just going to stand there as though everything he'd just laid before her was nothing?

"You don't *know* that you'll want to give up your adventures, Tommy. Once you get to India, you might not want to. You might not be done. And where would that leave me and you and any family we might have?"

"Why wouldn't I want to come home to you? We have a great time together."

"I want better than that for myself," she said, and her rejection of what he'd offered felt like a kick to the guts. Though she'd admitted she loved him, clearly she wasn't going to let that rule her.

The bonfire raged behind her, turning the red of her hair to fire, but the effect seemed like nothing compared to the fire that burned within her. Somewhere along the line, the woman he'd once dismissed as hardly worth his time had revealed herself to be fierce and brilliant, and for the first time he began to accept that Eliza might have plans of her own that truly had nothing to do with him. It was a very unwelcome thought.

He shocked himself then by saying, "What if I don't go back to India at all?"

"You have to. It's your heart's desire. And I have my own plans: I'm going to look for a house to buy outside Bath, where I can establish a much better place for the kinds of girls we were helping at Truehart Manor. Meg and I are going to call it Redstocking House. So you see, you and I will both be going back to lives we want."

"Why won't you believe I'll come back to be with

you?" he demanded. When she just left his words hanging there, he cursed himself. Why would she believe that when everything she'd heard from him had been about the life he wanted to live without her?

"I'm going to leave with Will and Anna tomorrow," she said calmly. "They'll see me back to London on their way to Stillwell."

"*What?*" Panic raced through him. "You can't just leave! We're married."

"We both know what would happen if I stayed with you, and I don't want that."

"But—things have changed." His mind racing, he seized on the practical. "You can't go. What about Hellfire Hall, and everything that still needs doing?"

"Mrs. Hatch will help you finish what we've set in motion. And then you can offer it to a renter."

She didn't want his house either? When, with her care and attention and that warmth that was uniquely hers, she'd made it into a home? How could she want to just abandon it to strangers?

"Eliza," he bit off, "there's a great deal more to say. I really want to be with you." He knew he was going about this all wrong, that he was rushing to keep up with something that was shifting inside him, but he couldn't seem to find solid ground.

While he'd been ready to admit that he loved her company, he'd refused to let himself see that there might be a very good reason for that. But now, as he watched the fire dance over her, he felt as though a whole new window on life was opening, letting in views he'd never dreamed he'd want.

"I understand that you believe that," she said, and

he nearly yelled with frustration. She didn't believe she could trust him to truly care for her.

He pushed down the awareness that he just might lose her and focused on sounding reasonable. "We need to be together just the two of us, without everyone else around." Then surely he could show her how he cared, show her she could trust him.

"That's not a good idea," she said. "And my mind is made up."

She went back to their guests, effectively sealing herself off from him.

He muttered a curse. What could he say to make her see she could trust that he only wanted her?

He had to find some way to make her listen, but it certainly wasn't going to be here, surrounded by their family and friends.

He stepped away from the light of the bonfire and made his way toward the manor, stopping inside to speak to Mrs. Hatch before he went to the stables for a horse. At least it was not yet too late at night to pay a call on Wallace Smythe. Time was of the essence.

As his horse picked its way quickly down the path to the Smythe manor, the sea beyond it glinted in the moonlight. The sea had always promised escape and adventure, but now Tommy was desperately hoping it might give him another chance with Eliza. He didn't deserve another chance, but he finally understood how much he needed it.

How had he been such a fool? Accustomed to relying only on himself because it was easier than accepting the messiness that deeper connections with other people brought, he'd kept things light and charming and fun, never allowing anyone else's needs to be more important than his own. Eliza had helped him see all that—and he'd seen a portrait of a man he didn't want to be.

He'd allowed selfishness and mistrust and, yes, pessimism to blind him to the best thing that had ever happened to him: Eliza. She'd made him see that he needed love if he was ever going to be the man he was capable of being. He needed *her*.

God, she was brave. She'd had the courage to tell him she loved him, and the unshakable nobility to leave him because he didn't deserve her.

He knew now that nothing could matter more than deserving her love.

His horse drew up in front of the Smythe manor, and Tommy jumped down and ran for the door. The butler was understandably surprised to see him at nearly ten o'clock at night, but he brought Tommy to his master, who was enjoying a quiet brandy at his library desk.

"Sir Tommy," Smythe said, standing, "what a pleasant surprise."

"I've come to ask a favor," Tommy said, his heart pounding with the need for the answer to be yes. "It's about that boat of yours that's been standing off the coast for the last few days."

Eighteen

As the time slipped by in the glow of the bonfire and the adults sipped mulled wine and laughed and talked and occasionally wondered where Tommy had gotten to, it finally dawned on Eliza that he'd left.

She supposed he'd been annoyed by their conversation, but still she was surprised.

"We had a disagreement," she told Will when he asked after his brother.

He sucked his teeth. "Let me guess: you waited until tonight to tell him you were leaving."

"Yes, but I'm sure that wasn't it."

"I wouldn't be too certain. He can't have been happy about it."

She thought of how Tommy had left so abruptly years before when she'd laughed at him, but this was totally different. They were mature adults, and even though she knew she couldn't count on him for the future, she didn't think he was childish. Though she had to acknowledge that she hoped he might be hurt enough to need a few minutes to himself.

But when Mrs. Hatch appeared to tell her that

Tommy had been called away on business, she reminded herself what a capacity for ignoring the truth had done for her in the past and refused to let herself think about him for even one more second.

When he hadn't returned by the time she went to bed, she admitted she was extremely annoyed that he could be so inconsiderate to both her and his family. And she was hurt, too—why not admit it? They'd become *friends*, but clearly that meant nothing to him. She counted sheep furiously until she finally fell asleep.

She awoke some hours later, and from the low position of the moon in her window, she supposed it was very late, or rather very early the next day. Something had awakened her, some sound, but though she concentrated, she heard nothing and sensed nothing—until a hand came over her mouth!

She screamed, but her muffled cry came out as nothing but an insistent grunt. She thrashed, trying to throw the intruder off, her thoughts racing. Who was he, how had he gotten in, what did he want? She screamed again, just as uselessly.

"Before you try to wake the whole manor, it's me."

Tommy? She stilled.

He took his hand away. She sat up, and the fury she'd battled at bedtime combined with her outrage at being treated thus infused her voice. "What on earth are you doing?" she demanded.

He sat on the edge of her bed. "I wanted to talk to you, but there are too many people around this place, and you're set on avoiding me."

Why couldn't he just let this go? She'd made her hard decisions and her plans, but he wanted to nibble at her resolve with his charm and make everything so much harder. She sagged back against the pillow. "We've already said everything. You just don't like that I'm leaving you, instead of letting you leave me."

"I'll admit your plans got my attention. But it's not just that. I—um—love you," he said in a rush, so that she could barely make out the words. They sent an initial thrill through her, but it died away just as quickly. They were just words, and they sounded awkward since he was only saying them because he thought they were what she wanted to hear.

"You don't."

"Yes, I do. I want to stay with you. I've decided not to go back to India at all."

"What? No." She sat up again. "You have to go. It's what you've wanted all along."

"What I want has changed."

She crossed her arms. "I don't believe you. And I don't want you to stay," she said, forcing the lie past her constricting throat. Anger warred with her hurt, and she stirred it up, needing the strength it could give her to protect her heart. "I have plans for a future that I can't wait to get started on," she told him bluntly, "and they have nothing to do with you. So you see, there's no place for you in my life."

He sighed, sounding as though the words that had cost her so much bored him. But what should she expect? He was used to looking out only for himself, and he didn't want to be truly affected by other people.

"Right," he said. She heard him fumbling for something.

"What are you doing?" she demanded.

"Kidnapping you." And before she could even squeak, he had a cloth tied over her mouth. She grunted angrily but he ignored her. He gave her legs a firm tug, pulling her flat on the bed, and then the demented man rolled her up in the blankets like a sausage in pastry!

He passed a rope around her body and tied it firmly though not uncomfortably, and then he picked her up and tossed her over his shoulder. With her arms and legs snuggly restrained inside the blankets, she couldn't move anything but her head.

Had he lost his mind?

Apparently, because he proceeded to carry her out of her room, down the stairs, and out to the drive, where a cart was waiting in the moonlight. He placed her gently on the seat and got in next to her.

"The cart is a bit rustic, so I'm sorry to say it will be far less smooth than the coach, but the coach was too much trouble for my purposes."

Too much trouble for a madman dragging a woman out into the cold, dark night? she wanted to yell at him, but all she could do was grunt some more. He chuckled.

"You're heaping curses on me, aren't you? And wondering what the devil I'm doing and where I'm taking you."

She grunted again, meaningfully.

"You'll see," he said unhelpfully. She felt almost certain he was smiling, and gnashed her teeth. Why was he doing this, the fiend? Was he trying to tease her into submission? She'd resist him to the end, if that was his goal, and she envisioned her brave refusal in the face of wicked seductions.

In a short time, she realized that they'd made their way down to the sea. She could hear the waves crashing against the beach.

Was he going to do away with her by dumping her, trussed up, in the waves? She didn't really believe it, but she was maddeningly frustrated that she couldn't talk.

He stopped the cart and got down and spoke to someone who'd apparently been waiting for him, instructing the man to return the cart to Hellfire Hall. Then Tommy picked her up and swung her over his shoulder again.

"I know it's killing you that you can't yell at me," he said as he moved toward the waves, "but it's only for a little longer. This last part will be a little tricky, though."

Tricky? Her whole marriage had apparently been a trick, because she hadn't known she'd married a madman.

He stepped into the waves, and the salt spray hit her face. He shifted his hold and pulled her off his shoulder, and just when she thought she was going into the waves after all, she felt the wood of a boat beneath her. It was a small rowboat with two men in it, and as soon as Tommy got in, they began to row. She turned her head in the direction they were going, and that's when she saw the ship, standing a little way off the shore.

The rowboat drew alongside and she was unceremoniously hoisted upward by means of some kind of chair, brought onto the deck, and propped up against the mast by gentle hands. Who *were* these men who were helping Tommy? Mercenaries he'd paid, who didn't care that he was abducting some poor, helpless woman?

"Captain Mulholland at your service, Lady Halifax," a calm, pleasant voice said amid the murky light. "Your husband will be along shortly."

Before she could even ponder this bizarre encounter, Tommy came over the side of the boat, exchanged a few low words with the captain, then picked her up again and brought her below to a cabin.

Several lanterns were lit within, and she could see that the space was tidy, of modest size, and almost pleasant. He laid her on the bed, then locked the door, turned, and gave her the most outrageous grin. She was not a violent person, but in that moment, she dearly wanted to smack him.

"Sorry about all this—well, sorry about the uncomfortable parts. I'm not sorry I kidnapped you—at least, not yet."

He grabbed the rope holding the blanket around her and unfastened it, then took the edge of the blanket and gave a jerk, rolling her toward the wall and out of her cocoon. As soon as her arms were free, she sat up and untied the gag.

"You beast!" she cried. "Are you out of your mind?"

He opened his mouth to speak and the ship jerked a little, as if a wave had hit it. He smiled. "Maybe, but only a little bit. I needed to talk to you."

"You couldn't have talked to me at Hellfire Hall?"

"Not with all those people around, and with you so studiously avoiding me and refusing to really listen."

The boat jerked again, and this time Eliza realized

why. "We're moving!" She scrambled off the bed, making for the door, but he caught her around the waist. "Let go! I have to get back to Hellfire Hall. We have *guests* to see to, and they're leaving in a few hours. And I'm leaving with them!"

"I left a note for Will," Tommy said next to her ear. "Our guests had a fine send-off last night at the bonfire. My brother can explain our abrupt departure to them." His mouth moved closer to her ear, and she tried not to shiver at the sensation, even though, despite everything, she craved it. "I'm entirely certain he and the rest of our family will be delighted that you and I have left for a honeymoon."

She blinked, hardly able to believe what he'd just said. "A honeymoon?" she repeated dumbly.

"Yes." He kissed the top curve of her ear. "We've had lots of time fixing up drafty old rooms, entertaining guests, and taking on the care of an orphaned boy, but we really haven't had enough time to just enjoy being married."

How could he do this to her? How could he tease her with the promise of a blissful honeymoon when he was going to India? But then she remembered what he'd said the night before, words she'd discounted as meaningless.

"What are you talking about?"

"I'm talking about how I'm not going back to India. At all. And before you tell me that I want to go—I don't. It took me a long time to see it, and I'm sorry I was so blind."

"To see what?" Her heart thumped wildly as she allowed herself to believe just a little bit that maybe he *had* changed.

He turned her to face him. His eyes held a look she'd never seen there before, and it made her heart race even faster. "That I don't need to travel the world looking for adventure because it's right here in England."

Her breath caught at the vulnerability in his eyes. "It is?"

"Yes," he said softly. "The thought of India used to give me a thrill, but I finally realized that you'd done something to that thrill."

She frowned. "That doesn't sound good. I would never want to stifle you."

"I didn't say you'd done something bad to the thrill," he said, cupping her cheek. "What I meant was that the thrill has grown larger. The adventure has grown larger. The real adventure—what scares me the most but also draws me more than anything ever has— is you. I love you, Eliza Tarryton Truehart Halifax."

Her mouth trembled. His words had gone right to her heart, like an arrow only he could shoot. "You do?"

He stroked her cheek with his thumb. "I do." He shook his head ruefully. "I don't know how I had convinced myself that despite having the time of my life with you, I needed to go back to India. But I was a pigheaded idiot who believed that the best way to go through life was not to get attached to anything with the power to truly touch me."

She had the power to touch him? "But what about the work that's been so important to you? How can you just give it up?"

His mouth tipped in a small grin. "In truth, my

experience puts me in a unique position to advise those who craft our policy on India. I'll have more than enough to do here in England."

"And being in India?"

"It was wonderful, but the world is full of amazing places I've yet to see. And I'd love nothing more than to share them with you."

Her heart melted a little more.

"You were right when you said I'd grown cynical underneath all the laughter and adventure," he said. "But it's not who I am."

"No," she said, a smile growing as she really started to absorb what all of this meant. "You're a very good, swashbuckling man who'll make the most amazing husband I ever could have wanted." She lifted up on her toes and wrapped her arms around his neck. "And the best man I could ever want to share a family with."

He claimed her mouth in a kiss that told of hunger and love and promise, and she kissed him back for all she was worth.

When they broke apart, he said, "You're the spring in my step and the wind in my sails, Eliza. And I can't believe I have the amazing good luck to be already married to you."

She arched her eyebrow at him. "If you'll remember, it wasn't luck. You swashbuckled me into this marriage, just as you've swashbuckled me into this honeymoon."

A wicked light came into his eyes, and she nearly clicked her heels with happiness. "You've only just begun to experience my swashbuckling." He scooped her into his arms, tossed her on the bed, and commenced doing deliciously wicked things to her.

Later, when they were lying sated on the bed and the sun had begun filtering in through the porthole, Eliza said, "Why did you sound so awkward when you told me you loved me just before you kidnapped me?"

"Because I'd never said it before," he said. "It *felt* awkward, speaking those words for the first time. But now I want to say them all the time. I love you, Eliza." He kissed her nose.

She'd never dreamed she could be so happy. "I love you, Tommy." She kissed his adorable cheek, which had developed an ungentlemanly shadow of whiskers that was just perfect for the man who was her very own brigand. "So, where are you taking me for this honeymoon?"

"Hadn't you guessed? Malta, of course."

"Malta!" She rolled onto her side and kissed him exuberantly. "Oh, Tommy, I haven't been since I was a girl! How incredibly thoughtful of you."

He grinned and slipped an arm around her shoulders. "It is, isn't it? I hear it's warm and extremely fine there this time of year, and I think we could use a few weeks of sunshine before we return to chilly old England. Rex will stay with Anna and Will while we're gone—I left him a note explaining about our surprise honeymoon."

"A holiday in Malta," she sighed, thinking of all the places she wanted to see again for the first time with him. "And I can't wait to tell you my plans for Redstocking House. We'll finish making Hellfire

Hall more cozy, too—won't it be wonderful there at Christmas? We can have everyone back to stay."

He kissed her. "You're very good at making plans."

"I am, aren't I?" She smiled, and her voice dropped several husky notches as she slid her hand across his warm chest. "But right now, and for the rest of my life, all my best plans will start with you."

Epilogue

Four Years Later

Dear Will,

I hope this finds you well and that Sam, now that he's passed the age of two, is no longer shouting "no" all day long at his older siblings.

All is as usual here, which as you know means controlled mayhem. Little Claire, having achieved the age of three, has announced that she's going to marry Rex. He was home for a holiday from school, and was very serious and gracious about the whole pretend wedding thing. Eliza and I are so proud of the young man he's turning out to be—it's hard to believe he was such a devil. He's been a good example to Claire, too, of how to be gentle with baby Nicholas when he drools on her favorite books.

Eliza is…amazing. In addition to being the most entertaining and doting mama our children could want (and the woman I adore more with each passing day), she's been working with Meg to get donations to start a second Redstocking House somewhere north of London. She sends her love, and we all look forward to seeing you next month for Christmas at Hellfire Hall. Tell Heck that it's his turn to help Rex arrange the treasure hunts for everyone. Inside, of course, now that it's cold.

Tell Anna...thank you. Those dresses she sent Eliza for our "honeymoon" years ago weren't the reason I came to see how I loved Eliza, but they certainly helped open my eyes, and for that I will always be grateful.

Your besotted, utterly
contented brother,
Tommy

Keep reading for an excerpt from the first
in The Scandalous Sisters series

The Beautiful One

ANNA BLACK GAVE A SILENT CHEER AS THE
carriage she was riding in lurched and came to an
abrupt stop at an angle that suggested they'd hit a
deep ditch.

Perhaps, she thought hopefully from the edge of
her seat, where she'd been tossed, they'd be stuck on
the road for hours, which would delay their arrival at
the estate of Viscount Grandville. She had reason to be
worried about what might happen at Lord Grandville's
estate, and she dreaded reaching it.

It was also possible she was being pursued.

Or not.

Perhaps nothing would happen at all. But the
whole situation was nerve-wracking enough that she
had more than once considered simply running off to
live in the woods and survive on berries.

However, several considerations discouraged her
from this course:

1. She had exactly three shillings to her name.
   Though admittedly money would be of no

use in the woods, she would at some point need more than berries.

2. She had agreed to escort her traveling companion, Miss Elizabeth Tarryton, to the home of Viscount Grandville, who was the girl's guardian.

3. If Anna abandoned her duty, along with being a wicked person, she wouldn't be able to return to the Rosewood School for Young Ladies of Quality, her employer.

Anna was nothing if not practical, and she was highly skeptical of the success of the life-in-the-woods plan, but the dramatic occurrences in her life of late were starting to lend it appeal.

"Hell!" said the lovely Miss Elizabeth Tarryton from her sprawled position on the opposite coach seat. Her apricot silk bonnet had fallen across her face during the coach-lurching, and she pushed it aside. "What's happened?"

"We're in a ditch, evidently," Anna replied. Their situation was obvious, but Miss Tarryton had not so far proven herself to be particularly sensible for her sixteen years. She was also apparently not averse to cursing.

Surrendering to the inevitable, Anna said, "I'll go see how things look."

She had to push upward to open the door to the tilted coach, and before stepping down, she paused to tug her faded blue bonnet over her black curls, a reflex of concealment that had become second nature in the last month. The rain that had followed them since they left the school that morning had stopped, but the dark sky promised more.

The coachman was already seeing to the horses.

"Had to go off the road to avoid a vast puddle, and now we're in a ditch," he called. "'Tis fortunate that we're but half a mile from his lordship's estate."

So they would soon be at Stillwell, Viscount Grandville's estate. *Damn*, Anna thought, taking a page from Miss Tarryton's book. Would he be a threat to her?

After a month in a state of nearly constant anxiety, of waiting to be exposed, she sometimes felt mutinously that she didn't care anymore. She'd done nothing of which she ought to be ashamed—yet it would never appear that way. And so she felt like a victim, and hated feeling that way, and hated the accursed book that had given two wicked men such power over her.

She gathered up the limp skirts of her faded old blue frock and jumped off the last step, intending to see how badly they were stuck.

The coachman was seeing to the horses, and as she moved to inspect the back of the carriage, she became aware of hoofbeats and turned to see a rider cantering toward them. A farmer, she thought, taking in his dusty, floppy hat and dull coat and breeches. He drew even.

"You are trespassing," he said from atop his horse, his tone as blunt as his words. The sagging brim of his hat hid the upper part of his face, but from the hard set of his jaw, she could guess it did not bear a warm expression. His shadowed gaze passed over her, not lingering for more time than it might have taken to observe a pile of dirty breakfast dishes.

"We had no intention of doing so, I assure you," she began, wondering that the stranger hadn't even offered a greeting. "The road was impassible and our coachman tried to go around, but now we are stuck. Perhaps, though, if you might—"

"You cannot tarry here," he said, ignoring her attempt to ask for help. "A storm is coming. Your coach will be stranded if you don't make haste."

His speech was clipped, but it sounded surprisingly refined. *Ha.* That was surely the only refined thing about him. Aside from his lack of manners and the shabbiness of his clothés, there was an L-shaped rip in his breeches that gave a window onto pale skin and thigh muscles pressed taut, and underneath his coat, his shirt hung loose at the neck. She supposed it was his broad shoulders that made him seem especially imposing atop his dark horse.

A stormy surge of wind blew his hat brim off his face, and she realized that severe though his expression might be, he was very handsome. The lines of his cheekbones and hard jaw ran in perfect complement to each other. His well-formed brows arched in graceful if harsh angles over dark eyes surrounded by crowded black lashes.

But those eyes. They were as devoid of life as one of her father's near-death patients.

Several fat raindrops pelted her bonnet.

"We shall be away momentarily," she said briskly, turning away from him to consider the plight of the coach and assuming he would leave now that he'd delivered his warning.

The rain began to fall faster, soaking through the

thin fabric of her worn-out frock. She called out to the coachman, who was doing something with the harness straps. "Better take off the young lady's trunk before you try to advance."

"No. That's a waste of time," said the stranger from atop his horse behind her.

She turned around, deeply annoyed. "Your opinion is not wanted."

The ill-mannered man watched her, a muscle ticking in his stubbled jaw.

A cold rivulet trickled through her bonnet to her scalp and continued down her neck, and his empty gaze seemed to follow the little stream's journey to the collar of her dampening frock. His eyes flicked lower, and she thought they lingered at her breasts.

She crossed her arms in front of her and tipped her chin higher. Not for nothing had she sparred with her older brother all those years in a home that had been more than anything else a man's domain. Her father had been a doctor and had valued reason and scientific process and frowned on softness, and she'd been raised to speak her mind. Life as a servant at Rosewood School was already testing her ability to hold her tongue, but this man deserved no such consideration.

"Is not your presence required elsewhere?"

"Where are you going?" he demanded, ignoring her.

"I couldn't be more delighted that such things do not concern you."

The stranger's lips thinned. "Who comes to this neighborhood concerns me."

"If you would move along," she said exasperatedly,

blinking droplets from her lashes, "we might focus on freeing the coach."

His gaze flicked away from her. "Drive on," he called to the coachman.

John, apparently responding to the note of command in the stranger's voice, disregarded Anna's sound of outrage and addressed himself to the horses. With a creaking of harness straps, they struggled forward. The wheels squelched as they found purchase amid the mud, and the carriage miraculously righted itself.

She sucked her teeth in irritation.

"See that you do not linger here," the man said.

"We are on our way to Stillwell Hall," she replied, thinking to make him regret his poor conduct. He might even work for the viscount.

He looked down at her, his face shadowed so that his rain-beaded whiskers and hard mouth were all she could see. "That's not possible. No one is welcomed there."

From inside the carriage, Miss Tarryton called, "Can we not proceed, Miss Whatever?"

Anna ignored her. "It certainly is possible."

"The viscount might not be in residence."

His words would have given her pause, except that when Miss Brickle had sent Anna off with her charge and a note for the viscount, she'd said that he was certain to be at Stillwell, because according to gossip among the mothers of Rosewood's students, he'd been in residence there constantly over the last year.

Though why this man should be so set on discouraging them from seeing the viscount, she couldn't imagine.

"I have it on good authority that he is. Evidently, sir," she said, "you have been raised by wild animals and so one must overlook your lack of interest in people, but I assure you Lord Grandville will wish to welcome us."

Something flickered in his eyes for the barest moment at her tart words, but his hard expression didn't change.

"No," he rasped. "He won't. Do not go there."

He turned his horse away and spurred it into a gallop across the field next to the road.

Anna found herself staring as the stranger rode off. And really, he *was* strange, because though he appeared to be a laborer, his speech was educated and his manner commandingly haughty. He might almost have been a gentleman, but he was too rough for that to be possible.

As the coachman climbed onto his perch, he gave a snort and called back to her, "'E's a friendly one."

"He probably keeps badgers as pets," she said, and mounted the coach steps amid the coachman's laughter.

Miss Elizabeth Tarryton, sitting composedly inside and looking as dry and untroubled as any princess accustomed to having things arranged for her, remarked, "Headmistress says ladies are above noticing the behavior of rough men. Not that *you* would know about proper behavior. Really, Miss Brickle ought never to have chosen a *seamstress* as a companion for the niece of a viscount. You—"

The girl hesitated, perhaps realizing how ridiculous additional comments would sound coming from someone who'd been discovered the night before kissing a lieutenant from the local militia in the school garden. When discovered by the headmistress, Miss Tarryton had almost proudly revealed that she'd reached the garden by climbing out a second-floor window. Miss Brickle had wanted the girl gone as soon as possible, before her scandalous behavior could taint the reputation of Rosewood School.

As the only other person privy to this escapade—she'd been up late doing the mending, needing extra time for the work since she wasn't actually very good at sewing—Anna had been assigned to escort Miss Tarryton to her guardian.

"Yes?" Anna prompted, surprised to find herself being addressed at all. The elegant Miss Tarryton, who looked like angelic perfection with her red-gold curls and her gown of pale apricot silk, had spent their journey gazing mutely out the window on her side.

The girl closed her mouth and returned to looking out the window, where the rain was now coming down heavily as the late afternoon edged toward evening. Anna would have felt sorry for Miss Tarryton, since she'd been hustled away from Rosewood so ignominiously, except nothing in her demeanor suggested she was dismayed about leaving. If anything, she seemed impatient to arrive at their destination.

They set off at a careful pace on the muddy road. Anna dried herself as best she could with a clean serviette from the now sadly empty lunch hamper. She didn't dwell on why the stranger had said what he had about Stillwell. Even if it were true, it merely suggested that Lord Grandville was a hermit, which could only be good news.

She would simply deliver his ward and then be on her way back to the school. It had been a month since she'd had to leave home so abruptly, and now, just when she'd been starting to relax her guard at Rosewood, she'd been sent on this unwanted journey.

A shudder rippled along her shoulders as a memory of curving pencil marks flashed through her mind, the lines of her own naked body caught in various positions on page after page of that appalling sketchbook. Images made without her knowledge. And three words written in garish red wax on the book's cover: *The Beautiful One.* Such an innocuous title for a thing that put her in danger of becoming the kind of woman no decent person could acknowledge.

Acknowledgments

As always, thanks go to my editor, Deb Werksman, and to all the hardworking people at Sourcebooks, especially Susie Benton, Rachel Gilmer, Eliza Smith, and Amelia Narigon, and the staff in the production and design departments. And thanks also to my fabulous agent, Jenny Bent.

And last but not least, I'm grateful to my husband, Mike, who is always incredibly supportive of my writing, and to our wonderful daughters.

About the Author

Emily Greenwood has a degree in French and worked for a number of years as a writer, crafting newsletters and fund-raising brochures, but she far prefers writing playful love stories set in Regency England, and she thinks romance novels are the chocolate of literature. A Golden Heart finalist, she lives in Maryland with her husband and two daughters.

Heir to the Duke

The Duke's Sons

by Jane Ashford

Life is predictable for a duke's first son

As eldest son of the Duke of Langford, Nathaniel Gresham sees his arranged marriage to Lady Violet Devere as just another obligation to fulfill—highly suitable, if unexciting. But as Violet sets out to transform herself from dowdy wallflower to dazzling young duchess-to-be, proper Nathaniel decides to prove he's a match for his new bride's vivacity and daring.

Or so he once thought...

Oppressed by her family all her life, Lady Violet can't wait to enjoy the freedom of being a married woman. But then Violet learns her family's sordid secret, and she's faced with an impossible choice—does she tell Nathaniel and risk losing him, or does she hide it and live a lie?

For more Jane Ashford, visit:
www.sourcebooks.com

A Gentleman's Game

Romance of the Turf

by Theresa Romain

How far will a man go

Talented but troubled, the Chandler family seems cursed by bad luck—and so Nathaniel Chandler has learned to trade on his charm. He can broker a deal with anyone from a turf-mad English noble to an Irish horse breeder. But Nathaniel's skills are tested when his stable of trained Thoroughbreds become suspiciously ill just before the Epsom Derby, and he begins to suspect his father's new secretary is not as innocent as she seems.

To win a woman's secretive heart?

Nathaniel would be very surprised if he knew why Rosalind Agate was really helping his family in their quest for a Derby victory. But for the sake of both their livelihoods, Rosalind and Nathaniel must set aside their suspicions. As Derby Day draws near, her wit and his charm make for a successful investigative team…and light the fires of growing desire. But Rosalind's life is built on secrets and Nathaniel's on charisma, and neither defense will serve them once they lose their hearts…

For more Theresa Romain, visit:
www.sourcebooks.com